THE HERO'S JOURNEY

12 steps to prevent cancer, heal your body

& restore your immune system

Nelson Lecuane

Published by Aset & Wsr
Editor: Sn Hrw & Snt Maat

This book is part of a series called The Hero;
The Hero's Journey
The Hero Entrepreneur
The Penguin Entrepreneur
The Hero Mother
The Hero Father
The Young Hero
The Hero Professional
The Hero Teacher
The 7 Principles of the Hero's Philosophy

The Hero's Journey is the first book of the series.

This book is dedicated to Richard Mathieson and Sue Miller.

Thank you for your kindness, your attention and generosity.
With gladness, I share this beautiful book, my goal is for it to become
yours and your relative's bridge to wellness and longevity

Contents

THE PURPOSE OF THIS BOOK 1

ABOUT THIS BOOK 7

THE MYTHOLOGICAL PERSPECTIVE 8

INTRODUCTION TO THE HERO'S PHILOSOPHY 19

CHAPTER 1 The Hero's Philosophy 25

CHAPTER 2 The Hero's Journey 51

CHAPTER 3 The Quest to Retrieve the Lost Vitality 56

CHAPTER 4 The Beauty and Mystery of Number 12 62

CHAPTER 5 Two Worlds - Two Philosophies 66

CHAPTER 6 The World of Maat, the Special World 76

CHAPTER 7 Citizens of the Special World 84

CHAPTER 8 The Circle of Influence 89

CHAPTER 9 Essential Characters 97

CHAPTER 10 The Roles of Essential Characters 102

CHAPTER 11 The Main Archetypes 112

CHAPTER 12 The 12 Steps of the Hero's Journey 254

Step 1 - Ignorance & La Dolce Vita 255

Step 2 - Signals & Diagnosis 269

Step 3 – Invitation 282

Step 4 - Refuse/Accept the invitation 288

Step 5 - Meeting the healer/mentor 299

Step 6 - Jumping into the ocean 310
Step 7 - The method, the philosophy 324
Step 8 - Ordeal, Battle, Rebirth 360
Step 9 Reward – Healing 376
Step 10 - Return 383
Step 11 Resurrection – Recovery 394
Step 12 - The Elixir 402
CONCLUSION How to Become a Hero 422
Bibliography & Further Reading 452
ABOUT THE AUTHOR 457

During a silent and transparent night, I started my journey of self-discovery. My quest was to retrieve a sacred, ancient and universal mystery.

It took me a while to understand the wise voices, the council, advice, teachings of sublime teachers, lovers who delight themselves by helping others to find lost lights and blissful, seducing smiles. I found the mysterious treasure hidden inside an ancient melody. It is beautiful, calming, charming, enchanting like a tranquil and silent summer sea. The treasure is a hero who continues to rescue the lives of men and women, children, families that are travelling inside 1000 sinking ships.

You are the hero, the treasure of your family, the architect of wonderful destinations. You are the hero, the light and saviour of blinded dreamers and intoxicated generations. You are the hero, the precious, essential mystery of your generation. Your roots are natural and ancestral. Smile, rejoice, dance because you are one of the heroes with a 1000 faces. A truly powerful and inspirational individual.

Nelson Lecuane

Disclaimer

The information in this book is provided only as an information resource and are the opinions of the authors about cancer treatments and mythology. Not medical advice. It is not intended to be a substitute for individual diagnosis, and treatment by qualified medical professional. Before embarking on any of the treatments described in this book, you should consult a qualified health care provider who will make a recommendation for treatment based upon on your medical history and current medical condition.

"Ok, two things to understand about quantum reality is that first of all, is that everything is made up of energy. It's all energy. Everything in the universe is made up of consciousness and energy. That's all there is. When you break everything down to assassins. Consciousness and energy. Your sickness that you presently have consists of consciousness and energy. Your marriage is consciousness and energy. Your career is consciousness and energy. What's happened to you in the past, is consciousness and energy. What will happen to you in the future is consciousness and energy. Get and understand very clearly, that everything is consciousness and energy, everything. And energy, here's where it gets very, very interesting, is, energy is not what it seems…

- John Kehoe: Consciousness & Energy – JohnKehoeMindPower YouTube channel.

Acknowledgements

A few years ago I fell in love with a subject called the Hero's Journey. When I looked into the subject, I learned that the key elements in a person's life are the characters, the people who help him or her to become a hero and succeed in life. During the early stages of my journey, I met people who played key roles in my life. Some of them came as investors, allies, and mentors. It took me some time to realise how precious their roles were. Looking back, I can see that they were mentors, helpers, threshold guardians, and allies. I was ignorant about life and its mysteries therefore I could not see the Gods and Goddesses, heralds, healers and helpers hidden in deeds and words. I was stuck in my own ego and blinded by the shadow.

I have met many wonderful people who have done their best to help me. They came at different times in my journey. Some of them dealt with the sincere seeker, others encountered the shadow that was created by a lack of cultural identity and self-knowledge. The shadow is not the real person. The shadow is the product of frustration and ignorance. I did not know myself, therefore, I failed to see the helpers, allies and mentors. I sincerely apologise to those who dealt with my shadow. I am very grateful to all of those who helped me to find and believe in myself.

I dedicate this book to Richard Mathieson and Sue Miller. Thank you very much for your kindness. I am also grateful to my parents and to beautiful and inspirational Leia. I am very grateful to Carlota from Merida. Angel Glez from Madrid. Muchas gracias hermano. Thank you to Keith Linton and his family. I am very grateful to Leia and Karen. Thank you very much indeed to Tim Mardon and Coronel Jose

Geraldo. I am also very grateful to Dr. Alexandra Marques Coelho. I am very grateful to Daniel Priestley for advising and inspiring me to become a writer. I am also very grateful to Dr. Rkhty Amen for helping us to discover the very rich culture of our ancestors.

I am also very grateful to Snt Maat Nfrt Mry Hrw for the endless hours, for your patience and your kindness. Muchisimas gracias hermana. Dwa Neferet.

Thank you to all the researchers, the pioneers and mentors who share their wisdom through books, lectures and YouTube videos. I am very grateful to the teachers who are striving to help families, children and fellow human beings to defeat the big monster. Dr. Sebi, Charlotte Gerson, Dr. Mercola, iHealthtube.com, Ty Bollinger, his family and the excellent team at The Truth About Cancer.

Thank you very much indeed to Dr Leigh Erin Connealy, MD for more than 30 years of dedication. Your book is a wonderful gift to humankind. Thank you very much indeed to the pioneers and Heroes Professor Thomas Seyfried and Dr Patrick Quillin. Thank you very much indeed for your wonderful work.

I am also very grateful to Rachael Linkie for her dedication and excellent books about health. The list of healers is endless therefore we cannot name all of them. We say thank you to the researchers and healers; Dr. Veronique Desaulniers, Chris Wark, Leonard Coldwell, Dr. Peter Glidden, Joel Furhman and to all the wonderful souls who are striving to help and heal others. Thank you also to all the teachers and mentors who contemplated and taught this wonderful and essential subject called mythology. A big thank you to the eternal Ka, and the soul of the grandmaster, the spiritual healer, the opener of the ways, the ferryman Joseph Campbell who dedicated his life to something bigger than himself.

THE PURPOSE OF THIS BOOK

In the summer of 2010 my father died. The death of my father was a difficult rite of passage for me. In the autumn of 2012, my mother died. More than 20 years before the death of my parents, I saw my brother being mercilessly taken by a disease. Following the death of my brother, I spent years being reminded of the power of an implacable monster called disease. This monster presents itself in several forms. It has several names. Virus, cold, blood pressure, migraines, anemia, liver disease etc. The monster is also known as cancer. Although it has many names, the monster has a common origin. The origin is called deficiency. In 2015 one of my best friend's father died of cancer. He was an Irish man, a very kind and hardworking man who loved his family. He had a family business and loved to spend weekends with his family.

In 2016 I became a father. From 2016 to 2018 I spent days and nights taking care of "the little one". It was a profound experience that transformed me. It reminded me of my parents who are no longer with me. It also made me think about the dangers which parents and children living in the 21st century face. Parents risk losing their children, children risk losing their parents, lovers risk losing their mates, students risk losing their teachers, mentors, guides and role models. Every human being living the 21st century is at risk of becoming a victim of the modern Minotaur that's destroying the bodies, the minds of family members, cutting lives of fathers and mothers. There is a risk but also an opportunity for heroism.

Another father taken down

In 2017 a father of two young boys and a young girl told me that he had stomach cancer. He lived in a well-kept house that's two doors away from us. I saw the fear in his eyes. He was stressed and shaken. I spoke to him several times about effective strategies, natural therapies used to combat the big monster. I told him to be brave, bold and to get busy healing himself. I gave him a book with a beautiful red cover. The small but beautifully written book contains a formula that helps a patient, a person, a non-pessimistic prospect to heal his or her body by flooding it with oxygen. The book is called "*The One Minute Cure*" The book was written by an American author called Madison Cavanaugh.

The frightened man was compelled to ignore my advice and the ideas introduced by the book. He was very scared. He felt powerless, impotent and publicly humiliated by a ruthless provider of pessimism. The man was not well informed about the monster. He was given chemo. He accepted it. He also had surgery to remove his stomach. It did not work. He died less than 2 years after the "official diagnosis".

The day before I learned of his death, I met a lady who told me that she had breast cancer. I met her 3 times on 3 different days, at 3 different locations. At the time when these intriguing meetings took place, we were in the process of writing a screenplay. Her appearance and story disturbed me. I decided to stop and reflect on the stories of the people that I was meeting and interacting with. I sensed that there was a mystery hidden in the events and experiences that were taking place around me. There was a logic, an explanation as to why I kept meeting people who were being attacked by the big monster. It was not the first time I contemplated the origins of cancer and its destructions. I had looked at the Minotaur before by contemplating other people's experiences.

From January 2014 to February 2018, I spent endless hours, afternoons, nights, days, weeks, months, questioning, researching about naturopathy, cancer, alkaline diets, and supplements. I bought books, watched lectures and documentaries delivered by experts such as Dr. Nicholas Gonzalez and Dr. Matthias Rath. I asked many questions and I got many answers.

My exploration was rewarded with intellectual gold. I learned a lot, however, I did not use the research. My primary purpose was to publish a philosophy dedicated to economics and entrepreneurial prosperity.

I love entrepreneurship, therefore I invested a great deal of time on that subject. The stories of death and pain caused by the big monster forced me stop and think. I reflected on my pain and the pain experienced by fellow men and women. I reflected on the unbearable pain experienced by children who have lost their parents, the desolate faces of husbands who lost their wives and the melancholic smiles of wives who have lost their husbands.

The havoc caused by the modern Minotaur persuaded me to change my plans. I resolved to make a positive contribution to other people's lives by sharing the ideas and strategies that I discovered. Helping others excites me. It stimulates my brain to think, reflect on profound subjects such as, alternative therapies, ancient history and longevity.

By contemplating the cyclical birth and decay of seasons, I learned that helping others is a reliable source of happiness. This philosophy inspired me to change my priorities in life. I feel really glad to positively contribute to a person's life. My meditations on complex and rich subjects such as "Religions of small societies" taught me that in order to successfully help others, we must first refine ourselves.

We could see ourselves as a mechanic that wants to fix a broken car. The healer, mechanic will have to fix, heal himself or herself first before trying to help, fix others. We cleanse the interior before the exterior. We can do that by departing from the ordinary world.

How to use this book

If the big monster has not attacked you yet, please keep reading. If you are currently battling a monster called cancer please go to chapter 12 and follow the 12 Steps to Longevity. I will also advise you to read the books "*Tomorrow's Cancer Cures Today*", "*The Cancer Survival Manual*" and "*Natural Strategies for Cancer Patients and Beating Cancer with Nutrition*". It doesn't matter whether you are healthy or not, you should read the whole book because it contains key principles. The principles and prescriptions proposed in this book are universal. They transcend race, gender, age, location, origin, social status etc. You can, could and should use essential principles, methods and techniques to empower yourself, your friends and your relatives. That's how you become one of the heroes with a 1000 faces.

the hero are there. What a person may lack is patience, discipline, a mentor and of course knowledge.

Origins of the word hero

The root word for hero is Hrw. This word is very ancient. It comes from Kmt (Kemet), also known as Ancient Egypt. Kmt is located in the North of Africa. When we talk about Africa and Africans we are talking about very, very ancient people and culture. In his marvelous book "*The World's Religions*" Professor Ninian Smart wrote the following:

"It is most likely that the first humans came from Africa... There was Homo habilis, the tool - user, and Homo erectus, the upright type, walking like us on two feet; and then perhaps 250,000 years ago, Homo sapiens, the knowledgeable one."

The idea of a hero is very ancient indeed. Every culture, race and country, every village, every family has a story or stories of heroes. Men and women who completed remarkable tasks such as giving birth to the first child of the family. The grandad who built the first house in the village, the auntie that wrote novels and made the family famous. "The grandmother who gave birth to the first baby in our family and started our genealogy. She was the first hero of our family."

Every movie, every house has a story that contains a villain and a hero. In the modern world every family has a member that's at risk of being attacked by a monster. The motif, the deeds of the hero or heroine are always very noble and commendable. An innocent person is attacked and must fight in order to save him or herself. The hero is someone who strives to save others. That could be your story. There will be a point in your life when you will need to step in and help someone to save his or her life. It could be your aged mother, your fabulous father, your beautiful sister, your lovely brother, your amazing husband, your charming wife, a dear friend or a nice work colleague. You cannot do it without the right tools and skills. You cannot do it alone.

A mother whose child is attacked by cancer or any other disease could become a hero by using specific methods and tools to help her child to fight the monster. A wife, a husband, a brother, a sister, a friend, a work colleague, a carpenter, a plumber, a mentor, an investor has the potential to become a hero. In order to defeat the monster and become a hero, a dreamer has to go on a journey. In our case, the journey will take the sincere seeker to the special world. The special world is the domain of alternative and natural therapies. Ancient remedies, rich mythologies and philosophies.

The hero has 3 key elements:

- Fear
- Desire
- An enemy

Fear

In our case, the patient who is suffering from breast cancer or any other sickness is the hero who has to fight the monster. He or she fears death and loss. There is a fear of death but also a fear of leaving young children without a breadwinner.

Desire

There is fear but also desire. There is a desire to become healthy, to recover, to be well again and live a long life. Every human being desires to be loved, to be wonderful, successful and beautiful. Diseases such as cancer destroy beauty, self-esteem and confidence. The monster destroys vitality, longevity and any type of prosperity. Cancer is a ruthless monster that does not care about age, gender or morality. Every ambitious human being would do well by striving to learn more about this monster. The desire to be healthy is universal and timeless. It inspired our ancestors to create refined poems, rituals and monuments. The subject of Mythology puzzles us today and will be the primary concern of the citizens of tomorrow.

The enemy of Aset

The third element that confronts every hero is an enemy. To defeat the enemy, the man or woman of our time has to become a healer. The greatest healer of the ancient world was a lady, a queen, a priestess called Aset. Her main enemy was her jealous brother, a principle called Sutek. Sutek practiced his craft in the North of Africa. The locals called him Sutek. After invading Kmt the Greeks changed his name to Set. He appeared in the Bible as Satan. He was not the only destructive principle of the ancient world.

In Ancient Iran the enemy was called Angra Mainyu. Angra Mainyu was a destructive force that corrupted the souls of human beings. Angra Mainyu was the enemy of everything that was good. The word Angra Mainyu is the root word for 'angry man'.

Cancer is a collection of angry cells that are keen to destroy anything in order to remain alive. We don't have to be victims of Angra Mainyu. We can protect ourselves, our friends and relatives by following the thread left by inspirational characters such as Aset. The required elements for heroism are within us. Many essential mysteries and principles were hidden in Kmt.

Kmt is the original name of the land today known as Egypt. In 332 BC Kmt was invaded by soldiers lead by a young man called Alexander of Macedon. The Greeks called Kmt, Egypt because they could not pronounce Het Ka Ptah, therefore, they said Aegyptus. Aegyptus was refined and became Egypt. Het Ka Ptah means, the temple of the spirit of Ptah. Ptah was the creative principle of the second capital of the empire. It was called Men Nfr. The Greeks translated Men Nfr to Memphis. That's how the people of United Stated got a city called Memphis. The main principles of Kmtic civilisation were Ra, his daughter Maat, his granddaughter Aset, his grandson Wsr called Osiris by the Greeks. Wsr became the prime model for many people and cultures. He was the principle of rebirth and divine kingship. Wsr was also the father of a boy called Hrw. Wsr is a very interesting principle. Wsr is the root word for Sir. Wsr was a member of royalty. An honorable individual. The Wsrian principle is still in use today.

A skeptic will gladly say that "mythology" are fancy stories. The answer to the skeptic would be; why do big corporations and intelligent investors use the word asset to describe their treasures?

The skeptic would also say, Myths are things that never existed. We would reply by asking the following question: Have you ever used the word minute?

Yes.

Do you know where the word minute comes from?

No idea.

The father of Ariadne was an aristocrat called Minos. Minos is the root word for minimal. The origin of the word is not Greek. It is African. The Kemites principle of fertility was called Min. From Min we get minutes, minimal, ministry, Minister. Minos plus the astrological sign Taurus gives us the "Minotaur" and many other words that we use every day.

Have you ever seen a British Prime Minister? The skeptic would have no other option but to reply yes to this question. Mythology is the source of everything, past, present and future.

Those who refuse to accept the truth will eventually become liabilities to themselves, friends and relatives. Aset and Wsr are universal principles. Aset is the mother, Wsr is the father. The essential seeds of the human family.

An essential asset

Aset is an essential and universal principle. She is also an excellent reference. She was the first queen of the ancient land, Kmt. She was also a wife and a mother. She was the wife of Wsr. Her husband was killed and cut into 14 pieces. After learning of her husband's death, she searched for his body and found it. She spent more than 2 months nursing and healing him. She succeeded and saved her husband from permanent and premature death. She became a role model for the ideal wife and healer. One of her titles was "Mut Wr, the Great Mother, "La Prima Donna" in Latin. The origin of the statement " The Madonna and Bambino".

Aset became the root word for assets. Precious people and things.

Like you, she was an asset. Aset was an asset to her family and culture. She started her journey as a daughter, a wife, became a widow, a healer, a mother. She completed the hero's journey and became an asset.

Any person who knows how to heal others is an asset to his or her people. A daughter who researches natural health on YouTube has the potential to become an asset to her mother, brother, sister, husband, father and anybody who interacts with her. She is the hero.

A big obstacle

The hero wants to achieve something. He or she faces formidable opposition. At first sight, the hero has no chance of winning. Hrw, the son of Aset, was a very young man who had to fight his uncle. Hrw vs. Sutek, David vs. Goliath, Satan vs. Jesus, Theseus vs. the Minotaur, Ishtar vs. Ereshkigal, Angra Mainyu vs. Ahura Mazda, Human beings vs. Cancer, Healthy cells vs Free radicals. Our research tells us that modern human beings are too detached from the mythological world, therefore they don't believe in the hero that's hidden inside them. Most people believe that they are powerless victims of one of the most vicious monsters in the history of the world. That's however a false perception, the product of mind programming and years of conditioning. You can defeat the monster called disease, old age, decay and sickness, poverty, dependency, diabetes... You are not a powerless victim. You have within you the seeds of ancient heroes. If you accept these ideas you are on your way to prosperity. "Yes and But" means the end of the journey.

The thread of Ariadne

Ariadne the daughter of King Minos spoke to Daedalus the great architect who built the Labyrinth of Knossos. She asked him to help her, not to save her life, but the lives of "others". Her goal was to get rid of a monster that destroyed her family and was about to destroy the lives of 14 innocent young people. Although the monster was her half-brother, Ariadne did her best to help Theseus, the Athenian hero who was prepared to sacrifice his life in order to save others. Ariadne gave Theseus a thread that enabled him to navigate the labyrinth.

That's the mythological message. You should do your best to heal yourself and heal others. That's the path to heroism and happiness. By learning how to save others you will get the clues on how to save yourself.

We are passionate about mythology. Mythology gives us clues about how to defeat the monster, disease, ignorance, the Minotaur. It also helps us to find the hero within us. We shall use mythological and philosophical lenses as well as personal experiences, to understand the character of this beast that's destroying families, children, friends, lovers, and generations. Cancer Research UK says: "That 1 in 2 people will develop cancer at some point in their lives." What about prevention or correction?

We believe that people who do nothing to prevent the development of free radicals are at risk of developing cancer. You don't have to be a victim of cancer or any other disease. You can defeat the monster by taking the right steps. Ariadne gave Theseus a thread which helped the Athenian dreamer to take the right steps. We give you a map that contains 12 steps. The heroes who cured themselves of cancer, migraines, diabetes have left threads.

Follow the threads left by successful heroes and you shall succeed. To become a hero you will have to go on a journey of self-discovery. You will discover small but very important details such as drinking a daily juice made of organic beetroot with a spoon of organic turmeric. Beetroot heals the liver. Turmeric removes inflammation and destroys free radicals. Turmeric also contains Curcumin. Both Turmeric and the liver are mentioned in mythological stories from Kmt, Ancient Greece and India. The story of Prometheus, for example, contains a hidden lesson about the vitality of the liver. Hrw the son of Aset and Wsr had 4 children. One of his children was a protector of the liver.

Enjoy the journey. The content of this book has the power to inspire you, as well as give you the tools, thinking and strategies for you to become the hero of your family, generation, company, organization, tribe, your inner circle and society. The opportunities and potential are there. We are very glad to share the journeys of the heroes who defeated the monster with you, your friends and relatives. Thank you for buying and reading this book. The key is in the application of the principles and the strategies prescribed. We are going to use;

- African mythology (Kmt) also known as Ancient Egypt.
- Sumerian/Babylonian mythology
- Iranian - Persian mythology
- Indian mythology
- Native American mythology
- Greek mythology

There is a forest near the house in which we live. A truly wonderful place that's ideal for meditation and reflection. People of all ages and origins use the forest to take walks and to meditate. I love being there. The home of the soul.

I enjoy the irresistible green and peaceful landscapes, I love to watch the agile and happy dogs running freely, I appreciate the delicious moments and memories, visions, conversations, experiences kindly offered by the forest and its strange sometimes mysterious citizens such as silent birds and timid squirrels. I love the ideas that come to my mind during my walks, I truly love the fresh breeze that fills my lungs with energy and essential oxygen. I also love the quietness and elegance, the natural beauty of the forest. It brings me millions, billions, trillions of wonderful ideas.

During a dry and warm summer sunset, I went to the forest to take a walk. I was happy, very happy. I was keen to spend hours walking, thinking, meditating, talking and listening to my heart. My mind was filled with ideas and visions about a book that we were planning to write.

Shortly after I reached the heart of the forest, I heard voices of people. They were walking behind me. I didn't recognise the voices therefore I kept walking. I remained quiet. As I walked, I realised that it was a man and woman. They were talking to each other. The sounds of their steps kept getting closer and closer to me. They got very close to me, then I heard the gentle voice of a lady. She was talking to a man. I kept on walking. I was very relaxed. "Hello", said an Englishman who appeared to be in his early 50s. "Hello, how are you?" I replied. "I am fine, thank you." He said.

The lady kept walking fast. She overtook me. She was walking very fast indeed. I greeted her. She failed to make eye contact instead she greeted me and kept walking fast as if she was about to miss a train.

The man and I were walking at the same pace. We found ourselves walking side by side. I looked at him and said "I made an exciting discovery that has the power to change your life. I would like to share it with you."

He looked at me and smiled. "What's the discovery?" He asked. "I think I have figured out how to remove disease from the body." The man remained quiet. We carried on walking side by side. The lady in front of us kept on walking fast.

"The secret is in the word enemy, what's the word that's associated with enemy?" I asked.

The man spent a few seconds in silence then turned to me and said, "Enema?"

"Yes." I said smiling. "You are 100% right." I was very pleased to hear his words. They confirmed my thinking. They were in harmony with my reasoning.

Enema is the keyword. I said... "If we look at the word enema we get similar words such as enigma and enemy. An enemy is an enigma, a frightening mystery. A disease is also an enigma. That's one of the reasons why people are scared of the word disease, illness, cancer etc.

An enema is one of the best ways to remove the enemy called disease out of the body. Enema is essentially another word for cleansing. We heal our bodies and minds through cleansing."

"Hum, I see, very interesting." He said. We kept walking towards the southern exit of the forest. I realised that we were heading towards the same destination. The paths of the forest are in the shape of a loop. They provide you with a cyclical experience. If you keep walking you will eventually end up in the place where you began. Although the forest is big and has many paths it will eventually lead you to the place where you started your journey.

We carried on walking and chatting. We spoke about natural health, natural healing, alternative therapies, organic foods, dependency and mineral deficiency. Shortly after we got out of the forest, the lady slowed down. She looked at me and said, "That's what I have. Breast cancer." "You have breast cancer?" I asked. "Yes." she said.

After learning about her condition, I spent 1 hour advising the lady about the steps that she could take in order to protect herself. It was almost half past nine in the evening when we finally stopped and said goodbye to each other. I was very happy to meet the couple. I was truly pleased.

When I returned home I reflected on the experience. I was shocked to learn that both husband and wife were sick. The wife had breast cancer. The husband suffered from diabetes. Both had no clue what do in order to get out of the labyrinth called "chronic diseases".

The man's wife was the 5th breast cancer victim I met in less than 12 months. It struck me that she was not aware of essential principles that could help her to defeat the big monster. She did not take supplements or engage in detox. These are basic tasks when it comes to disease.

I concluded that the best way to help the lady and anybody who wishes to learn about alternative methods to fight cancer, was to write a book. I decided to write a book about people who have defeated the monster, the heroes, the healers, and saviours of souls. The men and women, mothers, fathers who refused to be victims of a modern epidemic that's shattering lives and dreams.

Health is a fascinating subject. In my view, health is the most important subject a person can explore in life. You cannot succeed in life without excellent health. If you want to become a hero, to save yourself and your relatives from a painful experience, please keep on reading.

Get yourself ready to learn the secrets that have the power to transform you into a hero. The couple that I met in the forest prescribed to the victim's philosophy. The solution of their problem is called the Hero's Philosophy.

CHAPTER 1
The Hero's Philosophy

During a warm and fine spring morning, 22nd of March to be precise, I visited the Manchester Central Library with the goal of reading a book about Greek mythology. While I was there I met a lady who was battling cancer and the side effects of chemotherapy. I asked her how she was. She told me that she was trying to find an alternative method because "I can't take it anymore. It's too much, it's killing me." She said.

Me - How is your research going?

Patient 1 - There is so much information on the internet. I don't know who to trust, she said looking at me with desperate and melancholic eyes. I lost my hair, I am struggling to walk eat and talk. I don't know where to go from here. She had tears in her beautiful green eyes. I hugged and told her that she was on the right track.

Me - Many people believe that medication is the answer. I think differently. To understand complex subjects such as cancer, economics, love, life, friends, culture, we have to ask the right questions. In my view, one of the questions should be, what philosophy am I prescribing to? To cure yourself of cancer or any disease, you would have to become a philosopher.

Patient 1 - Philosopher? She asked. I am in pain. I need a remedy not a philosophy. I don't even know what philosophy is. I don't understand the whole thing.

Me - To understand a philosophy or a way of thinking you have to look at its roots, the origins. The people who created it. In your case that's the pharmaceutical industry and natural therapies. The fathers of "big pharma" or what people call the pharmaceutical industry, were a Scottish man called Andrew Carnegie and an American man called John D. Rockefeller. Carnegie and Rockefeller were billionaires who realised that they could control entire countries by creating a new industry that supplied false medication. After creating what's known as big pharma, they waged war on anyone who prescribed natural solutions. They lobbied governments to make it difficult to approve natural treatments. They also employed a man called Edward Bernays and instructed him to create propaganda that promoted drugs and targeted the natural "fear of death" which every human being has. Edward Bernays was the grandson of Sigmund Freud. He spent his entire life studying psychology and researching ways to mind control crowds. He wrote a book called "*Propaganda*" and invented the term PR, Public Relations. He was an expert in mind programming, brainwashing and mass control.

Edward Bernays created a PR campaign that persuaded women to embrace smoking. The campaign was called "Torches of Freedom" and took place during a large public demonstration in New York. Bernays put the words smoking and freedom next to one another. He also invented the idea of "War to restore Democracy". The union and employment of two conflicting words, an oxymoron, was a psychological ploy that worked beautifully. It also destroyed billions of lives and generations. Think of radiation and health. They are two polar opposites successfully sold through emotional branding and endless PR campaigns.

Whenever a celebrity is attacked by the Minotaur, the entire world is made aware. Nobody talks about prevention or restoration. Edward Bernays was one of the most influential tricksters in the history of the world. Every single "leading Media" organisation uses his tricks.

The fathers of big pharma were very ambitious, cynical, cunning and powerful people. They also created what people call private hospitals and medical patents. To mislead people they funded health charities, research organisations and medical schools. Whenever you take a medical drug you are prescribing to their philosophy. They were not very nice people therefore, their philosophies were not nice either. Their influence continues to this day. Their focus was on profit rather than health. Their companies caused unthinkable levels of suffering to billions of people around the world. Toxic drugs, wars, vaccinations, endless mind programming, social and psychological warfare through the media, psychic disruption are some of the strategies which they used to build their empires.

An expert in natural remedies called Dr. Aleksandra Niedzwiecki said that "big pharma makes more money than banks." Both Rockefeller and Carnegie became billionaires, very powerful people. They embraced a very destructive philosophy called Eugenics. They were very open about their views and plans for the future of the human race. They saw disease as a means to control population growth. Using ideas and techniques prescribed by Bernays, powerful corporations succeeded in persuading people to trust and prioritise the use of "deadly toxins" rather than "Mother Nature".

Rockefeller said: "Competition is a sin."

"Do you know the only thing that gives me pleasure? It's to see my dividends coming in."

The founders of big pharma were not interested in happiness or health. It was all about profit. Their goal was to make as much money as possible. Rockefeller and Carnegie rejected the ideas of ancient philosophers such as, Imhotep, the Greek Hippocrates, Indian philosophy, Ayurveda and modern Swiss called Paracelso. They realised that they could not make big profits with herbs and plants therefore, they said that doctors who prescribe herbs and plants should be sacked. Medical schools funded and controlled by their foundations were told not to teach natural health or discuss natural therapies. In today's very dynamic world, a Youtuber that's fanatic about health has more to say about micronutrients than "a qualified doctor." Google has indeed opened "the Pandora box."

One of the leading cancer doctors in the world, a remarkable man called Russell L. Blaylock said the following:

"The second myth circulating among oncologists is that the cancer patients must avoid taking antioxidants because these nutrients might interfere with conventional treatment. This fear is based on hypothetical grounds and not science."

The lady and patient was keen to learn more. I turned to her and asked the following question:

Me - Did you use natural remedies?

Patient - No, I was told that natural therapies don't work. A nurse that took care of me advised me to look into the work of a German lady who used oils and cheese to help cancer patients. She did not tell me the name of the lady. That's one of the reasons why I came here.

Me - Interesting, I think the lady's name was Johanna Budwig. I understand why you shunned natural remedies. Natural remedies are cheaper than conventional remedies. There is not much marketing around herbs because they are supplied by my Mother Nature, rather than a specific individual. They are free. Every year billions are spent on marketing new drugs. Many "new drugs" are very toxic and are removed from the market a few years after they are sold as "the new big thing". Turmeric for example, is a powerful anti-cancer agent. It is very affordable indeed. A prominent cancer doctor called Dr. Burzynski uses a therapy called Gene Therapy to fight cancer. He also uses Turmeric. He has been curing cancer for more than 30 years.

After creating a new industry, the owners of big pharma lobbied governments to persecute and destroy anybody who said that diseases can be cured through natural methods. In the world of health you have two philosophies. It doesn't matter what disease you have. You have to choose between the two:

- Economic philosophy - medical drugs, vaccines, surgery.
- Natural philosophy - herbs, cleansing and micronutrients.

Patient 1 - How does a philosophy affect cancer?

Me - Philosophy affects thinking, thinking affects behaviour. Your thinking affects your diet, your diet affects your health.

To answer your question properly we should look at the origins of philosophy. If you go to Ancient India you will discover an ancient and refined philosophy that was created and written long before Plato or

Socrates were born. Ancient Ethiopia and Kmt are excellent candidates for the birthplace of philosophy. Both countries have some of the oldest written languages in the world.

A king and a philosopher

A Persian King called Kurus whom the Greeks called "Cyrus the Great" was a remarkable philosopher. He loved plants and trees. His engineers created a sophisticated irrigation method which enabled the king to create wonderful gardens in the desert. The gardens were called Paradiso. Paradiso is the root word for 'Paradise'. King Kurus is credited with the invention of "Human Rights" He is the only non-Jewish person to be presented as a Messiah in a Jewish Bible. He was a philosopher who created one of the largest and richest empires in the history of the world. He was a philosopher and a very successful individual. Prince Charles is a lover of plants and gardens.

Me - Heard of the Chelsea flower show?

Patient - Yes. Everything makes perfect sense now. The Persian philosopher and king introduced gardening to modern Royalty.

Me - The culture is very ancient. Babylon and the Kemites, today called Egyptians already had gardens and swimming pools. Prince Charles is very open about his love for natural methods such as the Gerson Therapy.

The origins of Sophia

Wsr was the patriarch and King of Kmt. He was killed by his younger brother. The King's wife was called Aset. Aset was the highest priestess of the ancient world. She was a collector of wisdom and the perfect role model for matrilineal cultures. Wsr was a lover of Aset. Aset symbolised wisdom. She was known as the mother of libraries. After invading Kmt, the Greeks were inspired to develop their own culture from ancient principles that predated the invention of the Greek alphabet. They changed the names of the people, temples, cities, books and principles whom they called "Egyptian Gods". Wsr became Osiris, Dionysus and Seraphis. The leader of the country known as Nswt Bity was translated to Pharaoh. Aset became Athena, Djehuty became Hermes Trismegistus, and Hrw M Akhet became the Sphinx. Aset also became Sophia. In Greek philosophy, Sophia is the central idea of wisdom and religion. If you follow the sound of the name Aset you will eventually get into Sophia. The spelling might be different. The sound and the female principle are there.

The Greeks adopted aspects of African culture. A very matrilineal and nature loving civilisation. They did not fully adopt the culture, its rituals and principles because they were invaded and conquered by a patriarchal priestley tribe called the Aryans.

The Indo-European influence

"The invasions of the Indo-Europeans. These invasions come from the areas north of the Black Sea, and stretching along the great braising area. We had races, biologically plural, races. Speaking related languages. The Indo-European languages were first recognised as one family. In the 18th century in about 1782 or 83, by Sir William Jones who was the first westerner really, to make a study of Sanskrit. He was a judge in the court of Kolkata."

"And he recognised that the Sanskrit the language of India, was related very closely to Latin, Greek, the Germanic and Celtic languages. This is one family of languages with an enormous spread. And they were carried by these herding people, Nomadic herding people, who mastered the horse and then the war chariot. This indicates their Aryan, the differentiated Indo-European groups. The word Aryan meaning noble."

Joseph Campbell - Transformation of Myth through Time

Many thousands of years ago, the land today known as Greece was invaded by a tribe known as Aryans. Modern historians are unsure about the origins of the Aryan therefore they speculate that Aryans were the product of a union, an amalgamation of tribes from India, Iran and Europe. Aryans were a father, phallus worshiping people who placed a male creator at the center of their cults. Names such as Brahman, Zarathustra, Zeus, Kronos, Indra, Jupiter, Jove, Ahura Mazda, Shamash, Dyus, Dionysus, Deity, Dios and Deus refer to a male principle of Aryan origin. Aryans invaded mother worshiping cultures and changed their mythology.

For thousands, perhaps millions of years people across the world worshipped a female whom they called "Mother Nature". She was the main healer. Mythological characters such as Aset, Ariadne, Sedna, Rhea, Ishtar, Eve, and Gaia are symbols, memories of an ancient cult dedicated to the "Mother Goddess". The mother Goddess was more than a human being. She was the Moon, "La Luna", the soil. In certain cultures she was presented as the sky. She was the giver of children, lives, rivers, fishes, plants, seasons, stars and daylight.

Aryans changed the script and said that Jupiter, Jove, a male was the creator of the universe and the "father". The murder of Tiamat, a female principle from Babylon is evidence of the change.

Gilgamesh the King of Uruk refused to marry the priestess Ishtar. He accused her of murder and destruction. Enkido, the brother of Gilgamesh lost his purity after sleeping with a temple prostitute called Shamhat.

Societies and civilisations abandoned the stellar and lunar cults and calendars. They adopted solar calendars. Example "Gregorian Calendar". The Sun symbol of the solar cult became the central source of "everything in the Universe".

Aryans changed an ancient culture that centered on the "Mother". They also created a powerful society of priests. They invented languages, temples, schools, created laws and rich civilisations. They also changed the mythology and architecture of cities and countries which they invaded. In order to keep their power, powerful priests used literature to engage in character assassination of female priestesses.

A book called "*the Alphabet vs. The Goddess*" by Dr. Leonard Shlain explores this subject.

The ancient healer, the mother, successful saviour of souls was turned into an evil doer. Females ceased to be the saviour and became destroyers. Making females "Daeva", the root word for 'Devil' and 'Diva' was an intellectual and psychological strategy used to maintain social and economic power. The famous "Helen of Argos", a beautiful lady blamed for the war of Troy, is a reflection of Aryan influence. In India Kali also plays the role of a destroyer. She is the ugliest aspect of

Shiva. Kali is related to words such as California and thugs. Her followers were criminals known as Tuggies.

The female serpent, knower of ancient mysteries became an ally and personification of a female. There was a profound change in symbolic presentation and interpretation. In the North of Africa, in Kmt for example, a female and serpent were the guardians of the royal family and source of essential wisdom.

The Aryans turned the serpent into a source of evil and the main ally of a female. Years of endless propaganda and fear mongering have inspired many people to reject the idea that "Mother Nature" has the power to heal our bodies, minds and souls. Modern human beings don't trust in nature, they are afraid of nature. They would rather take powerful toxins rather than essential herbs and plants such as Graviola, Sea Kelp and Spirulina. The move from a female to a male creator had a profound effect on the consciousness of human beings. We became detached from nature. Such detachment is affecting our psyche and bodies.

After coming in contact with Africans whom they called "Ethiopians", Greeks were inspired to embrace the "Mother Goddess culture." They placed the female Aset as the central principle. The word Sophia means wisdom. Philo is the lover of wisdom. If you look carefully you will see the influence of the king they called Osiris. He was a lover of Aset. Aset saved him because she was wise. The patriarch of the Kemites was devoted to his wife. She personified wisdom. This union gave us the idea of philosophy. Love and wisdom.

The Greeks were inspired by the mythology and the story of Aset and her mythical husband Wsr. They went to Kmt to study in what is today known as the mystery schools. When they returned home, they created their own versions. The original name of the capital of the Kmtic Empire was Waset. The Arabs called it Luxor. The Greeks called it Thebes. There is a Greek city called Thebes located in mainland Greece. Greek intellectuals translated ancient text and changed names. Instead of saying WsrAset, they said PhiloSophia.

The name Sophia is associated to a female principle that has the wisdom to give birth to new ideas and essential principles. A philosopher is someone who gives birth to a new way of thinking and ideas. Kmt was the most advanced civilisation of the ancient world. From Kmt we got essentials such as medicine, architecture, theology, astrology and many other amazing things which the Greeks called Sophia. Over the centuries the name Sophia became an important and very influential reference. The modern world contains many examples of the influence of Sophia.

The wife of the former King of Spain is called Sofia. One of the richest museums in Madrid is called the Sofia Museum. There was a famous actress called Sophia Loren. Sophia is an essential and universal principle that transcends race, gender, social status, and birthplace. Everybody is in desperate need of a new Sophia.

The Greeks said 'philo' refers to a lover and 'Sophia' is wisdom. The lover of wisdom is a philosopher. The origin of philosophy is very important because it gives us a clue regarding the methods that each culture used to heal people.

Every culture has its own philosophy and philosophers. The Chinese use an ancient philosophy that focuses on herbs. The people of India use a philosophy that strives to heal the body, mind and soul. It is called Ayurveda. Native American Indians also use herbs, rituals and prayer to heal the body. In the Western world people are given drugs.

That's it. Patients are not told about the power of the mind, meditation, herbs, supplements and most importantly diet and cleansing.

The father of Western Medicine was a Greek man called Hippocrates. His name was the origin of the word 'hypocrite'. Anybody who wishes to become a doctor has to sign the famous Hippocratic Oath. Most doctors and patients are not told that Hippocrates was a student of Imhotep. Imhotep was one of the greatest philosophers of the ancient world. He was a very successful African doctor who cured more than 1000 illnesses using herbs. He was a key advisor to an Nswt Bity, pharaoh called Djoser.

The biographies of Imhotep and his disciple Hippocrates, are essential references for people who are interested in healing. Both men prescribed herbs and natural remedies. They were herbalists who used holistic healing to cure diseases. Their philosophies were based on "Mother Nature". They prescribed to the powerful idea that the natural world provides everything you need.

If you read ancient scriptures you will find wisdom about herbs, fasting and natural remedies carefully hidden in the Bible. The truth about the art of healing has been perverted for economic purposes. To understand the subject called health and disease, a person has to study and adopt the mindset of a philosopher, a thinker, a healer.

One of the main tasks of a philosopher is to ask intelligent questions. A philosopher is a researcher who is not satisfied with artificial answers. You should ask key questions such as:

- Are there any natural philosophies?
- Are they successful and documented?

- If yes, which book should I read?
- Who is the philosopher that I am dealing with?
- What does he or she prescribe?
- What's the origin of the philosophy that I am using?

These are essential questions. If we ignore the questions we will be forced to deal with the negative consequences that follow irrational thinking and lack of research. Whether you want to or not, you will consume a philosophy, medication, policies, ideas prescribed by somebody who follows a specific philosophy. Unless you create and follow your own. The economist, senator or MP working for the government follows a specific economic and social philosophy that will be reflected in his or her policies. The citizens of a country will be forced to deal with the effects of a government's philosophy. They could also use their own economic philosophies and create their own businesses.

If we look at the word 'prescribe' we learn something very interesting. 'Pre' means before. 'Scribe' is the writer. The word prescribe literally means before a scribe. Before a writer. Prescribe also means 'to give'.

A doctor is a scribe, a writer who has to give a prescription. A doctor has to write a prescription. We could wear the mask of a philosopher and ask;

What happened before the modern scribe started to prescribe medications?

The history of big pharma and the cultures of the ancient world gives us two types of philosophy:

- The victim's philosophy
- The hero's philosophy

Key questions;

- What happened to you before you met the scribe?
- What happened to you after you met the scribe and followed the prescription?
- What happened before the modern scribe came into play?
- The most advanced civilisations of the ancient word were Sumerian, Kmtic, Persian, Chinese, Japanese, Native American, Greek and Indian. They all valued scribes. What was the health philosophies of these civilisations?
- What were the prescriptions of men like Hippocrates?
- Should you use Turkish Tail to help your immune system?

Patient 1 - How do you find the right philosophy?

Me - You have to search. If you search you shall find. To become a philosopher you have to study other people's philosophies. To become a scribe, a writer you have to read other people's books. The God of Western philosophy was a man called Socrates. Socrates was the mentor of Plato. Socrates used a method that focused on questioning. He would go to a place called Agora and spend an entire day asking questions. Agora was the public square of the cities of Ancient Greece. Socrates' method was based on questions. That's the Socratic Method. To find the right answer to your challenges you have to ask smart questions.

Patient 1 - Who are the health philosophers of our century?

There are many. 3 years ago I read the biography of a remarkable lady called Charlotte Gerson. She was born in Germany on 27th March, 1922. When she was young she was diagnosed with tuberculosis. Doctors who prescribed to conventional medicine and philosophy told young Charlotte that her disease was incurable. Charlotte was very lucky. The young lady's father was a health philosopher. He knew how to cure diseases. He cured his daughter using natural remedies. Charlotte Gerson is still alive. Millions of people around the world prescribe and practice the philosophy created by her father; The Gerson therapy.

A great philosopher is someone who practices what he or she preaches. Dr. Mercola is a philosopher based in the U.S. Dr. Sebi was a philosopher from Honduras. Rene Caisse was a Canadian philosopher. There are many philosophers who explore the subject of health. You can find them by asking questions. Philosophy is a universal discipline that affects every single human being on the planet.

Amazon is a great tool to find excellent philosophers. If you search for a subject Amazon will recommend books related to a specific subject or author. Sites such as Amazon, Audible are a great strategy to discover literary excellence.

Patient 1 - How do you become a philosopher?

You don't need to go to university in order to become a successful entrepreneur. All you need is to use the correct economic, entrepreneurial philosophy. There are economic, social, moral, psychological, cultural, individual, collective philosophies. You don't need a piece of paper saying that you are a philosopher. You study and practice.

I am a self-educated philosopher. I didn't go to university. I am not a doctor, scientist. I don't even have a university degree. My philosophy does not come from the academic world. My philosophy is based on Mdw Ntr. Mdw Ntr is the root word for 'Mother Nature'. Please don't buy into my philosophy. Read, research and test. Our philosophy regarding health is very simple.

We believe that every human being is born a hero. The potential is there. We add a little bit of Indian mythology into the mix and say: The right thinking, the right mentor, the right action will enable you to become a hero who knows how to defeat the big monster called cancer.

The right thinking, right actions, right living are elements of Hindu and Buddhist philosophy.

Patient 1 - How do you develop your own philosophy?

Me - That's a very important question because if you don't develop your own philosophy, you will have no option but to use other people's philosophies. You will have to use other people's subscriptions. Become interdependent. I like the word amalgamation. A mixture. The cure of your disease is a mixture of different ideas and remedies. There is no such thing as a "cure" for cancer. A patient should try and use different methods. Healthy methods.

- Cleansing
- Herbs
- Meditation
- Supplementation
- Spiritual healing
- Organic foods

Patient 1 - What's more important, the person or the philosophy used by that person?

Me - You reject a philosophy. That doesn't mean that you reject a person. It's not personal. Saying no to a prescription or a person's opinion doesn't mean you hate people or doctors. A philosophy based on conflicts is very dangerous. It will help you to destroy your enemies but it will also destroy you. There are very dangerous ideas and practices that you should reject.

The most dangerous philosophers are people who don't practice what they preach. Plato created a very toxic philosophy. It is the most used philosophy in the world. There is a problem. It is very toxic and destructive. Plato never practiced his philosophy. He wrote and talked about it. When he tried to put his philosophy into practice, it caused so much destruction he was forced to flee the country in which he was trying to implement his philosophy. Plato was forced to flee Syracuse after courtiers rejected his ideas and influence. They saw his ideas as destructive. Plato's philosophy contains bad ideas and great ideas.

You should do your best to find a philosopher that practices what he or she preaches. It is very easy to prescribe medication then tell a person if the symptoms persist come back.

The benefits of cleaning your system

The king or queen of Kmt had a private doctor. One of the main tasks of the doctor was the administration of coffee enemas. Cleansing the liver was a key element of some of the greatest philosophies of the ancient world. They used natural elements to restore balance in the body. The word Mother Nature comes from Mdw Ntr. Ntr is the root word for 'nature', 'natural', 'natura', 'naturaleza'. Although we have advanced science we still need Mother Nature.

Patient 1 - Can you give me an example of a 21st century philosopher who studies the subject of health?

Go to YouTube and search for Chris Wark. He cured himself of cancer using natural methods. He does a lot of teaching about cancer. He is a lover of wisdom. He is a philosopher who knows exactly what he is talking about because his wisdom comes from experience. Someone who completes the Hero's Journey and heals his or her body becomes a philosopher. A lover of wisdom and natural methods to restore vitality.

Any type of prosperity and progress requires a philosophy. Philosophy is key because it affects your behaviour, your conduct, life, rituals, lifestyle etc.

Philosophy affects your choices, associations, actions and results. If you don't have a philosophy you are in trouble because you might be using an incorrect philosophy. There is no point criticising a person. You should look at their philosophy. Love or money? Refined or barbarian? Some of the most successful British politicians, journalists, intellectuals have something in common. They went to Oxford and studied PPE; Philosophy, Politics and Economics.

Patient 1 - How long does it take for a patient to become a philosopher?

Me - Philosophy is a way of life. 12 months of consistent application should be enough for a patient to get the basics, the foundations of excellent health and nutrition. You would spend the rest of your life being a health philosopher. In other words, you live your life according to specific philosophical principles. If we look at the life of one of the most influential philosophers in history, an individual who developed a very healthy philosophy, we can see 3 essential stages.

Please be aware that the name of a person changes when he or she reaches a stage of his or her personal, spiritual, intellectual biological and social evolution. For example, single, married, widow. One of the greatest philosophers of Ancient India is known as;

- Siddhārtha Gautama
- Bodhisattva
- Buddha

1. Siddhārtha was the patient who suffered from a spiritual, psychological sickness. He was a prisoner of illusion, delusion and confusion created by his father who was mainly interested in power. Siddhārtha's father was a philosopher who was interested in economics. Siddhartha was the patient.

2. After leaving his home and renouncing materialism, Siddhārtha became a Bodhisattva. Bodhisattva is another word for student. A Bodhisattva has the potential to become Buddha.

3. In order to reach the third and highest level of his spiritual and intellectual evolution, a stage known as Buddha, Siddhārtha had to renounce his old beliefs and way of life. The luxury, the opulent palace and its people were left behind. The same applies to a patient. The word Buddha means teacher. To become a teacher a patient has to renounce his or her old beliefs. You don't become a teacher unless you renounce your ignorance. It takes roughly 6 years for an initiate to complete his or her journey. To become a health philosopher, a patient should spend at least 6 years studying, meditating, researching and experimenting. The Hero's Philosophy is a practical philosophy. It's not theoretical. You have to do coffee enemas, fasting and juicing for the rest of your life. Buddhism contains an essential mystery. You don't spend 10 years proclaiming that you are a Buddhist. The philosophy becomes your spiritual water, something that you consume, drink and digest for the rest of your life.

Patient 1 - What happens if a person rejects a philosophy?

You have to deal with the consequences, which includes a painful and premature death. There are always pros and cons to everything in life. Medication or meditation? Processed or organic?

The ignorant and desperate individual does not have time for meditation. Instead he or she goes to a doctor and demands "a miraculous cure". A quick fix not meditation. The ordinary patient wants a quick fix, fast medication and fast healing. Such thinking is a violation of natural laws. Winter does not last 7 days.

The problem with the "quick fix" strategy is the following: you are where you are because of an incorrect philosophy. If you are not interested in renouncing your existing philosophy you are in danger of perpetuating the mistakes that brought you to the gates of death. Meditation requires a stop. You have to stop and think. Yoga requires a silence.

I recently met a lady in the forest who was suffering from cancer. She told me that she had no time to cleanse her liver because "I have to work". She gives priority to finance rather than biological and spiritual prosperity. It is a matter of time until the building, sacred temple that we call the human body disintegrates. If you don't stop and give your body the opportunity to heal, your organism will eventually force you to stop. I gave up my job, social status, and monthly salary in order to heal my soul and body.

You should stop, reflect, listen, and read. That's meditation. Philosophers spend a great deal of time meditating. If you reject the ancient philosophy called meditation then you have to deal with the chaos that comes from not thinking or reflecting. Chaos or harmony, triumph or tragedy, tears or laughter, longevity or brevity, life or death. You choose. Chaos creates stress. Stress creates disease. Disease creates disintegration, decay, gradual disappearance and a permanent dissolution called death.

Conflict or harmony

Two of the most successful modern managers in football are Pepe Guardiola and Jose Mourinho. They went to the same school in Barcelona. The school is called La Masia and is located in the capital of

Catalonia. Although they were exposed to the same philosophy, they have different approaches.

Mr. Mourinho adopted some principles of La Masia. Mr. Joseph "Pepe" Guardiola embraced the philosophy and principles taught by the school. Mr. Pepe Guardiola's teams seem to be more successful than those of Mr. Mourinho's. Mr. Mourinho's career is full of conflict and losses. From time to time Mr. Mourinho gets into disputes, arguments and public criticisms of his players. He is a very passionate and intelligent man who loves what he does. He was very successful during the early stages of his career. There was a point when his career experienced a sharp decline. Stagnation.

Mr. Guardiola's career contains many, many remarkable achievements. Mr. Mourinho seems to thrive on conflict. Conflict with the media, players, owners, referees, opposing managers. Mr. Guardiola's eyes are always on the big prize. Mr. Guardiola has never been sacked by a club. He is one of the most sought after minds of the game. His philosophy is very deep and enables him to achieve remarkable things wherever he goes. Wherever he goes he creates a revolution. His teams become models of intellectual and strategic evolution. An entire country and teams will change their style in order to match the beauty, elegance, harmony, perfection cultivated by Guardiola's teams. Teams managed by Mr. Guardiola achieve outstanding levels of success and refinement. As soon as he leaves, the team experiences a gradual decay. It doesn't matter how many millions a club spends, how many famous and experienced players it collects, it loses its light as soon as the philosopher known as Guardiola leaves.

A very interesting detail about Mr. Guardiola is the fact that he will instruct certain players to fast. He demands high-levels of discipline and commitment. Both managers are very successful and powerful.

They are two different individuals. Two different philosophies, two different personalities, two different journeys. One wins through conflict and a lot of destruction, the other refines and creates excellence based on harmony. They are both winners. What's the best strategy? Which strategy is ideal for the short-term? Which strategies are ideal for the long-term?

The book "*Natural Therapies for Cancer Patients*" has a very interesting statement. Doctor Russell L. Blaylock says that:

"Even more exciting is the discovery that many of the chemicals found in edible plants can turn cancer cells into normal cells, meaning that food components may indeed be used to reverse cancer itself. In addition, these same plant chemicals can reduce the complications associated with the conventional cancer treatments and enhance, sometimes dramatically, the effectiveness of these treatments".

Doctor Blaylock's philosophy inspires us to ask intelligent questions, such as, should we fight or repair?

Should we fight cancer or turn cancer cells into healthy cells using food and vitamins? Doctors who use natural ways will say "Use nutrition to heal cells." Those who prescribe to big pharma's philosophy will say "Wage war against cancer cells. Destroy them. Even if you have to destroy healthy cells."

Me - Do you know where the treatment known as chemotherapy comes from?

Patient - No, I don't.

Me - It comes from war and conflict. One of the books that every cancer patient should read is called "*The Cancer Survival Manual*", written by Rachael Linkie. On page 11 it says the following: "When doctors discovered during "World War One" that mustard gas destroyed bone marrow, they began to experiment with it as a way to kill cancer cells. Although they had little success with mustard gas, it did pave the way for modern chemotherapy - which involves the most toxic and poisonous substances anyone can deliberately put in their body."

Page 12 -The Cancer Survival Manual- Rachael Linkie

Chemo was the product one of the bloodiest wars in the history of the human race. Why would someone use a treatment that comes from conflict? It's all about philosophy.

Patient 1 - What type of health philosophies are there?

Me - There are many philosophies. Every writer creates a philosophy through his or her books and thinking. Sir Arthur Conan Doyle's philosophy can be found inside his books. Rachael Linkie's books contain a philosophy which would help a patient or a student to know more about the subject of health and cancer. Dr. Russell L. Blaylock's books present his philosophy. Dr. Blaylock is very experienced, he has more than 30 years of practical experience dealing with cancer. He has seen many things, many patients, and many changes. There are many philosophies and philosophers looking into the subject of cancer and healing. There is plenty to choose from. People who are ignorant about philosophy believe that their choices are limited. Such thinking leads to all kinds of irreparable biological and psychological havoc.

We can reduce health philosophy into two categories:

- Natural
- Artificial

There is a natural philosophy and an artificial philosophy. You can go to university and consume every single book about philosophy which you can find. That will make you a collector of ideas. Usually Greek ideas.

Natural philosophy comes from the observation of nature. Mother Nature is your best teacher. Aset, the female life giving principle is your ideal mentor and healer.

Patient 1 - What's the name of your philosophy?

Our philosophy is called the Hero's Philosophy. To create this philosophy we studied the journeys of people who successfully defeated the big monster called cancer. We practice the methods prescribed in this book. For example: I love fasting, I love dancing and helping others. I don't eat meat or starchy foods. Such habits are key elements of the Hero's Philosophy.

The Hero's Philosophy was designed to help you to become a hero of your family and circle of influence. Please remember that to become a hero, an outstanding individual who has the power to heal the mind and body, you will need to cleanse your mind and your body first. Please close your eyes and visualise your mind as the sky, your body as the Earth, you're the essential architect, "Brahman, the creative principle." You must find ways to create harmony, purify and nurture your body.

My mother's death was the catalyst, the bridge, the beginning of my beautiful, blissful and soul nourishing journey into the special world. I consciously jumped into the ancient and very rich world of natural health. It was not easy. I spent 8 months trying to do it "my way." I struggled until I discovered two mentors.

Fasting & cleansing

The first was a German man called Andreas Moritz. Mr. Moritz inspired me to do a liver cleansing program called a gallbladder flush. His method required abstinence from food. Mr. Moritz's philosophy was an introduction into fasting and natural self-healing. Although he never met me, his teachings initiated me into the ancient world of plants and natural philosophy. For the first time in my life I considered the idea of cleansing my liver. Mr. Moritz's was a crucial discovery. His ideas unlocked an essential and ancient mystery. A timeless memory and ritual carefully hidden in Kmtic and Greek Mythology.

The cleansing of the liver inspired the cleansing of the mind, soul, emotions and gradually my entire life and existence.

The second mentor was a sage called Dr. Sebi. Dr. Sebi also introduced me to fasting as well as an alkaline diet. His method requires high-level commitment. Dr. Sebi's philosophy includes long periods of fasting and the rejection of almost every single food from the ordinary world. Dr. Sebi's philosophy instructs the initiate to detach him or herself from animal protein, processed sugar, carrots, milk, meat, rice, pasta, starchy foods and a few other little devils.

Dr. Sebi's philosophy prescribes a large variety of herbs such as Cascara Sagrada, Burdock. The Sebian method also includes sea plants such as Sea Moss.

Inner and outer journey

When I started my journey I believed that my challenges were mainly biological. As I read the 7 habits of highly effective people and fasted, I realised that both psychological, spiritual dimensions required urgent care. I started two journeys: Inner and outer. One is invisible and the other visible.

The inner journey consisted in accepting the fact that although I spoke 7 languages I was ignorant. I didn't know the culture of my ancestors and this affected my spiritual health, self-esteem and confidence. I had to give up the lies called "official history." I love history and studied it at college. YouTube forced me to do some digging in order to find the true history of the world.

The outer journey

The physical journey required a change of location. I had to persuade myself to leave the wonderful and green Cotswolds in exchange for rainy Manchester. Resigning from my well paid job was also part of the outer journey. I voluntarily embraced economic scarcity. I started my life from Zero.

- No Education
- No Profession
- No Diet
- No Culture
- Only the desire to learn

These steps are important because if you are reading this book with the goal of healing yourself or learning how to heal others, you will need to go through an inner and outer journey. You don't have to change your address, however you will need to change your mindset, vocabulary and dietary habits. There should be a spiritual and physical quest. Giving up meat, carbs, TV, entertainment, junk music is not easy. It is necessary.

The spiritual quest is manifested through rituals, affirmations, readings and meditations. The contemplation of your ancestor's culture, history, healing practices is an essential step. The Druids, the Native American Indians were experts in natural medicine. The study of ancient mysteries is part of the Inner Quest. The inner journey is incompatible with TV watching, pop music, pointless debates, gossip, political intrigues and conflicts, breaking news and conventional thinking. The ordinary world, its citizens and ideologies are very toxic therefore should be rejected.

Key questions

- When are you going to start your spiritual journey?
- When are you going to start your Inner quest?
- When are you going to start your Outer visible quest?

CHAPTER 3
The Quest to Retrieve the Lost Vitality

During a quiet winter evening, an ancient queen was given the worst news which a wife can get. She was told that her husband was no longer alive. Rather than falling into an endless cycle of depression, the Queen, Aset left the imperial palace and went searching for the missing body of Wsr, her husband. She gave up luxury and security in order to find the missing body.

The first impression we get from the above story is that Aset was searching for the body of her husband. In psychological, spiritual and mythological terms the queen was looking for her own vitality. Her own mystery. The hero within. She was looking for the hero within herself. She embarked on an inner quest. When she left the country of her parents and grandparents, friends and ancestors, Aset was a widow. On her return she was received as a hero, the first virgin mother in the history of the world. She became a hero by rescuing and saving her husband. Her journey is essential for us because it contains clues. The death of her husband was in reality a call to adventure.

The loss of Aset's soulmate also symbolised a disease that needed to be cured, a body that was decaying and required purification.

The need of detox and purification was one of the reasons why her husband was "locked in a wooden chest" and thrown into the river "Hapi Itrw" Hapi was the principle of vitality and protector of the river known today as "the Nile".

introduced the world to the 24 hour system which is still in use today. Ra was the solar hero who brought light into the world every single day. The hero of the ancient world took 12 steps to complete the visible part of his journey. 12 steps were taken in the visible world and 12 inside the invisible. That's how we got the 24 hours system, the 12 signs of the Zodiac and the 12 months of the year.

Like the ancient hero and savior who transformed lives and landscapes by bringing fresh, youthful and irresistible light, you would have to take 12 steps in order to retrieve your vitality, prevent serious diseases and help a relative to overcome challenges brought by complex subjects such as cancer.

The 12 steps will also help you to get essential clues about the monster that you or your relative are fighting. If you live in a place called planet Earth, then you will be attacked by some form of malignant organism, bacteria, virus, infection etc. Cancer experts, such as Dr. Bita Badakhshan, M.D. from Iran says that;

"Viruses play a vital role in cancer."

Our environment, the soil, the air, the rivers and seas are very polluted therefore it has become almost impossible to escape disease. If it's not us, it's our relatives. If it's not our relative, it's our friend or a stranger that we saw on the Tube, Bus, TV or in a Newspaper. Almost every family is being attacked by the Minotaur.

Heroes are needed more than ever. There are global industries that make billions selling products that have the potential to cause cancer. Every single supermarket, fast food, takeaway shop, restaurant, hospital, clinic, school, train station sells something that has the potential to cause cancer. Researchers say that mobile phones have the potential to cause brain cancer through EMFs. Smoking, alcohol and many "alternative drugs" are known to be carcinogenic. The monster called cancer will not go away, because there are millions of people who have jobs, businesses that make products that cause cancer and generate profit at the same time.

Examples of profitable products that have the potential to cause cancer are: fast foods, bacon, beer, butter, processed cereals, breast implants, tattoos, fizzy drinks, farmed fish...

During the summer of 2018, prominent newspapers reported that the European Union, is restricting certain chemicals used in tattoos because its experts suspect that the ink used by tattoo designers has the potential to penetrate, contaminate and intoxicate lymph nodes as well as changing human DNA. Millions of people around the world make a living selling Tattoos. We live in a world in which processed foods are cheaper than books. Toxic foods are an essential ingredient of the "Global Economy."

The ambitious man or woman who wishes to live a long and healthy life has to become smarter. There is no other way. Ignorance or neglect will lead to an early and painful death. You are either a hero or a victim.

Please be aware that we are looking at disease from a mythological, philosophical and natural scientific perspective. Otto Warburg and Professor Thomas Seyfried provides us with the essential scientific perspective.

If we look back at the word 'philosophia', we discover a detail that escapes the ordinary eye. Philo is a lover. Sofia is wisdom. Philosophy is the study of Sophia. Sophia is a female principle. Mother Nature. The ambitious man or woman goes on a quest in order to learn more about Sophia, Aset, the Great mother.

You could and should research the benefits of herbs, organic foods, minerals, essential oils. Turmeric for example, contains a substance called Curcumin. Curcumin is essential because it turns cancerous genes off. Curcumin is a very powerful anti-cancer food.

Cabbages are essential because they contain Glutathione. A highly experienced healer, researcher and author called Mark Hyman says that "Glutathione is the mother of all antioxidants." Glutathione plays an important role in preventing colon, breast, prostate, liver and many other cancers. The quest to retrieve the lost vitality is also the quest to retrieve the hidden knowledge that's essential for a long and healthy life.

CHAPTER 5
Two Worlds - Two Philosophies

"The ordinary world is in one sense the place you came from last. In life, we pass through a succession of special worlds which slowly become ordinary as we get used to them. They evolve from strange, foreign territory to familiar bases from which to launch a drive into the next Special World."

- The Writer's Journey - Christopher Vogler.

The ordinary world

In 2016 I spoke to a lady whose husband was diagnosed with prostate cancer. She told me that before the diagnosis "we lived in a small town in the outskirts of York. Life was beautiful. We have two children, a baby boy and a 7 year old girl. Everything was fine until cancer came and destroyed our world. We had friends and relatives who were affected by the disease. We attended funerals of people who died of cancer. I know this will sound strange but we believed that cancer was something that happens to others. We were in such a bliss that we did not think we could become victims. We ate all kinds of foods. We ate butter, white bread, lamb, beef, etc. We did not buy organic foods because we thought it was costly. Soon after the diagnosis we realised that our decisions were wrong indeed.

We were not psychologically, biologically or intellectually prepared for the ordeal that followed our endless parties. We did not know what to tell our children. My husband got chemo and he did not cope. It was brutal and seemed to be getting worse by the hour. A friend whose father died of cancer sent me a link of a video on YouTube. I watched the video and a few others. For the first time in my life I realised how ignorant I am about the world. I realised how detached I was from the real world. We were lucky because my husband did not just want to be cured. He wanted to study, he did not want to die. He was willing to change, to learn, to become a student. I quit my job and became his nurse, main motivator and supplier of foods and supplements. The experience changed him. My husband became an excellent researcher. He would spend endless hours researching and then tell me what I needed to buy.

We worked hard, very hard for a long period of time. It was not easy. There were many grey days. I am glad to say that we succeeded. After 3 long years of daily juicing and cleansing, meditation and exercise my husband got the greatest news of his life. He is cancer free. My husband told me that his cancer was a message sent by God. We were told to stop partying, drinking and eating like Queens and Kings. That's exactly what we did".

Like many honest and decent human beings of her generation, the mother of two beautiful children did not realise that her family lived in the ordinary world. An artificial world carefully designed to make a person feel satisfied. The monster called cancer is a disease that requires knowledge of the special world. There must be a separation, detachment from the ordinary world, the visible world. The place where sweet food is the greatest food. It is not easy for an individual to depart, detach him or herself from the ordinary world because the majority of his or her friends and relatives are glad to live in the ordinary world. A toxic world which Plato called "the world of shadows."

I recently spent 45 minutes watching a cooking show on the BBC. The show was presented by one of the most famous female chefs in the UK. She was very pleased to present sugar, industrial salt, white bread, fried butter as luxurious food. I loved the filming and the presentation, I was shocked by the almost primitive diet prescribed to millions of people. There was no mention of organic or wholemeal foods. If you are going to eat starchy foods you could at least eat organic or wholemeal.

To heal our bodies and minds we must leave the world of appearances. Disease is a warning that we have spent too much time "enjoying, indulging ourselves". Disease is also an instrument which nature uses to force an individual to leave the ordinary world and get close to Mother Nature. The natural world uses both physical and psychological diseases to make people aware that it's time to move.

Theseus and the big rock

A hero called Theseus, the slayer of the Minotaur suffered from a psychological disease created by the absence of his father.

Theseus was born in a small village called Troezen. He was brought up by his mother Aethra. His mother was his main mentor. During one fine summer morning, Aethra asked her son to go to the pine forest that was close to the place where they lived. She asked him to move a big rock that was in the forest. Theseus accepted the invitation. He spent an entire summer trying to move the rock. When he finally succeeded, Theseus discovered a sword and sandals that were hidden beneath the rock. As soon as he moved the rock, Theseus made one of the greatest discoveries of his life. He got very excited and ran to his mother. He asked her who the owner of the sword and the sandals was. Aethra looked at her son and said "That's the sword of a king. Your father is the King of Athens." Aethra instructed her son "to go to Athens and meet your father", smiling she said "your father is Aegeus, King of Athens."

Shortly before he left, Aethra told her son to avoid the Coast road because "it is full of Bandits." The bandits, tricksters and assassins were trials and threshold guardians. The word Aegeus, the name of the father of Theseus, is the root word for 'Aegean Sea'. The rock which Aethra asked her son to move was an instrument of initiation. It symbolised ego, fear and ignorance.

Before he moved the rock, Theseus and his mother lived in the ordinary world. A small village called Troezen. Aethra was the first mentor of her son. She gave Theseus psychological and physical challenges, the trials and training in order to prepare him for the journey. That's the sequence that we have to follow. It doesn't matter who you are, your social status, your education, to succeed in life and be healthy you will have to move the rock.

An ambitious person who wishes to be healthy will be advised by his or her mentor to remove dairy, gluten, meat, processed sugar, toxins from his or her diet. The command "change your diet" is one of the many trials that every person that wishes to become a hero must overcome. Your diet is one of the "Bandits" which Theseus fought on his way to Athens.

Changing your diet is a form of departure. There is a departure from the ordinary world. A departure requires sacrifice and renunciation. It is almost impossible to read a book and watch television at the same time. One of them has to go. The old luggage has to be left behind.

The journey of the fool

The idea of departure is beautifully illustrated by the fool, the first card of the Tarot. In the Tarot, we see the fool carrying a very small bag. His bag is very light. He leaves his old possessions behind. Like the fool Theseus left Troezen with few possessions. He took with him a sword, sandals, and the psychological assets given to him by his mother. His luggage was very light for a traveler going on a long journey.

On your quest to retrieve your health and escape from premature death which would deprive you from being with your friends and relatives, you should not take your bad habits with you because they will derail your progress. They will slow you down and stop you from achieving your goal.

Anybody who is interested in health and longevity will have to leave the ordinary world. This departure does not have to be 100 percent physical. It can be done through books, recipes, lectures and videos. New information has the power to help the seeker to transcend and descend. You descend into the Nether and invisible world. The British lady from York spent 3 years nursing her husband. The destiny of her family changed after she watched an educational video on YouTube. That was her initiation.

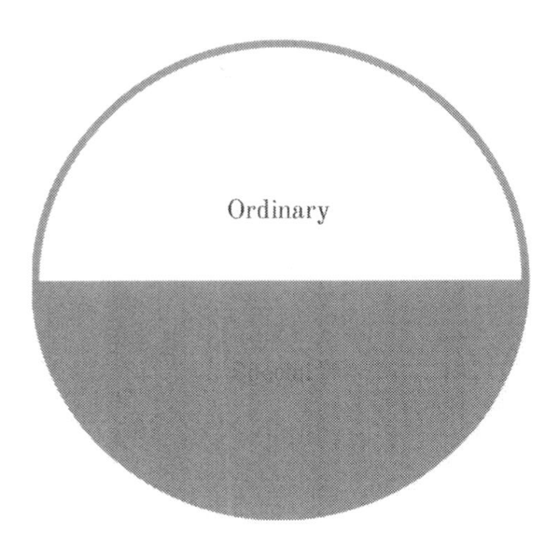
Ordinary

The world of illusions

The ordinary world is the familiar location, the world of illusions, the world of problems that have no solutions. The ordinary world is also the world of endless wars, political conflicts, breaking news, endless sources of pleasure and instant gratification. The ordinary world is also the world of perpetual fragmentation. The world of chronic diseases, surgery, radiation, processed sugar and a few other toxic things.

The ordinary world is a world that can be seen through the naked eye. The world of appearances. The ordinary world is ruled through the senses rather than intellect. Everything appears to be beautiful and fine. Many people spend their entire lives living in the ordinary world. People living in the ordinary world are not aware that there is another world, an invisible and richer world that contains endless gifts. One of the main tasks of a mentor is to lead a person to that wonderful location where every problem has a solution. That's not an easy task because the ordinary world is very addictive. It is the world of endless sugar, pleasure, distractions, conflicts and egos. People living in the ordinary world appear to be happy and healthy. If you speak to a citizen of the ordinary world, look at their habits you will realise that they are experiencing several forms of decay. There is psychological turmoil, addictions, inner conflicts, divorces and biological disintegration. They cannot save themselves unless they depart and embrace the Hero's Philosophy. They must descend and reject the idea of living a "Sweet and fat" life.

Saved by an experienced old lady

Patient 2 - "My name is Arnold. I live in Memphis. 7 years ago I started coughing blood and getting terrible headaches. I realised that something was wrong therefore I went to see my doctor. She sent me to the hospital to get tested. At the hospital I was told that I had lung cancer. I was a heavy smoker for 30 years. I knew where it was coming from. After the diagnosis I got very stressed. My health deteriorated. I got very sick. The people at the hospital told me that the cancer was spreading and that my liver was affected. The cancer was very advanced and there was not much doctors could do. I was told that I had less than 6 months to live. I went home and spoke to my wife. We decided to call our relatives and give them the bad news. We were very lucky. One of my wife's cousins works in a health food store. She knows a natural doctor who goes there every month to buy oils and supplements. She kindly introduced me to her.

I went to see the lady and told her my sorry story. To my surprise she told me that "we can help you". When I went to the lady's clinic. I was surprised how friendly and cheerful everybody was. The place was very welcoming. When I got there the patients and nurses were doing Tai Chi. Everybody was smiling and positive. I spent a week at the lady's home based clinic. I learned a lot about health, disease and detox. I was asked to give up 99.9% of my diet. I accepted the invitation. It saved my life."

Patient 3: Pamela Kelsey - "I was diagnosed with the cancer of the pancreas in 1975. I was told that I had 1 year and half to live. At the most. If I did chemo, possibly chemo, radiology, the different treatments that conventional medicine has. I chose not to do that after finding out about the clinic in Mexico." The Truth About Cancer - Episode 1 - YouTube

Pamela Kelsey is an entrepreneur based in the U.S. She was used to thinking outside the box, therefore it was not difficult for her to accept the call to adventure and jump into the special world. She was psychologically ready to depart. The special world for Pamela was located in Mexico. The clinic that saved her life was founded by a lady called Mildred Nelson. The special world is both material and immaterial, visible and invisible, ancestral and natural. The first departure is always psychological. The mistake which ordinary thinkers and cancer patients make is to focus on the physical departure. Although invisible the mental picture is more powerful.

The journeys of heroes such as Theseus, Ty Bollinger, Dr. Sebi, Charlotte Gerson, the man from Memphis and Pamela Kelsey reveal a very important secret. Those who wish to become heroes have to leave the ordinary world. To become a citizen of the special world a patient has no choice but to become a student. He or she has to be initiated into ancient and mysterious ways. The ways of the ancestors.

A person who wishes to become healthy, has to go somewhere in order to find something. Theseus went to Athens in order to meet his father. The man who had lung cancer had to go to a home based clinic. Pamela Kelsey had to leave the U.S. and travel to Mexico. Indiana Jones and Jesus went to Kmt, Aset went to Byblos, modern day Lebanon. There she found the body of her husband carefully hidden inside a tree.

Every person, every patient experiences 3 important stages:

- Separation - departure, detachment.
- Initiation - learning, discovery, instruction, re-education.

If these 3 areas are very strong disease will not succeed in destroying your body. Fear, stress and toxins create the perfect environment for the big monster to thrive.

Maat is the oldest psychological and spiritual system in the world. It inspired the creation of many social and moral systems including the 10 commandments. If you compare the 42 laws of Maat to the 10 commandments you will see where the authors of the 10 commandments got their inspiration from. The goal was to established personal and social order. A person who lived by Maat was guaranteed eternal life. A person who violated Maat was doomed to suffer. Time has changed, the principle however remains.

Maat is very interesting because it was not forced. A person had the freedom to either follow or reject Maat.

In today's world you can eat organic foods or reject them and consume junk food instead. Junk, GMO and processed food are the opposite of Maat, they have no life in them.

Why balance and harmony?

You might wonder why we are introducing you to Maat. We are introducing you to Maat to make you aware that to be healthy you need more than supplements, juicing, cleansing. You need principles and a balanced philosophy. You need a philosophy because a living being is not an island. A living being is a temple that has many rooms, altars and shrines. Every single shrine requires balance and harmony. Every single organ inside your body requires special attention. A human being is not just a stomach or a liver. There is emotional health, spiritual, social health, psychological health, intellectual health. That's why a holistic approach is always the best approach.

The key message of this chapter is that you should do all you can to be in Maat, balance, harmony with your external and internal environment. When a person is sick, he or she will have to go on a journey in order to find the lost balance.

We have to find Maat. People use different terms to refer to Maat. Balance, recovery, remission, cure etc. Finding Maat means finding balance. To find Maat you will have to be bold and judge your habits. This is a very personal and spiritual exercise. You have to become your own doctor. The official doctor should be seen as an ally who can help us to detect imperfections and confirm recovery. You should become your own judge and judge your habits. The good ones and the bad ones. The trial takes place inside the special world. That is inside your body.

Skin cancer and Curadem BEC5

Shortly after the end of a hot English summer, a friend approached me and told me that he was suffering from skin cancer. Before giving him my opinion I looked at the work of a prominent natural doctor called Bill Cham. I learned a lot by researching the world of Dr. Cham. I introduced the subject of Curaderm BEC5 cream to my friend who told me that he had skin cancer. For some peculiar reason he forgot to say thank you. I also suspect that he ignored the advice because "You are not a doctor."

He had the opportunity to become his own doctor. He was invited to become his own doctor. He doesn't believe in the hero inside him therefore he said no. He rejected the call to adventure, the invitation to find Maat. He had a tough time dealing with the side effects caused by conventional "treatments".

The world of Maat is invisible. Although we cannot see it, we know that it is there. You cannot see your cells and immune system however you know that they're there. The immune system belongs to the special world. The world of Maat. The idea of a special world is essential because it makes you aware that you are not just your body and the invisible self.

It creates the space for special people, special methods, special minds, special therapies and special things that cannot be found in the ordinary world. The special world is where the hero must go in order to find the strength, confidence, and the wisdom that will enable him or her to defeat the monster. The special world, is the home of essential and transformative mysteries. That's where you're going to find the gold called health, longevity and prosperity.

CHAPTER 7
Citizens of the Special World

The citizens, the characters who live in the special world are saviours and healers. In mythology they come in many shapes and forms. They are disguised and presented as villains and monsters, gods, animals, plants, muses, old women, old men, ferry woman, ferryman, musicians, fathers and mothers. In Greece we find the Minotaur, in Africa we find Sutek. In Iran we have Angra Mainyu.

To the ordinary eye, the Minotaur is bad. If we look at the Minotaur from a psychological, ancestral and mythological perspective, we learn that he was both a disease and a cure. Like Humbaba, the Minotaur was "a watchman." A guardian of ancient secrets and the path to heroism.

The Minotaur enabled Theseus and Ariadne to fulfil their potential. He was the cure for the conflicts that were destroying the family of Ariadne. Adriane wanted Theseus to kill her brother because she knew that he was a source of death and pain. The Minotaur was a curse and a cure. His death saved young Athenian boys and girls from premature death. The Minotaur was also a door that enabled Ariadne to escape the labyrinth built by her father.

"Why do you want the Minotaur dead?" Asked Theseus.

"Because he shames my family." Replied Ariadne.

When a person is told that you have such and such a disease the person is also being invited to go to war with a monster. There is a visible and an invisible monster. The invisible monster is the product of bad habits, emotional and psychological stress.

We could replace the word Minotaur with cancer. If we defeat the Minotaur we defeat cancer or a disease that's bothering us. The worst thing we can do is to give up the fight and allow fear to take over. We must go to the labyrinth and fight the monster that was created by endless bad dietary habits, environmental toxins and ignorance.

Humbaba

In Ancient Babylon, we get a monster called Humbaba. We are told that Humbaba was a big monster that lived in the forest. In reality Humbaba was a blessing in disguise. Humbaba was a threshold guardian. His role was to test Gilgamesh. Gilgamesh was psychologically unclean. When he went to the forest, Gilgamesh wasn't a good man therefore he killed the guardian of the Gods. The death of Humbaba was a violent crime. It was also the beginning of Gilgamesh's self-discovery journey and deep personal transformation.

The Gods and Goddesses, the kings and queens of the East and Western sky, were very upset with the two brothers. They decided to act. As a punishment for killing Humbaba, the Gods, Enlil and Shamash punished Enkidu. Enkidu fell sick and gradually descended into the world of no return. Gilgamesh was forced to watch the biological setting Sun of his brother. Enkidu was the only friend Gilgamesh had in life.

The death of Enkidu forced Gilgamesh to go on a journey of self-discovery. Before the arrival of Enkidu, Gilgamesh was a rapist. His mindset, his mentality was a disease for the people of Uruk. Humbaba was a cure in disguise.

One of the main stages of Gilgamesh's journey was the jump into the sea to retrieve the secret of eternal life. He took a plunge in order to purify himself. That was the real treasure.

After finding and losing the plant, Gilgamesh returned home and became a teacher. The hero left home as a psychologically sick man. He returned as a healthy person who was ready to heal others. Gilgamesh embarked on an individual journey on behalf of the collective. That's the secret.

Gilgamesh's disease was not biological. It was psychological. The sick man and woman living in the 21st century will prioritise the biological healing, the symptom and not the cause. The focus on the sickness of the body and ignorance of the spiritual, intellectual and psychological diseases is a mistake. Depression and self-hatred are known causes of biological diseases.

"A wake up call"

One of the most prominent natural doctors and healers of the modern world is a very intelligent man, called Dr. Rashid Buttar who has been helping cancer patients for more than 20 years. During an interview conducted by Ty Bollinger, Dr. Buttar said that most of his patients confessed to him, that the cancer which afflicted them was a blessing that inspired them to change their ways. "It was a wake up call". A call to depart from the ordinary world. Cancer could be seen as a blessing in disguise. If the person is able to stay calm and engage with the enemy, the survivor will become a wise and very healthy human being.

More than 8 years ago Chris Wark was told that he had cancer. The news were devastating and destroyed happiness and harmony in his family. Chris chose not to use chemotherapy and other conventional treatments. He went natural. He spent a great deal of time learning about foods and supplements. He succeeded in healing himself. He completed the Hero's Journey. After completing the Hero's Journey, Chris Wark created a YouTube channel and wrote a book that teaches and inspires others to believe and heal themselves. The ordeal turned him into a writer, teacher and healer. That's the psychological evolution of the Hero.

The cancer was a very bad experience but also an opportunity to learn. His persistence and desire to help others was rewarded with longevity and love. Through his YouTube channel and books, Chris Wark has inspired millions of people around the world to believe in themselves and use natural therapies. Chris Wark is an example of a citizen of the special world.

There is a very special and rich world introduced through mythology. There is also a special world that exists in our time. You should be aware and strive to be a citizen of both. One heals you psychologically, the other heals you biologically. The special world has many citizens. Some of the citizens of the special world are;

- Ariadne
- Aset
- Enkidu
- Gilgamesh
- Hero/Hrw

- Humbaba
- Maat
- Sedna, Shiva, Shamash, Spider woman
- Sekhmet
- Theseus
- Wsr
- Ra

You should be creative and find ways to detect your special world. Maat is the central character of our special world. Your special world is a healthy place populated by healthy people. It's not the ideal place for toxins or toxic people. Every special world contains special citizens.

CHAPTER 8
The Circle of Influence

"The Hero's Journey, I discovered, is more than just a description of the hidden patterns of mythology. It is a useful guide to life."

- The Writer's Journey - Mythic structure for writers
- Third edition, Christopher Vogler

The Kmtic symbol for the hero was a circle with a dot in the middle. The circle had many hidden meanings. It was a visible aspect of the hero who traversed the sky daily. It also symbolised;

- The creator
- The circle of influence
- The hero
- The source of light
- The eternal cycle
- The journey from obscurity, death to light
- The journey from sickness to health
- It was the birth and death of seasons
- The hero's journey

The source of light and hero, went on a daily and seasonal journey of self-discovery which started early in the morning and reached its climax at the sunset. That's when the hero became invisible. Modern psychologists and mythographers call the different stages the rites of passage. They are;

- Birth
- Growth
- Decay & transition

These cycles of life are also known as;

- Morning
- Afternoon
- Sunset

There is a more ordinary terminology used to define these stages;

- Childhood
- Youth
- Old age
- Past
- Present
- Future
- Winter, spring, summer, autumn

These rites of passage are natural. We have to experience them. We enjoy youth, then we grow old and experience a gradual decay. The big monster called disease violates the laws of nature and accelerates the decay of our organism. It shortens a person's life span.

The hero is the person who stands up and says "No. I am not going to surrender to you. I am not going to be tricked. I am going to learn how to fight and remove you from my body."

In order to be successful in our war against decay we need mentors who will supply us with words, images, clues, lessons, mysteries, unfamiliar names, tools which we can use to guide

> and save ourselves, our friends and relatives. We need resources that will enable us to free ourselves from the labyrinth.
>
> The labyrinth of Knossos was a dark and mysterious place. The same can be said about the world of disease and decay. A patient afflicted with disease will find him or herself imprisoned inside an obscure world. That's the labyrinth that creates the perfect space for the hero to manifest him or herself. We should not go there without the tools and wisdom supplied by an experienced mentor, a healer, a wise man, a wise woman, a medicine man, a medicine woman, a conductor of souls.

Joseph Campbell was a remarkable mentor. He gave us a circle of influence that illustrates the psychological, social, intellectual journey that we should complete in order to find the hero within us. At the end of our journey we shall attain "Individuation". We shall become complete and fulfilled individuals.

In his highly influential book the "*The Hero with a Thousand Faces*", Joseph Campbell introduced a diagram that illustrates the 12 steps that every ambitious person, every hero took in order to achieve his or her goal.

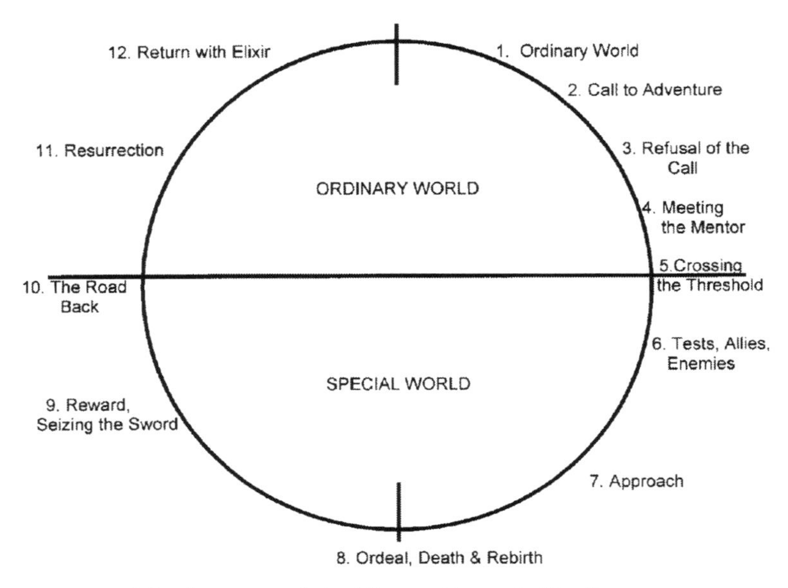

The Journey of the Hero - Campbell's diagram

The 12 steps are displayed in a circle, they are:

1. The Ordinary world
2. The Call to adventure
3. The Refusal of the call
4. Meeting with the mentor
5. Crossing the first threshold
6. Test, Allies, Enemies
7. Approach to the inmost cave
8. The Ordeal
9. The Reward
10. The Road back
11. The Resurrection
12. Return with the elixir

Christopher Vogler born 1949 in the U.S. is a prolific author, script writer and mentor. He is one of the millions of disciples of Joseph Campbell. During the early stages of his career Mr. Vogler had the opportunity to meet the mentor of many souls, the ferryman whose books, words and poetry lead generations to new destinations. Mr. Vogler wrote a very influential book called "*The Writer's Journey*". His book explains Campbell's philosophy using a very simple and easy to understand language. Joseph Campbell was an excellent storyteller. He was also an academic. Some of his terms are not easy to digest. They can easily become complex enigmas for the beginner that's taking his or her first steps into the special world, the very rich world of mythology.

Christopher Vogler is an excellent writer and story analyst. He operates in the very demanding world of filming and Hollywood. Mr. Vogler used the circle to illustrate the steps that a screenwriter has to take in order to write a great movie. His teachings also help a person to find him or herself in the world. Joseph Campbell used the circle to show the stages of psychological growth and the evolution that a human being has to experience in order to attain a stage which Carl Jung called "individuation." Christopher Vogler used the circle to illustrate the journey that an ambitious and creative person should take in order to become successful. The circle can be applied to many areas of life. We focus on health, the recovery or prevention of serious illness such as cancer. Joseph Campbell, Christopher Vogler and the Hero's Philosophy are tackling the same challenge. The goal, the vision is the same. To rescue an ambitious man or woman from the ordinary world. Our vision is to save others by giving them the right tools and clues about an essential and universal experience called the Hero's Journey. Below is Christopher Vogler's diagram.

Christopher Vogler's diagram:

Act I

Limited awareness

Increased awareness

Reluctance to change

Overcoming

Act II

Committing

Experimenting

Preparing

Big change Consequences

Act III

Rededication

Final attempt

Mastery

The diagrams, circles of influence are excellent tools for those seeking to understand their lives and their health journey. This book is dedicated to the journey of a patient, someone who either wants to defeat the monster, or prevent its arrival in order to enjoy optimal health and a long life. The Hero's Philosophy can be used together with conventional treatment. We advise you to do your research before deciding whether the philosophy is suitable for you and your loved ones. Please go to Google, YouTube, read books, talk to your doctor before deciding how to proceed.

It doesn't really matter whether you are sick or healthy. You need training about minerals, cleansing, juicing, essential supplements and the Hero's Journey.

It doesn't matter whether you are a farmer, a politician, student, mother, father, single, young, old, you can use the diagram to see where you are on your healing journey. You can also use the diagram to predict the future of your health. Stephen R. Covey said that "The best way to predict the future is to create it". You can create the best environment for your immune system to thrive by making small and essential changes related to your thinking and diet. It takes time to get into the special world. You have to be very patient either with yourself or your loved ones. There is a lot of learning and practice involved. Giving up carbs and animal protein requires a lot of discipline.

The Hero's Journey for people interested in preventing disease also contains 12 steps. The 12 steps correspond to each hour of the day, the 12 months of the year and the 12 signs of the zodiac. Your journey could take 12 months or 12 years. You can't complete the journey in 12 weeks. It doesn't matter how long it takes. You should start your Hero's Journey as soon as you can. The key is in the first step. Take the first step, reading, meditating, questioning, researching. You can do it by allowing your mind and soul to be persuaded and initiated. We are going to examine and discuss each element, each step that an ambitious person, who wishes to recover or prevent the loss of his or her vitality, has to take. Please remember that you cannot do it alone. You need to invite people to become citizens of your special world. We call such citizens essential characters.

CHAPTER 9
Essential Characters

"Every day the young and vigorous Re sailed in his boat, Mandjet on a fairly eventful voyage across the sky. The twelve hours of the day were personified as twelve solar deities (Maat, Hu, Sia, Asbet, Igaret, Seth Horus, Khonsu, Isis, Heka.)"

- P79 The Penguin Book of Myths and Legends of Ancient Egypt.

The language spoken by Aset and the people of her country was called Mdw Ntr. Mdw means words. Ntr means, principles, ancestors. Academics call a group of Ntr Gods. A Ntr is a principle, a sacred individual, a law that can be obeyed or broken. You can eat meat or chose to be a vegan. Eating meat is a violation of the principle, the Ntrt, Mother Nature called Maat. A Ntr is a male principle. Ntrt is a female principle. Ntr is singular. Ntrw is plural. In Mdw Ntr a 'W' is placed at the end of a word to make it plural. Nrtw refers to a collective.

The Ntrw are principles, eternal and essential laws. They are rules that govern the universe and have a profound effect on life. You can violate them. Nobody will take you to prison. You will however suffer the negative consequences created by your actions, words, internal visions and decisions. If you apply the principles in your life your chances of succeeding are very high. For example kindness, truth, honesty, intelligence, study, eating well are habits regulated by principles. Principles are your allies. They are eternal. They exist inside us. They are also around us. We see and talk to them every single day. My beautiful sister Snt Maat is a personification of the principle, Aset. The female principle. She has the potential to become a mother, a wife, a healer, a saviour, a priestess, an author, a teacher…

To fulfill her potential my sister would have to make sacrifices, delay gratification, embrace and follow timeless and universal principles. Principles are bridges to excellent experiences.

Conventional intellectuals call principles "Egyptian Gods", "Sumerian Gods", "Indian Gods", "Greek Gods", American, Indian, Chinese Gods, Native American Gods, Iranian Gods". They are not Gods. They are metaphors used to teach us important lessons. They teach us about life, psychology, ancient history. They also teach us about health by instructing us to look inside rather than outside. Principles lead us to the self.

An example of a principle connected to longevity was Ra. Ra was the main solar principle of the ancient world. Ra was always surrounded by the Ntrw. Some of Ra's allies were his children, others were his grandchildren. Ra is symbolised by the Sun. From Ra we get the words 'rational', 'radiation', 'ramifications', 'radio', 'rain', 'ratio' etc. The word radiation is important here. Do you use artificial or natural radiation? Natural radiation is free of charge therefore people are advised to stay away from the Sun. Artificial radiation generates billions. It comes with terrible side effects. Ra is the most reliable source of vitamin D in the world. Ra, the sunlight, affects every single living organism on the planet from ants and humans to plants in the deep sea.

Any rational person who wishes to be healthy will do his or her best to eat foods that are exposed to the Sun. Dates, grapes, mangos etc.

On page 112 of the book "The Cancer Survival Manual" by Rachael Linkie we're taught that "Vitamin D blocks the growth of blood vessels that feed breast cancer cells. Upping your vitamin D intake may also help to ward off breast cancer. A study at Birmingham University and St. George's hospital, London, discovered that breast tissue contains an enzyme that converts vitamin D to its active form, calcitriol, which is a potent anti-cancer agent."

12 allies

The 12 principles that guarded Ra were essential allies. Although he was extremely powerful, Ra could not exist and prosper without the help of his allies. In your journey that's your friends and relatives. Each Ntr, principle had a role assigned to him or her. They were all related to him. Maat was the central principle. She was the most important principle of the entire civilization. Maat was also the daughter of Ra. There was a spiritual but also a biological connection between Ra and his allies. You could stop here and ask: What's the connection between Ancient African mythology and disease?

The answer would be the structure, an efficient and intelligent inner circle. Ra succeeded because he had the support of 12 essential principles. Like Ra, the source of light and hero you will need allies. You don't have to be surrounded by 12 people, however you could have 12 books, 12 authors, 12 daily fresh organic juices taken for 12 hours during 12 consecutive months, together with 12 essential supplements. You could also have 12 mentors and 12 positive affirmations.

It doesn't matter who you are, where you live, how much money you have, you are a social animal. You cannot do it by yourself. You need a team. You need to build a smart, intelligent team around you. One of your tasks is to turn your relatives, friends into a team that's prepared to work together in order to help you to defeat the big monster. The biggest mistake you can make is to believe that somebody will do the job for you. Even the most experienced doctor and your main ally cannot drink the juices on your behalf. You have to do it. You have to go through the hero's journey and complete it.

Every person who comes in contact with us plays a role. He or she is a principle, a hero. We are blinded by cultural and racial bias therefore we fail to see the hero in front of us. You should do your best to turn your doctor, strangers and your relatives into an intelligent team that's ready to engage with the enemy called cancer.

The wisdom hidden in the story of Ra, the 12 hours and 12 principles is essential for a person who is battling a monster called cancer or wishes to prevent diseases. Please remember that you don't have to be sick in order to learn about health. The more you know about the origins of disease the brighter your future will be. The future is bright if there is no sickness in the family. Such vision is almost impossible to attain in the 21st century. We live in a very polluted world therefore we must study and be very careful about what we eat. We should also be very careful about the messages that we send to our mind and body because they affect our health. Almost every human being has a friend, a relative, a work colleague that's exposed to ignorance and toxins. There is plenty of room for tragedy and triumph. Ignorance leads to tragedy. Initiation and application are bridges to triumph. To succeed in life we need the contributions of essential characters. They are our essential principles.

During the fall of 2018 a friend sent me a link from the Guardian Newspaper. It was a story of a lady, a journalist that was trying to prevent blindness using the Gerson Therapy. She was on her second week and striving to remain disciplined and committed. A friend visited her and brought with him a pizza. She tried her best to resist the temptation. She put the pizza in the fridge and left it there for several days. In the end she ate the pizza and polluted her very clean environment.

Her friend was not an essential character or an Aset. He was a liability. A lover of pizza is not the ideal company for people who are trying to heal themselves from a serious disease.

CHAPTER 10
The Roles of Essential Characters

Earlier we introduced you to the circle of influence. The diagram that symbolises the ancestral hero who took 12 steps to complete a self-discovery journey. There is an extraordinary mystery hidden in the number 12. If we fragment the number 12 we get two essential principles. 1 and 2.

1. Number one is the pioneer, the father, the mother, the brave, the leader who sets things in motion.
2. Number two is the essential helper and healer that provides the psychological support that enables the leader to triumph. The mother.

In human terms number one could be a father, a husband, a mother, a wife. Number two could also be a mother, a husband, doctor, a sister, a daughter, a brother. They are the Sun and the Moon. They are the parents who are always surrounded by stars, their children. They complement each other. They are two pairs of opposites that support each other. 1 and 2 are more than characters. They are archetypes.

The pioneer

Arthur Conan Doyle was a remarkable man, the creator of Sherlock Holmes. He was born in Edinburgh on the 22nd of May 1859. Mr. Doyle was a pioneer that created a new industry. To his descendants Mr. Doyle is an essential archetype, a key reference. He is seen as a source of inspiration, ambition and excellence. He is an archetype that's introduced to every child of the family.

What exactly are archetypes?

A few years ago I read a book that explores the life and work of Carl Jung. Carl Gustav Jung 1875 - 1961. Carl Jung was a prominent Swiss psychologist who used mythology as one of the main foundations of his thinking and theories. He is considered one of the most influential psychologists of the modern world. He used the word archetypes to define ancient and essential characters that are part of the human family.

The word archetypes is related to the word Arcana, the first 22 cards of the Tarot. The Tarot has two types of cards. Major and Minor Arcana. The Major Arcana is very ancient, original and of non-European origin. The Minor Arcana is more recent and is not part of the original Tarot. It is said that the Minor Arcana was created by European aristocrats and members of secret societies that were based either in France or Italy.

The word Arcana means mystery. If we look at the word 'archetypes' we can see archaic. Archaic means ancient. Arcana,

Archetypes are ancient, archaic mysteries. In organic societies older people used to be the keepers of ancient mysteries. They were the main teachers, healers known as a medicine man and a medicine woman. For thousands of years, the medicine man, medicine woman, shamans were the sought after doctors who used herbs and rituals to heal the sick. They were the living archetypes, the ancient elements of the human family who knew the secrets of healing. They have been replaced by men and women who are trained to recommend laboratory made drugs.

The medicine man or medicine woman is an archetype. A guardian of ancient wisdom that used to fulfill essential roles such as the grandfather, grandmother, father, mother, older brother, older sister, mentor, guide etc. They were the pillars of the human family. They were also the healers who knew how to conduct ancient rituals.

One of the heroes who defeated a monster called cancer was a Canadian nurse called Rene Caisse. She was born in Canada and was very active during the 1920s. She became a healer after learning the secret formula used by an Indian medicine man, a shaman. The shaman was from an ancient Native American tribe called the Ojibwe. The man was a living archetype who knew the mysteries and rituals of Native Indians, that lived in the country which is today called Canada.

The subject of archetypes is very important because they are fundamental. Archetypes help us to understand the roles that we should play in life. The father, the mother, the hero, the villain, the helper, the healer are archetypes, models that can be found in every single mythological story and family. For example, Aset, Aethra, Ariadne, the spider woman, the Minotaur etc. These characters fulfil specific roles, "they do their duties" and inspire us to do our own duties.

Every single family, every single organization, every single society contains archetypes. The absence of archetypes causes a crisis in a person's psyche. It creates a psychological disorder called neurosis, anxiety, depression, fear, low self-esteem, self-hatred... That's one of the reasons why children should be close to their grandparents and be introduced to mythological stories. Neurosis creates psychic stress. Stress is one of the main causes of both mental and physical conditions.

Like the heroes of mythology you will need helpers, healers, teachers, villains, monsters. They are more than people. They are archetypes who could play an essential role in your or your relative's recovery. Archetypes could be seen as golden safes that contains precious gifts and invaluable mysteries.

Dr. Matthias Rath a specialist in Vitamin C is a living archetype. He works with a lady called Dr. Aleksandra Niedzwiecki. They are a team of highly experienced researchers that create natural plant based remedies. Dr. Matthias Rath and Dr. Aleksandra Niedzwiecki personify the medicine man and medicine woman. They also symbolise the wise mother and father who knows the secrets of herbs. Their research led them to discover a powerful compound called EGCG. EGCG is a crucial ally and weapon in the global fight against cancer.

The key roles played by archetypes are;

- The healer
- The helper
- The mentor
- The mother
- The old wise man
- The wise lady
- The villain
- The daughter
- The threshold guardian
- The Shaman, Shama woman
- The Ferryman, Ferry woman

There are certain archetypes that keep appearing in mythology. There is the old man, the old lady, the young man, the young lady, the monster, the helper, the healer, the mentor. There is also the priest and priestess, the source and sorcerer, the wise mother and a very successful trickster.

If you go to Ancient Greece you will find Ariadne. Ariadne fell in love with Theseus. She was the savior. She was also one of the mentors of Theseus. Ariadne was also the daughter of the main villain, King Minos. She was also the student of a sorcerer called Daedalus. She later became a wife and a mother. She symbolised an ancient principle, the 'mother goddess' and savior of souls.

Shortly before Theseus went into the labyrinth, Ariadne gave him the training, the keys, essential and lifesaving secrets. She gave him a thread that enabled him to find his way out. Without the thread

Theseus was doomed to die inside the labyrinth of Knossos. It was Daedalus, the clever, mad and dangerous scientist who made the thread. He was an ally of Ariadne and a victim of her father.

The principle of Aten

In Ancient Kmt there was a principle called Aten. Aten was the mentor and source of inspiration of a King called Akhenaten. Aten is the root word for 'ten', 'Athens', 'atonement', 'attempt' and many other words used in the modern world.

The universe is filled with essential elements, vitamins, archetypes, friends, relatives, teachers, mentors, apples, researchers. The task of an ambitious individual, patient and student is to learn from the archetypes. Archetypes give us an idea about the role that we should play in life.

- Are we victims or heroes?
- Are we perplexed or intelligent?
- Are we creators or consumers?
- What's the role of a mother?
- What's the role of a father?
- What's the role of a daughter?
- What's the role of a friend?
- What's the role of a teacher?
- What's the role of a mentor?
- What role should you play in your family?
- Are you the healer or the victim of disease such as cancer?
- Are you the supplier of intelligence or the money that can be used to buy organic foods and tools?

It is extremely difficult if not impossible to succeed if we don't know which roles we should play in life. The role of parents is to protect their children. In the 21st century many parents are unable to protect themselves, their children and grandchildren. Husbands don't know how to protect their wives, wives don't know how to protect their husbands and save them from minotaurs such as prostate cancer. They fail because they have no idea what's happening in the special world. In most cases there is no knowledge of diet or willingness to change. Many people play the roles of powerless victims. There is however a place for a hero. Someone who has the necessary wisdom to solve the problem. Every character, member of a family or community should play a key role. That's when he or she becomes an archetype. Archetypes solve several types of problems such as:

- Biological - disease
- Cultural - the methods of the ancestors
- Historical - knowledge of self
- Intellectual - what to do
- Psychological, spiritual - who are we?
- Social - what's my role?

We cannot succeed or complete our quest without archetypes. It is impossible. If you watch movies such as Star Wars, The Karate Kid, Million Dollar Baby, James Bond you will see the archetypes. In the movie Million Dollar Baby, Clint Eastwood plays the role of a trainer who helps a young lady to become a successful boxer. The film uses powerful principles. It replicates the role of the old man who teaches a young person how to survive in a hostile world. We need teachers, mentors to help us overcome obstacles. People who reject the wisdom of their mentors pay a heavy price. Many die prematurely after being exposed to powerful toxins that destroy the immune system.

Blinded by ego and ignorance

During the early stages of my journey I met a wonderful man who wanted to mentor and help me to grow. He gave me everything I needed: finance, logistics, moral and intellectual support. I had no knowledge of self and was striving to recover from depression caused by the death of my parents. I was blinded by the ego therefore I insulted my mentor. I rejected the call to adventure, the call to refinement and personal growth. It was a mistake. Unfortunately the rejection of mentorship is a mistake that many people make. Such attitude and error leads to failure in life. We cannot do it without archetypes.

The tragic journey of Icarus

We return to Ancient Greece and there we are told of a man called Daedalus. He was a prolific inventor of remarkable things. Daedalus tried to be the mentor of his son. After realising that he could not escape the open prison built by King Minos on foot, Daedalus set to work. He spent weeks collecting feathers. He used the feathers to create artificial wings. He tied the feathers together with wax. When his inventions were ready, he looked at his son in the eyes and told him not to fly too close to the Sun. The mentor told his student not to fly too high or too low. Shortly before they left, Daedalus looked at his son in the eyes and said:

"If you fly too high, the power of the mighty Sun God will melt your feathers and destroy your wings. If you fly too low, the ruthless waves of the ancient sea will wet your wings. If you fly too low the sea will drag you to its deadly waters"

After the instructions were given, father and son used their wings to leave Crete and the open prison built by King Minos. Everything was going according to plan until Icarus decided to enjoy himself. He ignored the instructions of his mentor and kept flying high. He broke the covenant. His decision was fatal. He got too close to the Sun. The wax melted and the feathers fell apart. Icarus fell into the ocean and drowned.

The story of Icarus is a warning to students. The message is very clear. Ignoring the instructions of a wise mentor will have devastating consequences. We should know and accept our limitations. The story of Icarus also teaches us that we cannot escape the labyrinth created by diseases such as cancer without the help and wisdom of a wise mentor. The stories of people who die after rejecting the instructions of a mentor and a natural healer are not something of the past.

The tragic journey of a healer's brother

From Los Angeles we are told the story of a man, an uncommon doctor. He was tall and elegant. Although he was in his 80s he had many daughters and sons. His children became mothers and fathers of beautiful boys and girls. This man had a wonderful mind. He was born close to a river. When he was a child he learned how to swim. He became a skilled swimmer. The beautiful, tall and elegant boy was afflicted by diabetes. Doctors told him that his sickness was incurable. He grew up and became a student, a lover of nature and beautiful plants that contain substances which heal the body. He learned the secret of plants which he used to heal himself and his patients. He was loved by millions of people who saw in him a perfect role model. An excellent teacher, mentor and healer.

One day the man's brother was diagnosed with cancer. The healer and mentor of many souls told his brother to change his diet and to stop eating starchy foods. He also told his arrogant and ignorant brother to use herbs to heal his decaying body. His brother rejected the instructions because "you are not a doctor". He believed in conventional treatments therefore he refused to change his diet or drink herbal teas. Like Icarus he fell from the sky and died. He died young and left behind innocent children and a grieving wife. His children were forced to grow up without a father in a very challenging word that's extremely difficult to master. The man died because he rejected the mentorship of an essential archetype.

CHAPTER 11
The Main Archetypes

Many thousands of years ago, Telemachus, the son of Odysseus was visited by an old man called Mentor. The old man encouraged young Telemachus to be brave, bold and confront his fears. Mentor told Telemachus "go and find your father". The old man was a personification of an ancient principle. He was an archetype.

The word archetypes was introduced by Carl Jung. A prolific author and dedicated student of occult and ancient wisdom. He used the word archetype to describe key figures found in mythology, the real world and the human psyche.

Picture a house with several floors. At the bottom of the house, there are certain objects and images. They have been there for millions of years. Every house in the world has such objects and images. They are primal. They are the ancestors, the names, blood types, the stories, pictures, memories, seeds, a grandmother, a grandfather, a cousin etc. They are the seeds of consciousness. In Ancient Kmt you find Maat, Djehuty, Ra, Sekhmet, Wsr, Sutek, Aset, Hrw.

They are universal and timeless principles. Most people call them Gods. Carl Jung called them Archetypes. Every Jewish person has heard of Abraham, Moses, the Promised Land. In India children are told stories about Vishnu, Indra, Brahma, the ancestral father and the great architect of the universe. Children from Native American Indian culture are told about an old lady called Spider woman. From Africa we got Aset, Wsr, Kayazimba, Obatala and many others. Every culture has archetypes. Every human being has a relative that looks like "one of our ancestors." The house which contains ancient images and memories is the human psyche.

If you observe your family and your surroundings you will find a father, a mother, the daughter, the brother, the sister, the cousin, the friend, the relative, the doctor, the nurse, the scientist, the grumpy neighbour, the gravedigger, the funeral director, the cancer specialist, the blood testing specialist, the herbalist, the bin collector, the student, the postman and postwoman. These are essential characters who play key roles. They help our psyche to remain intact.

We need these essential characters because they fulfill roles that we cannot fulfill. We need these characters to help us. We need to understand their psychology and the mythology hidden in them. If we refuse to learn we will fail. In the world of disease, there are certain people, archetypes that play key roles. A doctor tells you what's wrong, you get a specialist doctor who might recommend a treatment, a nurse who gives you the treatment. There is a patient, nurse, secretary and of course a mother, father, son and daughter. There is also the shaman, the medicine man, the medicine woman, the ferryman and the ferry woman.

In the very complex world of conventional treatments, we have the patient and the scientists who have been searching for the cure for more than 100 years. They have not found it yet. Even the most educated scientist will tell you that "We don't know how to cure 99.9% of diseases in the world". Should we look for alternatives? A plan B?

The Hero's Philosophy relies on key principles, research and mythology. The philosophy inspires you to follow the thread left by the man and woman that defeated the big monster. People who cured themselves.

In mythology, we have the heroes, the bad guys, the good guys, the mother, father, mentor. They are archetypes. The Ntrw, the gods, and goddesses are also there. The enemies and tricksters are also there. We should look at them in order to learn how they can help us. Mythology is the study of life. The union of health and mythology produces two types of archetypes.

- Visible
- Invisible

Among the visible, you have humans, fruits, and vegetables. In the invisible group you have vitamins, cells, micronutrients, tumors, viruses, emotions such as fear. They are essential and we should pay attention to both.

Visible archetypes:

- Daughter
- Doctor
- Father
- Financier
- Healer
- Herbalist
- Husband
- Mentor
- Mother

"It's not the cancer that really hurts people. Statistically, 42 to 46% of patients will die, that have cancer, will die of Cachexia, which is basically wasting of protein. They will basically lose all their lean body mass. That leaves between 58 to 54% of patients that didn't die of cachexia. The joke which is only maybe half funny, is that the rest of them die from the treatment. In another words, really nobody dies from the cancer. If you think about it, when patients get immune suppress when they have cancer, what actually takes them, liver failure, kidney failure, pneumonia, sepsis. But all these things are usually also associated with the person getting chemo and radiation."

- The Truth About Cancer; A global Quest - Episode 1

A few years ago I met a mother of two girls whose body was gradually destroyed by cancer. Her self-esteem was also destroyed. She did not survive the ordeal. She was a victim of the Minotaur that's eating the human race alive.

Both the mythological monster that attacked Greek virgins and the biological monster that's destroying organs and families have allies. We can win if we do our best to destroy the allies of the monster. Sugar, stress, toxins, bad diet, toxic emotional states, GMO and junk foods.

If we stop and reflect on the journeys of our ancestors we will come to the natural conclusion that we have three options:

1. Strive to become heroes.
2. Save our friends and relatives.
3. Do nothing, enjoy the sugar and become victims.

The third option is to give up, eat junk foods, toxins and sugar then spend 40 hours a week watching TV. That's the wrong strategy. We should learn as much as we can about the monster that's destroying families and generations.

The monster's main goal is to cause terror. Its main strategy is fear and ignorance. Fear causes stress. Stress is one of the main causes of disease. When we understand the psychological and biological strengths and weaknesses of the monster, we get clues on how to confront it. We remain happy. We avoid stress. We exercise and strive to be happy. We eat organic foods, we fast and do our best to remain jolly. That's the Hero's Philosophy.

The Trickster

"Tricksters were the anti-heroes of the world's myths. Greedy, lecherous and endlessly self-seeking, they still won grudging admiration for their quick wits - and sometimes for their skill in triumphing against the odds."

– The Great theme - Myth and Mankind – p66

In 2010 a father of two beautiful and ambitious girls was told that he had prostate cancer. He was given conventional treatment, surgery and radiation. He seemed to recover from the ordeal. Two years after the diagnosis he returned to work, and tried to have a normal life. It did not work. Four years after being told that his cancer was in remission, he fell gravely sick and died. He was tricked by a ruthless monster, which deprived him of seeing his girls growing up. Like many beautiful fathers before him, the man was struck by a silent assassin that's satisfied to lay dormant for many seasons.

A few years ago I met an ambitious lady. She is the mother of 3 beautiful girls. They were brought up well. They are elegant, eloquent and lovely. They are studious therefore they did well at school. One of the lady's daughters is an engineer. She told me she has two grandchildren. A lovely boy and a very happy and intelligent girl. She also told me that her grandchildren are anxious because they are growing up without their father. "They are not psychologically settled, said the lady". He was tall and vigorous man, a gentle giant. He was the authority. He loved his family. He used to take his wife and children on holidays to wonderful places such as Spain, Sicily,

Casablanca, Barcelona, Bombay, Athens, Los Angeles and many other exciting and exotic places.

I asked her what happened to your son-in-law? "He died 2 years ago." She said with tears in her eyes. "He got cancer when he was 24. He was given chemo and surgery. He believed, we all believed that he was cured. He spent 20 years working hard and bringing up his children. My daughter loved him. His mother and father also loved him dearly. His daughter, his friends, everybody loved him. My daughter misses him a lot. He was her first love. They got married 3 years after he got the treatment. 20 years later the cancer returned. It was stronger and more ruthless. It killed him in 5 days."

The lady's son-in-law was tricked to believe that the big monster was gone. Cancer is a trickster. It gives people the false impression that everything is fine. Cancer is not the only trickster in history to fool its victims.

The Fabian strategy

During the Punic wars, 218-208 BCE a remarkable Carthaginian general called Hannibal did the unthinkable. He crossed the Alps and invaded Rome. A small group of wealthy families that controlled the Roman Empire realised that they were dealing with a warrior of a different level. Hannibal was famous for his ability to inspire his men to fight to death. After realizing that they could not defeat Hannibal, secret societies that controlled the Roman Empire selected a Roman general called Quintus Fabius Maximus. They gave him an unusual mission. He was told "don't fight Hannibal because you will die. He is too strong for us. Go to the battlefield and destroy every single resource that his army will need. Break bridges, houses, burn entire villages, kill animals, cows and pigs, squirrels and chickens in order to deprive him of essential resources." Quintus Fabius went and did as he was told. His mission was to delay the arrival of Hannibal. He succeeded. While Hannibal and his men were busy dealing with the obstacles created by Fabius, a secret society back in Rome organised an army. By the time Hannibal reached the gates of Rome his entire army was exhausted therefore unable to fight.

The same happens to someone suffering from cancer. The Minotaur will gradually weaken the immune system. An immune system that's not taken care of will grow weak and lose the fight against free radicals.

The greatest general in the history of the world was defeated through trickery. Today the strategy used by Quintus Fabius is called the "Fabian Strategy". Quintus Fabius Maximus was a trickster. He tricked Hannibal to believe that he wanted a direct confrontation. He used conflict to lure Hannibal into a psychological and deadly trap. Cancer uses the same strategy. It persuades doctors to believe that direct confrontation is the best strategy. Direct confrontation is a short term solution. Healing the body is a long term goal which requires time and a lot of patience.

In mythology, we also find a character called the trickster. He is cunning, criminal, cruel and usually very successful. Think of Iago in Othello. He is a classic trickster. By the time the victim realises that he or she has been tricked, it is usually too late. That's what sugar and the big monster do. Families all over the world are tricked to fall in love with sugar. Sugar is everywhere. Sugar is also one of the main allies of the monster that we call cancer. Cancer loves sugar.

If you love sugar and are addicted to it then you have been tricked. It's never too late to learn and change. It's not easy to change however it is necessary. In most cases a change of diet and consciousness is an urgent task. Mythology warns us about tricksters.

In the book *"The Eternal Cycle"*, we learn about one of the greatest tricksters in Indian mythology. "Shiva was both benevolent and destructive. Those who dealt with him didn't know which mask he was wearing on a specific occasion."

Shiva was a trickster, always ready to trick his victims in order to get his way. Tricksters can be found in many fields. Sports, medicine, literature, politics, education. The trickster is a universal archetype. He believes that his or her happiness is above other people's wellbeing, therefore, he tricks them.

You can see the endless chain of destruction caused by a trickster. Everyday people are tricked to eat foods that contain sugar. Please remember that cancer cells cannot survive without sugar. People are tricked to love foods that are sweet. They are not healthy, they are sweet. They are also very dangerous because they fuel the growth of free radicals.

An experienced graphic designer, a filmmaker are tricksters who create wonderful adverts used to promote and sell dangerous and potentially cancer causing products. Sex and colours are used to trick people to fall in love with foods that contain shocking amounts of sugar and toxins. The consequences in the long-term are devastating. Many people enjoy pleasure today and pain tomorrow. People are also tricked to believe that they are powerless and that cancer is an incurable disease. I was of the same opinion until I watched the "Truth About Cancer" documentaries. The Truth About Cancer series told the story of a trickster who used cancer as a method to make a lot of money.

Dr. Fata - A prolific trickster

In July 2015, an American doctor called Dr. Farid Fata was jailed for 45 years. Dr. Fata realised that he could make a lot of money by telling people that they had cancer. He tricked people to buy and use chemotherapy and radiation. Every time he prescribed chemo for a patient he was paid by an insurance company. He told more than 500 people that they had terminal cancer. They got chemo and radiation and he was paid more than 17 million dollars by insurance companies. Men, women, children of all ages and origins fell for his tricks. Their lives were destroyed. He tricked them to believe they had terminal cancer and urgently needed radiation and chemotherapy. He is a trickster who played on his victims fears. The subject of cancer is not just biological. Disease of any kind is also a psychological experience. The product of addictions and a negative mindset.

It doesn't matter the name or severity of the condition that's afflicting us, there is always a psychological dimension involved. Millions of people are tricked to believe that the monster has left the body. They are given a temporary relief and happiness. Although the symptoms go away, the cause remains.

A few years ago I read the biography of a man, a powerful, intelligent and very wealthy man. He was very successful indeed. The father of 3 wonderful children. 1 boy and 2 girls. When he was young the man created a technology business. He became wealthy, very wealthy before the age of 30. He loved his work. He was passionate about excellence, marketing and computer science. One day he felt uncomfortable and had difficulties in emptying his bladder. He went to a doctor and was told that he had pancreatic cancer.

He was diagnosed in 2003. In 2004 he had surgery and a tumor was removed. In 2009 he got a liver transplant. He was very happy about the surgery. He continued to work. In 2010, his health started to deteriorate. He experienced a visible decline. He was forced to take medical leave.

He died in 2011. The ambitious man, a beautiful man with a beautiful mind was tricked by a monster called cancer. It tricked him to lower his guard and believe that he was healed. Both the surgery and transplant were temporary solutions. Cancer is one of the biggest tricksters in the world. It has the power to trick you to give up and surrender. Cancer is a warning. A method used by nature to tell you that you should stop doing what you have you been doing for the last 20/30 years. "Cancer is a nature's telephone call telling you that it's time to change."

Master of false impressions

10 years ago the brother of one of my school mates, was told that he had lung cancer. He went to the hospital and got chemo. He returned home and seemed fine. He carried on smoking. Two years

later he was dead. Cancer tricked him to believe that he was fine. It gave him the false impression that it was gone when in reality it was still inside him.

The big monster called cancer is an excellent candidate for the title "greatest trickster in the world". It tricks many people to believe that "it's gone." It also tricks people to believe that it's incurable. Such beliefs generate high-levels of stress and fear.

What can you do? What are your options? How can you save yourself?

Mythology gives us a clue. The Ancient Greek architect Daedalus is a key reference.

How did Daedalus escape the fury and trickery of King Minos?

Daedalus was very smart. He tricked the trickster. He created artificial wings and used them to escape. He couldn't escape by land therefore he found a way to escape by air. King Minos had no airplanes, therefore he could not stop the intelligent inventor from leaving the open prison.

That's the key lesson, wisdom, beautifully hidden in the story of Daedalus. When it comes to cancer you have to find a way to trick the greatest trickster in the world. How do you do that? You invent and adopt a healthy diet. You overcome trials and all kinds of psychological and physical challenges.

1. You eat well - if you can adopt a vegan and organic only diet, do it
2. Exercise
3. Avoid toxins

4. Take the necessary supplements such as vitamin D3, Iodine, Selenium, Zinc, Alphapolic acid, Glutathione, Milk Thistle, Turmeric
5. Study, read and research the subject
6. Avoid stress
7. Research and reading will give you confidence
8. Detox, detox and detox
9. Fast
10. Give up meat and dairy products and animal protein. Leave animals alone. Like you, they have the right to be alive. They have relatives as well.
11. Practice positive affirmations
12. Embrace mind power, epigenetics and a powerful philosophy called "Inner engineering"

Every year I spend at least 3 month eating raw organic foods only. It's not easy. It is necessary. If I can do it, surely you can do it as well. Raw foods are an excellent source of longevity, Vita.

Are you prepared? If you aren't then prepare yourself - Move the rock

The idea of preparing yourself to a big challenge is very ancient. Before he went to Athens, Theseus spent several months trying hard to move a big rock. When he finally succeeded, he started his journey towards Athens, the capital where his father lived. On his way to Athens he fought bandits, ruffians, tricksters and experienced villains. The rock and the fights were his training and preparation for the great battle. The obstacles were his initiation. The bandits, and the rough road were threshold guardians, designed to ensure that he was prepared for the next stage of the adventure.

Shortly after he arrived in Athens, Theseus started a new adventure, he went to Crete in order to fight the Minotaur. It was a difficult journey, a very challenging battle. He fought bravely and won. Theseus won because he was prepared. He was not afraid of the Minotaur because he had spent 1 year preparing himself. Like Theseus, you can prepare yourself by changing your diet, detoxing and reading as much as you can. There is a website called Audible. It contains many audiobooks written by experts on alternative therapies. If you don't have time to read, you can at least listen to wise mentors.

There are two methods of preparation that you should adopt:

1. Psychological

You can prepare yourself psychologically by researching and reading about the causes and every single method used to treat cancer. You can look at traditional methods such as chemo, radiation and surgery. You can also research about less known methods such as Essiac, Gerson therapy, apricot kernels, detoxing, supplementation and essential oils. One of the best ways to prepare your body is by using methods prescribed by naturopaths. You could study Naturopathy. You could contact a naturopath and ask for advice. Get training. Ask intelligent questions, pay people to educate you about the subject that is central to your present and future

2. Biological

One of the best ways to prepare yourself biologically is through practice.

- Exercise
- Coffee enemas
- Fasting,
- Yoga
- Running
- Swimming

These are excellent ways to protect your body. Avoid exposing your body to toxins such as cigarettes, drugs and alcohol. Never lower your guard. Things such as processed, artificial sugar and stress should not be part of your life. That means no drinking, no smoking and no chemicals.

Exercise is essential because it eliminates stress. Reading is essential because it eliminates ignorance. Juicing is essential because it cleanses the blood and brings in fresh oxygen to essential organs. You should research about oxygen therapies and use them whenever you can. Organic foods are essential because they contain vitamins. Please remember that the word vita means life in Latin.

If you are attacked by the monster you should never fall under the false impression that a brief treatment is enough. When a monster strikes, you need to design a long-term plan dedicated to health. You trick the monster by eating well, living well and thinking well. You trick the monster by doing the right things. By pursuing Self Mastery. There are no shortcuts to heroism and longevity.

The Victim

"I knew a man, a common farmer, the father of five sons, And in them, the fathers of sons, and in them the fathers of sons. This man was a wonderful vigor, calmness, beauty of person. The shape of his head, the pale yellow and white of his hair and the beard, the immeasurable meaning of his black eyes. The richness and breadth of his manners. These I used to go and visit him to see, he was wise also. He was six feet tall, he was over eighty years old..."

- Walt Whitman - The Body Electric.

I also knew a man, a beautiful man. He was strong and happy. He was a builder who loved his work. He was a hardworking man. He worked very hard therefore his family was never in need. He loved his work and loved his friends also. He was an extrovert. He loved his wife and his 3 children. I spoke to him several times. I visited him and learned about his goals, visions, and intentions. Unfortunately he also loved to smoke and enjoy a drink with friends.

I am sad to say that the man is no longer alive. He died after being struck by cancer. He had lung cancer. Doctors told him to get surgery and chemotherapy. He followed their instructions. There were some painful conclusions. He went to the hospital and spent a few weeks there. When he returned home he was not the same person. He lost his vigor. The manly manners, the bravery, the self-esteem and confidence were gone. The energy in his eyes was also gone. He became a pessimist, his pace changed. He became a depressed patient. He gave up, he lost the passion for living.

The man, the husband, the father of 3 young children was the victim of the big monster called cancer. He was 50 something when he died. He has gone into the invisible world of eternal silence. He left behind countless Pandora boxes filled with sweet and unique memories. He lost a great battle. Perhaps the most important battle of his life.

The man was a victim of a monster. He was not the sole victim. His children are very young. They are not 18 yet. They lost a mentor, a protector. They lost the king of their house, his wife lost her companion, her best friend and owner of her heart. His friends lost their mate, his employer lost a valuable asset. Cancer does not just destroy one single person. The wonderful man or woman, the patient is not an Island. The Minotaur destroys anybody who is close to the patient. That's one of the reasons why allies should start the Hero's Journey as a prevention strategy.

In the world of diseases there are two types of victims:

1. The first victim is the patient who fails to win the greatest battle of his or her life.
2. The second victims are the relatives, the brothers, the children, lovers, parents, friends, wife, husband, neighbours and anybody who cares about the patient.

There is a physical and psychological loss. There is also a personal and a collective loss. The families and children left behind are forced to grieve the loss of wonderful souls. The ambitious men and women of our century will do their best to avoid becoming victims of the big monster. They could and should become initiates.

Patient 4 - "I was very young when my mother was diagnosed with breast cancer. I was 11 at the time. I did not understand what was really happening.

I saw the transformation in my father's face. The whole thing changed him. One day he was very happy. The following day he was crying like a baby. The experience of losing my mother, devastated my father. Seeing my father crying traumatised me. My mother did her best to remain "normal". She had 3 doses of chemo. The treatment destroyed her. She lost a lot of weight, hair and beauty. My mother was tall and very beautiful. She had dark hair and beautiful brown eyes. Her experience was a brutal lesson about health and death. I was forced to learn a lot in a short period of time.

Looking at it today, I can say that it was a blessing in disguise. 20 years after the death of my mother, I was told that I had the same disease. I was offered the same treatment given to my mom. I gladly refused. I had seen a lot.

I have a degree in Computer Science therefore it was not a big deal for me to resign from my well paid job in order to focus on the biggest challenge of my life. I was scared but also keen to heal myself. I read every single book and watched every single video that I could find about breast cancer. I spoke to survivors, I emailed and called some of them. I spoke to people in Australia, New Zealand, Africa, China, U.S. Russia and China. I re-educated myself about the causes and the best ways to fight cancer. After 2 years of enemas and juices, organic foods, I went to the hospital and was tested. I was over the moon when they told me that I was 100% cancer free. I cried non-stop for 2 hours."

There are heroes, many heroes who stand up and fight the monster. They refuse to become victims of the Minotaur. The lady's mother was brutally murdered by cancer. Her mother's death was a call to adventure. She accepted the invitation to learn and change her habits. She succeed. She cured herself. Her experiences helped her to transcend, descend and evolve from victim to hero. Her story is not unique. The ancient world has a wonderful tale of a female who said no to the big monster that was keen to destroy her family.

Theseus got into the world of the Minotaur as a victim. While he was there he fought and succeeded. He got in as a young man and got out as a man a hero, a leader.

Many patients are told that they are another victim and that their lives will be short. Very few people tell them that they have the potential to become heroes.

A human being living in the 21st century will at one point in his or her life go into a hospital or clinic. Like Aset the ancient African Queen and Theseus the Greek hero, they will become patients. Will they get out as a healthy people? Will they become heroes? Will they die as victims? What's stopping people from being healthy in a highly developed age?

- Diet?
- Economics?
- Fear?
- Ignorance?

There are people who refuse to be victims of cancer. They are heroes who accept the call to adventure. The call to learn, to say no to sugar. They choose to fight rather than to die in pain. The following words are from a YouTube video called "Lonnell's Holistic Approach to Prostate Cancer - Cancer Survivor Story" on The Truth About Cancer YouTube channel:

Lonnell - "I was diagnosed with prostate cancer in the year 2000. The first challenge I faced was accepting the diagnosis. It was given rather abruptly. Matter of factly, and I recall the urologist saying you've got cancer and he explained three possible options. I could have surgery or chemotherapy or radiation. He said, when would you like to schedule for surgery? And I said I need time to think, to process this. I haven't thought about it, I haven't asked God what I should do. So just give me some time and then I will respond. Dispensed chemotherapy and chemotherapeutic agents. It involved putting on rubber gloves and a mask and I knew that it was toxic and it had a severe effect on the body. I knew that this was not something that I would choose to do. A strategy that God gave to me was three-fold and it centered around three verbs that I employ. It was to;

- Watch
- Fight
- And pray.

And much later, I learned that this was a holistic approach in that I watched what I ate, I watched what I thought, I watched what I spoke. It was dealing with the physical body so that's part of it, but then there were other factors that contributed. And that's in terms of the fight that dealt with the emotional aspects of the soul, mind and the body. There's this great mental fight that you go through. I think of it as the fight of my life."

When a person or patient reaches the second stage of the Hero's Journey, he or she will be told that their body or immune system has lost the fight against the big monster. The big monster has many names. Cancer, cold, aids, breast cancer, colon cancer, pancreatic cancer, liver cancer, lung cancer, brain cancer, malaria, diabetes... When the verdict, the result of a clinical test is delivered the patient becomes aware of his or her own mortality. The news that you are being attacked by a deadly enemy creates fear and stress. Depending on the person who is giving the diagnosis, the patient will either feel lost of fearful. If a salesperson is trying to sell you something he or she will always play into your fears. Salespeople, actors, actresses, writers, politicians, journalists, filmmakers are aware that a human being pays attention to 3 types of emotions. They are basic and affect every single person in the world. They are;

- Conflict
- Desire
- Fear

These 3 primal emotions are used in many industries to lure people and compel them to make decisions. Advertisers tell you to, "Buy this product otherwise you're at risk of dying. Vote for this person otherwise we will be attacked by terrorists." The fear mongering is used to trigger collective fear. Fear can be very destructive. It has the power to make people do the unthinkable. Fear also pollutes the immune system. It creates stress. Stress enables disease to prosper.

The word cancer is feared by many people. They fear cancer because they don't know what cancer is. We fear what we don't know. The enigma. Most people who fear cancer have no idea how the monster behaves, who are its allies. Many people are also ignorant about the best methods which can be used to defeat or prevent the arrival of the monster. Ignorance is one of the biggest sources of fear. Fear is damaging because it leads to stress. Stress is one of the main causes of cancer and "chronic diseases".

There is an intellectual ecosystem, a kind of labyrinth that requires negative thinking, emotional storms, stress, toxins, ignorance and deficiency. If you are aware of the labyrinth and its elements your chances of succeeding are very high indeed.

The Hero

"A Hero is someone who has given his or her life to something bigger than oneself" Joseph Campbell

"

During the last decade of the 80s a girl who was suffering from advanced kidney cancer was introduced to a healer. The parents of the sickly and frail girl, told the healer that "Our daughter has terminal cancer. We have tried everything. Can you help us please?"

The healer accepted the "call to adventure" and initiated the girl into the principle of resurrection. The girl recovered and lived well for many years. The girl, her parents and the healer were heroes. The girl's parents kept searching for the lost vitality. They did not surrender and say "Ohh Gosh, this is life." They kept looking for effective solutions. That's a hero act. The searching. The parents of the little girl realised that they needed to speak to a modern day Aset. "The knower of all secret ways and words of potency"

A prolific author and ferryman called Joseph Campbell said that "heroes are people who dedicate their lives to something bigger than themselves." They do it after experiencing pain, the loss of a close relative, someone whom they truly treasure. Their experiences become the central focus of their activity, profession and inventions. They turn their experience into a craft. It becomes the origin of their visions and intentions, a job. Something which they do for rest of their lives. Many of them succeed in defeating the Minotaur then spend the rest of their lives inspiring, educating, helping and showing others how to get out of the labyrinth. They are driven, selfless, bold, brave and creators of wonderful projects which reflect their inner beauty.

To understand the steps that turns a patient, a sincere seeker, a dreamer, into a hero, we should avoid looking at people through conventional lenses and vocabulary. Conventional thinking says: “He is a patient who is suffering from cancer. He, she, is a victim of cancer.” This is basic terminology. We need to think outside the box and use a more ambitious vocabulary, a mythological language and psychology. We could change the paradigm by seeing a patient as someone who has the potential to become a hero, an initiate, a student, a sincere seeker. We remove the word patient and replace it with hero or sincere seeker. We could see cancer as a monster, a Minotaur, Satan, or a whale that has a big belly.

Wherever there is a monster, there is a space, an arena that’s ready to accommodate a battle, a confrontation between the hero and the monster. The word patient is usually associated with someone who is weak and suffering. Someone who is in pain. The sincere seeker is someone who wishes to end suffering. The hero is looking for something. He or she is not waiting for something. Conventional thinking says, “I am waiting for the results of a test”. The hero would say, “I am creating the right environment in order to get excellent results.” The first is reactive. The second is proactive. Aset did not wait in order to get the final news about her husband, instead she stood up and went looking for his body. That’s a proactive approach. Theseus did not wait for the Minotaur to come to Athens, he went to Crete to meet it. That’s a proactive approach.

Types of heroes

We have two types of heroes;

- The visible hero
- The invisible hero

We also have;

- The successful hero
- The tragic hero

The tragic hero

I met a lady who was married to a charming man. She loved him. She was faithful to him. She committed her life to him. When they met, her future husband was a young man with no purpose. She helped him to become a mature person, a responsible man. She became the mother of his children, his priestess and goddess. They got married. She became the wife and he the husband. They enjoyed 30 years of pure bliss. One fine summer afternoon her husband was told he had stomach cancer. Both husband and wife did not have healthy eating habits. They did not read books. They did not visit libraries frequently. The diagnosis forced them to change. It clouded their vision, polluted their hours and shattered their hopes of a long and sweet life. The big monster challenged them to learn new skills and embrace a new mindset and philosophy. They were asked to depart, to go to a new place and be initiated into a new diet, vocabulary, a new way of living. They rejected the invitation. They said no to the call to adventure. Their story became a tragedy. They became victims rather than heroes.

The husband's health declined. He lost his vitality and the ability to inspire his family to pursue wealth and tranquility. The man died prematurely.

The lady became a widow, her children became orphans. The lady is a fine example of a tragic hero who failed to fulfil her mythological potential. She didn't have the necessary tools to save her husband from premature death. She failed to become a hero because she didn't have the tools and the clues left by her ancestors. She didn't have the necessary thread. She failed because she didn't know Ariadne, the giver of essential keys, that open the doors of a world that is very mysterious and rich at the same time.

The successful hero

In Greek mythology we learn about Perseus. He was the son of a single mother called Danae. Danae was imprisoned by her father, a cruel King called Acrisius. Acrisius is the root word for 'a crisis'. Acrisius wanted to prevent his daughter from giving birth, therefore, he imprisoned her. Danae was confined to a dark room that had a small window. She was beautiful, sweet and irresistible.

Zeus, the son of cruel Kronos, fell in love with her and penetrated the room where she was confined. He took the form of a beautiful sunlight and impregnated her. 9 months later she gave birth to a blessed, beautiful and brave boy who was destined to achieve great things.

Danae gave birth to a boy. She called him Perseus. Perseus is the root for 'pursuit', 'persuade', 'persuasion', 'prosecutor'. Perseus became a hero. He rescued his mother after she was kidnaped by a cruel ruler called Polydectes. Danae was a successful hero. She gave birth to a boy. Her son was not a victim of a cruel king. Perseus was a successful hero who saved his mother after she fell into the hands of a tyrant who wanted to marry her by force.

The heroes who defeated a monster called cancer

Chris Wark is a cancer conqueror from the United States. He is an author and founder of chrisbeatcancer.com. He is another fine example of a successful hero. He cured himself of cancer using natural remedies. From Germany we get the story of a Dr. Gorter. He cured himself of an aggressive cancer. After completing the Hero's Journey, Dr. Gorter created a clinic that helps people to defeat the big monster.

Failure to retrieve the lost vitality

Orpheus was the son of a Thracian King called Oeagrus. His mother was a muse called Calliope. Orpheus was very talented. Orpheus was the finest musician of his time. One fine afternoon his wife was bitten by a poisonous serpent. Keen to save his wife from premature death, he went to the underworld and tried to rescue his wife. After charming and conquering the heart of the queen of the underworld, he was allowed to take his wife back to the world of the living. He was also given very clear instructions. He was told not to look back. That was the condition, the covenant that he signed with the king of the world of the dead. Shortly after he reached the world of the living, he looked back to check if his wife was still following him. It was a fatal mistake. He violated the agreement and paid a heavy price. Orpheus was also a fine example of a tragic hero.

Although he failed to rescue his wife, Orpheus has an important lesson to teach us. Orpheus teaches us to pay attention to details and to follow the instructions of our mentor. The King of the world of shadows, told Orpheus not to look back. Orpheus violated the command. If a mentor says 13 glasses of organic juices a day, the student should drink 13 glasses of organic juices a day. Both the tragic and successful heroes have important lessons that we should not ignore. The tragic hero fails to retrieve the lost vitality. He or she returns home without the Holy Grail. The secret of longevity. The successful hero, returns home with the elixir. We can learn from people who survived and those who didn't manage to defeat the monster. Both have powerful wisdom to share with us.

Rene Elliot the organic Londoner

"The hero, therefore, is the man or woman who has been able to battle past his personal and local historical limitations to the generally valid, normally human forms."

Joseph Campbell - The Hero with a 1000 faces, page 14

During the early decade of the 90s a young lady decided to create her own business, and pursue her dreams of becoming an entrepreneur. She was asked to choose between her heart and economics, health or profit. She said yes to the invitation to follow her heart and the desire to help others.

A successful hero accepts the call to adventure and departs from the world of ordinary thinking. Rene Elliot is an ambitious entrepreneur based in London. In 1995 Rene founded a supermarket called Planet Organic. Planet Organic represents a complete departure from conventional thinking. Planet Organic stores sell organic foods and hundreds of life saving supplements, delicious organic desserts. Rene Elliot is a successful hero who fulfilled her potential by helping others to stay healthy.

During a hot summer day in August 2018, I bought a bottle of water from Planet Organic, the branch located in Kensington, tube station Bayswater. When I looked at the text on the bottle, I was surprised to learn that the;

- Water is locally sourced
- BPA free
- 100% recyclable

Planet Organic reflects the standards and vision of the founder. An ambitious entrepreneur who is keen to provide ambitious people with organic foods and essential supplements. Such vision is a complete departure from the thinking behind every big supermarket. More than 90% of foods sold in conventional supermarkets are GMO and non-organic. That's the ordinary world. Rene Elliott is the hero who departed from the conventional, ordinary world and returned with an elixir called Planet Organic. Like Rene you could become the hero of your generation. How do you do that? Simply "Follow your Bliss" and the thread left by those who came before you.

The successful hero is a kind of a modern shaman or shama woman. He or she is a conductor of souls, a visionary that is keen to reject the ordinary, in order to attain the extraordinary.

Defeating a monster called cancer is an extraordinary achievement that requires a psychological, biological, financial, intellectual investment.

"A shaman's training also involves private and secret instructions from a master about the professional law as it is understood within that community. The trainee studies the nature of the spirit by learning the story or myths about them. A shaman in training also receives instructions in medicine and plant life. Learning techniques for warding off death or restoring the dead back to life. This notion of restoring life and health is an intimate part of the shaman's role in many cultures. In his or her initiation the shaman undergoes a sickness in order to prepare him for healing others."

- Religions of Small Societies by Ninian Smart, narrated by Ben Kingsley

THE HUSBAND

"My name is Catherine, I live in central London. My husband was the director of a global law firm that has offices in London. 4 years ago I was told that I had cervical cancer. 1 year after the diagnosis, my husband resigned from his very well paid job in order to be with me. He sacrificed his high flying career in order to save me."

"Dana & Ed's Fight Against Invasive Ductal Carcinoma - Treating Breast Cancer - Cancer Survivor Story" - Truth About Cancer YouTube channel:

Ed - "Her and I began watching the series the first night. After the first night of watching, I think I sat through the whole thing with my mouth hanging open because suddenly so many things made sense to me. Just common sense and the questions raised in there, the history of the cancer, pharmaceutical industry and stuff was just very common sense. And it's like light bulbs going off in my head."

That's the testimonial of a husband whose wife was diagnosed with breast cancer. Both husband and wife became successful heroes because they re-educated themselves about the subject called cancer. They watched the series and got the clues on how to get themselves out of the labyrinth.

"The Truth About Cancer" is a project founded by Ty Bollinger and his friends. Ty Bollinger's organisation was the school, the temple that initiated and helped the husband to free himself from ignorance. In the world of cancer ignorance means death. Ed's wife won the greatest battle of her life thanks to many people. The Truth About Cancer and of course her husband, were essential archetypes that guided her towards the light. A 21st century husband doesn't have to be a magician or a shaman. He has to be wise. His wisdom will inspire his wife to remain calm and stress free.

A battle for husband and wife

Lana - "It was jaw dropping, he's right, we sat with a box of tissues between us and it flooded us. And I got to be honest with you, it wasn't for me. It was for all the people we knew that have lost their battles. His father lost his and I just looked at him and I said, if the people that aren't here today would have had this information they may still be here. That was huge. I knew I was gonna be okay. You guys did that for me, The Truth About Cancer did that for me."

The journey of the victims, patients, students and heroes that defeated a monster called cancer, teaches us something very profound. It doesn't matter how old we are, our origin, our profession we will need to re-educate ourselves about health and cancer.

During the summer of 2017, I met a husband who was suffering from diabetes. His wife was suffering from breast cancer. The couple were being attacked by monsters. Both husband and wife didn't have a clue about juicing, cleansing, detoxing, minerals etc. The lady that was battling cancer refused to learn. She persisted in clinging to her ego and ignorance. Such psychological flaws can be fatal if not addressed and corrected. Rejection of wisdom leads to ignorance. Ignorance is a bridge to premature death.

The psychological strength of the husband

Ed - "What I really didn't count on was the emotional aspect of this thing. I so underestimated that. It just sucks the life right out of you for a while. I just can't stress enough how strong that part of it is. Once you get through that, once I heard her say I'm gonna be fine. It's like you let your breath out and it's just such a difference."

The words of a husband who became a successful hero are priceless for people interested in longevity. They reveal a very close relationship, loyalty between two people who were under attack. They started their Hero's Journey as victims. They were offered radiation and other conventional treatments. They rejected the invitation. They learnt as much as they could about the Minotaur. The learning, the training, the initiation, helped the ambitious couple to succeed. The husband's words remind us of the need to be emotionally prepared. The fight against cancer is more psychological than biological. "Once I heard her say I am gonna be fine." This was the statement that enabled the husband to remain calm and get the right energy to support his wife. The key word is energy.

John Kehoe said that "Everything in the Universe is made of consciousness and energy. That's all there is. Your sickness that you presently have consists of consciousness and energy... What will happen to you in the future is consciousness and energy..."

The husband's initiation

What is initiation? To understand the meaning of the word initiation we look into the etymology of the word Culture. If we divide the world Culture into two words, we get Cult and Re. Cult means hidden, Re is the visible aspect of an ancient creative principle. The grandfather of Aset. The cult of Re refers to the hidden circle of Re, the invisible family of Re. Each member of Re's family is a principle. Anybody who wishes to understand Re has to be initiated into the circle. Initiation simply means training, education, discovery of hidden principles.

Cult of Re = Culture. Someone seeking wisdom about natural ways to heal his or her body has to be initiated into a new culture that values the power of pHlants. The cult of Mother Nature. The word for beginning in Portuguese is Inicio. Iniciar means to start. Initiation refers to a beginning. To initiate is to start something. In our world to initiate means to start the learning process.

Students of an ancient culture

The learning centers of Ancient Africa were called Mystery Schools. People from all over the world went to Kmt to learn the mysteries of life. Two prominent Western intellectuals spent more than 20 years being trained by Kmtic priests. They became some of the influential thinkers of the Western world. They were Pythagoras and Plato. Their teachings and philosophies came from a very ancient world. Pythagoras, for example, spent more than 10 years in Kmt.

The husband of a lady who is battling cancer will need a philosophy dedicated to health. Philosophy is preceded by initiation. We are referring to an intellectual initiation that will inspire a departure, rejection of old beliefs, ignorance and bigotry that has the power to turn a hero into a powerless liability.

The ambitious husband will find a mentor, a teacher, a ferryman, a ferry woman, a healer and conductor of souls, who will teach him how to become a hero. The other option is to remain ordinary. Watch TV, drink alcohol, ignore the signals, reject the call to adventure then become a widow. The 21st century environment is very demanding. It requires an expert in detox and liver cleansing not a drinker or smoker. Husbands living in the 21st century can busy themselves with economics, sports, golf etc. These are excellent hobbies. They are necessary pursuits. There is, however, the need to be wise because we are living in challenging times. The ambitious husband will find a mentor. He will become a student of alternative therapies. He will get clues by reading, listening and adopting a new philosophy, the Hero's Philosophy.

A well informed husband will become an essential asset to his family. If he refuses to learn, the husband will become a liability because he will have no chance against the big monster. The monster called cancer is ferocious and will not be defeated by tears and lamentations. The conflict requires intelligent and carefully planned actions.

A husband living in the 21st century has to wear many masks. He is the king who is ready to do whatever he can to protect his queen. He's the mentor who is ready to lead and teach his family and friends. The husband is also the student who knows the secret of herbs. He's also a seeker of new ways of solving problems. He is a philosopher who asks intelligent questions.

Watching great documentaries, such as the Truth About Cancer is an excellent strategy and initiation into a new world, a new way of thinking and successful living.

Key questions

- Who is the mentor of the husband?
- What does the husband know about breast cancer?
- What kind of books does the husband read?
- What kind of diet does the husband follow?
- What kind of content does the husband consume daily?
- Is the husband the main mentor of the family?
- Does the husband drink or smoke?
- Is the husband psychologically and intellectually prepared to face the monster?
- Is the husband willing to give up old habits?
- When was the husband initiated into the subject of health?
- Is the husband a citizen of the special world?

THE WIFE, MOTHER, THE PRIESTESS & SAVIOUR

"The best known of these mother goddesses is probably one venerated in the countries of the eastern Mediterranean. She went by different names...

To the Sumerians she was Inna, to the Babylonians Ishtar, to the Phrygians of Anatolian Cybele, to the peoples of Syria and Lebanon Astarte. In the Greek world, some of her attributes turned up in Artemis, others in Aphrodite and Demeter. The Romans identified her with Gaia, Ceres, and Tellus. Everywhere she was the Great Goddess, the Queen of Heaven and she generated a special kind of religious awe."

- p63 The Great Themes - World Myth

When I was a teenager, my family and I lived near the house of a migrant family. The father, the patriarch of the family, migrated from an African Island called Cabo Verde. The mother was a Portuguese lady. She was short, beautiful and friendly. The couple had two children, one boy and one girl. The boy was called Bruno, like the famous Florentine rebel Giordano Bruno. The couple had a beautiful and truly charming daughter called Edna. Edna is beautiful, very charming indeed. Many boys fell in love with her. She was my classmate at school. I was very shy therefore I never told her that she is very charming.

Until last year I was not aware that the name Edna came from a very ancient principle. The principle is called Sedna. Sedna was the mother "goddess" of the American Native Indians. She personified " Mother Earth", the source of life, health, longevity and prosperity. Sedna was the mother of heroes.

A hero that overcame many trials

Hrw is a Mdw Ntr word. Hrw was the son of Aset. Hrw also means daylight. Hrw became Hero in English. Heroi in Latin. When he was young Hrw was stung by a scorpion. He was on the verge of death when his mother rescued him. Hrw experienced many trials. The greatest was the fight against his uncle Sutek. The two spent many years fighting for supremacy. The ego vs the Hero.

An analysis of the journey of Hrw and his mother Aset reveals a precious secret. The victim's journey. We have a boy who lost his father and was bitten by a scorpion. Then we have a victim who lost her husband. She fought and defeated the monster called death. One of the challenges that she faced was imprisonment. Sutek imprisoned his sister in law in order to stop her from fulfilling her potential. In the journey of Aset, imprisonment symbolises the psychological struggle that every hero has to overcome. The cruel Sutek, locked his sister-in-law in prison, in order to prevent her from finding the body of her husband. She was freed by her allies. She carried on searching and managed to save her husband. The monster tricked her. She lowered her guard. The monster returned and striked again. She fought back and saved her husband for the second time. Shortly after saving her husband, Aset faced another formidable opponent. Disease. A scorpion attacked her child. She worked hard and succeeded in rescuing her son.

The journey of the ancient queen and mother of the Hero was not an easy one. Your journey or the journey of your relative will not be easy. It doesn't matter what you wish to accomplish, the Hero's Journey is never easy otherwise everybody would complete it. Aset was forced to evolve from victim to hero several times.

Aset is an essential archetypal character. She was a wife, a mother, a warrior, a healer and a very wise mentor and sister. She was the archetypal suffering wife who is not prepared to accept the death of her husband. She is a member of a universal family which Joseph Campbell called "The Hero with a Thousand Faces". A 21st century wife and mother who is not interested in reading and studying will face formidable psychological, financial, biological, social and emotional challenges. Some of these challenges are created by the big monster.

After spending 50 years drinking alcohol, milk, smoking, eating meat and all kinds of processed and GMO foods, the body and immune system of a modern husband will eventually disintegrate. There will be signs followed by a diagnosis.

Queen Hecuba

From Ancient Greece we get the story of Queen Hecuba. She paid a heavy price for the folly of her son called Paris. Queen Hecuba was the Queen of Troy and wife of King Priam. She was also the mother of Paris, the young man who seduced Helen the wife of Menelaus. Menelaus was the younger brother of Agamemnon. Agamemnon was the King of Argos. The love affair between Paris and Helen was a herald of war. Although Queen Hecuba was aware of the deadly conflict that would follow the arrival of Helen, she did not impose herself. She did not use her influence and try to persuade Paris not to surrender to lust. She paid a heavy price. Her entire family was slaughtered by the Greeks. Hecuba lost everything she had. She became a slave after rejecting the call to adventure. The call to learn and transform the consciousness of her family. She was asked to step in and become a leader. She didn't step in and her family was destroyed. Queen Hecuba was a fine example of a wife who failed to save her family from complete disintegration. She was a tragic hero.

21st century women and wives face a similar risk. The monster might be different. The Greek Queen's main enemy was war. One of the main enemies of the modern wife is cancer. Both cancer and war cause separation, destruction and death. A 21st century wife faces a different type of war. A silent and deadly war that requires planning and study.

The importance of learning

Learning creates the space for a refined experience and existence. A 21st century wife does not have to suffer the destiny of Hecuba. She can learn how to protect herself and her family.

Months before writing this book we interviewed several ladies and asked them to share their wisdom about mythology, cancer and longevity. One of them told us that, "My husband has blood cancer." When we asked the lady what books do you read? She told us that "I don't read very often".

We told her that the monster that she is fighting requires a lot of research and dedication. We also told the lady that vitamin C, Curcumin, Lysine, Cruciferous extracts, Selenium were essential terms that she should master.

Unknown to her the lady was on the first stage of the Hero's Journey. Ignorance is the greatest enemy of any living being. If the patient and the nurse are ignorant, the monster called cancer has the advantage. Ignorance limits a person's choices. The hero who embarks on a journey with the goal of defeating cancer should read as much as he or she can about the subject.

The philosopher should ask key questions such as;

- What makes cancer prosper?
- What foods are the best foods to fight and prevent cancer?
- What types of foods should be avoided by a person affected by cancer?
- What kind of music should a person affected by cancer listen to?
- What kind of places should a person affected by cancer visit?
- What are essential minerals?
- How do you prevent cancer?
- What steps should I take after being diagnosed with cancer?
- What books should I read about the subject?
- What are micronutrients?

A powerful wife

Cancer Survivor Story - Tom & Peggy - Stage 4 Squamous Cell Carcinomas - The Truth About Cancer YouTube channel:

Tom - "My personal journey began in 2013. I've always been a gym rat, I ran marathons. I was a go-getter I'm an army vet. I was a police officer. Stressful jobs and then I got into litigation and again stressful jobs. I ate pretty healthy but that all came to a screeching halt in December of 2013, where I had a lump on one side of my throat. Ultimately it got needle biopsied and then surgically it was biopsied. And they told me I had stage 4 squamous cell, I had a neck cancer. Which had metastasized. Actually the primary was in the middle of my neck. The lump over here (points to left right side of his neck) was part of the metastasis and I had it on my left side as well."

Peggy - "Seven days prior to Tom's diagnosis of stage 4 squamous cell cancer, I was given a diagnosis of stage 1 non-metastatic breast cancer. So December 10th 2013, was the day that had all really hit home because as Tom said his foster mom died of multiple myeloma, his birth mother died of pancreatic cancer, his dad died of lung cancer, uncles, grandparents, and so forth and my mother had four primaries. But there's no comparison between taking care of people you love with cancer and having a doctor point their finger at you and saying you have cancer. To say it felt like the world stopped and there was no sound in the world, would be kind of the understatement of the century when the phone call came in and he told me he had stage 4 cancer. I just, I couldn't believe that it could even be possible, this was a steel Adonis. 6 foot 3, 225 pounds, marathoner, gym rat, I mean you should have seen the shoulders and the neck on him.

We thought we were eating well. We were thinking we were doing right by ourselves, we were never overweight. Whatever maladies we had we didn't think we're serious I had asthma and allergies, no big deal that's not gonna kill you right. One time he picked up a boat and he popped the vertebrate in his back and I couldn't get him to take an aspirin, you know. That's what a tough guy we're dealing with here. I thought I had seen the worst I could see with my mother, with what she went through. The last of hers was also squamous cell cancer also in her tongue, also HPV positive, so not from smoking and drinking. Not from living a bad life neither one of them. The one before that was, she had breast cancer, the one before that was non-Hodgkin lymphoma and the one before that was melanoma. I thought I had seen it all. I had slept on hospital floors. I had been through so much with her, but there was just no comparison to what it was like with him.

We decided against full protocol because it would have involved him taking cisplatin which would have left him profoundly deaf, which would have meant that his work as a litigation manager would have been over. The alternative drug that we selected was a biologic class drug called Erbitux. I read the drug monograph because for 12 years my primary clients were the drug companies. That's the kind of marketing research I did and I worked on vaccines and I worked on every class of drugs except for oncology. I did only one study in 12 years on oncology but I interviewed literally thousands of doctors and patients, nurses, hospital administrators, insurance company executives, anybody who could have anything to do with marketing a drug I interviewed them. And I really thought I had seen it all and I read the drug monograph on the Erbitux and it said that it would cause a skin reaction that would look like acne, right? And the oncologist, the medical oncologist who was formerly a researcher at Mayo Clinic and at Scripps said yeah you'll be teasing him about looking like a teenager.

Well, it started out that way and inside of two weeks it had burnt every bit of skin off of him from here (points to chest) up over the top of his head all of his hair, down inside of his elbows in the back of his knees. You looked liked you've been dipped in sulphuric acid and I had to bring him to the emergency room because the drug has a black box warning for anaphylactic shock and he wasn't breathing. And he was so swollen he couldn't see his nose from here to here (points at left side of nose to the right side), or his chin from here to here (points at her chin and collar bone). That's how swollen he was. Took him to the emergency room in Virginia Beach, ER doctor was pushing 50 years old, looked at him and said: Oh my god what is this, I've never seen anything like this in all my life. And he wanted me to tell him what had happened. He had never heard of the drug, we made the phone call to the medical oncologist. Who didn't answer and the best they could do was shoot him full of Benadryl and put the paddles on him....

We learned about it from Truth About Cancer because, when we first got diagnosed friends who were into holistic living said you need to get on a raw vegan diet Non-GMO immediately which we did. For as long as he could do, but once the radiation began he wasn't able to chew because so much tissue was destroyed. So I was blending everything and throwing it in a blender and we got hooked up with the Life Extension Foundation and we did their pre-cancer protocol of vitamins and minerals and supplements. We at some point in time, and I wish to God I could remember how, actually I think God just tapped me on the shoulder and here this is The Truth About Cancer, get on this website. And started looking at what was on the website and you know so that's pushing four years ago now..."

This is a testimonial of a couple that worked together to defeat the big monster. Their journey is crucial because it shows us that we cannot do it alone. Without his wife the man would have not survived. She refused to be defeated. She urged doctors to take him to the emergency room. She read the labels in order to learn about the potential side effects of the toxins that were given to her husband. After being given powerful and toxic drugs, Tom lost consciousness. When he woke up he didn't know what had happened to him. There was only one person who could tell him the truth. That person was his wife Peggy.

She was the also the person who prepared the juices for him. She was the hero who saved him from a premature death. Peggy is an essential asset. A wife that saved her husband from premature death.

In mythology the wife of the hero, the wife of the patient, the sufferer, is usually very powerful and wise. Aset was both psychologically and intellectually stronger than a modern wife. Ishtar was also psychologically very strong. She descended to the world of "No return" and rescued her husband.

The challenges faced by a wife living in the 21st century cannot be ignored. In the ancient world a husband went to war. He could die, survive or get injured. In the 21st century the husband is at risk of dying from many diseases such as cancer, diabetes, cardiovascular disease, stroke etc. A modern wife is at risk of seeing her husband's body and life, present and future disintegrate, therefore she should do all she can to learn about the "Truth About Cancer". The modern wife could find and adopt a philosophy dedicated to longevity. To succeed an ambitious wife has to complete a learning program. Learning about health is more important than fighting for a career.

Aset was called the mother of libraries, she was very wise. She was also called the high priestess. She was a psychologist, an activist as well as an active optimist. She was mentally strong therefore well prepared to deal with the challenges that every human being is destined to experience. Initiation is one of the best strategies that can be used by ambitious modern wives. After the 13 missing pieces of her husband's body were collected Aset spent 70 days healing him. She spent 2 months and 10 days initiating her husband into a new culture. This is a very important detail. The mighty king was saved, initiated by his wife.

Where can a modern wife go in order to learn how to become a healer?

The website www.theherosjourneyhealth.com is a library that contains essential lessons and ideas. A great place to start.

Departure - Initiation - Return

“The famous Belgian anthropologist Arnold Van Gennep studied various rites of passage and he found that they typically involve 3 stages.

1. First there is a separation from the old way

2. Gennep's second stage has since been called “the liminal stage. From the Latin word ‘liman’, meaning threshold.

3. The third stage is reaggregation. Said in another way. A person is first separated from the community to be interwoven with deeper meanings connected to the spirits and the creation of the world. The person then re-enters the community and reconnects with the way the world ought to be. The first initiation occurs after birth...”

- The religions of small societies by Professor Ninian Smart, narrated by Ben Kingsley.

In African and Sumerian mythology wives play the roles of successful heroes. Ishtar and Aset succeeded in saving their husbands. They rescued their husbands from the tormenting world of the dead. To achieve their goals they descended to the nether world. Please pay attention to the word descend. A passenger that's travelling in London and is keen to get from Baker Street to Aldgate will have to descend into the underground. The treasure which the sincere seeker needs is inside the invisible Nether World.

After being humiliated and forced to get naked, Ishtar saved her husband and brought him back to the world of the living. Her journey was not easy. She had to make many sacrifices. The same strategy could and should be used by modern wives. The endless hours of television, cheap foods and worship of materialism will turn an intelligent individual who has the potential to become a hero into a liability. Time should be invested in studying the weaknesses and strengths of the modern Minotaur. The more prepared you are, the better for yourself and your family, community, generation, spouse and future.

Initiation is crucial, because when a person is told "you have cancer", a race against time begins. There is stress, fear, anxiety. There is not much time for contemplation, reading or thinking. Cancer is not a monster that should be ignored. The monster must be stopped, the sooner the better. In the story of Aset, Danae the mother of Perseus, Aethra the mother of Theseus, Ishtar the wife of Tammuz, we are told that the mother and wife had the wisdom and power to save her husband, the patient. The mother is the first hero. She gives birth to the child, helps the husband to attain maturity and longevity. She is the priestess who initiates the hero.

The modern wife can experience initiation through reading, research and application. Coffee enemas are an initiation into an ancient ritual dedicated to cleansing the body of harmful toxins. The initiated man and woman will develop personal healing rituals. In India, priests, priestesses and ordinary beings, use daily Mantras and affirmations to attract positive energies and feelings. Mantras are ancient rituals, fragments of a universal mythology that continues to transform people's lives today.

An ambitious wife could learn and create healing mantras and rituals for the entire family. The essential stage which we call initiation lasts between 12 to 24 months. It is a wonderful and life changing experience.

The Wise Lady

"The spirit of the seasons was only one of the aspects of the pervasive feminine principle in myth. So universal was the cult that some scholars have postulated the existence of a single Great Goddess, worshipped under different forms and different names around the world."

- The Great Themes - Myth and Mankind p62.

"The mother of our songs, the mother of all our seed, bore us in the beginning of things, and so she is the mother of all types of men, the mother of all nations, she is the mother of the thunder, the mother of the streams, the mother of trees and all things, she is the mother of the world and of the older brothers, the stone people, she is the mother of the fruits of the earth and of all things, she is the mother of your younger brothers, the friends and the strangers, she is the mother of our dance paraphernalia, of all our temples and she is the only mother we possess, she alone is the mother of the fire and of the Sun."

The Kagaba people - Colombia
- The Religion of Small Societies, Professor Ninian Smart, Audible

Paintings of women from ancient civilisations have something very rich, a mysterious and ancient beauty, a silent music, an irresistible song hidden in them. It is a wonderful melody that pays tribute to the smile of a muse, a goddess, a wise teacher, a female, a saviour, a healer of souls. She is an ancient archetype called the old wise woman. She was the medicine woman of the entire world, the nurse of generations and populations. Wherever we go, we find cults, temples and wonderful monuments dedicated to her.

Many years ago American filmmakers produced a documentary about a remarkable man called Harry Hoxsey. They said;

> *"Medical authorities claim Hoxsey is a hoax. They outlawed the therapy in the United States without a scientific investigation... Mildred Nelson founder of the Hoxsey Clinic in Mexico. The Hoxsey nurse Mildred Nelson took the treatment from Texas to Tijuana in 1963. Her Biomedical Centre was the first alternative clinic to go from the US to Mexico. She has been treating cancer with Hoxsey for 40 years. She claims impressive results."*
>
> \- Hoxsey: The Quack Who Cured Cancer - How The AMA & FDA Shut Down 17 Cancer Clinics YouTube

One of the main characters of the documentary "The Quack Who Cured Cancer" is an old lady called Mildred Nelson. She appears several times on the film to talk about her journey and the journeys of her patients. She was an expert on the subject of cancer and whenever she talked she exhibited confidence, authority, elegance and magnanimity. In the film we see her walking. There was an elegant music and pace in her steps. We also see her smiling and inspiring, healing and transforming souls. Her pace is majestic. She has the pace of someone who knows exactly what they are doing and where they are going. She was not an ordinary person.

Mildred Nelson was the personification of an ancient guardian and keeper of a wisdom that has been passed from one generation to another. She was a prominent citizen of the invisible but very special world.

Without realizing, Mildred Nelson played the role of the ancient mother, the ancient Ntrt, the ancient "Goddess" who knew how to heal her children. The archetype of the old lady appears in many mythologies. In some stories she doesn't play a prominent role. She is in the background. While living in the ordinary world, Mildred Nelson rejected her role. She saw herself as a powerless nurse who could not help her own mother. For many years she played the role of an obedient and ignorant victim who believed in the "official scientific versions". Her journey changed when she met her mentor, an old man called Harry Hoxsey. She didn't know how powerful she was until she met her mentor. That's what happens to many potential heroes. They fail to fulfil their potential because they are too busy enjoying the deceptions and distractions thrown at them. The pleasures of the ordinary world.

The life of a human being changes when a nasty reminder called the big monster shows up. In mythology and theatre, incidents are called heralds. They appear on the scene to make an announcement. In the ordinary and ignorant world they are simply called "the big C".

Heralds

Heralds are essential allies. They give us clues about transformations, changes which are about to take place. Like the town crier, the newsreader of ancient societies, the herald stands up and shouts "it's time to change". A herald appeared in the life of Mildred Nelson in the form of cancer that attacked her mother.

Mildred Nelson's mother became very ill. She had what doctors called terminal cancer. Mildred Nelson was against natural therapies. Her mother's cancer journey changed everything. Her mother's sickness lead the nurse to Harry Hoxsey's Clinic. It also led her to her mentor and the opener of the ways. He initiated her, and showed her how to heal a body attacked by disease. His influence on her thinking was profound.

It gave her a new vision, a new energy, life purpose and mission. It inspired her to change her profession and personality. When her mentor died, she grieved then took decisive steps to perpetuate his vision of healing people. She opened a clinic outside the U.S. To this day, the clinic remains active in Tijuana.

Her decision to continue the work of her mentor was a reflection of a principle called the Mother Goddess. Her mentor helped her to find the ancestral self, the hidden hero that exists inside every human being. The life purpose of every female is deeply connected to the soil in which they walk every day, Mother Earth. Mildred Nelson became a healer, a hero, a savior who had no time to engage in intellectual confrontations. She realised that she would be forced to spend years fighting people who are stuck in the ordinary world. She did not want to fight. She wanted to heal people, therefore, she went to Mexico and opened a clinic. The clinic continues to heal people to this day.

Every single person who spoke to her saw and experienced the ancestral energy of an old wise lady who knew how to heal. Without realising, Mildred Nelson's patients spoke to a sister, Ariadne, Aset, Sedna, Aethra, Danae, Queen Tye, Spider woman... She was the living archetype of the old wise lady.

The important detail in her journey is the fact that she did not want conflicts. Most females don't want conflicts. They want to realise their potential. They are driven into conflict through violent ideologies, social engineering, entertainment and powerful cultural tools such as Hollywood and crime dramas.

The quest to find the light of the soul

In the famous book called "*Coming Forth by Day to Light*" incorrectly called "*The Book of the Dead*" we see the husband of Aset, the ruler of eternity seated. Behind him, there are two ladies, two sisters, two nurses, two healers. They are called Aset and Nbt Het. Nbt Het means "the lady of the house".

The name Aset means throne. She was the bridge to coronation and kingship. The king was impotent until his sisters rescued him from perpetual obscurity. Untrained eyes will give all the power to the king. The king seems powerful. We assume he is the ruler until we learn that the two ladies standing behind him, were the nurse and healer who saved him from permanent death. They are archetypes, the "old wise women". The wise nurse, sister and saviour.

Mildred Nelson worked as a nurse for many years. She moved from conventional medicine to natural medicine. She was more successful in the natural world. She evolved from a powerless nurse to a powerful healer, a hero who dedicated her life to the task of curing cancer. "Something bigger than herself".

Kronos and chronic

Skeptics will argue that cancer is a chronic disease. The word chronic is of Greek origin. Kronos was the husband of Rhea and the leader of a generation of titans. Kronos had a terrible personality and very bad habits. He was obsessed with power. In order to prevent his children from being more powerful than him, he ate them alive. He swallowed them. He was a tyrant who castrated and deposed his own father. Kronos had a terrible habit which eventually contributed to his downfall. He died because he could not control his appetite.

There are many Kronos living in today's world. They have very bad habits such as smoking and eating junk food. Like the father of the Titans, they are architects of their own downfall. They spend years swallowing the wrong things, foods, drinks and substances which will eventually cause the disintegration of their immune system.

It is a matter of time until their immune system gives up. Kronos is the root word for 'chronology', 'chronic', 'chromium'. Kronos means time. It doesn't mean incurable. It takes time for a disease to be eradicated. Many patients are told that "cancer is a chronic disease";

Mildred Nelson disagreed and rejected the labels incurable and chronic. She spent more than 40 years helping people to defeat the monster. She was a hero, a ferrywoman, a rescuer of souls, an opener of ways to prosperity and longevity. She was a Mother Goddess, an Aset, a modern day Artemis. Her name is a wonderful song, a delicious memory that belongs to eternity. Be bold, follow her thread and strive to become an asset to your family, generation and community.

Queen Afua the wise lady, an Aset

"It took me two 21 day cycles to detox myself of all the diseases. It was like a revelation. I woke up and I said I don't have to be sick anymore..."

"Greetings and warm welcome. I am Queen Afua and I have been working as a holistic health practitioner for four decades. And in those decades I have written 6 books on holistic health. It was 1969 when I started on my journey and I was 16 years of age. I was a dancer. I was a singer. My life was to be an artist but I was also sick. I had chronic asthma, eczema, hay fever, arthritis, headaches, monthly PMS. I didn't know when or how I was going to get better. My medication was increasing, my injections for my asthma were weekly. I was progressively getting worse. I was invited to go on a healing retreat, and it changed my entire life."

- My Story: Queen Afua - Queen Afua YouTube Channel

Queen Afua is one of the leading healers of her generation. She is in her mid-60s. She is very well known in New York. Queen Afua is a living archetype. She has the image of an ancient mother. She is also the image of wisdom, health, and commitment. She is also a wonderful model of the wise wife who knows how to heal her husband and her family. She started her journey as a victim then evolved and became a hero. Her journey is similar to the journeys of many heroes who cured themselves from "chronic diseases". Every one of us starts as victim of an injustice, a disease, a crime, a misunderstanding, a cabal, a conspiracy, a conventional conclusion etc.

Queen Afua completed the Hero's Journey. She was ignorant until she was 16 years old. She was tricked to believe that she was destined to be an entertainer, a famous person. She had the signals and diagnosis that emerge on step 2 of the diagram, the circle of eternity. She paid attention to the signals, the suffering voices of her body. She confronted the monster rather than pretending that everything was ok. That's the cardinal sin of the modern diva who is too busy to be initiated into the natural ways of the ancestors.

Queen Afua's initiation started when she was invited to go on a healing retreat. In mythology that's the departure, separation. Departure is followed by initiation. She was initiated into an ancient culture. Upon her return, she became an asset to her community and family. The return is an essential element of the sacred sequence. It gives the hero the opportunity to make a living healing broken hearts, bodies, souls and families. The hero becomes the Tree of Life. Whatever he or she says, is valuable and has the potential to save the life of a person.

The experience and wisdom that she gained at the retreat was life changing. She accepted the call to adventure and was taken to an ocean called holistic health. She was cured and decided to become a healer. Young people who interact with her today see an aged lady who knows how to heal the body. They have in her an excellent role model who completed the Hero's Journey. She is the personification of an ancient mother. The wise old lady and wife. One of the heroes with a 1000 faces.

Queen Afua is a prolific author. The titles of her books give us clues about her philosophy. The titles are:

"Sacred Woman, Heal Thyself and Circles of Wellness"

She is a Hero who learned the ancient art of healing and makes a living sharing the wisdom. She is an Aset.

Charlotte Gerson - An authority

"In other words, the body is normally organised in order to heal, yes, the body has a built-in natural defence healing mechanism, and Dr. Gerson was definitely of the opinion that the only thing you have to do is restore and rebuild the body's healing mechanism. Which is being suppressed and damaged by the chemicals and the pesticides and the fungicides and the poison in the water. The fluoride that they put in the water and things like that. These things poison and damage the body's defenses. Actually, when the defenses are in order, your immune system, your enzyme system, your hormone system, your essential organs like the liver and the lungs and the brain and the heart. If those organs are in order cancer is impossible, you cannot have cancer. The body has too many powerful defenses so that cancer is first of all completely avoidable and secondly, even in advanced situations totally curable."

- Charlotte Gerson on Cancer and Disease - YouTube Jay Kordich

In 1977 a young man called Steve Jobs and his friend Steve Wozniak agreed to create a small business which they called Apple. In the same year, another young man called Muhammad Ali was at the peak of his boxing career. In 1977 a 55 years old lady created a company which she called The Gerson Institute. The lady's name is Charlotte Gerson. Charlotte Gerson was born on the 27th of March 1922 in Germany. Her father was the famous medicine man Dr. Max Gerson. The main mission of the company that she created was to help people to fight and defeat a monster called cancer and many diseases considered chronic, incurable or terminal. The main product of the company was a method, a refined philosophy developed by her father. Her father was persecuted and poisoned for striving to heal people. She was perfectly aware of the trials and obstacles that would certainly follow her. The skeptics, the implacable competitors, the pessimists, the tricksters, the money makers, sales people…

Charlotte Gerson is one of the many heroes who defeated a monster called cancer. "She dedicated her life to something bigger than herself". She became the wise old lady. As of the writing of this book Charlotte Gerson is 96 years old. She is an old lady who travels around the world to teach and share wisdom about the secrets of longevity. Many skeptics have a lot to say about scientific proofs.

You can get busy discussing scientific proofs or you could look at philosophers who have mastered the art of living well. All you need to do is to observe the journey of Charlotte Gerson. Many skeptics and experienced doubters will reject the idea that nature has the power to defeat the big monster. It's all about chemicals and the big 3, "Cut, radiate and burn, then wait and see what happens."

Although she gave up medical insurance and stopped seeing a doctor many years ago, Charlotte Gerson is 96 years old. She is a highly experienced and dedicated healer. She is the old wise lady, the old wise woman who knows how to restore Maat, balance. She is an expert in helping people to cure cancer.

> *"It is a scientifically verifiable fact that the Gerson Therapy cures cancer as well as almost any other chronic degenerative disease."*
>
> - Charlotte Gerson - Dying to Have Known YouTube documentary
>
> - Gerson Media

Meeting the mentor - the healer

One of the most important levels of our circle and philosophy is stage 5. It is called meeting the mentor. Stage 5 is when the patient, the student meets his or her teacher. The wise healer who will initiate him or her into natural ways to heal disease.

We pay attention to the training that the mentor gives to the student or patient. If the mentor is a female she gives the training, wisdom because she's wise. The old wise lady is a fragment of Mother Earth and an ancient culture that remains vital for the existence and prosperity of human beings. Her knowledge comes from the natural world rather than the academic or scientific world.

In Canada we find a nurse called Rene Caisse. Like many heroes Rene Caisse's life changed when she met her mentor. The female healer plays the following roles;

- Healer
- Herbalist
- Leader
- Mother
- Nurse
- Rescuer
- Saviour
- Teacher
- Wife

We cannot afford to ignore this archetypal image of the old wise lady.

The urgent question confronting us is the following;

Who is initiating females in the 21st century?

"We have a wonderful story of a little boy 8 years old who was of a group of 7 other kids. All of them had sarcoma. He came to Mexico to the Gerson Clinic, pale, very thin, no hair, bald and quite sick with pain. He was put on the Gerson therapy, sent home. The mother reported that within 3 months the tumor was gone. Not only that, two years later he was a strapping young fellow with lots of hair. He was growing, he was happy at school. More important yet. He recovered while the other 6 children in the group who had received chemotherapy and only chemotherapy were all dead."

If we look at the story of the boy from the Hero's Philosophy perspective, we see the difference and benefits of living in the special world. The boy and his family lived in the ordinary world. The world of ignorance. He got the signals and diagnosis. He was given chemo and in spite of the extreme pain that he experienced, the monster called cancer did not go away. After realising that the methods of the ordinary world were causing more pain and damage than healing, the parents of the boy decided to take their son to the special world. There he met an old wise lady who initiated him into ancient mysteries.

The wise lady introduced him to a therapy called "The Gerson therapy". A philosophy given to her by her father. She healed him. She fulfilled her role of "the wise old lady" who knows how to restore vitality and health.

Charlotte Gerson was initiated at a very early age. During her teens, Charlotte was diagnosed with tuberculosis. She was expected to die because tuberculosis was considered a "chronic incurable disease". Charlotte's father was a medicine man. He did not buy into the conventional view about health and disease. He used the same method which cured his migraines to heal his daughter. Using the method prescribed by her father Charlotte confronted the big monster. She won. Mrs. Gerson spent many years working as a secretary for her father. He mentored her. When Charlotte Gerson's father died she spent a few years raising her children. She completed the hero's journey related to motherhood then she opened a clinic dedicated to healing cancer patients. She helped many people to defeat the big monster.

"Back in 1978, I thought I was in good health living a very normal life. My husband discovered a lump in my breast. So we went to a gynecologist and we went to a surgeon. The surgeon did a biopsy. He said you have cancer and you will have surgery in two days. I got a pamphlet in the mail. I still think it's a miracle. The pamphlet said that Charlotte Gerson was going to give this lecture for the national health federation on cancer. So I said; I might as well go and listen because that's another way. I listened to her and everything she said made sense."

- "Dying To Have Known" documentary - Gerson Media

The above testimony is of a lady who was cured of breast cancer after completing the Gerson therapy. The therapy was introduced to her by Harward Strass, the son of Charlotte Gerson and the grandson of Max Gerson. We have 3 heroes who defeated the big monster using the wisdom provided by Mother Nature.

Max Gerson = Severe migraines

Charlotte Gerson = Tuberculosis

A lady = Breast cancer

The mythical role

"Yet the need for a female goddess of healing and compassion was far from limited to the Levant. The Chinese had an equivalent figure in Guan Yin, goddess of mercy and still one of the most popular figures in the Daoist pantheon. Like Mary, she is often shown bearing a child in her arms..."

- The Great Themes - Myth and Mankind

Charlotte Gerson, Rene Caisse, Veronique Desaulniers, Ariadne, Queen Afua, Aset, Spider woman, Sedna, Guan Yin, are a personification of the mythological and ancient "mother of all things, fruits and trees", worshiped by the Kagaba people. In the ordinary world, Charlotte Gerson is the mother of two children, a boy, and a girl. In the special world, she is the mother of many healthy children and leader of healthy souls. She has spent more than 40 years teaching, inspiring, healing and saving people from all over the world. She travels the world to lecture and make people aware of the powerful and natural methods discovered by her father. She is one of the many heroes who defeated the monster called cancer. In 2008 she was invited to share her wisdom about health. She said the following:

"I don't have a doctor, I don't go to the doctors. I avoid doctors. That's the reason for staying healthy. Chemotherapy has never healed anything. Chemotherapy does not restore the body's ability to heal, it poisons it further. It weakens the immune system. They make huge money on it. The pharmaceutical companies pay doctors to prescribe chemotherapy."

- Charlotte Gerson On Cancer And Disease - YouTube channel
- Jay Kordich

Rene Caisse the old wise nurse

"Tremendous sums have been raised and appropriated for official cancer research during the past 50 years, with almost nothing new or productive discovered. It would make these foundations look pretty silly, if an obscure Canadian nurse discovered an effective treatment for cancer."

Rene Caisse - Tomorrow's Cancer Cures today

p123 - Allan Spreen, M.D.

During the first decade of the 1920s a Canadian nurse called Rene Caisse made a remarkable discovery. She was taking care of an 80 year old woman who had migrated from England to Ontario. The nurse and patient were chatting when Rene noticed a scarring on the lady's breast. How did you get that scar on your breast?

The patient smiled and told Rene that the scar was caused by breast cancer, a disease that she had contracted "30 years ago". Rene was shocked because in her experience "people with breast cancer don't live long. How did you manage to live 30 more years after the diagnosis?"

The patient told Rene that a medicine man, a Native Indian who lived in Ontario gave her a remedy, a tonic that cured and saved her from premature death. She patiently told Rene Caisse that doctors diagnosed her with advanced breast cancer. They told her the only option she had was to remove the breast. The English lady and her husband were poor. They did not have the funds to pay for conventional treatments. The English migrant decided to trust the Native Indian man who knew ancient ways of curing diseases. She gladly accepted the remedy given by the healer. She drank the tea daily and within a short period of time the tumor started to gradually disappear. The English lady was cured of what conventional doctors called "deadly and incurable disease." With the help of the medicine man, the English lady succeeded in defeating the big monster.

Mrs. Caisse asked the patient if she was happy to share the recipe and details of the remedy that saved her life. The patient gladly shared the wisdom. Rene Caisse wrote down the names of the herbs.

The experienced Canadian nurse was given the opportunity to put her knowledge into practice when her mother was diagnosed with stomach and liver cancer. The prognosis was bleak. Rene's mother was not expected to live long. Doctors told Rene Caisse's mother that they had no means to save her. Upon hearing the doctor's words, Rene Caisse asked the doctors that were treating her mother if she could use the "remedy from the Native Indian man". The doctors agreed.

Rene Caisse used the herbal tea to cure her mother who lived another 18 years after being attacked by the big monster. Doctors who heard the story of Rene Caisse asked the nurse if she could use the same remedy to help their patients. Rene Caisse agreed to help. She travelled to many places and helped doctors to save their patients. 8 doctors whose patients were cured through Essiac tea, wrote a letter to the governing body asking the "big boys" to allow "Essiac tea" to be approved as one of the standard treatments for cancer in Canada. Their request was denied. Although the request was rejected the popularity of the Essiac tea grew. Many people contacted Rene Caisse and asked for help. She helped them and did not charge a single dollar for her services. Her charity did not please the competition. Big business lobbied for Caisse to be prosecuted. This strategy forced her to go underground. She spent 50 years healing people for free.

Rene Caisse's mother and her aunt were the first but not the last patients who enjoyed the benefits of Essiac tea. Thousands of people from all over the world started to use Essiac tea as a weapon to fight the big monster. Rene Caisse became a global healer.

What is Essiac?

Essiac is a play on words. It is the name Caisse spelt backwards. The tea can be easily found on the internet and in natural health shops such as www.essiacproducts.com

Rene Caisse was persecuted by the government and big businesses who did not prescribe to her natural cancer cure. In order to escape prison, she went underground and continued to help cancer patients. She experienced the ordeal, stage 8 of the hero's journey. Rene Caisse refused to charge for her services. Her goal was spiritual rather than financial. The formula for the healing Essiac tea includes:

- Burdock root
- Indian rhubarb
- Sheep sorrel
- Slippery elm bark

Heroes like Rene Caisse are essential references for ambitious men and women who wish to prevent cancer or repair a damaged immune system. She is the mythical mother who gives inspiration and confidence to a patient. She was a female who cured breast cancer, liver cancer, diabetes, and other diseases labelled incurable. Like Mildred Nelson, Rene Caisse was a nurse, therefore, she was seen as a reliable source. Her main priority was not money.

Her actions were in Maat, harmony with her job, her profession, vision and life purpose. Anybody who is affected by cancer would get a boost of confidence and optimism by knowing that there are females who cured cancer using natural therapies. Rene Caisse could also be seen as a mentor to females who wish to protect their families. She personify Aset, Artemis, Ariadne, Sedna and many other female principles.

A modern shaman or shama woman

Rene Caisse and many healers play the role of the medicine man or medicine woman. The ingredients used in Essiac tea, were given by a shaman. In ancient culture, the role of a healer was played by a shaman or a shama woman. The Portuguese word for flame is 'chama'. Chama is also the verb to call. A shaman used to go to a village and perform a ritual that had profound psychological and social implications. It was a method, a ritual used to initiate the community. The ritual was also designed to heal the collective by sharing ancient wisdom. It also prepared children for the challenges of life. In order to enter the special world, a shaman drank a liquid, an elixir that enabled him or her to transcend. A shaman was the medicine man or medicine woman who knew the secrets of herbs.

Origins of the word Shaman

"In many small societies the Shaman is an elite figure, drawn to his profession either because of heredity or because he has had a vision, or an especially significant dream."

The Religions of Small Societies - Professor Ninian Smart, narrated by Ben Kingsley

Llama is the Spanish verb to call. A shaman or shama woman's main role was to call "the spirits of the ancestors" to come and heal the family, the community, the inner circle.

We find fragments of shamanism carefully hidden in modern languages such as, Italian, Spanish, English. To ask what's your name in Italian? You would say, "Lei come si Chiama." Shama, flame, is also the root word for 'showman', 'showoman'. To ask what's your name in Portuguese you would say "Como te chamas?" The principle of Shama is carefully hidden in the question.

Where does the whole idea of shama come from?

Can we trace this word to antiquity?

Yes we can. Ancient Babylon is an ideal place to go.

After becoming victims of their king, a rapist called Gilgamesh, the people of Uruk prayed to the Gods, and asked for help. Their pantheon had a powerful creative and solar principle. His name was Shamash.

The book "*The Ultimate Encyclopedia*" written by Arthur Cotterell and Rachael Storm says the following:

"Shamash was the Babylonian God of the Sun, who saw all things and thus also came to be regarded as a god of justice and divination. Known to the Sumerians as Utu, his light uncovered every misdeed and enabled him to see into the future."

A shaman or woman shaman is a reflection of a universal mystery known and practiced by people from different cultures. A shaman or shama woman goes into an initiation ritual where he or she first gets sick, and experiences a temporary death. After his or her death, the healer learns how to heal the sick, the brother, the sister, the father, the husband, the family, the community.

When they fall sick, modern citizens go to the pharmacy rather than to the medicine man or woman. The goals and priorities have been changed by events such as the industrial revolution, invention of TV and advertising. There are more toxins and less natural solutions. The shama, flame, fire, sunlight, has been replaced by pharma. We also find fragments of Shamash carefully hidden in modern words such as 'charming', 'Schumer', 'summer', 'Sherman', 'chairman', 'Simon'. One of the most prolific modern Jewish Historians is a man called Simon Schama. A shaman or shama woman is a light bringer. A weak immune system will gradually lose its light. It will need a shaman or shama woman. Someone who knows how to restore the flame. The light of the sun. (IV Vitamin C and Vitamin D)

Pharmakeia and Al-Kemet

Whenever something is wrong with our body we go to the pharmacy. When we look at the origins of the word pharmacy we discover that it comes from Greek, Pharmakeia. Pharmakeia means to poison.

What about the chemist? Where does the word chemist come from?

Chemist came from an incorrect pronunciation of the word Kmt. When Arabs invaded Kmt in 7AD, they could not pronounce Kmt therefore they said Al-Kemet. Al-Kemet became Alchemy. That's where we got the idea of a chemist. The chemist of antiquity used organic means to fertilize the land. The modern chemist uses chemical methods to "fertilize the land." Methods such as chemotherapy are meant to fertilize the land. The result is brutal to the land, the body, the mind, the immune system and the future of the individual involved.

Heroes such as Rene Caisse are a source of inspiration for women who wish to either learn how to defeat a monster or how to protect their "lands" through natural means.

The English lady who migrated to Canada initiated a nurse who later became one of the greatest healers of her generation. The patient played the role of a mentor, an Aset, Aethra, Ariadne and many other mythical healers and mentors.

Rene Caisse was trained by a lady who was in the last season of her life. The meeting between the nurse and patient can be seen as a meeting between mentor and teacher. That's the initiation which Joseph Campbell discusses in his books. There must be a form of initiation. It doesn't matter how old we are, we have the power to become heroes, we have the power to change our mindset, we have the potential to learn. It's never too late to learn new skills. It's never too late to be initiated into essential mysteries.

The healer and shama woman Rene Caisse, was an adult when she learnt about the healing tea. It's never too early or too late for a person to be initiated into the mysteries of a specific culture.

Leigh Erin Connealy, a muse, a healer from California

Beautiful lady, wonderful teacher, blessed be thy sacred soul.
I was truly delighted to explore your work.
It inspired me. It gave me the keys and clarity.
It showed me how to get out of the modern labyrinth.
We the sincere seekers, your students, are very grateful for your kindness and your dedication to the subject of restoration.
Grateful we are for your endless hours and many years dedicated to healing and purification.
Magnificent, marvellous, majestic are your intentions, your purified Imagination.
Crucial knowledge, and life saving initiation.
For the healing of the soul, the mind, the body, and the sacred family.
Dr Connealy, you are a prime bridge to longevity.
Thank you for your clarity and sincerity.
Yours is an ancient and essential role and protective principle.
You are a fragment of a universal mystery. Our ancestors call her Maat, Ariadne, and Sedna.
The mother of seasons, the healer, conductor of souls.

The source of sublime years and history.
The memorable light, saviour of lives and a source of liberty from a lethal Agony called disease.
Excellent is the music hidden in thy books.
Like the blue clouds in a tranquil summer sky,
It is a source of peace and emotional harmony.
Your words and your beautiful work are an essential melody.
They are educational and inspirational.
They are also the key. The life saving choice which the man,
The woman, and the wounded warrior living in our polluted and perplexed century can and should use to save his or her life, to save the lives of his or her children, sister, seducer, friends and sincere seekers.
Beautiful teacher, thank you for your time and kindness.
Thank you for your powerful books and your refined experience.
Your wisdom and voice are essential mirrors, powerful tools, and bridges for the ambitious father,
The ambitious mother, the romantic lady, the marvellous muse, the child, and the stranger who is keen to prolong his or her existence.

Leigh Erin Connealy is the author of the wonderful and essential book called "The Cancer Revolution, A groundbreaking program to reverse and prevent Cancer"

The remarkable journey of Maurizio Sarri & Zig Ziglar

Maurizio Sarri was born on the 10th January 1959, in Naples. He is one of the most admired football managers in the world. Mr. Sarri has a very interesting biography. He has coached some of the biggest and most successful clubs in the world. Mr. Sarri started his coaching career in 1999. He was 40 years old when became a professional manager and landed his first big job.

Zig Ziglar was considered one of the greatest personal development coaches in the world. Like Mr. Sarri, he also started coaching when he was 40. Their journeys teach us that it doesn't matter how old you are, or where you are, you can always be initiated into the Hero's Philosophy. The key is in the application, ambition and dedication to excellence.

THE MENTOR

"One formula 1 driver famous for his complete focus and meticulous attitude is Sir Jackie Stewart. As I mentioned earlier, aged just 17 I found myself racing in Formula 4 and it was during that period that I received an unexpected phone call from Jackie. The one I initially suspected it was a wind up from my mates. Fortunately, it was not a prank call and instead it lead to that incredible opportunity for me to drive at Paul Stewart racing. As I have explained there were good races and bad during my time with that team. But being around Sir Jackie was always the most remarkable experience. Clearly, being mentored by Sir Jackie in terms of racing was a massive experience and learning curve. However it was also absolutely fascinating watching and learning from him away from the track. Seeing how he handled himself in life and in business."

- David Coulthard - The Winning Formula.

David Coulthard is a very successful man. He is successful in motor racing, business and in life. In his book "T*he Winning Formula*" he wrote that he could not have achieved his goals without the guidance of his parents and many men, women and mentors that he met during his exciting personal and professional journey.

The word journey is a bridge to mythology. We must study mythology because mythology is the mirror of life. Every myth contains a student and a mentor. A mentor is someone who will help us to rewrite the stories of our lives. One of my mentors is a wonderful man who is based in the Cotswolds. I met him in the early stages of my journey. I was ignorant and trying to overcome an emotional storm caused by the death of my parents. I didn't see how valuable he was. I was very fortunate to meet him. The short period of time which I spent with him will positively influence me for the rest of my life. He is a refined man, intelligent and dedicated to his family. He gave me essential clues about how to enjoy a refined existence. Just by observing him I learned a lot.

The stories of our lives have been told and written many thousands of years ago. All we need to do is to follow the instructions. In both mythology and the ordinary world, the role of a mentor is vital.

The first goal of a person who is suffering from a disease could be meditation not medication. Meditation on key principles, such as causes, potential helpers and healers, guardians of ancient solutions. That's a Buddhist approach to self-healing. Every patient needs a prolonged re-education because the human organism requires time to return to its ideal state. The refined memory of a mentor will inspire us to meditate on effective solutions and natural medicines.

Mentors in mythology

In mythology as well as movies there is always a key character. A mentor, a guide, a ferryman and ferrywoman. In Karate Kid, Kazuki Miyagi is the mentor of a boy bullied by his schoolmates. Aset was the mentor of Hrw. Aethra and Ariadne were the mentors of Theseus. Utnapishtim and his wife were the "preservers of life" and mentors of Gilgamesh. Max Gerson was the mentor of his daughter. It doesn't matter what kind of challenge you are currently facing. You cannot solve it without the help of a mentor.

A simple task such as changing a tyre requires a mentor. The mentor is someone who wrote the instruction manual on behalf of the company that sells the seats. Some of the most watched videos on YouTube, show people how to complete important tasks, such as;

- How to change a car tyre?
- How to remove bacteria in your mouth
- How to cure herpes
- How to create a business

We need mentors because they help us to clarify the how, the what, the when, why and who. Who should we talk to about prevention? What's the best book on the subject?

The idea of having a mentor, a "preserver of life" is very ancient.

The word mentor came from Greek mythology. In the Odyssey, Telemachus, the son of Odysseus was visited by an old man. The old man introduced himself as Mentor. That's where the word mentor comes from. The old man gave Telemachus the call to adventure. He invited, instructed the young boy to "be brave, be bold". He also told the boy "Go and find your father". The old man who introduced himself as Mentor was in reality the Goddess Athena. The ancient mother goddess, the protector, the savior, who saves children from starvation by giving them breast milk. She also helps boys to become men.

Athena disguised herself as an old man in order to play the role of the old teacher. She loved Telemachus' father and was keen to help his son. The boy was depressed and anxious, he needed a mentor. She disguised herself as an old wise man called Mentor. She mentored the boy and helped him to overcome psychological and physical difficulties. She prepared a ship for him. She also helped him to create an experienced team.

A very ancient principle - MentuHotep

The word mentor can be traced back to Kmt. One of the main principles of Kmt was called Mentu. "Mentu" is the guiding principle, "Hotep" means satisfied. The goal of a student is to satisfy his or her mentor, by following instructions. There was a very successful Kmtic ruler, Nswt Bity (called Pharaoh by Greeks) called Mentuhotep. He adopted Mentu as one of his mentors. He succeeded by striving to satisfy his mentor. Success in life is usually associated with training, education, discipline and initiation. That's why we all need a mentor. We cannot do it by ourselves. We need wise people to mentor us. The same applies to health. Anybody who wishes to heal his or her body will need a mentor. The ideal mentor is someone who thinks outside the box.

If you read many books, watch many videos you will eventually get multiple mentors. The more mentors you have the better. The same thinking applies to the world of cancer. Mentors are sources of excellent choices.

Ty Bollinger

Ty Bollinger born 19th January, 1968, in the United States. Is a prolific author, teacher and speaker, researcher and seeker. He runs an educational project called "The Truth About Cancer". He is an expert on natural ways to heal cancer. Ty has many mentors who gladly share their wisdom with him. Every mentor that speaks to Ty, takes him into a very rich world, the special world. The dedicated student will one day become an excellent mentor. Mentors in mythology tend to be the old man or the old lady. They can also be a frog, a horse, an eagle, a tree, a prodigious child, a serpent etc. They come in many ways and many forms. They symbolise experience and wisdom. Ariadne for example, was a young mentor who got her training from an old man called Daedalus. A mentor does not have to be defined by age or gender. Rene Caisse had 3 mentors.

- An English lady - initiated by a medicine man/shaman
- A natural doctor - who showed her a healing herb
- A medicine man from the Ojibwe tribe - initiated by his ancestors

Rene Caisse was shown the plant that cures breast cancer and many other diseases by a male natural doctor. Rene had many mentors.

Mentors come in many shapes and forms. They might be younger or older than you. From a higher or lower social class. The key is the source of their wisdom and experience. Gender or origin doesn't matter. Alexander of Macedon's mentor was Aristotle. As soon as Alexander started to ignore the advice of his mentor his life and career suffered a decline. The tragic journey of Alexander of Macedon who died at the early age of 33, teaches that mentors are essential archetypes.

You will not win one of the greatest battles of your life without a mentor. It's not going to happen. Please remember that the word hero comes from Hrw. Hrw was the son of a lady called Aset. Aset was the main mentor of her son and sister. A mentor is an asset to his or her student. When attacked by cancer or any other disease a person has to become a student. The victim will fall into depression, decline and despair. The student will succeed after following specific instructions of his or her mentor, a teacher who knows how to inspire and repair.

How to get out of the intellectual and psychological Matrix?

When Theseus went to the labyrinth, he was also going to a very complex matrix. Ariadne was the mentor who gave him the keys and the thread that enabled him to get in and get out. A mentor knows how to get you out of the Matrix. That's what makes him or her an essential Aset. In the film the Matrix, Morpheus is the mentor of Neo. In life, movies and mythology the hero has a mentor or mentors.

The root word for Morpheus can be traced to Orpheus. A man who tried to be the mentor of souls. Both Orpheus and Morpheus are saviours of souls. The word Morpheus and morphine are related to death. The Latin word for death is Morte. Both Orpheus and Morpheus are conductor of souls. They risked their lives to save people. They played the roles of essential archetypes called mentors.

The central point of Neo's journey takes place inside the kitchen of a lady called "Oracle." Neo goes to the Oracle in order to know who he truly is. One of his mentors is a lady, the mother of essential mysteries.

She is the healer who helped him to find the truth about himself. The truth set him free.

In Ancient Greece powerful kings and queens used to go to the Oracle of Delphi in order to clarify essential questions about their future. Their journeys remind us that even members of Royal families need mentors. See yourself as a member of your own royal family. To either prevent or correct the damages caused by monsters such as a cancer you will need many mentors.

Key questions

- Who is your mentor?
- What's the culture of your mentor?
- How rich is the experience of your mentor?

The Daughter, the victim & the saviour

Rene Caisse's mother was 72 when she was diagnosed with liver cancer. She was given only days to live. She was saved by her own daughter who gave her a special tea.

There was a very ancient city called Troy. It was located in modern day Turkey. The Queen of Troy was a lady called Hecuba. Hecuba had many children. Before the arrival of the Greeks, Queen Hecuba was a very happy wife and mother. She was married to an aged and powerful King called Priam. Her life changed when her son called Paris returned home with a beautiful Greek lady called Helen. Both Paris and Helen were tricked by the Gods to get into a love affair that was doomed to end in tears. Helen was married to a man called Menelaus. Menelaus was the brother of a Greek King called Agamemnon. The Greeks waged war on Troy with the goal of rescuing Helen and destroying their main economic competitor. Troy was a very powerful and rich city. The two armies were led by experts in war therefore a stalemate ensued.

The war lasted 10 years. The Greeks realised that they could not defeat the strong and experienced Trojan army through conventional strategies therefore they tricked them. They created a large wooden horse and filled it with soldiers. They left the horse outside the gates of Troy as a parting gift. The Trojans fell for the trick. They brought the fake horse inside their walls then spent the evening partying. They got very drunk and slept. Their sleep was disturbed by piercing screams of men and women who were being slaughtered, stabbed and tortured by the cunning and cruel Greeks.

The Greeks attacked every single person they could find. Women, children, soldiers were all butchered. The event became the central myth of the Western world and consciousness. Homer the writer and narrator of the Epic became the mentor of prominent, professional, prolific poets and public speakers. When the war ended Queen Hecuba became a prisoner of war and a slave. Her male children were killed. Some of them fled and went to Italy.

One of Hecuba's daughters was called Polyxena. Polyxena was sacrificed. She was killed by the son of Achilles in order to serve as a slave to the ghost of Achilles. Polyxena became the victim of cruelty and violence. Euripides gave us the details of Polyxena mother's grief in his book "*The Trojan Women*" and "*Hecuba*". Polyxena was the unlucky daughter who lost her life after being consumed by a monster called war. In Greek mythology, disease is presented as war. There is a deadly conflict between a monster and a hero. The same happens in cancer and disease.

Many daughters living in the 21st century are at risk of losing their lives. The big monster doesn't care how old a person is. Cancer is ready to attack everybody. Especially people who don't take the necessary steps to ensure that the gates of their immune system are closed. A modern daughter does not have to be a victim of extreme cruelty, ignorance and disease.

A daughter living in the 21st century could and maybe should learn the essential skills that will help her to prevent or defeat the big monster. Many young women and daughters living in the 21st century are at risk of getting breast cancer, thyroid disease and many other health challenges. They are also at risk of losing their parents to cancer. They should strive to become an Aset rather than a Polyxena. Young women could save their lives by learning and adopting a healthy lifestyle, reading and avoiding cancer causing foods that contain processed sugar.

In 2012 a publishing company called Agora Health Limited published a book called "The Cancer Survival Manual. Tomorrow's cancer breakthroughs today." The book was written by Rachael Linkie. On page 20, the prolific and experienced author wrote: "Green tea helps destroy breast cancer and esophageal cancer cells." Ambitious daughters could initiate themselves by reading books such as the one written by Rachael Linkie.

The opinion of an experienced healer

The text below was extracted from the YouTube channel iHealthTube.com.

Dr. Bob DeMaria is pointing out the negative effects caused by mineral deficiency.

"Your liver has cells in them for physiology called kupffer cells. Kupffer cells eat unwanted unfriendly bacteria, viruses in cancers cells. So if your liver is not functioning you're going to have a greater potential to have cancer. I'm going to throw out two thoughts to you right now. They are two of the most important items I'm going to share with you right now to prevent cancer. There's a term called Apoptosis. We are being led to believe that genes or lack of gene function, is the main reason of all the diseases. Well, I know and you know RNA and DNA, that's how we work. If you go to the American Cancer Society website, they'll say the leading cause of cancer is altered DNA. There are two elements that are just so critically important.

The very first one is Iodine. Iodine is not just for the thyroid gland. Iodine is for breast tissue, ovaries, and testicles in men. Iodine literally will turn the gene that's been on, off that promotes cancer. Apoptosis is limited cell life. Iodine keeps cancer cells in check. That's important."

1st Iodine

"I spend time in Japan. The average Japanese woman consumes about 12 milligrams of Iodine a day. From sea vegetables and from fish. It's not about the soy, it's about the sea vegetables and fish. Japanese women are not very big by the way. So they consume 12 milligrams of Iodine a day and I consume 12 milligrams of Iodine a day.

Now just because we're telling people to go and take Iodine now, doesn't mean you go out to the health food store and buy Iodine. You've got to be really logical and wise about this. We do a TSH, T3, and T4, that's a blood test for the thyroid. If your T4 is less than the midline, we may supplement with Iodine but there are other things we like to do first. You can also do a urine Iodine loading test. In other words, we make people take no vitamins at all for 4 days. We do a pre-test, we have them urinate in a cup or container then we have them take 50 milligrams of Iodine and for the next 24 hours literally, catch that Iodine. We want to see how much is excreted... You should excrete 95% of it. Most people I see they excrete about 35% that means their bodies holding on to the Iodine. That is the most scientific way to assess someone for Iodine.

We supplement accordingly. Now if you take Iodine too much too fast, and you have Bromine, Fluorine and Chlorine in your bodies... Bromine comes from hot tubs, Fluorine comes from toothpaste, water.

Chlorine comes from water. That's one of the reasons that we promote shower dechlorinators.

You know, most everyday people in the United States, they stand in a 4 x 5 gas chamber, I mean glass chamber. Breathing in toxic chlorine gases. Chlorine compromises thyroid function. If you don't have enough Iodine you're going to have a greater potential not to have the gene working that stops cancer cells."

2nd Vitamin D

"The second is vitamin D. Vitamin D and Iodine work hand in hand to keep cancer in check in the human body. What has science been telling us for the last 30 years? To stay out of the Sun. The Sun is your friend."

Dr. Bob DeMaria gives us two clues on how we can prevent cancer.

Vitamin D and Iodine.

These supplements support the immune system therefore they should be used by both males and females. Especially daughters who wish to enjoy long and healthy lives.

The Wise Man

"His role is precisely that of the Old Wise Man of the myths and fairy tales, whose words assist the hero through the trials and terrors of the weird adventure."

Joseph Campbell - The Hero with a 1000 Faces, page 6

Aset, Ariadne, Luke Skywalker, Karate Kid, Harry Potter, Rene Caisse, Charlotte Gerson all learned from an essential archetype, called the wise old man.

George Lucas is an American filmmaker and writer. He was born on 14th May 1944, a year before the end of the Second World War. He is the original author, producer and director of Star Wars. When he was young George Lucas was keen to find a mentor to guide and help him to become a great writer and thinker. He asked a writer called Joseph Campbell to be his teacher and mentor. It was Mr. Campbell who helped George Lucas to create Star Wars by introducing him to the subject of the Hero's Journey and mythology. When Joseph Campbell met George Lucas he was at the pinnacle of his career. The old man fulfilled the role of a mentor by sharing his wisdom.

A person who wishes to become healthy and happy should also seek a mentor. Ideally an expert in natural healing, micronutrients and essential supplements. The old wise man could be a member of the family who thinks outside the box. It could also be someone who you meet through books, videos, lectures etc. Although we have never seen the wise Native American Indian man, who initiated the patient of Rene Caisse, we use his wisdom to prevent cancer by drinking the famous "Essiac tea". By learning the story of Rene Caisse we discovered the old wise man, the shaman whom the English lady called "the medicine man".

Movies are full of examples of old wise men. A rich example is in the movie Star Wars. The main characters in Star Wars are Darth Vader, Luke Skywalker, Princess Leia and Obi-Wan Kenobi. If we look at the etymology of the word 'father' we discover some interesting details. In Old English a 'faeder', meant a person who begets a child, also "any lineal male ancestor; the supreme being. From Proto-Germanic "fader" Old Frisian 'feder', Dutch 'vader', Old Norse 'favir', Old high German 'fatar' - German 'vater': in Gothic usually expressed by atta), from Pie "pater-: father"...

To get the true origins of the world father we must look at ancient cultures and languages. In Kmt the word for father was Itef. The character 'f' gives us a clue. In Ancient Persia, we discover that the leader of a religious cult known as Mithraism was addressed as father.

In India the followers of the Persian spiritual leader called Zoroastro are called the Parsi. Parsi is also spelled Parsee (later transformed to Pharisees). The Greek word for father is Pateras. The characters F and P lead us to many ancient names used to address an old wise man who plays the role of guardian, teacher and father. P leads us to papa, F leads us to father, fratello faixa, family etc.

Darth Vader is the father who is ruled by a shadow. He chooses to be faithful to a system rather than to his heart. His young son is the hero who strives to fight the forces of evil. Vader is the Dutch word for father.

A modern version of Hrw and Ra

The character called Skywalker was inspired by Kmtic mythology. The priests of Kmt wrote that "Ra took 12 daily steps to cross to sky." The young hero is called Skywalker. His name contains two keys words. Sky and Walker. Like Ra he goes on a journey of self-discovery. His mentor was an old man called Obi -Wan Kenobi.

It doesn't matter what kind of biological challenge we are facing, we should always look for a mentor. Mentors have the keys to the labyrinth. The wise old man is a teacher who has completed the journey and knows the secrets of healing and life.

One of Ty Bollinger's mentors was a man called Nicholas Gonzalez. Dr. Nicholas Gonzalez was one of the world's top experts on cancer. He studied journalism and wrote for a prominent newspaper. His life changed when he met an old wise man called Dr. Kelly who initiated him into a new culture that uses nature to heal diseases. Dr. Kelly became a mentor after using diet, coffee enemas and supplements to cure himself of an aggressive liver cancer.

Like the heroes who defeated the monster called cancer, you will also need a mentor, a teacher.

Where do you find the wise old man who knows the mysteries of health? Where is that person?

In today's world, the old wise man can be found online. On YouTube, Amazon, in bookstores and through the advice of intelligent friends. Some of the wise old men who knew the secrets of herbs are no longer alive. Although they are no longer alive their wisdom remains. They have disciples who practice and teach their mentors techniques. Many of them wrote instructional books and delivered lectures. Linus

Pauling, Dr. Sebi, Otto Warburg, Max Gerson were some of the wise men who dedicated their lives to the subject of natural health.

There are many wise old men who are still alive and have knowledge about healing. The list is very long. We will mention a few names here:

- Edward G. Griffin
- Joseph Mercola
- Robert Gorton
- Dr. Matthias Rath
- Jonathan V. Wright
- Andrew Wei
- Allan Spreen M.D.
- Russell L. Blaylock M.D.

Dr. Matthias Rath, born in 1965 in Stuttgart, Germany specialises in cardiovascular diseases, vitamin C and essential extracts which can be used to fight cancer. Dr. Matthias Rath is based in Europe and has a foundation called Dr. Rath Health Foundation

Stanislaw Burzynski is based in the U.S. and is known for dedicating his entire life trying to find a cure for cancer. Dr. Keith Scott Mumby, Dr. Leonard Coldwell... The list is very long indeed.

Every country and continent has wise men who dedicated their time and talents to the subject of health. The old wise men of our time are known as independent researchers. They write books and have their own clinics and formulas. In 1974 Edward G. Griffin wrote a book called "*The World without Cancer*". There are many old wise men who have dedicated their lives to the subject of healing. They are not necessarily old. They are wise and highly experienced. You should explore and study their philosophy. You should learn from them because that's how you become well versed on the subject. I have adopted the philosophies of many wise old men and women. I feel great. I feel happy and healthy. I am confident about the future. Intelligence gives you confidence regarding the future. An old wise man has the right intelligence.

Some of the wise old men who have transitioned are, Otto Warburg, Jay Kordich, Dr. Sebi, Max Gerson, Samuel Thomson, Nicholas Gonzalez. They wrote books and shared their wisdom.

When we contemplate these archetypes we start to think about solutions that are outside the box. Their ideas and words will inspire you to think differently.

Joseph Mercola, a pioneer

One of the most experienced natural health doctors is a man called Joseph Mercola. Dr. Mercola was born on the 8th of July 1964 in Chicago.

"I have always been passionate about health. I started exercising in 1968 which is 50 years ago and I am still exercising and that was one of the primary motivations to go into medicine. To learn more about health. Unlike most of my classmates who were focused on disease, drugs, and surgeries, I was the oddball focused on wellness and getting people healthy because if you are healthy disease disappears. Unfortunately, I got caught up on the conventional paradigm. I was a pharmacy apprentice for a half a dozen years before I started medical school. And really bought it, hook, line, and sinker and really embraced the drug model and was heavily prescribing after I graduated and started my practice in 1985. But still, I was passionate about health. Just did not understand that drugs are not the way to achieve it. Eventually, I came to network with a group of physicians in the American Academy of Environmental Medicine and found that there were other physicians out there who understood this.

That transferred to other organizations. I started my mentoring in natural health therapies and approaches. Concurring with this, also in 1968 I started my first computer programming for training COBOL. I have also been passionate about technology. In the mid-1990s and started a website in 97. I was an early adopter and started an email newsletter and gave it to my patients."

The above paragraph is a fragment of Joseph Mercola's Hero's Journey. He spent years swimming in the world of conventional medicine. One day he met mentors who helped him to jump into the world of natural health.

Today Joseph Mercola is one of the leading natural health practitioners in the world. He has been healing and teaching people for more than 20 years. His website attracts more than 20 million users a year. He is the archetypal wise teacher who has collected essential wisdom and is happy to share it. His website is a treasure trove for people interested in healing and wellness. The website is called www.mercola.com

Dr. Sebi

"It is oxygen the body needs, not rice or beans or a piece of meat. Oxygen, that is the fuel of the body."

- Dr. Sebi - Rock Newman interview

Alfredo Bowman was born on 26 November 1933 in Central America in a country called Honduras. When he was a child Dr. Sebi was told that he had "chronic" asthma and diabetes. His diabetes were severe and made him impotent as well as obese. His life was a misery until a friend advised him to travel to Mexico and talk to an old wise man called Alfredo Cortez. Mr. Cortez was a natural healer, a herbalist, a Shaman. Although he was in his late 70s when he meet his student, Mr. Cortez was happily married. He had more vitality and energy than the obese and diabetic young man who was standing in front of him. He knew the source of vitality and healing properties hidden in plants.

When Mr. Cortez was introduced to Alfredo Bowman he smiled and asked: "Where do you come from?" Mr. Bowman said that" I am from Honduras." Mr. Cortez was not happy with the answer and kept asking, "Where do you come from?"

Mr. Bowman kept saying that he was from South America. "I cannot help you." Said Mr. Cortez. "Why" asked Mr. Bowman? Mr. Cortez looked at him and asked, "where did you come from?" "I am from Africa." Said Mr. Bowman. "Now we can talk." Said the Mexican healer.

Mr. Cortez understood that disease is both a psychological and a biological challenge. Self-knowledge affects a person's confidence. Obese people tend to have a low self-esteem. That's one of the reasons why they find happiness in junk foods. Dr. Sebi was Obese and diabetic when he met his mentor for the first time. We should never ignore the importance of self-esteem and its impact on health.

Senor Cortez also understood that "you cannot give 1 type of medication to everybody" because people have different blood types and biological structures. Women for example find it more difficult to tolerate Chemotherapy than men. On the 25th of October 2018, the website of Dr. Matthias Rath published an article that says, " A new study has found that women undergoing chemotherapy treatment for cancer suffer more toxic side effects than men"

When he was young Mr. Bowman lived with his mother and grandmother. His grandmother used to call him Dr. Sebi. Her words were prophetic because in spite of not having a medical degree her grandson learned how to cure illnesses using herbs and fasting. His philosophy transformed him into one of the most famous and influential doctors in the modern world. He popularised a subject called the alkaline diet. He was also a remarkable role model because he cured himself of diabetes. He completed the hero's journey then he returned to heal others.

When Dr. Sebi stood in front of Mr. Cortez he was obese, tired, sick and ignorant. These are some of the qualities experienced by people who are not well. Dr. Sebi was in his early 30s at the time. He was impotent and tired. "I was angry, very angry." He had spent most of his life traveling around the world in order to find the cure for diabetes.

Dr. Sebi's life changed when Senor Cortez asked him, "what's your diet?" The mentor's question was very simple and profound at the same time. It was an essential instrument of research.

"I eat meat, rice, chicken. I drink milk". "Hey" said, Mr. Cortez. "That's not the diet of an African. Rice does not come from Africa. Chicken was invented in Holland. Chicken is hybrid. Rice is a hybrid food. It causes anemia. Change your diet and you will be healthy again. Stop eating starchy and hybrid foods because they attack your organism. Stop eating rice, bread because they are starchy and attack your immune system. Hybrid foods cause anemia and circulation issues. You must eat organic, alkaline foods only. No rice, no chicken, no bread, white pasta. Animal proteins and sugars should be removed. Stop eating carbs for a long period of time."

Dr. Sebi was shocked. "No bread, No meat? Where will I get proteins from?" Mr. Cortez looked at his student and said "If you want to eat bread eat spelt bread. If you wish to eat pasta, eat spelt pasta. Don't touch processed pasta or processed food. Avoid gluten and carbs. You must become 100% vegan and eat alkaline foods only. You must fast for at least 3 months every year. Fast and drink herbal teas while you fast."

The instructions were difficult to follow because Dr. Sebi was addicted to junk food. He was told that in order to cure himself of diabetes he would have to renounce more than 98% of his diet. That's the journey that everybody who wishes to be healthy should contemplate. That's the hero's journey, detachment, separation from old habits, thinking and food. Dr. Sebi was told to stay away from processed carbs. Why?

The human organism turns carbs into glucose. Glucose is a fancy word for sugar. It is almost impossible to heal the body while consuming sugar at the same time. A sick body needs rest. A patient that's serious about his or her health has no option but to give up carbs for a prolonged period of time.

Novak Djokovic and the power of carbs

Novak Djokovic was born on the 22nd of May, 1987 in Belgrade, Serbia. Novak got into tennis at a very young age. For many years he struggled to win tournaments. He used to collapse during matches, that meant he was unable to finish matches and win tournaments. He struggled for many years. One day a Serbian mentor who saw him collapsing in the middle of a match, contacted him and said. "I know what's wrong with you. You are gluten intolerant. Stop eating foods that contain gluten. Stay away from carbs." Djokovic followed the advice. He changed his entire diet. His career took off. He became number 1 tennis player in the world and winner of more than 13 grand slams. Djokovic's parents own a pizza business. He grew up eating carbs. He had to depart from the habits, world and diet of his parents in order to find Maat, balance that enabled him to become a great champion.

Departure

When you watch movies or listen to stories you are usually told about a man, a woman and sometimes an animal, such as "The Lion King" that leaves home and goes on a long journey. That journey is the journey of self-discovery. The person usually leaves home as an ordinary person, a sick person then returns as a healthy individual. A hero. Dr. Sebi left home as a diabetic and migrated to the United

States. He lived in California and from there he traveled to Mexico. In Mexico, he met his mentor and healer, Mr. Cortez. Talk to any ignorant sceptic about diabetes and you will be told that diabetes is a chronic disease that has no cure. Dr. Sebi cured himself of diabetes and obesity then opened a clinic that helped people to cure cancer, diabetes, blindness, paralysis, aids and many other diseases. To achieve his goal, he had to first defeat the shadow that was inside of him. It was the shadow that inspired him to be obese and addicted to food.

Like many natural doctors, Dr. Sebi was hated by his competitors. He was charged with fraud. He was taken to court by the U.S. Government. He was not the first or the last old wise man to be taken to court. Max Gerson, Rene Caisse, Harry Hoxsey and many heroes who used natural medicine to help patients were also taken to court.

Dr. Matthias Rath has been taken to court more than 150 times because of his research. Healing others was Dr. Sebi's passion. He helped many people to change their diet and lives. He was one of the heroes who defeated the big monster called disease.

Dr. Sebi is an essential reference because he was the hero who cured himself of diabetes, impotence, and schizophrenia. His methods are very simple therefore easy to follow.

They are;

- Alkaline foods only
- Fasting
- Herbs
- Juicing
- No starch or animal protein
- No carbs or processed foods

"It is oxygen the body needs, not rice or beans or a piece of meat. Oxygen, that is the fuel of the body".

This quote was taken from Dr. Sebi's interview on the Rock Newman Show, where he discussed his path to healing and how he continued to spread wisdom to help others. According to him "our conventional understanding of diet and health is the main cause of the ailments in the modern world. Dr. Sebi went on a 90 day water fast, no food, only alkaline water from the Cusca plant. This plant has a ph level of 9, meaning it contains a high level of oxygen. His long term fast was a remarkable experience. He was not bedridden. He was traveling, giving lectures and creating programs to help people. His message inspires the following thinking: The body can survive and thrive on the right fuel. If you do not feed your body with the right fuel, you will create dis-ease because your body will struggle to cope with the imbalance.

Dr. Sebi performed the role of the old wise man. He was very ancient. He spent more than 30 years researching the benefits of herbs and fasting. He did not just research, he practiced what he preached. He is the mentor, the wise old man who comes to give you essential clues about diabetes, cancer, sickle cell and many other diseases. He cured himself of diabetes. That's an essential clue.

A politician who defeated a big monster called disease

Dr. Sebi was not the only Hero who succeeded in defeating a big monster called Diabetes. From the UK we get the story of a prominent politician called Tom Watson. During the second week of September 2018, Mr. Watson, a senior leader of the Labour Party, told several media organisations that "he reversed type 2 diabetes through diet and exercise." When asked about how he felt after completing his Hero journey, Mr. Watson said that "I feel great, I feel absolutely fantastic. Chilled out. I feel like my IQ has gone up. I feel younger. It's a great feeling."

Key questions

- What steps did he take in order to heal himself?
- What did he recommend?
- How did he manage to cure himself of diabetes?
- What herbs did he consume?

Max Gerson

"This is a short story on the brilliance of Doctor Max Gerson and his disease curing therapy. Doctor Gerson was born in Germany in 1881 and studied internal medicine before he immigrated to America. During his childhood in Europe, he had a fascination with studying soil. And how adding chemical fertilizers affected the food, soil, and our health. Spurring his interest in Internal Medicine. During his time in school, he developed severe migraines so he put his knowledge of food and toxicity to the test.

After playing around with the elimination diet for a couple of years he was actually able to halt his migraines. He then began to use this diet he found with his patients, then in 1918, a patient came back to him stating that his migraine disappeared but also that his skin tuberculosis was cured by it too. This was a major breakthrough of the time because skin tuberculosis was thought to be incurable. So the word quickly spread.

In 1924 he was invited by a famous lung specialist to do a clinical trial of the Gerson diet and he ended up curing 450 out of 486 patients who had skin tuberculosis. That's over 99% success rate. The world's leading medical journal published this story establishing the Gerson therapy as the first cure for tuberculosis. Dr. Gerson then left Germany came to America and established a clinic and got to work."

- Extract from - Max Gerson YouTube channel - Destroying the Illusion

Max Gerson was a doctor who suffered from migraines. His story is very interesting because he was the healer who needed healing. A doctor that needed a doctor. That's the journey of 99.9% of natural healers. They start their journeys as patients. Dr. Gerson went to a doctor and complained of severe migraines. His GP told him that he would have to spend the rest of his life "coping" with the pain. He rejected the invitation to remain a long-term patient. He refused to be a victim.

We are going to observe the journey of Max Gerson through the Hero's Philosophy.

1 - Ignorance and La Dolce Vita

The first stage of the hero's journey is ignorance. The man, the woman is ignorant about big business, the history of conventional medicine, the history of natural medicine, the history of politics and the importance of vitamins and micronutrients.

2 - Call to adventure

There is an event in the hero's life, a discovery that shakes a person's beliefs. The potential hero finds him or herself inside the "Belly of the Whale". The candidate is invited to get deep into a subject called health and disease. For Max Gerson the invitation came in the form of a disease called migraines, at the time migraines were considered incurable.

6 - Jump into the ocean

Stage 6 of the hero's journey is jumping into the ocean. Max Gerson was forced to jump into an ancient ocean called natural healing. There he discovered the power of coffee enemas and supplementation. During his research, he also became aware of an Italian lady who cured herself through diet. Others people's experiences gave him valuable clues, and threads. He followed the thread given by the Italian lady. He jumped into the ancient Ocean called "Natural healing."

After jumping into the ocean, Max Gerson discovered that the use of coffee enemas and natural foods enabled him to create a formula. The research inspired Max Gerson to create one of the most famous methods of healing diseases. The method is called the Gerson therapy. It took more than 50 years to discover and organise the different elements of the Gerson therapy.

The Gerson therapy is used by prominent people, such as Prince Charles and a few Hollywood actresses such as Gwyneth Paltrow. There are many clinics around the world that specialise in the Gerson Therapy. Japan, Mexico, Hungary, Spain are some of the countries that have clinics that use the Gerson therapy to cure diseases such as cancer and diabetes. Max Gerson became one of the most popular and prominent medicine men of his generation. His therapy "allows people to do it at home."

The Gerson therapy in Japan

A Japanese doctor who developed colon cancer that spread to his liver saved his life by using the Gerson therapy. After completing the hero's journey he taught his colleagues how to use the therapy to cure cancer. The Gerson therapy is one of the "Official" methods used by doctors to cure cancer in Japan. Below is doctor Hoshino's testimonial:

"My name is Dr. Yoshihiko Hoshino about 16 years ago, I suffered from colon cancer. I changed to Gerson therapy. And over these 16 years I continued to take the Gerson therapy, the metastasized liver cancer disappeared. I underwent ultrasound echo examination and after this examination there is no metastasized cancer, in the liver over these 15 years. Over 500 patients with cancer who visited here Loma Linda Clinic. At first we like to try a statistical analysis. This statistical analysis is already well under way on these 500 cancer patients treated with the Gerson therapy and well over half of them are curing or recovering. The scientific tracking of data is over a period of years and continues."

- From the YouTube channel Brewed strange - Scientific results of the Gerson Therapy.

Max Gerson was a fine example of a hero who defeated the big monster called disease. His formula is very simple. "Disease is caused by deficiency and toxicity." Eliminate toxins and cleanse your body, take essential supplements and you will prosper. Max Gerson's therapy is founded on a statement by a German scientist who said that "Disease cannot exist in an alkaline environment." Anybody who wishes to become the hero of his or her family should read the book written by Max Gerson. Gerson's ocean is very rich indeed. It contains books, documentaries, clinics, lectures and detailed instructions regarding health, micronutrients, vitamins and supplements.

The Shadow

"The archetype known as the Shadow represents the energy of the dark side, the unexpressed, unrealized or rejected aspects of something."

- p65 Shadow - The Writer's Journey, Christopher Vogler.

A few years ago I went to see my dentist. I got my teeth cleaned. I spent 1 hour with the hygienist. When I finished I went to the reception and paid. While I was waiting for the machine to process the payment, the receptionist looked at me with curious eyes and asked:

"What do you do for a living?" I told her that I write books about all kinds of subjects. My favorite being entrepreneurship. She smiled and asked,

"What are you working on right now?"

I told her that I was researching a subject called natural health. It's very interesting indeed. Very simple but also very deep.

"My friend", she said, "Is suffering from cancer. She had a very difficult time. Got 5 doses of chemo and the treatment did not work. She tried everything. She is currently on a clinic trial. She has been struggling for a long time."

"Wow, sorry to hear that" I said.

"We are very worried" said the receptionist. "We suspect she will not make it to Christmas. She lost her hair and weight. It's not very nice. The whole affair is heartbreaking. What would you advise her to do?" Asked the receptionist.

I replied and said that "I would strongly advise her to go to YouTube and search for a documentary called "The Truth About Cancer". That's the starting point. Education is the first step. Your friend has to complete the Hero's journey. She could go to a temple and meditate, think, reflect then accept the invitation to change her thinking and diet. That's her main disease. She should say yes to the first stage, the first part of the ancient and sacred sequence. It is called departure. Departure is followed by initiation. Your friend has to study subjects called health and cancer."

"What books do you recommend?" Asked the receptionist.

Great books

There are many books, "*Natural Strategies for Cancer Patients*" by Russell Blaylock is a must. She could also buy a book called "The Gerson Therapy, written by a lady called Charlotte Gerson. "*Beating Cancer with Nutrition*" is a must. The book was written by Dr. Patrick Quillin. His book is a classic in the world of natural healing. "*The 9 Steps to Keep the Doctor Away*" by Dr. Rashid Buttar is another must. Dr. Matthias Rath is another must have.

"*The Truth About Cancer*" by Ty Bollinger, "*The Cancer Survival Manual*" by Rachael Linkie. "*The Cancer Revolution*," "*Radical Remission.*" There is plenty of material. We have an online library dedicated to cleansing and prevention strategies.

Your friend could and should depart from ordinary thinking and strive to learn as much as possible. There is no point in telling her to change her diet and detox if she is not going to follow the advice. Cancer is a very intense experience that requires a deep immersion into the world of learning. It's not something you do in 7 days. It can take years for a person to recover. If the person is not willing to do the rights things then both the patient and healer will struggle.

I took the lady's email and sent her every single link that I could find about the subject. Cleansing, remedies, books, lectures. I sent the email on Friday and got busy with my own life. I expected a reply. There was no reply. There was no thank you. I got busy with my life and carried on studying and reading. There was not even a thank you for your time. I did not mind, or take it personal. I am very busy person who likes to read and study. I realised what was going on.

Two years later I met a lady who told me that she was suffering from breast cancer. I felt sorry for her. I gave her excellent advice and links on the subject. I did not get a thank you from her either. There was no recognition or signs of gratitude. I got busy with my own life and carried on reading and writing. It did not bother me. I recognised the rejection to the call to adventure.

6 months after meeting the third patient, I started to plan my second book. I was talking to my sister about the hero's journey and its mysteries. We were discussing the details of the hero's journey when I stopped and said:

I just realised something very strange. I spoke to 6 people who were in the midst of very brutal chemotherapy treatments. I told them about the Gerson therapy, supplements, books and cleansing. They pretended to love the content, however, none of them said thank you. They pretended to be listening. They were not interested in learning because learning is associated with the desire to change. Disease, depression, despair, fear of death have the power to intoxicate the psyche, the soul, mind, and the thinking of a patient. Learning and Healing go together "like love and marriage." You can't have one without the other.

I told my sister the story of a man, a family man who told me that he had stomach cancer. I saw him as a friend, therefore, I was worried. I went to his house days before he got chemo and told him to look into YouTube and do the research. He did not pay attention to my words. He rejected the advice. He got chemo and surgery. It didn't go very well. I saw him weeks after getting chemo and his entire body was transformed. I went to his house and told him about enemas and herbs. I asked him to take notes. He told me to write everything on a piece of paper then drop it into the letterbox.

I bought a book called the "*The 1-Minute Cure*" then went to his house and knocked on the door. His wife came and I gave her the book. She said "thank you. I will show it to my husband".

I don't remember the man coming to me and saying thank you. At one point I got the impression that I was disturbing him, therefore I stopped going to his house. I was shocked when his wife told me that he died. I was shocked to learn about his death. I thought he had an effective plan B.

I like to talk to people, go for long walks and reflect on my experiences. During my walks I kept asking myself; what stops people from receiving the help they desperately need and what stops them from saying thank you? What's the cause? Why do they cling to ignorance and ego?

The shadow is the barrier, an obstacle to healing

I read two books that helped me to understand the character whom psychologists called the shadow. They were "*Dreams and reflection*" by Carl Jung and "*The Writer's Journey*" by Christopher Vogler.

I bought and read the book The Writer's Journey. I love the book. It contains a chapter called, "The Shadow". Mr. Vogler explores the subject of the shadow beautifully. His book made me think of celebrity chefs. Some of the famous chefs on television use shadows to lure audiences. They don't care about the health of their audiences. They seduce their audience's shadows through toxic, tasty and unhealthy foods. They also make a living promoting unhealthy, sweet foods. The message is clear; Fall in love with sugar and meat. Eat like a king and forget your longevity. Enjoy "Carpe Diem."

The Writer's Journey helped me to understand what happens to certain patients, people and personalities, policemen, prominent politicians, popular TV presenters and powerful characters who allow shadows to ruin their careers and lives.

On page 66 Christopher Vogler wrote the following:

"The shadow can combine in powerful ways with other archetypes. Like the others archetypes, the shadow is a function or mask which can be worn by any character."

The mask of a person who refuses to learn

Please pay attention to the word mask. Many people who believe that they are healthy will not take advice easily. They would rather cling to their ignorance than accept the call to adventure. They will wear a mask and neglect their own health.

When someone is attacked by cancer three things tend to happen.

1. The person will recognise and accept that "I need help".
2. They will become very stressed and afraid
3. They will refuse to learn and contemplate alternative therapies

The patient will go to a doctor and demand a "quick fix", a pill or some "effective remedy". There is a small detail missing here. The detail is the word 'change' or 'learn'. I need help is not the same as I need to change. I need help is not the same as I want help. I want help is not the same as I want to learn. The patient will say I need help. The shadow will say I don't need change. There is a collision. Two personalities, with two different visions. If the shadow is the most dominant personality the patient is in big trouble. Cancer cells could be seen as shadows of healthy cells. There is a point when they become dominant. If they are not removed from the body, they can lead a person to death. The shadow which affects a person's personality has the power to blind the patient and lead him or her to premature death.

That's a final and forced departure from this world. The shadow rules a person's life through ego, arrogance, ignorance and a lot of pretending.

"You don't succeed by demand you succeed by deserve." - Jim Rohn

The above statement is very interesting. Jim Rohn was the mentor of Tony Robbins, Les Brown and Mark Hughes founder of "Herbalife". Very successful entrepreneurs. Jim Rohn told his audiences that;

"You have to deserve success, you have to do something in order to deserve success. You have to do the right things. You don't succeed by demand."

The same thinking applies to health. It's not enough to get doses of chemotherapy and radiation. A patient could and should change his or her diet. There is a group of patients and dreamers who will reject the invitation, "The call the adventure". The call to adventure is a call to give up the 10, 20, 30, 40, sometimes 50 something years of bad diet, bad habits and ignorance. There is a group of people who will hold into the old self. They refuse to depart, leave the ordinary world.

I remember going to the hospital to get a blood test and seeing a man wearing a light blue patient's gown. He was standing at the main entrance of the hospital. Although he was clearly suffering from a serious health condition, the man was smoking. It was a very strange image. To see a patient who is also a smoker. The man at the hospital entrance was unable to give up old habits, addictions and bad education. A bad habit and an addiction will create a new personality. A toxic and unhealthy shadow. This personality is the shadow.

Macbeth is a fine example of a shadow. He was a successful general who turned into a prolific murderer. If the patient does not take the necessary steps to start a journey of self-discovery, the shadow within him or her has the power to destroy everything. The shadow is a negative ego, a psychological and invisible disease that's more powerful than cancer. It blinds the patient, it leads him or her to self-destruction. Macbeth was the architect of his own downfall. Rejection of organic foods, and the sacred sequence departure, initiation and return could have serious consequences in a person's life.

Sutek - Satan the greatest shadow

The people of Kmt used a character called Sutek as a metaphor of a shadow. Please remember that the word 'Sutek' is the root word for Satan. Sutek is the greatest shadow in the history of the human race. Sutek was the younger brother of Wsr, the husband of Aset. Sutek was a member of the Ancient Kmtic royal family. He was powerful and respected. He was also jealous. Something happened that changed him. He became greedy and started to pretend. He killed his brother then proclaimed himself as the new Nswt Bity, the leader of the two lands.

There is a powerful lesson hidden in the journey of Sutek. After spending 8 years fighting Hrw, the son of his older brother, Sutek realised that he was on the wrong path. After realising that he was heading towards self-destruction, Sutek surrendered to the energy of the hero and changed his ways. He became a protector of his grandfather, the solar principle Re. Re is the root word for 'return' and 'reformation'. There was an evolution in Sutek's personality. The journey of Sutek also teaches us that the shadow is a trickster. If we don't eliminate the shadow and persist in clinging to ignorance, stupidity and ego, we risk becoming victims of the big monster. Smoking, drinking, junk food, animal protein, mineral deficiency, exposure to toxins, psychological and physical stress, are some of the main causes of cancer in the world. Please remember that Sutek, the shadow and the hero are two aspects of the same personality. Their battle is internal. It takes place inside all of us every single day.

The archetype of the shadow is universal. Hours before he was stabbed to death, Julius Caesar greeted and embraced the same men who were plotting his downfall. He did not realise that he was dealing with shadows. Shadows pretend to be someone who they aren't. When the big monster called Cancer is around there is no point in pretending that I can keep the same old habits and be healthy at the same time. In order to cure himself of Diabetes, the British Politician Tom Watson gave up "the great diet" and exercised daily.

There are people who are just too proud of themselves to learn new things which have the potential to same them. When disease strikes they refuse to let go the old self. They refuse to change. The consequences are devastating.

I met a lady who told me that she had breast cancer. She also told me that she was too busy to detox. Every time I mentioned the name of an author, she interrupted me and said, "I know that, I have seen that, I have heard". She said that "Coffee enemas are bad for your health." She also refused to say thank you for the advice. Her strategy was daily physical exercise. Exercise is great and necessary, it is a powerful way to heal the body. It helps the mind to release endorphins. Physical exercise is also a tiny, a very small fragment of a health program. It is not the whole program. There is always the need to cleanse the psyche, cleanse the soul, change our diet and learn. That's how we eliminate the shadow.

A person who is told that he or she has cancer, has less than 2 years to change his or her eating habits. A lady once told me that she could not do enemas or take time off work because "I love my work, I have to work". She gives priority to money rather than health. That's an example of a person dominated by the shadow. If you persist in offending your body, disease will eventually force you to stay home. Many people refuse to buy organic foods because "It's too expensive." The same people have no problem buying expensive TV's, expensive clothes, mobile phones and cars.

There are many people who don't have cancer, however, they smoke. Cigarette companies are very kind. They write on the box;

"Smoking causes lung cancer".

The smoker is too proud to listen. He or she is dominated by the shadow. A shadow also stops people from reading. They refuse to read, to learn to grow and change. The shadow is very powerful and has the power to block a person's progress.

I lost my mother, my father, my brother, friends, and relatives to diseases. The whole subject of life, death, disease triggers a strange energy in me. It's a call to adventure. When someone says "I am not well", the healer in me steps in and tries to help. I don't care whether a person is a male or female, Christian or Jew, Muslim, Chinese, Australian, working class or wealthy. I do my best to share what I discovered on YouTube and the books that I read, because I am passionate about being healthy.

Over time I realised that a bad diet, addiction to TV, lack of reading, stress, materialism, cultural ignorance creates a shadow. A shadow is very dangerous because it blinds the individual. You can tell people who are controlled by a shadow:

Hey there is a train coming your way and you should get off of the track as soon as possible.

The shadow in them will look at you and laugh as if you are stupid. I used to eat bacon until I read that bacon is one of biggest causes of cancer in the world. I read an article on the BBC food website that explored the subject of bacon and cancer. I believed in the content, therefore I stopped eating bacon. I have not touched meat for over 10 years and I don't miss it. The shadow that was in me loved bacon. I had to win that internal battle order to eliminate the desire to eat bacon.

Christopher Vogler has more to say about shadows. On page 68 of his book he wrote;

"Like the other archetypes, shadows in a person's psyche may be anything that has been suppressed or neglected or forgotten. The shadow shelters the healthy, natural feelings we believe we are not supposed to show. But the healthy anger or grief if suppressed in the territory of the shadow, can turn to harmful energy that strikes out and undermines us in unexpected ways."

After my parents died I developed a shadow. I started to attack and insult people close to me. I realised that I was toxic. I could not explain to others what was happening. They could not understand it either. I did not grieve properly therefore I accumulated a lot of anger. I had to get out of the world of business and take some time to grieve. It took me 1 year to get over it. In the end I felt lighter and happier. I got rid of the shadow that was clouding my vision and thinking.

Becoming vegan also helped me a lot. Fasting helped me to remove biological and emotional waste out my body, mind and soul.

Before you try to help yourself or somebody who is close to you, you should stop and ask key questions. Do your research by asking the following questions;

- Am I dealing with a shadow or the original self?
- What's the psychological state of this person?
- Where are they in their hero's journey?
- Are they aware of their potential?
- Are they interested in longevity?
- Are they wearing a mask in order to hide the true state of their life and health?

People will wear a mask and pretend that they are strong and can do it by themselves. An ordinary person cannot become a hero without the help of others. The allies, the archetypes, and essential characters.

Shadows might be created for financial reasons, self-esteem, culture, race, ignorance and pure arrogance. If someone is not healthy, it's not a good idea to embrace the shadow. Some people refuse to believe that natural remedies are effective. I know people who refuse to eat vegetables. Natural foods are natural remedies. They are not magic pills. Natural remedies require time to take effect. It's not a 7 day miracle cure. You have to spend months sometimes years doing the right things.

A friend introduced me to a mother whose 15 year old boy was given chemo. I said to her, now is the right time to get into a healthy diet and cleansing. This is the right time for the Gerson therapy. She looked at me as if I was truly stupid and replied: "My son is fine, thank you". The mother was under the control of the shadow.

If you listen to Charlotte Gerson's interviews in which she discusses the subject of cancer, you will realise that she is serious when she talks about detoxing and removing toxins from the body. There is no need to pretend that we are superhuman. We are human and will do well to accept the fact that we have weaknesses and shadows that must be eliminated. Christopher Vogler is a great teacher. He said:

"A shadow may be a character or force external to the hero, or it might be a deeply repressed part of the hero." - p68 The Writer's Journey - Christopher Vogler

Key questions

- Are you allowing a shadow to block your own growth and development?
- Are you allowing a shadow to make you arrogant, impatient, unpleasant, ungrateful and sick?
- Are you allowing a shadow to ruin your life?
- Is your shadow created by your social and financial status, race, age, gender, nationality, addictions, terrible habits?
- Is your shadow addicted to substances?

- Was your shadow created by TV programs, political ideologies, junk food and junk music?
- What do you in order to refine your spiritual health?

Allies & enemies

"Heroes on their journeys may need someone to travel with them, an ally who can serve a variety of necessary functions..."

- p71 The Writer's Journey - Christopher Vogler

To understand these essential archetypes called "allies & enemies", we must return to the palace of Knossos, the home of King Minos and his family. There we find a young man, and a young lady. Theseus the son of King Aegeus, and Ariadne the heir of the Minos dynasty.
On page 54 of the book "Triumph of the Hero" we are told the following:

"He quickly retracted his steps through the maze, using the twine to guide him. When he emerged, Ariadne was waiting for him. She had managed to obtain the keys to the prison in which the other Athenians were held, and she distracted the guards long enough to allow Theseus to free the comrades."

Theseus was an ambitious Athenian that was keen to end the supremacy of Crete. He was an enemy of King Minos, the father of Ariadne. Ariadne and Theseus were nobles. The Persian word for noble is Aryan. That's the root word for 'Aria', air in Italian, 'Aristocrat', 'Aristoteles' and 'Ariadne'. Ariadne was the daughter of a king. She was a noble woman who decided to help an ambitious young man. She was an essential ally. Without her Theseus and the 14 virgins were doomed. The same thinking applies to a patient.

Every cancer patient will need allies. Please be aware that the cancer is the Minotaur that's keen to destroy the patient, his or her family, friends and relatives. Many cancer patients around the world consider Ty Bollinger and his team essential allies. Below are fragments of Ty's journey.

The Quest for The Cures - Episode 1 - YouTube channel The Truth About Cancer:

"Hi this is Ty Bollinger. I want to tell you my story about how cancer has affected my family. 1996 I visited my father. My wife Charlene and I visited mom and dad at their house and we didn't know he was sick. He had had stomach aches, no other physical symptoms really at that point. He doubled over in pain that night and we took him to the hospital, it was in San Antonio Texas. A few hours later the doctor had gone in for surgery. They thought it was gallstones. The doctor came out and said that dad had cancer and it was all over his stomach. So we asked the doctor what we should do. And he said, we should take his whole stomach out, we should remove it. So we did. And then over the course of the next 25 days my dad bled to death, from the surgery. 19 blood transfusions in 25 days. He died on July the 25th 1996.

That was my introduction into cancer and into what I call the cancer industry. After dad died, within the next seven years I lost my grandfather, my other grandfather, my grandmother, an uncle and a cousin to cancer. Then in 2004 was the straw that broke the camel's back. My mother died of cancer. And interestingly I had been researching for many years at that point, natural cancer treatments, but at that point when you're thrown into the mix and you really just don't know what to do. There were so many relatives there. The surgeon was frantic, the doctor that treated mom was a close family friend and he said we need to cut her stomach out.

The same thing they did with my father. So they did, we did, we opted for surgery. And unfortunately mom died of a stroke several months later, that most likely resulted from the surgery. That was what really got me to where, in a position personally I needed to get this information out to people. Like I said I've been researching for the last 7 years since my dad had gotten sick, and I had accumulated a lot of information. Thousands of hours of research. And I decided at that point that I needed to put it into a book. My goal in publishing my book in 2006, was just to honour mom and dad so that they didn't die in vain so, that people could be empowered with this knowledge. So that if their mom or dad is diagnosed with cancer, which according to the World Health Organization, if you're watching this 1 in 2 men, 1 in 3 women they're watching this they're going to be diagnosed with cancer.

If you're diagnosed with cancer and you have the knowledge that you need to make a good decision on how you're going to treat it. That was my whole goal. I didn't know that eventually this would blossom into something that I did full-time, and be able to help literally tens of thousands of people across the world. I'm very grateful for that but that wasn't my plan. Fast forward to 2014 the current year. In March I talked to a couple of friends and we had the idea, that we should go across the country, travelling to see the smartest people and get their opinion, their protocols. The smartest doctors, some of them, on how to treat cancer naturally. So we did."

Like every hero that came before him, Ty's journey started after he accepted the call to adventure. Earlier we introduced you to the subject of a quest, the pursuit of a secret formula, a vision that has the power to heal the individual and the community. Ty Bollinger's quest was to know how to defeat the Minotaur using natural means. He wanted to know if there was another option, a different way. The word way leads us to ancient China. There we discover a powerful spiritual philosophy called "Tao Te Ching." "The Tao is a way", another way to understand life and the universe. Ty Bollinger was looking for another way to heal the body and save lives. Tao Te Ching is a refined and highly sophisticated philosophy. That's what Ty Bollinger discovered by developing excellent relationships with great allies.

Departure

Ty Bollinger followed the hero's path. Every sincere seeker starts his or her journey as a victim. The believer who has the potential to become a hero departs, leaves his or her home with the goal of finding the secret of longevity. Aset, Gilgamesh, Theseus, Prince Arjuna the leader of the Pandavas, Mildred Nelson and many heroes left the ordinary world and went on a quest. Ty Bollinger left his home and travelled to many cities and countries, in order to meet his mentors. The hero who is battling a monster will also have to embark on a quest. He or she is fighting a ruthless monster. The patient is at war with an internal enemy that's not prepared to negotiate or surrender. The patient has to adopt the mindset, thinking of a military general. Every general, every strategist needs allies. Even the confident and well trained Theseus, the slayer of the Minotaur could not do it alone. It was Ariadne who distracted the guards and opened the gates of the labyrinth.

Theseus was a brave young man. He was also ignorant about the secrets hidden in the labyrinth. He had no clue how find the Minotaur. He was destined to die. The labyrinth was a dark place carefully designed to imprison anybody who got into it. Ariadne the daughter of King Minos fell in love with Theseus and decided to help him and the 7 boys and 7 girls who were destined to be eaten alive. Shortly after he descended to the labyrinth, Theseus was given a thread by Ariadne. The thread was crucial as it helped Theseus to find the entrance and the exit of the labyrinth. The thread was a gift that Daedalus gave to Ariadne after she asked him to help her. Without the thread Theseus was doomed to spend the rest of his life wondering inside the labyrinth of Knossos. The lesson is very powerful indeed.

Key questions

- Who are your allies?
- Who gave you the thread which you are following?
- Who gave you the keys of the world in which you are living?

Theseus' biggest enemy was not the Minotaur. It was ignorance, the knowledge of how to get in and how to get out of the labyrinth. Theseus succeeded because he got the help of 4 allies.

- Daedalus
- Ariadne

- Aethra - Theseus' mother
- Aegeus - Theseus' father

That same strategy should be applied to cancer or any other challenge. Cancer is a big enemy. It requires skills in biology, knowledge of herbs, essential oils, finance, science, strategy and psychology. The fight against cancer or any other disease is not a solo journey. The cancer and health industry is a labyrinth. Most people have an idea how they get in. Many patients, mothers, parents, brothers, sisters, uncles, grandmothers, wives, husbands don't have a clue how to get out. Refined philosophies are threads that enable the suffering man or woman to become a hero.

Ty Bollinger is a remarkable example of a modern hero. His family was almost decimated by the monster called cancer. After losing his parents and grandparents, Ty decided to act. He did not just act. He spent more than 7 years researching and learning. The key word is learning. More than 7 years of initiation resulted in wonderful documentaries, lectures and books.

The number 7 is a very rich esoteric number. We find it in mythology, literature and organised religion. Utnapishitim, the mentor of Gilgamesh asked his wife to bake 7 loaves of bread for Gilgamesh. Aset spent 70 days healing her husband. King Minos used to feed virgins to the Minotaur every 7 years. In the Bible it said that the world was made in 6 days and on the 7th the creator rested. Today we have 7 days of the week. Historians speak of the "magnificent 7". The body of Wsr the successor of Re and husband of Aset was cut into 14 pieces. That's 7x2.

The pain and wisdom which Ty Bollinger collected from his experiences inspired him to create an organization called "The Truth About Cancer". The goal of the organization is to educate and help people not just to understand but also to learn how to fight and win the greatest battle of their lives. Ty is not a doctor. He is not a filmmaker. He realised that he could not achieve his goal without the help of others. He worked with his wife and friends. Together they created an excellent and dynamic team. They contacted as many natural health experts as they could find and asked for help. In order to accomplish his goal Ty flew to many countries and met experts, experienced healers who make a living helping people to defeat the Minotaur. Experienced healers, saviors of souls, researchers, teachers and authors became his allies and mentors. They supplied him with essential wisdom that he used to save many lives. The principles that we call allies can be found in many areas of life. They are in mythology, sports, schools, secret societies, aristocratic families...

The winning formula

In his book *"The Winning Formula"* David Coulthard teaches us an important lesson about teamwork. He shares his experiences and the lessons that he got from Formula 1. Formula 1 racing is one of the most competitive sports in the world. A single team requires more than 800 people. Most of them work "in the factory." An F1 team also needs excellent suppliers, planners, strategists etc. They are all working to support 1 driver. The leading driver. Even the most talented driver in the world cannot win a race or a championship without the support of his team.

"Naturally people often ask what is like to drive a Formula 1 car. There is no doubt that it is a fantastic experience to drive something as light and powerful as a Williams, Maclaren or Red bull around the streets of Monte Carlo or an iconic circuit such as silver stone and Monza. However it is not a solitary experience that everyone imagines, because every step of the way I am supported by a group of people who are much more clever than I am. I am only one link of the chain that leads to success and it all requires a team effort from start to finish. Every day of the year, every minute of every the day."- The Winning Formula - David Coulthard

The message from heroes found in both mythology and the modern world is very clear. You need to build a winning team.

People who have completed the Hero's Journey could become your greatest allies. They can tell us what they did in order to overcome obstacles. A dreamer who wishes to become a hero will have to build a successful team. Every single member of the team plays an important role. You will have to become a leader of souls and delegate. Ask people to do what you cannot do. You cannot fulfil every single task therefore you need a team. Cancer is a big and powerful monster. The task of removing the monster from the body is a big project. It's like building a new house, you need architects, engineers, plumbers, gardeners, diggers and all kinds of experts. The monster called cancer should not be confronted by one single person.

I remember talking to a tall man who was suffering from diabetes. I told him that "you should not drink beer if you suffer from diabetes". He looked at me and laughed. His friends were happy to buy him beer. Were they allies or liabilities? You need allies. Your allies might be younger than you. They might be of a different race, different gender, lower social status, culture. It doesn't matter. You need allies. You need good people who are willing to help you in any way they can.

The subject of enemies and allies is very interesting because we find visible and invisible enemies. As well as visible and invisible allies.

Invisible enemies

- Tumours
- Addictions
- Ego
- The shadow
- Ignorance

Visible enemies

- Artificial sugar
- Canned foods - canned tomatoes
- Farmed salmon
- GMO Foods
- Pop Corn
- Pop/fizzy drinks
- Processed meats
- Processed foods
- Refined sugar
- Soda

Visible allies:

- Archetypes

During the last days of spring 2018 I spoke to a lady who had colon cancer. I was explaining to her why people insert coffee through the rectum. She stopped and said, "That's harmful, there is nothing wrong with drinking coffee." I tried to share my experience, I said "When we drink coffee it goes to the upper stomach then to the lower stomach. When it reaches the lower stomach the coffee becomes acidic." She was keen to argue about something that she had never tried or researched. Her wisdom was the product of speculation, therefore, I did not explore the subject further.

I realised that I was talking to a shadow, the voice of arrogance and ignorance. When a person is unwell he or she should wear the mask of a student. An ambitious dreamer should listen to every single expert before making a decision. Experienced shoppers don't go to a single shop and buy an item. They spend hours searching both online and offline. Some people spend 12 months searching for the best deal. The same strategy should be applied to your health. There is another powerful strategy which you could use. Turn your relatives into allies. We get clues about this strategy in mythology.

Theseus was born in Troezen. He lived with his mother. For many years, his mother was his main ally. She was the hero who brought him into the world. She was also his main mentor, his main adviser. First she instructed him to go to the pine forest and move the rock. When the first task was completed she advised him to go to Athens. When he arrived in Athens and introduced himself to his father he got a new mentor and ally. When he arrived in Crete and met Ariadne, he got another mentor and ally.

Ariadne spoke to an old man called Daedalus and asked him to help her. It was Daedalus who created the thread which Ariadne gave to Theseus. Theseus had many allies. Among them were relatives and strangers.

Aset the Kmtic Queen, priestess, and healer was helped by her sister, her nephew, her grandfather and one of her father's loyal servants. A principle called Djehuty. Djehuty was the principle of wisdom and right speech whom the Greeks called Hermes.

Aset's main allies were:

- Djehuty
- Her grandfather
- Her nephew
- Her sister
- Her son Hrw

If you look at the journey of Aset and Theseus you will learn an important lesson. The hero's main allies came from outside. Two of his allies, his mother and father, came from within the family. You should strive to turn your relatives into your main allies. Please remember that when it comes to cancer crying won't help you. People have to read and research. Your allies should strive to remain positive and optimistic. The big monster loves stressed and depressed people.

How do you turn your relatives into allies?

Lord Krishna told prince Arjuna, "do your duty."

It's very simple. Give them specific roles and goals. Your husband could be the person responsible for buying organic foods and the necessary tools for juicing and enemas. Your son could be the person responsible for supplements. Your daughter could the person responsible for preparing the enemas. She could also ensure that the coffee is medicinal and organic. Enemas require distilled pure water. Your wife could be responsible for vitamins and juicing. Your friends could be the researchers. Your oldest son could be responsible for implementing the method and the diet. Your best friend could take the role of motivator. He or she could research the best motivational videos, books and audiobooks. You could be responsible for preparing raw foods and essential powders. You should do your best to build an ambitious team made of people who are happy "to do their duties," rather than simply crying and being depressed. The task of recovering from a disease is a big task. It's not a solo journey.

If you build a team and give roles to each member of your team, you will end up with powerful people around you. The mistake you can make is to believe that you will defeat the monster by yourself. It's not going to happen. The majority of experts will come from outside your family. The majority of Ty Bollinger's allies are health experts from around the world. If you don't give roles to your friends and relatives they will become depressed and stressed, deluded and confused. A sad and gloomy environment will help the big monster to prosper. The big monster called cancer or disease doesn't care whether people cry or moan. When the monster strikes you should sit down and plan. Diagnosis means war. A clever warrior is advised by powerful, proactive and very intelligent allies. You could think outside the box and use technology as one of your main allies.

Essential tools

A few years ago a friend introduced me to a machine called Kangen. Kangen is the name of a Japanese inventor who realised that tap water contains more chemicals than oxygen. He mediated on the subject. Rather than going to the streets, protest and demand clean water, he created a solution. He got himself busy and invented a machine that turns tap water into oxygenated water. Alkaline water. The machine is called Kangen.

His machines are used by very wealthy people. Very wealthy people such as Bill Gates tend to live long lives. They think differently and follow specific principles, a specific philosophy. They see and use technology as allies. They use machines such as Kangen. To defeat the monster called cancer, you will need the right tools and resources. Kangen water is a great ally. There are many machines and if you invest your time researching you will find amazing tools that will help you to either prevent cancer or heal and repair your immune system. There are affordable machines that turn tap water into ozonated water. There is a very interesting healing method called oxygen therapy. This method uses a machine to help patients to consume high quantities of oxygen. It is a powerful machine. Many athletes use this therapy to recover from injuries. The method is also called hyperbaric oxygen therapy because the patient spends several minutes inside a hyperbaric chamber.

Every hero needs tools. You need tools. Juicers, computers, paperbacks, audiobooks, an ozone water machine, an oxygen water machine, air purifiers, an enema kit. Luckily the tools that you need don't cost a fortune. You don't have to be a millionaire in order to get

The Greek word Kratia means power, rule. In Latin it became Cratia. From Cratia we got 'Cracy' . Aristo+Cracy means the rule, the power of the Aryans. The people of ancient India called their land AryaVata. That means the "Land of the Aryans"

The Vedas were the sweetest things an Aryan could hear or consume. They were sacred scriptures and intellectual food used to heal the soul and initiate societies. In the Western world the Vedas have been replaced by physical food. Ayurveda medicine is a philosophy that uses food as medicine to heal the body. Food is a fragment of the philosophy and not the main element of the ancient Indian science. In Western medicine food is not even part of the equation. This idea is gradually changing.

From Sanskrit and Ayurveda medicine we got 3 key words. They are "Vata, Pitta, and Kapha." These 3 words are known as Doshas.

What are Doshas?

The website teaindia.co.uk says that doshas are "Driving forces in your body that determine your constitution/Prakuti (in Sanskrit), also referred to as your mind/body- or Dosha - type. You are born with a unique balance of the three doshas that make up your constitution (just like your fingertips)..."

From "Dosha" we got a word that's essential for our investigation. The word is "Dolce". Dolce means sweet in Italian. From "Dosha" we also got "Duchess", "Duce". It means Duke in Italian. The fascist Benito Mussolini was known as "II Duce". We shall focus on "Dolce Vita," sweet life. That's the name of the first step of the Hero's Journey.

We will contemplate the first step of the Hero's Journey. This is the first step which the heroes who defeated the big monster called cancer took. To understand this step we shall return to the Himalayas circa 563 - 480 BC. There we find a Prince called Siddhārtha Gautama. His father was a very wealthy man who was advised by a sage that his son was destined to be a spiritual leader, a shaman, a philosopher, an ascetic, a healer. His father did not want his son to be a mystic, a vegetarian, a monk, a mendicant and medicine man. He wanted the young Siddhārtha to succeed him, to become a powerful king and take care of the affairs of the state. Keen to distract his son from his life's mission, the father created an environment made of endless illusions. Endless parties with a large number of beautiful women and good food. There were endless celebrations, parties and streams of pleasure day and night. The young prince was brought up in a controlled environment. An artificial reality that had nothing to do with the real world. He was blinded, imprisoned by the senses and shadows. Shadows that make the ordinary world appear attractive.

Everything was going according to plan. The king was happy, satisfied, confident that the plan of flooding the luxurious palaces that he owned with sensual orgies would do the trick and blind his son. One day everything changed after the young prince asked his charioteer to take him out for a picnic in the local park. The charioteer obeyed. He prepared the royal carriage and took the prince away from the beautiful prison that his father had spent years creating. The prince and his loyal servant departed. Shortly after the pair left the imperial palace, the domain of magnificence and pleasure, the young prince saw an old man. For the first time in his life, the prince saw a weak man who was struggling to walk and stand. He was very poor and very old.

As soon as he saw the decaying man Siddhārtha asked his charioteer to stop. What's happening to that man? He asked visibly shaken. "That's old age." Answered his charioteer. "Old age? What is old age?"

The charioteer and loyal servant used the truth to initiate the Prince into the real world. The truth liberated the prince from illusion and confusion. The trip to the park was the beginning, the catalyst of Siddhārtha's transformational and heroic journey.

The struggling old man was the first of the 3 visions which helped the future Buddha to awaken.

The journey of young Siddhārtha helps us to understand what's happening to many people in today's world. Although they are surrounded by technology, computers, and luxury, many people are sleepwalking to the grave. They are ignorant about the 4 pillars of health.

- Diet
- Mind
- Culture,
- Philosophy

Modern human beings are surrounded by endless distractions, illusions and fabrications provided by prolific and experienced tricksters. Modern citizens are given 24-hour breaking news, endless sports events, cheap junk foods, political intrigue, gender wars, free and psychologically intoxicating music. We are also given violent video games that distort our reality, plenty of drugs and alcohol to intoxicate our immune system and psyche. GMO and processed foods corrupt our biology and gradually destroy our vitality. Many people are stuck in the world of ignorance. They have no clue what their bodies and minds need in order to perform and deliver excellence. Blinded by made up beliefs and false history, they neglect their health and pile 1000's of hopes on a "quick fix" pill.

A few months ago, the morning of the 25th July 2018 to be precise, I was taking a walk in the forest when I met a young and beautiful British couple. The young lady was tall and charming. She wore a wonderful light blue dress and fine red shoes. Her companion was shorter than her. He was jovial. He was wearing a light green shirt and yellow shorts. They were happy, very happy. The weather was excellent, pleasant. The skies were blue, the soil was dry and soft. It was hot, very hot. I saw wonderful, gentle and fragile birds playing on top of tall trees with green leaves. We were enjoying a very unique and memorable English summer.

The charming and smiling couple looked like people who were in their late 20s. They were both very friendly. As soon as they saw me, they smiled and greeted me. I reciprocated their kind gesture and greeted them. For obvious reasons, we chose the weather as our main muse, our main subject and source of inspiration. Smiling, the young gentleman looked at me and said "This is a very unusual English summer. There is no rain or grey clouds, "It is very nice." Said the young gentleman. He also told me his work colleagues were complaining about the heat. "They kept moaning and saying it's too hot" he said smiling.

I smiled, paused then commented on his story. They are missing the point I said. They should complain about the fact that they are not getting enough Sun. The Sun is good, a very good ally. The Sun is also the father and mother of all living beings and healthy things. The Sun is a giver of precious gifts that have the power to save our lives and the lives of our children, brothers and sisters, parents, grandparents, friends and strangers. The Sun is one of the most important allies a person can have in life. "Why?" he asked. "I was told that the sun causes skin cancer. I paused, reflected on his statement then replied. That's another ploy to move you away from Vitamin D. If you spend 10 hours under the scorching Sun , you might get skin cancer. There are many caucasian people living in South Africa. They don't die of skin cancer.

The Sun is the most reliable source of vitamin D. Did you know that women who are vitamin D deficient are at risk of getting very aggressive breast cancer?

"Really!" exclaimed the young lady. I didn't know that. Yes, I said. The majority of people living in England are vitamin D deficient. Vitamin D is essential because it helps the immune system. England is not a hot or sunny country therefore vitamin D is difficult to find. We don't get 90 days of strong sunshine in this country. Vitamin D is a gift of the Sun. It is free and essential. People of African origin who are vitamin D deficient get very aggressive breast cancer. Many develop extremely large breasts. That's a clear sign that their thyroid is suffering from vitamin D deficiency. Many women who have breast cancer also have a problem with their thyroid. Iodine and vitamin D prevent such problems.

Vitamin D helps the immune system to prevent and fight cancer. The young lady was visibly surprised and pleased. "I did not know that," she said. "That's very interesting."Replied her companion. I looked at his black eyes and said; "Your colleagues should be begging to be allowed to go for a walk in the Sun. Workers go to work at 8am and leave at 5 or 6 pm. They drive or use public transport to get home. They are not exposed to the Sun. They have very low levels of vitamin D. Their immune system will gradually lose its ability to protect them against all kinds of viruses, bacterias and diseases." Our conversation was delightful. I was inspired to share the research of Dr. Mercola with the young couple. Smiling I said that, "An American doctor called Dr. Mercola, looked into the subject of vitamin D."

Dr. Mercola wrote the following:

"Most cancers occur in people with a vitamin D blood level between 10 and 40 ng/mL, and the optimal level for cancer protection has been identified as being between 60 and 80 ng/mL. Research shows having a vitamin D blood level above 60 ng/mL lowers your risk of breast cancer by more than 80 percent, compared to having a level below 20 ng/mL." Source is www.mercola.com

The Sun is the most reliable supplier of the most important vitamin in the world. "How do I solve that problem?" Asked the young lady.

You should take a supplement called D3. That's essential. You should take a vitamin D supplement every single day. Especially in the winter because sunlight is very scarce. Vitamin D deficiency is linked to many types of cancers and diseases such as breast cancer, liver cancer, colon cancer, hyperactive thyroid etc. You are too beautiful and young to be unwell." "Thank you." She said smiling. You are a charming man said her smiling companion. A few minutes later we reached the exit of the forest. We shook hands, smiling, we said goodbye to each other.

Ignorance and La Dolce Vita

When Theseus arrived in Crete, he had no idea where the Minotaur lived. He was ignorant about the Minotaur, the labyrinth and its deadly traps. He had no clue what was really going on. The same can be said for many people living in today's world. They gladly consume GMO foods without questioning its origins. They are also ignorant about cancer and its deadly traps.

The journey and experience of Theseus is universal, many people in the world are not aware that vitamin D plays an essential role in preventing and fighting cancer. They are ignorant and detached from natural world. They should be forgiven for their ignorance, because ignorance is a natural state of the human experience.

La Dolce Vita is the first stage, the very first step of our intellectual and biological journey. Babies have a similar experience. The sweet and fragile baby that smiles to her mother doesn't know the meaning of the words mother, father or employment. Mother and father are intellectual tools used by adults. Citizens of our age are also very busy people. They never research about health until they are forced to do so. By then it's almost too late. Many wonderful human beings are too busy enjoying La Dolce Vita therefore they are not aware that cancer is a disease of the immune and psychological system.

"If I had to pick the one thing, and only one thing, that is most important to defeating cancer, it be would immunity. We know that people who have immune deficiency diseases, such as AIDS, also have a significantly higher incidence of cancer. The same is true for transplant patients, since they have to take special drugs to suppress their immunity." - Page 195 - Natural Strategies for Cancer Patients by Russell Blaylock, M.D.

Cancer vs. The Immune System - Cancer Tutor YouTube channel:

Ty Bollinger - "One of the things that's pretty much without dispute, is that the immune systems plays a big role in the prevention of disease. As a matter of fact, the immune system is really your first line of defence against pathogens, against the bad guys that come in and try to invade your body and make you sick."

Dr. Rashid Buttar, D.O. - "So cancer first and foremost is a problem with the immune system. You cannot have cancer if you have an intact immune system."

Dr. Ben Johnson, M.D., N.M.D., D.O. - "One of the things that I do is I begin to un-impede their immune system because every cancer patient, their immune system has missed the cancer. So it has missed it, and so you have to un-impede their immune system and then you have to stimulate it back into action."

Dr. Sunil Pai, M.D. - "With all our patients whether its cancer or any kind of chronic disease. It's always about lowering inflammation and improving and increasing your immune system response. Because your immune system has to fight, fix and repair against anything."

Dr. Bradford S. Weeks, M.D. - "It'd be logical to argue that in an intact immune system, there would be no room for cancer."

Dr. David Brownstein, M.D. - "The immune system can do its job surveil for foreign substances and foreign bodies, and get rid of that and you know, it can keep cancer at bay. When the immune system gets disrupted I think that's when bad things start happening to us."

Dr. Keith Scott Mumby, M.D, Ph.D - "Many people and I'm one of them see cancer as basically a disease of the immune system. Especially in our modern world, I don't think there's any way your gonna stops cells firing off and going wrong and turning into rogue cells. It's just too many toxins. But a good immune system will pick them up very quickly and eliminate them. So in a very strong sense, cancer is a disease of the immune system. So you want to do everything in your power to help the immune system, that means you know the right kind of nutrients that will help it, it also means removing the stresses that will stop it working."

Immune system

Our friends and relatives, brothers and cousins, sisters, aunties, work colleagues are busy trying to succeed in all kinds of ways. They are not aware that vitamin D is one of the most important vitamins in the world. Vitamin D3 is a powerful ally of the immune system that you cannot afford to ignore. Low levels of vitamin D cause serious damage to the immune system. The immune system is the first and last defence against any disease. Doctor after doctor, healer after healer, hero after hero proclaim that "Diseases are in one way or the other associated with low-levels of vitamin D". In women, deficiency of vitamin D disrupts the thyroid. It leads to inflammation. Inflammation leads to cancer.

Many people are extremely busy trying to meet the demands of life and of a very competitive society therefore they miss small but very important details that could save their lives and the lives of their friends and relatives.

Before the diagnosis, the hero is usually busy trying to prosper in the world of ignorance and materialism. A mother will be busy taking care of her family. She will also be busy trying to advance her career. A father is usually busy trying to overcome emotional as well as economic challenges. Such challenges demand time, something which most people don't have.

The first step of the hero's journey is indeed ignorance, "La Dolce Vita." This step takes place in the ordinary world. The ordinary world is the world of appearances. The world of economics, career, pleasure, competition, corruption, consumption, contamination, chronic illnesses and addicted consumers. During the first step of his or her journey, the hero lives as an addicted consumer. He or she is addicted to sugar and endless distractions such as entertainment, political dramas and societal goals. Everything appears to be fine. Pain and discomfort will appear and shatter his or her dreams and delusions.

A natural state of ignorance

We come to the world as small fragile babies. We don't remain babies. Like organic plants, we grow and become teenagers and adults, husbands, wives, old wise teachers and later memorable ancestors. We must grow, learn new skills and adopt a new mindset. The refusal to stop being ignorant has dire consequences for both the individual and his or her family. Biological and physical growth should be followed by intellectual growth. Please remember that disease is the product of a psychological, emotional, intellectual and biological decay.

In his lectures, essays and books Joseph Campbell talked about separation, initiation, and return. The smart dreamer who wishes to become a hero should find a way to separate him or herself from the ordinary world, ordinary thinking and ordinary experiences. The ambitious person should accept the fact that we are all ignorant and need to learn. Accepting one's ignorance is the first step. Ignorance and arrogance could lead to pain, desperation and a painful season followed by a painful and permanent departure.

One of the main tasks of ambitious people is to depart, detach themselves from the world of ignorance. Departure is an essential step taken by every single hero, ancient and modern. The first step is the ideal stage for research and re-education about health and vilitaty. In the story of Theseus for example, we learn that he departed from Troezen and went to Athens.

The key supplements used to prevent a complete collapse of the immune system are:

- Beta Glucan
- Black seed oil
- Chlorella
- Glutathione
- Reishi mushrooms
- Selenium
- Spirulina
- Turmeric
- Turkey Tail Mushroom Powder (Coriolus)
- Vitamin C
- Vitamin D
- Zinc

- IV- Vitamin C

According to experienced healers and health experts, cancer takes many years to develop. It's not something that happens in 7 days or 24 hours. Those who are aware that they are on the first stage of their health journey could take proactive steps to prevent the development of the big monster. Dr. Mark Hyman wrote a wonderful book called "*The 5 Forces of Wellness: The Ultra prevention System for living an Active, Age defying, Disease Free life*". The book introduces a powerful philosophy called "Ultra prevention".

Rejection of the artificial "Dolce Vita" is in itself a great strategy to prevent diseases. The first step of the Hero's Journey should be a temporary rather than a permanent address. We should free ourselves from ignorance as soon as possible.

Step 2 - Signals & Diagnosis

"It was April 2009 and I had found a lump on my breast."

- Tamara St. John, Author and Hero

The second step of the Hero's Journey is a very important step. In order to become a hero and win the battle against the monster called disease or cancer, you cannot skip any of the steps. You cannot pick and choose. You cannot say, "I want to remain ignorant. I will do nothing and I will be ok." You should not say, I don't want chemo then sit and do nothing. It doesn't work that way. You should pay attention to the second step.

The second step of the Hero's Journey is called Signals and Diagnosis. Too many toxins and a lack of minerals will create the right conditions for disease to prosper. Deficiency will become chronic. The first signs are known as symptoms. The human body gives the patient clues about what's going on inside of his or her body. An excellent example of signals is the color of your urine. When urine turns yellow that's a sign that the body lacks water and you are dehydrated. The solution is clean water. Our body is constantly talking to us. Cancer in the body is a sign of deficiency. The solution is micronutrients and cleaning not toxins.

"Yes, well in 2009, it was April 2009 and I had found a lump on my breast. And because I was busy getting my Master's degree and I was almost finished. I was going to finish in June of 2009. I said Ok, I knew what it was in the back of my mind. I was like ok, well, I can't deal with this now. I am busy getting my degree. So I put it on the back burner. And then in May of 2009 I lost my job. So, now I was unemployed and with cancer. I was like, I still cannot think about this right now, I have a month until I graduate, so I was putting it on the back burner. Well, in that time of two months, it had actually spread to my lymph nodes. So I had 5 or 6 lymph nodes underneath each armpit and everything was, it visible and swollen. And by that point, everything was throbbing all across my breast area and it was really painful. Difficult to sleep and then it was itching at the site of the lump on my breast. And so, by the time I finally graduated, I just you know, because I didn't have any insurance and I didn't have any money. So I just sat in front of the computer and I cried and I said; you know, God you put this on me for a reason so you gonna have to help. And I just asked him what do you want me to do? Lead me in the right direction to what's going to heal me naturally. Because there was no way. I saw my mother going through chemo and radiation like 30 something years prior when I was like 12 years old. There was no way I was going to do that."

Tamara St. John M.B.A - author of "Defeat Cancer Now" - www.tamarastjohn.org

Tamara St. John is one of the heroes who defeated the big monster. In 2009 she was busy striving to complete a Master's degree. She was also busy trying to meet the economic demands of the country in which she lives. In the U.S. if you have no money, you struggle to get the attention of doctors. The medical industry is deeply linked to the insurance, financial industry. Tamara was also trying to meet the demands of her university. Such demands created stress.

Tamara was very stressed indeed. She lost her job and that created more stress. All this negative energy was channeled into her body. She was given warnings, signals that something required urgent attention. Her body became mineral and vitamin deficient. It gradually lost its ability to fight foreign pathogens. It started talking to her. It gave her signals that something required urgent attention.

Instead of stopping and taking care of her body she chose to carry on, to pursue the goals of the outside world, the ordinary world.

That's the strategy which most people take. After 10, 20, 40 years of consuming foods loaded with sugar the body will ask for support, resources, supplements. Tamara and many people of her generation ignored the "call to adventure". She ignored the signals. If you read the signals given by your body and do something about it, you will require less time and less money to defeat the monster. Prevention is a great strategy. When prevention fails you attack the monster by detoxing and bringing in more minerals. You go to war with everything you have at your disposal. The war could last 3 months or 3 years. It doesn't last 30 days.

The second stage of the Hero's Journey is a warning that a change is required. Every single person will at one point in his or her life reach the second stage. Most people panic. Others simply ignore it. They are too busy to listen to their own body. It's the wrong strategy.

Signals given by the body should never be ignored. Signals are not the disease, they are a method that the body uses to tell us to change, eliminate and add something new. There is an inner conversation between the body and the person. The body screams and says: please give me micronutrients, cleanse me, take care of me. The body spends years giving signals. They come as inflammation, difficulty in sleeping, allergic reactions, rashes, tiredness. Stomach ache, unexplained weight loss are some of the signals that the body uses to tell us that it is lacking vitality. If a person ignores the signals he or she will be forced to deal with the "disease". Disease comes with pain, stress and accelerated disintegration.

An American historian and archeologist called James P. Allan has spent more than 40 years looking at the foundations of Kmtic civilisations. In his book "*Middle Egyptian*" he wrote the following: "The Ancient Egyptians had very specific ideas about human nature. In order for every human being (including the king) to exist, five different elements were thought to be necessary.

- The body
- The heart
- The shadow
- The ba
- The ka
- The name..."

- Page 99 Middle Egyptian - James P. Allan

The people of the ancient world were in harmony, Maat with their environment. They believed that a person has a body, a heart, a shadow, a soul, a spirit and a name. These were considered the 5 key elements that a person needed in order to be complete. The body is a vessel that holds the heart. The heart is the house of emotions. A spiritual person must have a relationship with his or her soul. If a person is in harmony with his or her soul, he or she will get the signals and will quickly understand that there is a deficiency in body. A person who is in tune with his or her soul will also accept the call to adventure. The call to gradually abandon the ordinary world, its diets, illusions, addictions and destructions.

The second stage is crucial because it makes the person aware that there is a need for a deep personal, intellectual, social and biological transformation. Smokers will start to cough blood, alcoholics will see the color of their skin change to yellow. That's called Jaundice and it is a sign that the liver is not healthy. Women will notice a lump in their breast. Men will struggle to empty their bladder. These are signals which the body uses to tell us, that the powerful and wonderful machine that we call the human organism needs repair. It needs rest, fasting and cleansing. The body will strive to talk to the soul. Many people living in today's world are detached from the spiritual, mythological and biological self. They either miss the signals or worse they ignore them because "I am too busy." A damaged body will struggle to function. Like a very old Ford Mustang, the body, vehicle to new experiences will gradually come a stop.

As soon as they realise that something is wrong with their bodies, many people panic. They allow themselves to be consumed by fear. Fear brings in stress. Stress is one of the major causes of disease. It causes more damage to an already damaged body.

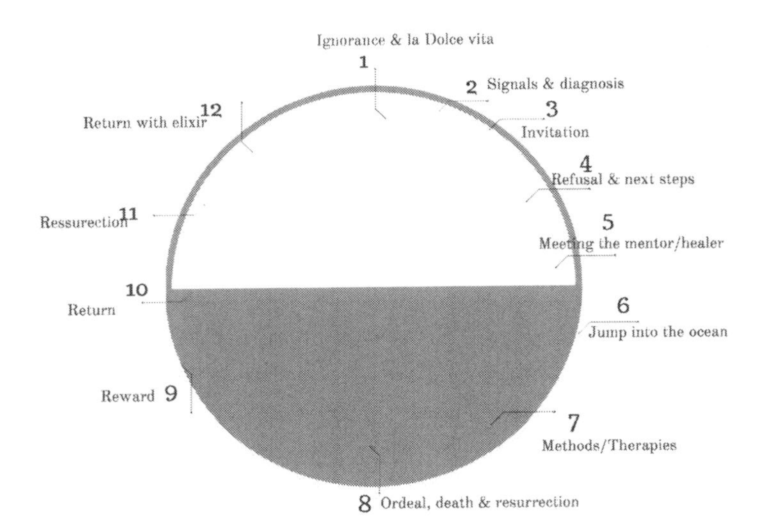
Ignorance & la Dolce vita
1
2 Signals & diagnosis
3
Invitation
4
Refusal & next steps
5
Meeting the mentor/healer
6
Jump into the ocean
7
Methods/Therapies
8 Ordeal, death & resurrection
Reward 9
10
Return
Ressurection 11
Return with elixir 12

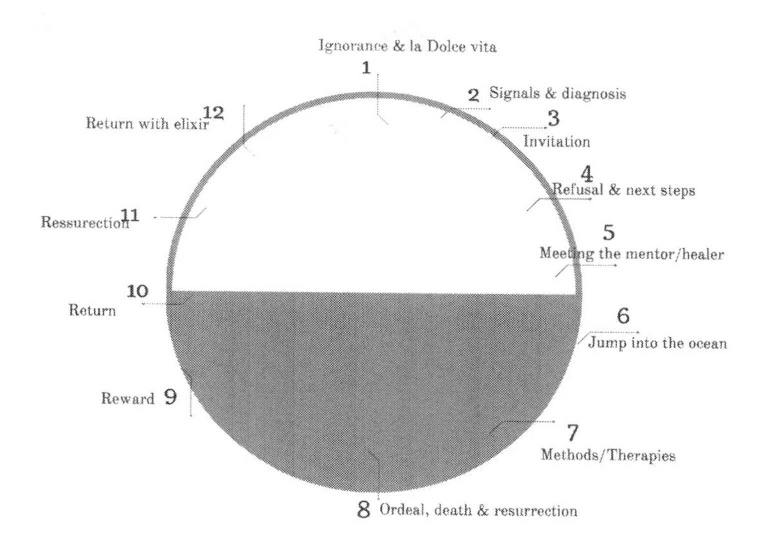
Ignorance & la Dolce vita
1
2 Signals & diagnosis
3
Invitation
4
Refusal & next steps
5
Meeting the mentor/healer
6
Jump into the ocean
7
Methods/Therapies
8 Ordeal, death & resurrection
Reward 9
10
Return
Ressurection 11
Return with elixir 12

Step 3 – Invitation

"I texted my friend of many years and said: You will need to do at least 12 coffee enemas and drink 13 glasses of organic juices every single day for at least 2 years. He texted me back and told me that he could not do 12 enemas a day. I reflected on his answer and concluded that I could not rescue him from the belly of a violent and merciless whale called cancer." - A British healer from York.

Every step is essential. During the first two steps we experience ignorance followed by signals and then a diagnosis. For people and patients who are ignorant about the subject called cancer, the second step of their journey produces fear and stress. There is no need to panic. Step 3 is an invitation. Do you take chemo or natural compounds?

In the third step of our healing journey we receive the invitation. We either get into the belly of the whale and fight, or we are annihilated, destroyed by toxins and free radicals.

We contemplate the journey of a hero who shared his experience with The Truth About Cancer YouTube channel. Lonnell from the U.S. was given the dreaded news more than 10 years ago.

"I was first diagnosed with prostate cancer in the year 2000. (The) first challenge I faced was just accepting the diagnosis. It was given rather abruptly. Matter of factly, and I recall the Urologist saying you've got cancer and he explained 3 possible options. I could have surgery, or chemotherapy, or radiation. He said when would you like to schedule

the surgery? And I said, I need time to process this. I haven't thought about it. I haven't asked God what I should do. So I, I... just give me some time and then I will respond."

Lonnell's invitation was a brutal experience. He was given 3 options: Chemo, radiation or surgery.

They were all conventional and carried severe side effects. He was an experienced man who saw many friends and relatives being ruthlessly destroyed by the big monster. He knew the side effects caused by the 3 options presented to him, therefore he said no to the invitation. As you read this book, millions of men from all over the world who are over 40 years old will get an invitation similar to the one given to Lonnell. A person's life experience as well as spiritual and emotional health plays an essential role in whether he or she accepts the invitation. People who have not done their homework about nutrition and health will incorrectly believe that their options are limited.

Step 3 is the invitation to change, change of diet, ways of living, emotional diet, psychological diet, social diet, intellectual diet. It is a profound transformation. In mythology the seeker who wishes to become a hero is asked to purify him or herself. Almost every person who has seen the side effects of chemotherapy and radiation is tempted to reject the invitation. That was the case of Tamara St. John after her self-diagnosis.

"...Because there was no way, I saw my mother going through chemo and radiation like 30 something years prior when I was like 12 years old. There was no way I was going to do that."

When she was a teenager, Tamara St. John saw her mother being ruthlessly attacked by the big monster. She also saw her mother losing her hair and gradually being eaten alive by the monster. She also saw the side effects caused by the medications that her mother took. It was a traumatic experience that she was keen to avoid. Tamara's experience was a blessing in disguise. Her mother's ordeal was an invitation to learn more about effective natural therapies. The experience broke her heart. It also forced her to take a proactive approach to health, life and longevity.

In 2010 and 2012 I experienced the premature deaths of my parents. I don't want the same to happen to my children and friends, therefore I read books and spend hours researching foods that are excellent for the body and mind. The death of my parents was an invitation that I could not ignore. It was the death of my mother that moved and inspired me to reject the temptations of the ordinary world.

If we look at the signals and diagnosis of both Lonnell and Tamara St. John, two heroes who defeated a monster called cancer, we can see that step 3 has a very strong psychological dimension. Spiritual and emotional health are very important because they influence a patient's decision.

From sceptic to healer and preserver of life

Mildred Nelson is undoubtedly one of the most successful heroes and healers of the modern world. The 3rd step of her journey is very interesting. She was pro-conventional treatments. She did not believe that a big monster such as cancer could be defeated through natural remedies. She was a professional nurse who labelled natural healers

"Quacks". The diagnosis and severity of her mother's cancer forced Mildred to contemplate alternative therapies. She tried to persuade her father to give up the idea of seeing a natural doctor. The sickness of her mother was an invitation for the entire family. As soon as she saw her mother recovering Mildred switched sides. She became a student of the same man she used to despise.

There was a policeman who enjoyed himself arresting Harry Hoxsey. He arrested Harry more than 50 times. One day his brother was attacked by the Minotaur. Both the policeman and his brother went to a Hoxsey clinic. After the policeman's brother was cured something remarkable happened. The policeman became Harry's greatest defender and ally. He became Harry Hoxsey's defence lawyer and did it for free. "Seeing is believing."

A diagnosis is also an invitation for a patient and his or her family to change their beliefs about health and healing. It's not an invitation for one person. Cancer is a collective experience.

Every single hero that has defeated the big monster, Mildred Nelson, Charlotte Gerson, Rene Caisse, Max Gerson, Dr. Sebi, Tamara St. John was invited to change. Max Gerson was invited to change his entire diet and way of thinking. Mr. Gerson went to a Medical School therefore he believed in conventional treatments. He had to renounce his beliefs and education. He had to depart from the ordinary world. A patient that's in pain incorrectly believes that he or she has no time to change. "Give me a pill or an injection and restore my health." When a person is in pain he or she wants a quick solution not a prolonged treatment. Many people want the healing, not the

Hero's Journey. There is problem. The Hero's Journey has 12 steps not 3. The project called "healing my body" is always a long-term goal.

Many people fail to overcome the challenges presented in this step. Please remember that in order to become a hero a person has to overcome trials, challenges, difficulties. Every single patient will be invited to

- Take conventional treatments
- Or go solo and use natural remedies.

There are no exceptions. Old, young, man, woman, single, married, poor, rich, tall, short, all of us will be invited to change our ways. Whether we want or not. The Hero's Journey is a universal experience, it affects every living being. Every year birds have to fly to different continents in order to escape the harshness of winter. They have been doing that for millions of years.

What's the ideal time to accept the invitation?

The ideal time to accept the invitation is before the big monster manifests itself. Before the diagnosis. This is the ideal time to change. Theseus did not meet the Minotaur then get the training. He got the training then met the Minotaur. In the ideal world you should learn how to protect your immune system then strive to heal yourself, a friend, a work colleague or a relative. There is an ancient, universal and eternal sequence. The second stage of the sequence is also the stage of fulfillment. After accepting the invitation you will learn how to fulfill

- What else is there?
- What do I do next?

When a patient reaches stage 4 of the Hero's Journey a formidable opponent emerges. Negative thinking supported by fear. The fear of death paralyses many people.

On 12th August 2018 the Guardian published an article entitled: "Cancer: 1 in 4 patients too scared to seek help over symptom."

Cancer is an invitation. An invitation to get into two different worlds.

- Conventional medicine or alternative medicine.
- Ordinary world or special world.

Many people are not even aware that there is such a thing as alternative medicine. I was not aware of the word naturopathy until I started reading about the subject. One of the most important questions of this stage is what's next?

- I don't want chemo or radiation - What's next? - Step 5
- I will go solo and try to heal myself - What's next? - Step 5
- I will use a natural therapy - Which one? Step 7

Any person who finds him or herself on stage 4 is forced to make a choice. What's the best choice?

The best choice is the Hero's Philosophy. The Hero's Philosophy has two parts;

- 1 The hero, that's the person and then the philosophy. A hero is someone who is prepared to learn, to change, to face and overcome difficulties.
- 2 A philosophy is something that requires learning, patience, time, experimentation. Max Gerson spent more than 30 years refining his philosophy.

A Hero's Philosophy is not an empirical philosophy. It is a practical and performance-oriented philosophy. Many things have to be done. Ideally the right things. Books have to be read because disease and cancer are both biological and highly intellectual subjects. You won't be able to save everybody because there are many people who don't want to either listen or adopt new ideas. Sadly some patients want a quick fix, a 3 month fix for a problem that took 20/30 years to mature. The reward, healing comes on step 9 of the journey not step 3 or step 5.

Step 4 is also the stage of the hermit, the silent, lonely thinker who takes time off to learn as much as possible about the tricks and weaknesses of his or her enemy. Talk to conventional doctors, friends, relatives. Talk also to natural doctors, research as much as possible. Please remember Jim Rohn's advice,

"Whatever you do, make sure it is the product of your own conclusion."

The worst thing you could do is to reject the invitation from both life and your body. Talk to your doctor, ask questions. Contact professionals and ask for advice. Every single philosophy, therapy has its pros and cons. Research is one of your best allies. Some cases require conventional treatments because the "tumor is too big" and must be removed immediately through surgery. Coffee enemas are a great strategy to prevent the development of tumors. Glutathione is a powerful ally that's activated by coffee enemas. Intravenous Vitamin C is also an excellent strategy used to stop the development of tumors.

Refusal in mythology & movies

In mythology and movies, the hero is also given the opportunity to choose. In most stories the hero first rejects the call, then he or she changes his or her mind. The same happens in the real world. Ty Bollinger interviewed a lady who used to sell pharmaceutical drugs. She was not keen to use alternative therapies until she read Ty Bollinger's and Chris Wark's books. In movies we have the scene of Neo in "The Matrix". The hero rejected the invitation to join a team of ambitious individuals. It did not take him long to realise that he had made the wrong choice. Shortly after saying no to the invitation, he saw unfriendly "Men in Black" looking for him. They were assassins.

From Ancient Greece we get the story of Orpheus. Orpheus went to the underworld in order to save his wife Eurydice. The King of the underworld was persuaded by his wife to allow Orpheus to rescue Eurydice. The King of the Dead agreed with one condition. "Go all the way and don't look back." Orpheus agreed. He took his wife and started the return journey to the world of the living. He got out first. Keen to see whether his mentor was telling the truth Orpheus looked back. He violated an essential principle therefore he lost his wife forever. She was one step away from reaching the world of the living. Orpheus' story is essential for anybody who finds him or herself on stage 4. Orpheus violated the agreement which he made with his mentor.

During an interview Charlotte Gerson said "The biggest mistake that people make is to keep switching from one therapy to another."

Stick to one therapy, one method. Research; study then make a decision. The Gerson therapy is very intense. It's not the cheapest either. It is necessary, documented and used in many homes, clinics around the world. Stage 4 is the stage of adoption. At this stage a person will reject a method and adopt a new philosophy. It doesn't matter whether he or she chooses natural or chemical, the patient will be initiated into something. The individual will get into a new culture that has its own rules and special characters.

Two options

- There is the Hero's Philosophy prescribed by people such as Dr. Veronique, Dr. Matthias Rath, Dr. Gonzalez, Dr. Johanna Budwig, Ty Bollinger, Patrick Quillin, Dr. Rashid Buttar, Max Gerson and many others = I am a hero
- There is also the victim's philosophy = This philosophy persuades people to believe that "I am a victim."

In his masterpiece the "Hero With a Thousand Faces" Joseph Campbell warned us about the consequences of saying no to the call.

"Because I have called, and ye refused... I also will laugh at your calamity; I will mock when your fear cometh: when your fear cometh as dissolution, and your destruction cometh as a whirlwind; when distress and anguish cometh upon you... for the turning away of the simple shall slay, and the prosperity of fools shall destroy them."

- p49 "The Hero With a Thousand Faces : Refusal of the call."

Please remember that at this stage you should be proactive. It doesn't matter what philosophy you choose. You will need to detox. You either detox and remove every single toxin in your body or you face the consequences caused by a toxic environment and the refusal to learn the mysteries of the special world.

The power of vitamin C

"Case One: A 51 year old woman with kidney tumours refused conventional treatment and instead, received 65 grams of IVC twice each week... After 10 months of IVC, her tumors were gone and her cancer remained in complete remission for four years." - Page 136 - Tomorrow's Cancer Cures Today - 25 secret therapies from around the world.

If you say "No" to conventional treatment you will need to be very diligent, committed as well as patient. It can take more than 10 years to cleanse your body completely. Intravenous vitamin C is not something you do yourself. You would have to contact a qualified doctor to help you to get high doses of vitamin C into your organism. This philosophy was pioneered by Dr. Linus Pauling and his colleague Dr. Ewan Cameron in 1966. Dr. Matthias Rath is a disciple of Linus Pauling.

Key questions

- Are you prepared to change your diet?
- Are you willing to become a philosopher?
- Which philosophy are you going to use?
- Why are you going to use that philosophy?
- Are you prepared to move to the next stage of your journey?
- What's your plan of action?

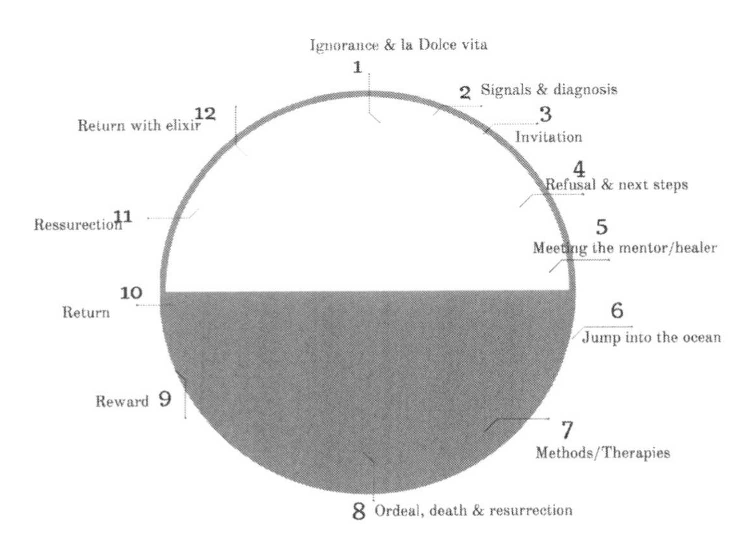

STEP 5 - MEETING THE HEALER/MENTOR

"Mentors are often former Heroes who have survived life's early trials and are now passing on the gift of their knowledge and wisdom."

- p40 - The Writer's Journey by Christopher Vogler

The above statement is vital. It helps us to understand a crucial relationship that should take place in step 5 of the Hero's Journey. In mythology we get the word 'mentor'. In the special world we get the word 'healer', 'medicine man' or 'medicine woman', 'shaman'. In the ordinary world we get the word 'doctor', 'oncologist', 'consultant', 'physician' etc. Professor Ninian Smart's book "*The Religions of Small Societies*" says that:

"One of the most important and central figures of small societies is the Shaman. The word shaman itself comes from Siberia. It signifies a kind of prophet who is prone to have spiritual experiences and visions and who is trained to become a religious leader... The term Medicine man essentially refers to a medicine man among North American and other aboriginal peoples."

We will draw a line and put 3 dots. They will enable us to see the power of having a great mentor.

- Dot number 1 is at the beginning. That's the person who wishes to become a hero. In this book, that's the patient or the person suffering from cancer or any other disease. It could also be a person who wishes to prevent disease.
- The second dot is the mentor. That's the herbalist, medicine man, medicine woman, natural doctor or naturopath. He or she stands in the middle of the line. The mentor is the bridge to the future.
- Third, at the end of the line we have the monster. The monster is standing in front of the future. The monster is the obstacle, the trial which the dreamer must overcome in order to become a hero, a happy, healed and a very healthy person.

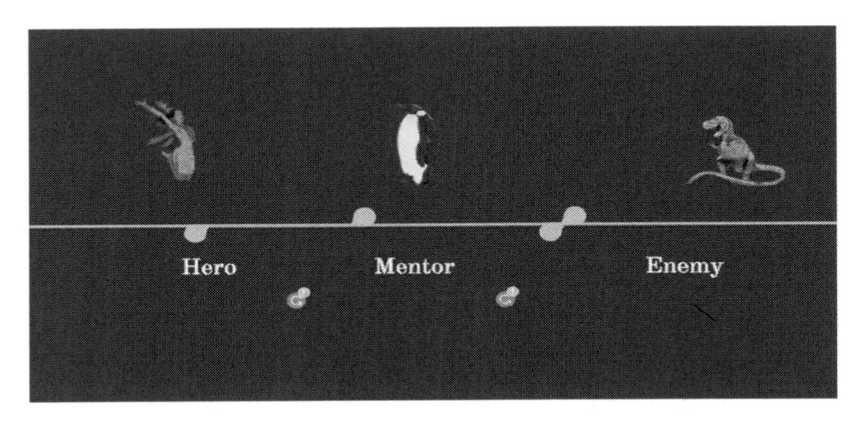

The monster is a barrier, the obstacle to progress. Cancer or disease does not want the hero to reach the desired destination called optimal health or remission.

Please remember that the hero starts his or her journey as a sincere seeker. The first experience is a psychological event that will motivate the patient to pursue success.

The patient, the person who is being attacked by the monster will not make it without the help of a mentor. A mentor could be called a doctor, a healer, a naturopath, a helper, an expert. Although the names and terminology change, the role remains. Step 5 is when the patient who wishes to become a hero is introduced to the mentor. The patient cannot survive the traps inside the labyrinth without the thread, the help, the advice, the wisdom which the mentor spent years accumulating. In Theseus' story for example, the thread of Ariadne was invented by an old man called Daedalus.

The Midas touch

The mentor is crucial because or he or she has the Midas touch.

King Midas was the ruler of a Greek state called Phrygia. He was powerful and popular. He was loved, adored, cherished by his people. King Midas enchanted the heart of God Dionysus, the principle of fertility. The pleased God Dionysus told King Midas that he could ask for whatever he wished and that all of his wishes would be granted. Impressed, the spoiled king told his new patron that, "My desire is to have everything I touch to be turned into gold." The King's wish was granted. Thereafter everything King Midas touched turned into gold. His relatives included.

From the legend of King Midas we get the following expression, "the Midas touch." A mentor, a healer who knows the secrets of herbs, juices, the immune system and minerals, has the Midas touch. Whatever he or she touches turns into health, pure gold. After drinking the tea prescribed by the Indian medicine man from the Ojibwe tribe, the mother of Rene Caisse enjoyed a long life. The mother of Mildred Nelson also enjoyed a long healthy life after "falling into the hands" of a medicine man called Harry Hoxsey. In today's world many dreamers experience complete recovery after using the therapies of Dr. Rashid Buttar.

A modern Midas

Ty Bollinger's series called The Truth About Cancer are a treasure trove for any ambitious human being who is interested in excellence. One of the diamonds of the series is Dr. Rashid Buttar. He is a fine example of a modern Midas. Some of his patients are people who have been told that their cases are terminal and that they "have few months to live". Some of them arrive at his doorstep with badly damaged immune systems. After years of neglect and toxic living the psychological and biological structures of a patient will be seriously damaged. Only a highly experienced philosopher and mentor has the necessary wisdom and the resources needed to restore Maat, balance and harmony in the temple.

Self-initiation

Tina Baird was on her last legs when she read 3 books which initiated her into the special world. Keen to stop the decline and fall of her health, she contacted Dr. Buttar and asked for help.

The Truth About Cancer Episode 6 - YouTube:

Tina Baird - "The beginning of last year I was doing blood tests every six months. And my blood tests came back elevated. And so went in for another bone, CT scan and PET scan this time and found it in my spine, I mean no erm sternum and a spot on my left hip. I did one round of chemo and then at that point, that's where Ty Bollinger and Chris Wark and even Kelly Turner's book "*Radical Remissions*" had just come out. And it was just released and I saw it on the day I went in, for my round and couldn't get the book in time.

So I had that first round of chemo, and came home that day got the book and started reading the book and that's when I stopped chemo. And talking with Chris I asked him who he recommended, if he knew of anybody here in the Charlotte area and he recommended Dr. Buttar. And that's how I got to Dr. Buttar. I think it was God just saying you need to, you need... there's another option for you and so that's when I said ok, stop. I don't care what happens you know, I've got to look at something else, someone else is speaking to me, someone else higher is speaking and I need to listen. I just know I would not be here today. Not at all. I wouldn't have made the 12 rounds. The 12 treatments."

That's the testimonial of a sincere seeker, an initiated lady, and a student who prescribed to the Hero's Philosophy. Her testimonial reveals a very interesting secret. The esoteric number 12, the 12 steps which an initiate has to complete in order to reach the zenith of his or her journey.

If you had the opportunity to speak to Tina Baird and many patients who were initiated by Dr. Buttar they would gladly tell you that he is their hero. "He saved me from premature death". He is a fine example of a hero who defeated the big monster. Dr. Buttar's philosophy took many years to refine. His experience gave him the Midas touch.

Dr. Buttar's philosophy

Dr. Buttar - "Our goal in this 4th step is target acquisition. That we want to acquiesce the target, we want the body to identify the cancer as being foreign because right now the cancer is mimicking a fetus and it's saying hey hey I'm supposed to be here and that's when you see cancer secreting Alpha-fetoproteins... Even though it may be a male, it doesn't matter because it's trying to show the body that I'm ok you don't have to be worried about me, I'm supposed to be here. So we want the body to identify the cancer as being foreign. And the way we do that is through AARSOTA. And that stands for Autogenous, Antigen, Receptor, Specific, Oncogenic, Target, Acquisition.

This 4th step is to acquiesce the target meaning having the body identify the cancer and being able to do what it needs to do, to follow the way that the ultimate engineer designed our bodies. Our bodies were designed to identify cancer. When the body's immune system starts doing what it's supposed to do. But because the immune system first is dysfunctioning, it can't do that so we move on to the 3rd step which is immune modulation. And then with the 4th step now the immune system may be strong and able capable to fight, it doesn't know what it's supposed to fight, who the enemy is. That 4th step AARSOTA is designed to allow the individual's immune system to identify the cancer as being foreign."

Philosophers such as Max Gerson, Charlotte Gerson, Dr. Rashid Buttar, Dr. Veronique Desaulniers, Ty Bollinger are bridges to the special world. The mentor, the teacher, the healer's main goal is to introduce you and your relatives to an exciting, refined and very special world. This mission, task, duty is very ancient. In both mythology and the physical world, the healer strives to teach his or her student how to save themselves from an early death, pain, and misery. The presence of an experienced mentor is enough to trigger "the placebo effect". The placebo effect is essentially mind power applied to sickness. The presence of an experienced and successful healer helps the patient to see the finish line. There is a positive psychological transformation. 100% of the cancer conquerors and heroes who spoke to Ty Bollinger said that his documentaries and the words of "experts" helped them to see that there is another world. A world of endless possibilities. They got the "Placebo effect."

Gilgamesh and the preservers of life

The life of the ancient King of Uruk changed on the day he met Enkidu, the orphan who grew up in the forest and ran with the gazelles.

"He entered the city of Uruk - the - Town - Square, And a crowd gathered around. He came to a halt in the street of Uruk- the -Town - Square, All gathered about, the people discussed him: Enkidu with his foot blocked the door of the wedding house, not allowing Gilgamesh to enter. They seized each other at the door of the wedding house, in the street they joined combat, in the square of the land."

p16 - The Epic of Gilgamesh -
Penguin Classics - Translation by Andrew George

Enkidu was a stranger who was keen to save a woman from being raped by the King of Uruk. Enkidu's behavior shocked Gilgamesh. For the first time in his life, Gilgamesh realised that there was someone

brave enough to challenge him. This person was not only nice, he was prepared to risk his life in order to save others. Enkidu's attitude was an essential lesson. It taught Gilgamesh about morality, and friendship. Enkidu was a citizen from a different world. He brought with him a new culture, a new way of doing things. A new mindset.
That's exactly what happened to Tina Baird. Weeks before she met Dr. Buttar, Tina Baird was exhausted, very depressed and ready to die. Her life changed when she met a mentor who practices the philosophy of the ancients. A natural philosophy that's based on restoration rather than destruction. A mentor is a bringer of a new culture. He or she is the light, a bridge, the red carpet that leads a dreamer to the future.

Please remember that Enkidu was born in the forest. He spent his entire life living with gazelles. He was brought up by animals therefore he spoke their language. He was a deeply spiritual and natural being. He ate plants and drank the waters of clean and calming rivers. He was a pure gentleman, good and precious as gold.

Gilgamesh grew up in the city. He drank beer and ate bread. He delighted himself with meat and the blood of animals, victims of cruel sacrifices. Enkidu was the mentor that taught Gilgamesh how to live in harmony with Mother Nature. Enkidu symbolises the subconscious mind. He is the messenger who came from the forest. Gilgamesh is the ego, the spoiled person who believes that "I am entitled to the cure". Enkidu was both the mentor and the healer. When he died, Gilgamesh grieved for the first time in his life. That was a sign of a profound psychological transformation.

- Enkidu came from the forest - Special world
- Gilgamesh lived in the city - Ordinary world

A close look at the epic of Gilgamesh reveals an important detail. Enkidu was not only a nice gentleman, he was also a vegetarian. He lived in perfect harmony with animals, plants, clouds, rivers and natural landscapes. Enkidu was in harmony with himself therefore, he did not have the terrible habit of eating meat. Enkidu's arrival in the city of Uruk represented the death of Gilgamesh's old self. He was sacrificed in order to make Gilgamesh aware that he was on the wrong path. In the end, Gilgamesh became one of the greatest mentors of the ancient world. The Epic of Gilgamesh is one of the most profound and beautiful poems of the ancient world. It used to be recited in the houses of aristocrats, nobles, foreign merchants, kings and queens. At first sight the Epic of Gilgamesh has nothing to do with cancer or disease. If we look deeper we will realise that Gilgamesh's mentor first cured him psychologically and then biologically. Gilgamesh's thinking symbolises a disease. He was saved by his mentors "the conductors of souls."

Gilgamesh was blinded by his ego therefore he was unable see the destruction caused by his mentality. He needed more than 1 mentor in order to change his ways. Without a mentor an ambition seeker will fail to grasp the irresistible and immeasurable meaning of the essential and very seductive Universe called "the special world". A mentor is a magnificent lighthouse. He or she is a vehicle, a glimpse of the endless and eternal vitality that exists in the special world. The very ancient, mysterious and mystical world of Maat.

Meeting Dr. Rashid Buttar resulted in a profound physical and psychological transformation, a metamorphosis that saved Tina Baird from complete disintegration. Meeting her mentor was Tina Baird's beginning of her body's regeneration. The resurrection principle, step 11 of the Hero's Journey, was activated as soon as she spoke to her mentor. Lucky are the seekers who grasp this ancient principle called mentor.

The meeting between mentor and student, patient and healer is also the reunion of two worlds. The ordinary and the special world. The mentor lives in the special world, his or her student lives in the ordinary world. The mentor rescues the sincere seeker from the world of artificial, foods philosophies, promises and remedies.

- Gilgamesh = Ordinary world
- Enkidu = Special world
- Tina Baird = Ordinary world
- Dr. Rashid Buttar = Special world

Key questions

- Who are you in your journey?
- Are you Gilgamesh or Enkidu?
- Do you eat animals or plants?
- Do you drink beer or alkaline water?
- Do you have a mentor?
- What kind of mentor do you have?
- What's the influence of your mentor in your life?
- What kind of subjects does your mentor explore?
- What kind of books does your mentor recommend?
- Do you have a one-to-one relationship with your mentor?
- What did your mentor achieve in life?

- What makes your mentor the ideal role model?
- Is your mentor an expert on health matters?
- What are you mentor's family values?

Key references for mentors and authors:

- Allan Spreen
- Charlotte Gerson
- Mildred Nelson
- Linus Pauling
- Dr. Matthias Rath
- Dr. Nicholas Gonzalez
- Dr. Rashid Buttar
- Dr. Sebi
- Dr. Veronique Desaulniers
- Rachael Linkie
- Rene Caisse
- Russell Blaylock
- Joseph Campbell
- Johanna Budwig
- Queen Afua
- Leigh Erin Connealy
- Patrick Quillin
- Russell L. Blaylock, Md
- Thomas Seyfried

Step 6 - Jumping into the ocean

"Gilgamesh, on landing, had to listen to the patriarch's long recitation of the story of the deluge. Then Utnapishtim bid his visitor sleep, and he slept for six days. Utnapishtim had his wife bake seven loaves and place them by the head of Gilgamesh as he lay asleep beside the boat. And Utnapishtim touched Gilgamesh, and he awoke, and the host ordered the ferryman Ursanapi to give the guest a bath in a certain pool and then fresh garments. Following that, Utnapishtim announced to Gilgamesh the secret of the plant: "Gilgamesh, something secret I will disclose to thee, and give thee shine thine instructions: That plant is like a brier in the field; its bottom, like that of the rose, will pierce thy hand. But if thy hand attain to that plant, Thou wilt return to thy native land."

- p159 The Hero with a Thousand Faces - Joseph Campbell.

The journey of Gilgamesh reveals a beautiful mystery. The second line says; "then Utnapishtim bid his visitor sleep, and he slept for six days." Number 6 is half of 12, the circle of influence, the Hero's Journey, the ocean that contains the essential mysteries. On step 6 the patient and initiated man or woman jumps into the ocean, the special world, the world of ancient mysteries, the school, the temple, the clinic of the ancestors.

On his quest for longevity and immortality Gilgamesh met a ferryman called Ursanapi. It was Ursanapi who introduced Gilgamesh to the couple that survived the ordeal known as the "great deluge."

After realising that conventional treatment was not working, Tina Baird contacted Chris Wark a man who cured himself of cancer and asked him to lead her to the right mentor. Chris Wark played the role of the ferryman, who ferried the sincere seeker to the healthier side of the river.

Gilgamesh was introduced to Utnapishtim by Ursanapi, a ferryman. The ferryman or ferrywoman of our age is someone who knows a healer, a philosophy, a therapy. The consultant, oncologist is a ferryman, ferrywoman to the very toxic world of drugs. Ty Bollinger is a ferryman. A ferryman or ferry woman has the potential to become a healer of souls. After reaching stage 6 of his or her quest the seeker who wishes to become a hero will be initiated.

On stage 5 the student is given psychological trials by his or her mentor. The trials were meant to prepare the individual for a very profound experience. The trials are tools, means of initiation. They are a method which the mentor and healer uses to educate his or her patient. Commands such as "stop eating cooked foods, detox, take such and such supplement, stop watching TV, drink such and such juice" are examples of trials. If the patient refuses to complete a trial "because I can't" he or she will fail on his quest to retrieve the lost vitality.

Theseus the slayer of the Minotaur was asked to move a rock that was in the pine forest. After moving the rock he was told to go to Athens. As soon as he arrived in Athens his step mother Medea, ordered him to go and cleanse his body and hands in the river Kephisos in order to purify himself.

After completing the first stage of the psychological and emotional initiation, the once very sick, depressed but resolute sincere seeker will voluntarily present him or herself as student of a mentor who has mastered modern and ancient secrets, that have the power to restore balance in a decaying body. Stage 6 is the point of no return. It symbolises a complete separation from the ordinary world. Nothing will be the same again after the hero jumps into this ocean.

"Meaning once you have crossed that line you have to live your life a certain way."

Dr.Rashid Buttar - The Truth About Cancer

The patient who is given doses of chemo or radiation will never be the same again. The sincere seeker who goes to a Gerson Clinic will think and live differently. A Gerson Clinic is a special world. Citizens of the ordinary world are appalled by the idea of "putting coffee up your bum." The same people are more than happy to eat the flesh of dead and tortured animals. They are also pleased to eat the children of drugged cows, pigs and eggs of suffering chickens. Cleansing is essential. It doesn't matter what kind of sickness you wish to prevent or remove, it is impossible to heal the body without cleansing. The sincere seeker who is keen to save his or her life gladly accepts the call to adventure, the invitation to jump into a world that believes in the power of Mother Nature. That's exactly what Betsy Dix and her husband did. The suffering and stressed couple initiated themselves by listening to Ty Bollinger, the ferryman whose parent's death forced him to jump into the ocean.

We don't jump into the ocean because we want to. Life forces us to jump. Wsr the husband of Aset and oldest son of Nut and Geb was locked into a beautifully decorated chest and thrown into the river, Hapi Itrw. The intelligent human being is the one who takes the

The Canadian hero Rene Caisse, spent many years swimming in an ocean called "conventional medicine." One day her mother was diagnosed with liver cancer. Doctors from the conventional world told Rene Caisse that her mother could not be cured. She spoke to the doctors and asked them if she could try a tea which a Native Indian medicine man gave to one of her former patients. The doctors agreed and the rest is history. The remedy from the Native American Indian man came from a 'foreign ocean', an organic culture that believes in the power of the great Mother such as Sedna. In Ireland she was known as Brigid. The mother of Brigid was called Dana. Both mother and daughter were principles of fertility.

A living being attacked by a disease will be given two options:. Remain in the ordinary world or jump into the special world, the ocean.

Modern or ancient - Natural world or chemical world

The horse of the grandfather of Harry Hoxsey was a very lucky being. After it was struck by cancer, its owner allowed it to wonder in the wild. It was allowed to remain in the natural world where it ate healing herbs that impressed its owner. The herbs later became an integral part of the Hoxsey's tonic. Methods such as chemo, radiation, surgery belong to a specific type of ocean. The Gerson therapy, Essiac, detox, supplementation, oxygen therapy belong to a different ocean. There are many types of oceans. Which one is ideal for you? The best answer to the question is initiation, re-education and training.

New oceans in education

Ambitious parents who wish to help their children to succeed financially, biologically, socially, intellectually and psychologically use a very effective strategy. They send their child or children to a private school, a private academy that has the necessary resources to help a child to develop, socialise with children from wealthy families that will become leaders of powerful organisations. In England private schools such as Eton and Harrow are oceans that almost guarantee a successful financial and professional future to its students and customers, usually wealthy parents, aristocrats who wish to place their little ones in the "pole position of the social order." Oxford University is a fine example of a very old and rich ocean that produces an almost endless list of influential minds, thinkers, economists, journalists, politicians, researchers and authors.

New oceans in sports

Barcelona FC is one of the most famous and successful football clubs in the world. Barcelona FC has a school called "La Masia". La Masia is a factory of talent. It is more than a school. It is an ocean that has a unique philosophy that enables ambitious youths to prosper. It doesn't matter what type of quest or purpose a person is pursuing, the ambitious seeker cannot prosper without a refined philosophy and strong intellectual foundations. Such assets are usually found inside private oceans or industries.

Healing the body and the soul

In order to find the secret of immortality, the Sumerian hero Gilgamesh was asked to jump into a bottomless sea. Bottomless means that there are many possibilities, many options. In today's world people use the word therapies.

The Hero with a Thousand Faces, Joseph Campbell - p159

"Ursanapi ferried the hero out again into the waters. Gilgamesh tied stones to his feet and plunged. Down he rushed, beyond every bound of endurance, while the ferryman in the boat. And when the diver had reached the bottom of the bottomless sea, he plucked the plant, thought it mutilated his hand, cut off the stones and made again for the surface. When he broke the surface and ferryman had hauled him back into the boat, he announced in triumph:

Ursanapi this plant is the one...
By which Man can attain to full vigor.
I will bring it back to Erech of the sheep pens ...
Its name is " In his age, Man becomes young again."
I will eat of it and return to the condition of my youth"

Gilgamesh, the King of Uruk, Son of Ninsun and Lugalbanda and older brother of Enkidu was not the last hero to delight the hearts and ears of his audience.

Betsy Dix's triumphant announcement

"We're doing some of those tests as we speak and all of parameters, my blood work of a healthy 30 something year old. So this is really great news. My energy, my colour, all of those things, my liver my kidneys are all functioning at 100% and like a healthy individual would be. And so we're very grateful that the cancer markers are so very low."

The Penguin Philosophy

Our school teaches a philosophy called the penguin philosophy. To help students understand this philosophy we start our sessions by telling the story of two ambitious human beings who jumped into an ocean. They wanted to become successful entrepreneurs therefore they resigned from their Monday to Friday jobs and jumped into new waters. A new ocean.

The river contains 3 types of characters;

1. The Dreamer - who wishes to realise a dream.
2. The Dinosaur - who wishes to beat the competition. They survive but don't thrive.
3. The Penguin - individuals who embrace evolution. They thrive.

Dreamers are people who wish to accomplish a goal. They have a quest, a desire, therefore, they jump into an ocean. They sacrifice short-term security and pleasures in order to enjoy a wonderful future. The second group of people are Dinosaurs. Dinosaurs are ex-dreamers who rejected the idea of evolution. They jumped into the ocean and embraced a competitive philosophy rather than a creative philosophy. They evolved and became Dinosaurs. Dinosaurs spend their lives struggling to survive. They waste their energy and resources trying to beat the competition. They reject evolution and new ideas. They use orthodox ideas only, a thinking that leads them to extinction, premature death and final departure from their village, home, city and family.

Before jumping into an ocean, dinosaurs were excited dreamers. They were full of enthusiasm. They had dreams and visions of prosperity. A few weeks, sometimes months after touching the waters of the new industry, a new ocean, dreamers experienced a transformation. They became dinosaurs. They became negative and pessimistic. Dinosaurs are doomed to extinction. They are intellectually, psychologically and biologically stuck. They are prisoners of their egos and ignorance. Although they're physically strong they will become victims of time and seasons.

The third group of people are Penguins. They are dreamers who embraced evolution and learning. They evolved and became penguins. They are individuals who thrive. Penguins live outside the ocean. They succeed by creating rather than competing and consuming. After saying yes to evolution, they mastered the process of change and growth. They became the masters of the two worlds and architects of wonderful things.

A person attacked by the monster called disease will go through a similar journey. He or she will be asked to choose between remaining a dinosaur or becoming a Penguin. Spending 2 year eating raw organic foods and doing coffee enemas are some of the strategies used by Penguins. Dinosaurs will keep eating sugar and smoking as if nothing took place. They will eventually become extinct because their biology is weakened by toxins and free radicals. An excellent questions would be. How do I become a penguin?

You don't just become a penguin. You must jump into the river, an ocean and learn the mysteries. Like Gilgamesh you should have "a bath" in order to purify your mind and body. In ordinary terms the bath is called detox. That's a short introduction to the Penguin philosophy. The penguin philosophy can be applied to many areas of a person's life. The Penguin philosophy is fully explained in the book

"The Penguin Entrepreneur." Our goal is to publish the book in January 2019.

It doesn't matter what kind of biological challenge you are facing. In order to heal your mind and body you will need to "take the plunge" and immerse yourself into a new ocean. An experienced healer of bodies and souls has his or her ocean. For example, Linus Pauling used high doses of vitamin C to restore a damaged immune system. Dr. Buttar, Dr. Matthias Rath, Charlotte Gerson, have their own clinics. The clinic is an ocean that contains essential tools and remedies.

Step 7 - The method, the philosophy

"I have been treating cancer patients with nutritional supplementation for the past thirty years and have never seen a single case of tumour-growth acceleration or interference with conventional treatments." - Natural Strategies for Cancer Patients by Russell L. Blaylock, M.D.

The heroes of the ancient and modern world used specific methods to defeat a big monster. Aset the African Queen and mother of the hero, used herbs to heal her husband. Gilgamesh used the Tree of Life to heal his anxiety about life and death. Theseus used a sword to kill the Minotaur. If the monster that you are battling is called disease you will also need a method, a way to defend yourself, a friend or a relative.

Below are some of the most successful methods used by heroes that defeated the big monster. The majority of the methods can be found in the wonderful book called "*Tomorrow's Cancer and Cures Today -25 secret therapies from around the world.*" The book was written by Allan Spreen a scientist, author and researcher.

The method, philosophy and therapy

The method is essentially a philosophy, a way and a weapon which the ambitious man or woman will use to fight the monster called cancer or any other disease. An example of a method or philosophy are IV Intravenous injections of vitamin C. They are a very powerful method to fight cancer. Dr. Allan Spreen, wrote the following:

"Only markedly higher doses of vitamin C will selectively build up as peroxide in the cancer cells to the point of killing them, and these tumor - toxic dosages can only be obtained by intravenous administration."

Every hero uses a method, a therapy, a philosophy to fight and overcome challenges. The adopted method will eventually become a way of life. You can't and shouldn't spend the rest of your life using chemo. You could however spend the rest of your life using the Gerson therapy, IV vitamin C, Rene Caisse or any of the methods listed below. The idea of not eating meat is not something that you do for 12 months only. Abstinence from animal protein should be something you do for the rest of your life.

Contrary to popular opinion there are more than 30 different methods, ways which you can use to fight or prevent the arrival of the big monster. The best time to learn is always before diagnosis. That's step 2 of the diagram. We love the word prevention.

The more educated and informed you are about natural healing and the Hero's Philosophy the happier your future will be. Please remember that a cancer diagnosis causes high-level stress and fear. Cancer is also an economic strategy. You could be forced to spend £100.000 or more during the first 12 months of a natural therapy. If they are not consumed, acquired, gradually organic foods, juicers, essential supplements and books could eventually become an expensive enterprise. They are vital and cannot be avoided. Start small, that's the secret. Start with one supplement then develop your discipline.

The best strategies are prevention and a proactive approach. You could prevent the prosperity of the big monster by learning about the subject and using some of the effective methods such as daily consumption of Curcumin, Essiac tea, Zinc etc.

"The influence of a vital person vitalises you" - Joseph Campbell

In the summer of 2016 I met a mentor whose thinking changed my life. I was on a 2 years startup entrepreneurial journey. I was struggling to make ends meet therefore I started searching for an effective philosophy that would enable me to increase my sales. I was running a small 1 man's business that provided film production services. Keen to find a solution to my predicament, I went online and searched for great books for entrepreneurs. I discovered a book called "*Entrepreneur Revolution*". The book was written in 2013 by a London based mentor and successful entrepreneur called Daniel Priestley. I read the book and listened to the audio version. I was very impressed indeed. The book contains a powerful yet very easy to understand philosophy. It advises ambitious individuals to strive to become a "key person of influence" by creating "high quality intellectual property." The philosophy is very powerful. I was attracted to it.

It made me stop, reflect and then change my entire paradigm. I initiated myself into his philosophy by reading and listening to his book several times. I took the plunge and immersed myself into the book and Daniel Priestley's ocean. I embraced every single idea prescribed by the author. I contacted Daniel Priestley and thanked him for his kindness and wisdom. He invited me to attend one of his conferences. I gladly attended the conference. I met the healer and his team. I also met fellow travellers, dreamers who were seeking, refined ideas and experiences. The healer of minds, the Australian Shaman is a very charismatic and kind teacher. He gave me a book called "*Become a Key Person of Influence*". I was very grateful. The key person of influence contains details of his philosophy. They are;

- Pitch
- Publish
- Product
- Profile
- Partnership

This is the method, the philosophy which Daniel Priestley prescribes. It inspired me to become a writer. It forced me to stop doing business the "old way". It changed my paradigm and helped me to become a better person. It saved me from financial poverty.

Central to Daniel Priestley's philosophy is the idea that you "must create intellectual property by becoming a writer." This is the method taught by his schools. It doesn't matter what a person aims to achieve in life. The ambitious and organised dreamer needs a method. A philosophy. That's step 7 of the Hero's Journey. Every successful healer and mentor has a philosophy that took years to develop and refine.

In 2016 I had serious financial problems that needed an urgent and long-term solution. There are many mentors that provide life coaching services. Daniel Priestley introduced me to a strategy that has the power to solve my problems not just in the short but also in the long-term.

The idea of becoming a writer is very challenging. It requires a complete change of both habits and thinking. It took me 3 years to implement the philosophy. The same thinking applies to healing. It's not a 7 days task. The dreamers who wish to become heroes will have to develop many habits and remain loyal to a specific philosophy. Dr. Rashid Buttar has a powerful philosophy which he uses to help people to become heroes. He is also a prolific author.

Let's look at some of the methods used by successful healers and conductor of souls, bodies and minds. Please remember that there are millions of healers around the world. We find them in India, Africa, Asia, Europe, Australia, China etc. It is impossible to name all of them in this book. The best way to learn more about a specific philosophy, therapy and method is by contacting the creators of that therapy. Example; you should take the plunge into the Dr Rath foundation, the Gerson Institute. You could contact them and ask smart questions.

Method 1 - The Matthias Rath foundation - Dr. Aleksandra Niedzwiecki, Ph.D.

"During the course of our research we came to the conclusion that there can be two sets of micronutrients that show documented efficacy against cancer, we call it synergie 1 which contains multiple nutrients that contains vitamins, amino acids, trace elements and plant extracts that have been shown to be effective against a variety of cancer types.

Synergy I Multiple Nutrients:

- Vitamin C
- Lysine

- Proline
- EGCG
- Quercetin
- N-acetyl cysteine
- Vitamin B6
- Selenium
- Copper
- Manganese

Another synergie compound that contains only selected plant extracts, such as;
Synergy II:

- Curcumin
- EGCG
- Quercetin
- Resveratrol
- Cruciferous extracts

They are two sets of micronutrients that showed this very potent anti-cancer efficacy."

For more details please contact Dr. Rath Research Institute -
The above lecture is called "Webinar on natural control of cancer featuring Dr. Aleksandra Niedzwiecki: World Cancer Day 2016."

Method 2 - Dr. Rashid Buttar

Dr. Rashid Buttar - "We have a 5 step program which has been evolving since 1997. But the 5 steps I'll outline. The first is systemic detoxification. You have to clean up the body. If you don't detoxify the body then there are too many things in the way for the body to function correctly and most of these toxicities are causing a detrimental effect on the body that increase oxidative stress etc and etc. So what we know as poisons, there's different mechanisms of how these poisons affect the body. You're probably familiar with, I know you're familiar with the 7 Toxicities, my whole philosophy. That I have all the different toxicities and it goes from heavy metals... the 4th one is energetics like electromagnetic radiation, microwave energies this that and the other. And cell phone radiation a big one. The 5th one is the most important in my opinion and that's emotional psychological toxicity. The 6th one is foods. Not what we're consuming because that falls into the 1st and 2nd... but the 6th one is foods, what we do to the foods. Which I know is near and dear to your heart. The radiation, the homogenisation, the pasteurisation, the genetic modification of foods. All these things we do to food and change the basic modular structure of these that we take into our body to sustain ourselves. These are severely, severely, detrimental to the body. And then 7th toxicity is spiritual. So these toxicities that I'm talking about that's the first step, we deal with all those things."

In the 6th episode of "The Truth About Cancer" Ty Bollinger shared the core philosophy of Dr. Buttar.

- Ty Bollinger - "Dr. Buttar shares with us his 5 step protocol for treating disease.
- The first step is detoxification.
- The next step, step number two is physiological optimisation.
- Step number 3 is immune modulation.
- Step number 4 is target acquisition.
- Step number 5 which he says is probably the most difficult is maintenance.

Now step number 4 is target acquisition. Dr. Buttar uses a vaccine that's called AARSOTA. It's a completely non-toxic vaccine." - Ty Bollinger

We examine the words of an experienced philosopher. He said "The 5th one is the most important in my opinion and that's emotional psychological toxicity."

Many people will wonder why the Hero's Philosophy contains mythology. If understood and applied correctly mythology has the power to heal a toxic psyche. I am pleased to say that I have not watched TV for 20 years. I feel healthy, psychologically, intellectually, emotionally, socially and biologically. The subject that we call disease is very detrimental to the psyche. A sick person will gradually develop a negative personality that's addicted to negative ideas, fear and in most cases depression. A diagnosis turns many positive people into depressed and sometimes manipulative individuals. It is extremely difficulty to heal a damaged body while ignoring a toxic psyche.

The Kemites, builders of the world's oldest and richest empire said, "As above so below". The mind and the body should be healthy and in perfect harmony.

We embrace the teachings which say that the ordinary world is unhealthy. We cannot escape the influence of the ordinary world. The ordinary world is also an integral section of the special world. That's one of the reasons why every hero returns to the ordinary world after completing the Hero's Journey. The successful patient, the hero will become the master of the two worlds. That means he or she will be able to say no to bread, processed sugar, pasta, rice, hamburgers, cheesecakes, beer, wine and many other sources of disease destruction and decay.

Method 3 - Dr. Veronique Desaulniers

"Trigger number 4 - Emotional wounds. Although the complex relationship between psychology and physiology is not clearly understood scientists are well aware that a psychological stress affects the immune system... Start your day with a glass of clean water with a juice of one lemon powdered vitamin C and powdered magnesium..."

- Heal Breast Cancer Naturally

One of the most refined heroes of her generation is a very inspirational mentor called Dr. Veronique Desaulniers. In her book "*Heal Breast Cancer Naturally*" she prescribes 7 essential steps to prevent and heal breast cancer.

The 7 steps prescribed by Dr. Veronique are:

- "Essential number one is, let food be your medicine.
- Number two is detox. To reduce your toxic exposure.
- Essential number three is to balance your energy.
- Essential number four is to heal your emotional wounds.
- Essential number five is to look at biological dentistry because your teeth have a huge impact on your health.
- Essential number six herbs and supplements and vitamins boost your immune system.
- Number seven in really practicing true prevention."

Extracted "From The Truth About Cancer - A Global Quest Episode 2":

"So one of the reasons I'm doing the work that I'm doing is because there's so much information out there, where does a person start? Because you know, do I detox first? Do I do this? Do I do that? What herbs do I take? So I developed a program. It's a seven step program called "The Seven Essentials." And it's so simple that anybody can apply it.

1. So the first one, essential number one is, Let Food Be Your Medicine. We know that food has a huge impact on our genetic expression. We know that it can literally turn on specific cancer-protective genes, we know that through the science of epigenetics and nutrigenomics.

2. Number two is to detox. To reduce your toxic exposure. We live in a toxic world, we can't deny that, but there are things that you can do specifically to help support the detoxification pathways in your body and to prevent all the toxins from entering into your body.

3. Essential number three is to balance your energy. You know we're energetic beings, and so what can you do to keep that electricity and that energy flowing properly? Chiropractic care, acupuncture, exercise, proper sleep, making sure that your hormones are balanced, because hormones are very key in so many hormone-driven cancers.

4. Essential number four is to heal your emotional wounds. You know, learn to nurture yourself and to love yourself, to forgive yourself and others. Manage your stress better, you know, let go of the past, because if you, keep stuffing those emotions inside, you know you're are going

to grow a tumor. You either grow your life or you grow a tumor. You know, so you have to change that emotional component.

5. Essential number five is to look at biological dentistry because your teeth have a huge impact on your health. You are connected, your teeth are connected to your organs through your meridian system. What you have in your teeth affects your health, because if you have toxic amalgams in there it's causing toxicity in your body.

6. And then we look at essential number six which is, you know, there's specific herbs and supplements and vitamins that can really reduce your toxic load, that can help heal the cancer, actually kill cancer cells, and boost your immune system.

7. Ok and lastly, is essential number seven in really practicing true prevention. Traditional medicine, unfortunately, does not really teach prevention and does not know about prevention.

There are many ways and different technologies that can detect cancer when it's at, you know, the size of a pinhead instead of waiting until it's the size of a lump or a bump that you can detect on an X-ray or on a mammogram. Thermography for example can read the physiological changes that are going on in the body. There are specific blood tests like the cancer profile which measures the HCG hormones, and the PHI which is a malignancy hormone, TK1 enzyme, the ONCOblot test which can also determine cancer when it's just the size of a pinhead in the body. That's true prevention. And so if you can stay on top of your health by monitoring and not just guessing about your health, but making sure that you're moving in the right direction, there is no reason to fear cancer."

Method 4 - The Gerson therapy

Two years ago I discovered the story of Max Gerson. I bought his book and read it. I also bought Charlotte Gerson's book and read it. I started to apply some of the elements of their therapy. I can personally say that coffee enemas and daily supplementation combined with juicing saved my life. I am a great fan of coffee enemas. I spent 1 year doing daily enemas, juicing, taking supplements, reading and listening to experts.

Coffee Enema and cleansing

A great strategy to cleanse your colon and liver. I use the Gerson therapy as a prevention strategy. Like many other therapies the Gerson philosophy is ideal for both treatment and prevention. This therapy is ideal because you can do it yourself and in your own home. The book "*The Gerson Therapy*" by Charlotte Gerson is an essential read for anybody who is interested in the Gerson's philosophy and natural therapies.

In the Gerson therapy the liver is the most sacred organ. It is given 100% attention every day for 2 consecutive years.

The book "*The Gerson Therapy*" written by Charlotte Gerson says the following:

"As we added, Dr. Gerson included such procedures as medicine like nutritional supplementation and liver detoxification...

Seriously ill patients usually spend a minimum of three weeks at the Gerson hospital before returning home. If a patient is not in an advanced pathological condition, two weeks at the hospital may be satisfactory and sufficient. Still, in order to fully restore the body, the patient must continue the strict therapy for a suggested minimum of two years." - p376

Page 379 of *The Gerson Therapy* says: "Recommended Juicers... The most popular juicing devices among Gerson patients is the Nowalk Model 270 Ultimate juicer manufactured by Nowalk Sales & Services."

Programs from personal experience

The Truth About Cancer YouTube channel tells a wonderful story. The journey of a hero who healed himself from prostate cancer. Below are some of the methods that he used.

18 years ago Lonnell was given what most people consider the dreaded news. It was in fact an invitation to change and jump into a new ocean. When he reached step 2 of the Hero's Journey, Lonnell was told that he had prostate cancer. According to conventional doctors prostate cancer is one of the most difficult monsters to fight. Many men who suffer from the cancer of the prostate are given radiation seeds. The treatment has long-term side effects. Difficulty to urinate and impotence are some of them. On stage 3 of his journey, Lonnell was invited to choose between radiation, chemo or surgery. Lonnell was at peace with himself. He was psychologically healthy therefore he knew he had to take time off to meditate and reflect. Being a spiritual person he was able to connect with a higher order, a higher voice, his intuition, his Christian God and father.

"...I knew that it was toxic and had a severe effect on the body, and so I knew that this was not something that I would choose to do."

After rejecting the invitation to use conventional methods Lonnell moved to step number 5. He refused to be a victim. Instead he chose to be a student. He initiated himself into the special world by watching "The Truth about Cancer" documentaries. He remained calm and studied the subject carefully. His research gave him clues regarding the best path to follow.

"A strategy that God gave to me was threefold, and it centred around 3 verbs that I employ.

- It was to watch,
- Fight
- And pray.

And then much later I learned that this was a holistic approach. In that I watched, I watched what I ate, I watched what I thought, I watched what I spoke. And so, you know, it was dealing with the physical body so that's part of it but then there were other factors that contributed. And that is in terms of fight. And that dealt with the emotional aspects of the soul. The mind, the will and the emotions. And so there's this great mental fight that you go through. I think of it as the fight of my life and actually I was fighting for my life. And a lot of that was mental and overcoming factors, overcoming negative emotions. One of which was fear. Overcoming that and so that was part of the strategy. And then the other part was the spiritual aspect which involved prayer and reading of the scriptures and looking to the scriptures to find specific principles that I could apply in my particular situation. So it was holistic in terms of body, soul and spirit..."

Lonnell used a holistic method to defeat the monster. He eliminated conventional foods from his diet and added new ones. He then got into detoxing, juicing, fasting, supplementation and raw foods. Raw foods was a great strategy. One that's used by the majority of heroes who succeeded in defeating the Minotaur. He realised that the monster requires sugar in order to thrive and by stopping eating foods that contain sugar he succeeded in starving cancer cells. He did not take medication in order to avoid toxins. He searched for biological, spiritual, psychological and intellectual balance. Lonnell used "The DVD's and documentaries the Truth About Cancer" lectures as a school, a manual of self-initiation, the temple, the house of sacred mysteries. The excellent and lifesaving work of Ty Bollinger, his family and friends enabled Lonnell to initiate himself and jump into a very rich ocean. The Truth About Cancer is more than a YouTube channel. It is a temple in which anybody who wishes to defeat the monster can have sessions of initiation and learn what others did in order to save themselves.

In Ancient Africa believers used to go to a temple. In Ancient Greece people went to a place called "the Oracle of Delphi". The word Delphi means "womb". The Oracle symbolised the mother goddess. "The Ocean that contained everything that was to come."

Many people living in today's world use platforms such as YouTube and Amazon, to initiate themselves and discover essential mysteries about life and health. Please remember that there is a universal sequence. Departure, Initiation, (fulfillment) and Return.

Lonnell's stage 5, meeting the mentor was very rich. This is what he said about his mentors and initiation:

"I was doing well and then I heard about The Truth About Cancer and it was an incredible blessing to me. Opened up a world of other possibilities whereby there could be different approaches to treating it and so I think of The Truth About Cancer as a kind of lighthouse. You're in this stormy sea and you know, dangerous waters, and there's this lighthouse that shines, that provides incredible resources and makes you aware of other possibilities. So it's informative, it's educational and it is an incredible resource. And so I appreciated that but in addition to that it is not only educational but it is also inspirational in that it brings you in contact with people who have tried other possibilities and who've been successful in overcoming that. And so those are the two aspects that have particularly meaningful to me, is that it has been a source of education as well as a source of inspiration for me."

Lonnell had a quest. He wanted to defeat the big monster. To achieve his goal he took strategic actions.

"...One of the things I did, was I eliminated red meat from my diet and dairy products and I increased raw foods, green vegetables, especially phosphorus vegetables, broccoli, cauliflower, green vegetables. In addition I also took a supplement called Chlorella, which is a green supplement. And that would be avoiding fat foods. Another nutritional as well as a product that has anti-cancer fighting substances in Kombucha. Kombucha which is a tea that's rich in probiotics. And I learned to make it so I would have my own home brew."

Five key steps that helped Lonnell to win the greatest fight of his life.

1. A liquid - herbal tea (Kombucha) - the elixir
2. A Diet change - elimination of red meat and dairy products - introduction of raw foods
3. Herbs
4. Spiritual & biological balance - gratitude and at peace with the self
5. Supplementation - Chlorella

To learn more about Lonnell's journey please watch the video on the YouTube channel - The Truth About Cancer: "Lonnell's Holistic Approach to Prostate Cancer - Cancer Survivor Story."

Below is a list of methods that you could check and see if they are suitable for you. Please be aware that every single country has heroes. If you search you shall find them.

Dr. Nicholas Gonzalez

Enemas and diet - Enemas, supplements and a diet that meets the biological requirements of the dreamer. Please read the book "*Nutrition and the Autonomic Nervous system*" by Nicholas J. Gonzalez - www.thegonzalezprotocol.com

Dr. Matthias Rath

Please visit the Matthias Rath foundation website. Dr. Rath and his colleague Dr. Aleksandra Niedzwiecki are experts in natural anti-cancer compounds. Dr. Rath is also a prolific author and lecturer.

Dr. Sebi

Fasting, herbs, alkaline foods that contain oxygen. Elimination of toxins and hybrid foods. Please read the book "*Alkaline Herbal Medicine: Reverse Disease and Heal the Electric body.*" by Aqiyl Aniys.

Dr. Sebi was an expert in herbs, fasting and alkaline foods. He was a prolific lecturer.

Rene Caisse

Essiac tea - please contact www.essiacproducts.com for more details.

Ed McCabe and Oxygen therapy

Hydrogen and Oxygen therapy - Please read the books for reference "*Flood Your Body with Oxygen*", "*The One Minute Cure - Ozone & Oxygen.*"

Hoxsey therapy

Herbal tonic, organic diet, cleansing (please contact the website for more details).

Dr. Russell L. Blaylock, M.D.

Please check the book "*Natural Strategies for Cancer Patients.*"

Leigh Erin Connealy, M.D.

www.connealymd.com
Cancercenterforhealing.com

Essential oils

Cannabis oil and essential oils, such as Frankincense are used as supplements by many heroes. This method includes cleansing, elimination of toxins, organic fresh fruits and vegetables.

Dr. Robert Gorter - Cologne

"I am a doctor then I became a professor at the University of San Francisco and Berlin. I am myself a survivor of an aggressive form of cancer, now for 44 years and I've treated myself as my own patient with immunotherapy. Because of this I have always had a great interest for the treatment of cancer patients…" Dr. Gorter runs a cancer clinic based in Cologne Germany. Like Dr. Veronique, he is a healer who healed his own mind and body. Dr. Gorter specialises in immunotherapy.

Re-education

Websites and YouTube channels are excellent sources of education, inspiration and information about effective methods.

There are several methods which you can use to fight the big monster. The above are some of the most popular methods used in the Western World. Should you use these methods even if you're healthy? Yes. You can always take a proactive rather than a reactive approach to life.

There is nothing wrong in taking a proactive approach to protect yourself and your family. The most effective method to defeat the big monster is prevention. Eliminate foods and toxins that create the right environment for the monster to prosper. Take supplements and minerals. Detox and be happy. There are many people who don't have cancer however they drink tonics such as Essiac tea. Natural remedies are good for the body. You don't have to be on stage 2 of the Hero's Journey, symptoms and diagnosis, in order to eat organic foods, juice and detox. The intelligent and ambitious person will be proactive and protect his or her immune system.

Dr. Johanna Budwig's philosophy - The Budwig Diet

"Flaxseeds and flaxseed oil contain substances that promote good health, particularly alpha - linolenic acid (ALA), an essential fatty acid that is beneficial for heart disease, inflammatory bowel disease, arthritis, and a variety of other health conditions. In addition to ALA, flaxseed also contains a group of chemicals called lignans which appear to play a role in the prevention of cancer. "In fact, researchers have found that a diet supplemented with flaxseed may reduce the formation, growth of prostate, breast, and skin cancers (melanoma) in mice... In general the cottage cheese, flaxseed oil involves mixing 2 tablespoons of cottage cheese with one tablespoon of oil. The daily recommendation is for 6-8 tablespoons of oil, but Dr. Budwig recommends working your way up to the full daily amount..."

- Pages 31 - 32 Tomorrow's Cancer Cures Today - 25 secret therapies from around the world by Allan Spreen, M.D.

Dr. Burzynski's philosophy - Gene therapy

"Today the Burzynski Clinic offers alternative cancer treatments for over 50 different types of cancer, including colon, pulmonary, breast, prostate, head and neck, ovarian, pancreatic, esophageal, hepatic, renal, bladder, brain, malignant melanoma, lymphoma, and many others. In addition to Antineoplastons and gene - targeted medications, the Burzynski Clinic has dietary specialists staff to recommend specific diets according to your individual genetic needs.
The Burzynski team also recommends taking supplements like curcumin (see chapter 9) that help keep tumor suppressor genes functioning normally."

- Page 109 - Tomorrow's Cancer Cures Today - 25 secret therapies from around the world by Allan Spreen, M.D.

The scientific perspective & a Hero called Thomas SeyfriedThe Metabolic therapy

"You shall hear how Hiawatha
Prayed and fasted in the forest,
Not for greater skill in hunting,
Not for greater craft in fishing,
Not for triumphs in the battle,
And renown among the warriors,
But for the profit of the people..."

- The Song of Hiawatha - by Longfellow, Page 55

The beautiful and mystical book written by Longfellow tells the story of a young man who goes into the forest in order to fast. He wanted to heal his spirit. He wanted to find the sacred self, therefore he fasted. Time has passed, but this ritual remains relevant. Dr Thomas Seyfried is a hero and pioneer who has "dedicated his life to something bigger than himself", finding the solution for the challenges caused by cancer. He introduced to the world a powerful therapy that is changing how natural doctors look at cancer. The method is called "Metabolic Therapy"

"What a terrific person, what an amazing researcher who has dedicated his life to really looking at things in a different way and is making such an incredibly good progress in really trying to re-educate us in terms of the paradigm underlying cancer as a generality. I think it is good to take a step back often times and look at the broad strokes that might be involved"

- Dr Perlmutter on Dr Thomas Seyfried:

"There has to be a change here. We are spending billions of dollars on this disease and the incidences continue to increase, the number of deaths per day. Why is this? What's going on here?

It's my view that we have misunderstood what the nature of disease actually is. And this disease actually. This is what I want to focus on, I want provide you with data, evidence to show what we think the disease ... what it is."

Provocative question

Is cancer a nuclear disease, a metabolic genetic disease or a mitochondrial metabolic disease?

This question is very important because the answer will change the way we study and try to manage the disease. The academic and pharmaceutical industries view cancer as a genetic disease. This view is what we call dogma. Cancer as a genetic disease is a belief, an unshakable belief identified as a health dogma.

I teach biology at Boston College and all the books on biochemistry and cell biology talk about cancer as a genetic disease involved with oncogenes, tumour suppressed genes, and similar areas. The dogma is in all the academic text books. Medical students are indoctrinated into thinking and studying cancer as a genetic disease. It's the fundamental basis for the pharmaceutical and academic industry. It's in their grants and approaches and things like this. Is that right though?...

According to the dogma, it's a combination...

Mitochondria, I am going to talk more about them in a minute. These are the little organelles inside the cell that generate energy in our body. You can completely shift the tumour genetic. The cancer type can be changed by moving these mitochondria around regardless of the kind of nucleus. Whether it's a tumour genetic or non tumour genetic nucleus. These finds are incompatible with semantic mutation of cancer. I only gave you a snapshot of many, many studies that I pulled together for the first time. When you see this data for the first time, one after another, you say to yourself, "what is going on here?".

Does the people who run the genome project know about this? Often times they ignore it. They don't discuss this. Here it is

- Normal cells beget normal cells
- Tumour cells in red, beget tumour cells

What is responsible for this dysregulated growth? Is it the mutation in the nucleus as the dogma states or is it something to do with Mitochondrial abnormality in the site plasma…? Because they are abnormal also in the tumour cell, these tumour cells don't have normal energy metabolism.

What's happening is that normal mitochondria can suppress the formation of the tumour. Whatever the gene mutations happen to be, they are not the driver of this disease. Yes, we are focusing on that.

If somatic mutations are not the origin of cancer, then where does cancer comes from? How do we get cancer?

Warburg, the leading biochemist of the 20th Century, had it pegged a long time ago in Germany.

Warburg said, "Cancer arises from damage to cellular respiration". When we breathe, we inhale and we exhale. This is our respiration, our cells respire. We get our energy from oxygen and we burn fuels. Cancer cells have defective respiration and must compensate in some way. The cancer cells gain energy through fermentation gradually compensating for insufficient respiration. Fermentation is a primitive energy source that existed before oxygen came on the planet.

"Older people are more prone to cancer than younger people, because that organelle gets damaged with age"

If all cancers are a type of mitochondrial metabolic disease, what therapies might be effective for managing tumours?

Calorie restriction is effective. What brought us to the idea? What's going on here?

A metabolic cancer intervention that involves total dietary restriction, but differs from starvation. People say Dr. Seyfried does starvation studies. No this is not true although Kahil did complete starvation studies. Dr. Seyfried encouraged calorie restriction that is very therapeutic. These are his words, "You don't starve to death. People say I have not eaten for 3 days, I am starving to death. You are not starving to death. My students ask how long are you going to go before you eat again? How long are you going to live without eating? Ohh 2 days. I say, are you going to be dead in two days if you don't eat?…"

The body maintains minerals and nutrients and will not starve and you will not die. Fasting enhances mitochondrial biogenesis and OxPhos. Also If you stop eating, the mitochondria go through this Autophagy procedure…

Reduce blood glucose - When we stop eating, blood sugar goes down for most of us. Obviously, you are not eating anything. If we stop eating, two days, I should be unconscious lying on the floor writhing around, what happened? How come I am not doing that?

Because insulin goes down and glycogen comes up, you start mobilising the fats after a couple of 36 hours to get rid of the glycogen. The fats go to the liver and the liver breaks up the fat. The process is like pulling long loads of fatty acids out of a wood chipper. The product is these water-soluble ketone bodies that are transported to the brain. Next, the brain will burn ketones and glucose. The ketones release the pressure from the fact that you are low on blood sugar. This is an evolutionary conserved adaptation to starvation, otherwise we would have been wiped out as a species. Humans evolved to starve. Starvation is a pathological state. It is a period when therapeutic fasting moves to starvation which is pathology and that's very dangerous...

Beta hydroxybutyrate acetoacetate - fat products broken down by water, powerful energy metabolisers that allow our bodies to function at maximum energy efficiency but only when glucose levels are down.

Water broken down products of fat powerful energy metabolisers that will allow our bodies to function at maximum energy efficiency but only when glucose goes down...

This has occurred in all kinds of humans with all kinds of cancer. Brain cancer is linked to blood sugar. It doesn't mean the blood sugar causes the cancer, butt if you have the tumour it will grow faster when blood sugar levels are higher. When the sugar is higher, the tumour is going to grow larger because of the fermentation of blood sugar.

Anti-tumour effects of calorie restriction

Anti Angiogenic - Mukherjee et al, Clin, CancerRes, 2004
Anti Inflammatory - Mulrooney et al, PloS ONE, 2011
Pro Apoptotic - Mukherjee et Al Bri. Journal Cancer 2002

You want to kill rogue cells by the tumour cells dropping dead. You don't want to blast the whole environment and kill vital cells and organs along with the tumour cells. The ketogenic diet calorie restriction kills the tumour cells through a pro-apoptotic mechanism which is truly nice because it targets only the cancerous cell. Stark contrasts to the standards of care...

The problem with calorie restriction is the name itself. People that have cancer are under a lot of mental stress. They are in duress. When you tell the poor guy to stop eating for like 3 weeks, he doesn't want to hear that. We can achieve the same kind of metabolic manipulation with ketogenic diets.

What is ketogenic diet?

A lot of controversy. Ohh this ketogenic diet? What is a ketogenic diet?
Basically, the diet comes in all sizes and shapes and you have to be careful. It's basically a low carbohydrate diet. It is high fat with moderate protein; you get a lot of energy per milligram of food. Ketogenic diet in my view should always be consumed in restricted amounts. Do you know the interesting thing about this way of eating? If you eat fat, the human brain triggers the feeling of being

full. There are hormones in our bodies and brains that respond when we eat fat that causes us to naturally restrict our food intake. This is very important in reducing blood sugar levels that cause cancerous tumours to grow.

- Blood Glucose and
- Blood Ketones

"Wow!" people say, "you eating a diet that has no carbohydrates in it". One or 2% sometimes zero carbohydrates are allowed. How is it possible you are maintaining high blood sugar when you are eating a diet that has no carbohydrates in it?

Where is the sugar coming from?

It comes from the liver.

If you eat too much fat you get insulin insensitivity and the blood sugar stays high. You got to cut the blood sugar down a little bit. Once the blood sugar goes down the ketones go up. Here is a guy eating the ketogenic diet and you ask "Are you getting ketones from this?". Yes, he is getting ketones. The ketones have increased and he is peeing, releasing them through his bladder. As fast he is making the ketones, he is peeing them out. When you restrict the diet now, the ketones are staying in the bloodstream. They stay in much higher concentration. High ketones levels are extremely important. When you can get them high enough, they will absolutely kill the tumour cells. Dan D'Agostino and I showed this and several others...This is very interesting because the pharmaceutical industry has a big platform on developing drugs that kill tumour cells. Drugs used to kill the tumour are very toxic and expensive. You can get rid of the tumor too if you can get the ketones high enough. All you must do is lower your blood sugar which increases your ketones.

Here is the plan

- You get the blood sugar down.
- You get your ketones up.
- You get to this zone of so-called Metabolic Management and we are trying to achieve that…"

You want to achieve Metabolic Management.

Ref: Youtube channel - TheIHMC – "Thomas Seyfried; Cancer; A Metabolic Disease with Metabolic Solutions"

Books - "Cancer as a Metabolic disease", Thomas Seyfried. "Tripping over the truth", Travis Christopherson. "Keto for cancer", Miriam Kalamian.

In 1931 a German scientist called Otto Warburg won the prestigious "Nobel Prize in Physiology for his discovery of the nature and mode of action of the respiratory enzyme".

Dr Warburg's research led to the correct conclusion that "cancer cells use glucose as their main food. "They need sugar to survive and cannot survive in an Oxygenated environment". That's why the hyperbaric Oxygen therapy is used together with the Metabolic therapy.

Almost 100 years later, a follower of Otto Warburg has spent more than 20 years following the thread left by the German Hero. His name is Professor Thomas Seyfried. Professor Thomas and his team discovered the second key element needed for the prosperity of cancer cells. Cancer cells don't breathe, they ferment. They also consume glutamine. Glucose and Glutamine are the main fuels of cancer cells. Cut out glucose, carbs, sugar and glutamine and you destroy the food supply of cancer cells and they die. "Tumors shrink and cancer cells die without the use of powerful and expensive drugs that come with severe side effects"

Dr Thomas and his team also discovered that cancer is not caused by genes but by damaged mitochondria. If you repair the mitochondria you will enable your body to heal and destroy cancer cells.

How do you repair damaged mitochondria?

Dr Thomas and his team based at Boston University spent many years dealing with cancer patients. They followed the instructions of an American doctor called Russell Wilder. In 1924 Dr Wilder was working at the Mayo Clinic, he developed a diet that successfully treated epileptic patients. Dr Wilder realised that calorie restriction and therapeutic fasting enables the human organism to repair internal damage. Prolonged fasting starting at 3 days for females and 4 days for males activated a self healing mechanism that's carefully hidden inside the human body. When the liver is deprived of carbs it turns fat into energy. During the first 2 days of fasting the practitioner gets a few headaches as the brain struggles to free itself from addiction to glucose and carbs.

"Brain cancer, liver cancer, stomach cancer, colon cancer, breast cancer are in reality one single disease caused by a damaged mitochondria" You can prevent and manage the disease successfully through therapeutic fasting. The longer the fast, the more benefits a person gets. "A human being can fast up to 40 days. After that it becomes pathology"

After 4 or 5 days of therapeutic fasting, ketones come into play. Ketones enable the body to heal damaged mitochondria and destroy free radicals. Ketogenic diet, calorie restriction and supplementation are great strategies to prevent cancer. This method is in perfect harmony with the lifestyle of the Hunza tribe from Pakistan/Afghanistan. Therapeutic fasting is an essential element of their culture. They enjoy long and healthy lives. They also consume Apricot kernels which contain high levels of B17 Vitamin.

Dr Seyfried also stated that if a person's cancer is very advanced then another strategy is required. There is the Before and After stages which cannot be ignored.

The Metabolic therapy consists of ketogenic diet, Hyperbaric Oxygen Therapy and Don (a drug that reduces glutamine, the second main fuel of cancer cells). Both Dr Seyfried and Dr Warburg's work are compelling evidence that genes are not the cause of cancer. There are many causes of cancer. The main culprit is damaged mitochondria. Dr Seyfried has more than 20 years' experience dealing with advanced cancer of the brain and cancers that affect other organs. His teams, which are based in countries such as Egypt and Turkey, are getting 'incredible results' by employing therapeutic restriction combined with elimination of glutamine and glucose.

Dr Seyfried's work is essential for ambitious human beings who wish to prevent cancer. He is also a great reference for patients who wish to manage cancer naturally.

In one of his lectures Dr Seyfried recommended a book called "Keto for Cancer" The book was written by Miriam Kalamian - Edm MS CNS.

During step 6 of his Hero's Journey, Dr Seyfried jumped into a river called Academia. After spending many years inside the academic world he realised that many academics who look into the subject of cancer are 'blinded by a Dogma that says cancer is caused by genes, therefore they spent a great deal of time and money looking into the wrong place"

He also stated that "the Metabolic Therapy is not financially attractive to big pharmaceutical companies therefore it is not given credit. Scientists who refuse to pursue the Gene Theory as the cause of cancer struggle to get funding and face formidable obstacles to get their trials approved. "It will take 100 years for conventional doctors to adopt Metabolic Therapy because it is very simple and does not require all the drugs and toxins given to people all over the world." Thomas Seyfried is a Hero who jumped into the special world and returned with an elixir called Metabolic Therapy. His book is called "Cancer as a Metabolic Disease, On the origin, Prevention and Management of Cancer"

High fat and cancer

Please be aware that Ketogenic diet is a short term strategy. Consumption of high level fat is linked to cancers such as breast and colon cancer. The key element of the metabolic therapy, fasting, can be used as a long term strategy. If you can manage to fast for 5 or 10 days every month you will enjoy a long and healthy life.

A study conducted by Rowan T. Chlebowski, MD, PhD, revealed the dangers of prolonged consumption of fats. The study found that women who consume high quantities of fat get aggressive breast cancer and struggle to recover after the diagnosis. Fasting, taking supplements such as green tea are great strategies to prevent cancer. The Ketogenic diet was designed to help people who struggle to fast for long periods of time. If you cannot fast, please make sure you avoid carbs such as bread, pasta, potatoes, processed cereals, junk food. The metabolic therapy is a powerful strategy that requires abstinence from carbs. A raw and organic plant based diet is an excellent strategy that's in perfect harmony with the metabolic therapy.

Essential supplements used by healers

- Apricot Kernels
- Ayurveda philosophy - plant, herbal - holistic
- Broccoli extract
- Cannabis oil - CBD
- Chinese herbs
- Coriolus Versicolor - Turkey tail mushroom
- Curcumin (Turmeric) - supplementation & anti-inflammation
- Glutathione
- Green tea
- MD-Fraction Maitake mushroom
- Selenium
- Vitamin C
- Vitamin D3

For more names please check our website

www.theherosjourneyhealth.com

Please do your research before using any method listed here. Consult your doctor and request professional advice before using a specific philosophy, method.

Education about the subject

- Thetruthaboutcancer.com
- Glidden Healthcare - YouTube
- Chrisbeatcancer - YouTube channel
- iHealthtube.com - YouTube channel
- Amazon - books
- Audible - search for cancer
- Breastcancerconqueror.com

A diagnosis creates stress and a sense or urgency. You should never be stressed. Stress creates disease. You can avoid headaches by studying and taking small but powerful strategic steps. Re-education and meditation is a great place to start.

Step 8 - Ordeal, Battle, Rebirth

"Now the hero stands in the deepest chamber of the Inmost Cave, facing the greatest challenge and the most fearsome opponent yet. This the real heart of the matter, what Joseph Campbell called the Ordeal. It is the mainspring of the heroic form and the key to its magic power."

- Page 155 of The Writer's Journey by Christopher Vogler

Tamara St. John said the following:

"I immediately started Budwig in June of 2009. And within a couple of weeks the lump started going down and the pain got less and the throbbing got less. So I knew something was happening, something was working. By June I was already sleeping like 15 hours a day. I was that exhausted. And always like in a fog. So I know that the cancer was pretty advanced at that point. Especially because it spread to the lymph nodes. And then about a couple of months later I started to add apricot kernels and then added in juicing, and starting to detox my body and of course exercising a lot. Going hiking and getting out in the Sun. Doing stuff like that. I started healing."

An interesting detail in Tamara's journey is "Going hiking and getting out in the Sun." She got closer to Mother Nature and vitamin D.

Stage 2 of the Hero's Journey, signals and diagnosis is the level in which the patient experiences psychological violence created by fear and stress. On stage 8 the hero will experience psychological and physical violence. The monster that has been gathering forces will finally show itself and demand immediate attention.

"About September 2009 a rash appeared around my neck in the form of a ring. And I didn't know what was going on. So I talked to Doctors. I talked to Biochemists and I talked to other people with cancer. And other people had told me that that's the epidermal growth factor receptor. It's the rash that comes out when you have cancer in your body. And it will come out while your body is detoxifying from cancer. Not everybody gets it because it is more prevalent in HER 1 type cancers, so advanced stage breast cancers or non-small-cells lung cancer. So that came out and I asked these people, well, how long is it going to take until it goes away? Because it was really itchy and nothing was helping it. You know, I put Aloe Vera or anything on it. Nothing was working. And they said, when all the cancer is gone in your body the rash will disappear. And it took over 7 months from that point until it finally disappeared. Sometime in April 2010 is when it finally you know, was going away." - Extracted from iHealthTube.com YouTube channel: She Cured Her Breast Cancer - Here's How!

The call to adventure and initiation

Tamra St. Johns said that "It took 7 months from that point until it finally disappeared." The esoteric number 7 appears again.

During her teens Tamara St. John saw her mother battling the side effects of chemo and other conventional treatments. The experience traumatised her therefore she decided not to use chemotherapy. She rejected the invitation to jump into the chemical world. She used natural methods to defeat the monster.

When she reached stage 8 of the Hero's Journey, Tamara had a direct confrontation with the monster. The rash that appeared around her neck was evidence that something was fighting against her. It was also a sign that what she was doing was working. The monster was dying. The death of the monster causes what healers call "the healing reaction." The body reacts and strives to remove toxins and dead tissue. The rash was a signal that her efforts were being rewarded. The positive attitude, juicing, detoxing, meditating and reading were producing the desired results. There were times in which she doubted her own abilities, therefore, she contacted mentors. She was not the first hero to question her own potential.

Bhagavad Gita

The Ancient Indian epic called "Bhagavad Gita" tells the story of Prince Arjuna, the leader of the Pandavas. Prince Arjuna's army was battling the forces of evil. Although he was the most skilled archer of his generation, the prince almost surrendered to self-doubt. Shortly before the battle started Prince Arjuna turned to his charioteer and asked for reassurance. He told his loyal friend that he was not confident enough to fight and win a war that would restore Dharma in the country. Unknown to the prince, the charioteer was Lord Krishna, a wise principle and an ancient mentor. Lord Krishna told the prince to believe in himself and fight in order to restore balance and harmony in the land. The command was "Do your duty and don't be attached to it."

In the book *The Eternal Cycle - Myth and Mankind* we read the following;

"Leading Pandava warrior Arjuna paused before battle, filled with doubts. Krishna, his princely charioteer, eased his worries by advising him on what he should do in conflict. Then, to Arjuna's great astonishment, he revealed the divine reality within him." - p84

"As a warrior it was Arjuna's dharma - his proper and essential quality - to fight and be brave. He should perform his duty, but with a sense of detachment from personal reward. He must go resutely into battle."

- *The Eternal Cycle - Myth and Mankind*

The internal, invisible enemy

The story of both Tamara St. John and Prince Arjuna teaches us that on step 8 of his or her journey the hero will face two enemies. They are both internal.

The 1st is the psychological enemy created by fear, negative words, negative thinking, stress and pain.

The 2nd enemy is the cancer itself. The big monster is ruthless. There will be times in which the big monster will appear to be winning. Many heroes talk about pain and fear. If we follow the thread left by heroes who completed the Hero's Journey, we will learn a very important lesson. We need mentors to inspire us to keep fighting.

Prince Arjuna had a very important task to complete. Being mortal he hesitated. He was almost capitulating when his mentor stepped in and gave him encouragement. The story of the prince reminds us that we need allies and mentors, healers of souls to inspire and rescue us from invisible labyrinths. We need someone who will motivate and give us the necessary tools to succeed. On step 8 the hero will need every single resource available to him or her. Books, juice machines, supplements, happy and positive friends. The hero will also need a strategy.

A general and a warrior

We cannot win wars without strategy and strong will. The fight against cancer is the Greatest War that a person can experience in life. War against cancer is not just biological. It is emotional, psychological, financial, social, generational and global. On step 8 the hero could wear the mask of a general.

Every general uses a strategy. Military strategies are used in business, economics, politics, education and many other areas of life. Although every human being uses strategies daily, most people are not aware that they are strategists. Strategic ignorance leads to chaos.

When it comes to war there are two types of strategies;

- Western strategy - Direct assault and conflict orientated
- Chinese strategy - Indirect assault, intellectual warfare

The foundations of Western strategy can be seen in conventional medicine, games such as chess and football. Chess is a linear strategy. There is an objective. A goal. The goal is always to defeat the opposing army by encircling the king. When the king is encircled and cannot move he is forced to commit suicide. It's called checkmate. Chess relies on direct confrontation. To get close to the king an army has to make many sacrifices. Many pieces have to die. To win a chess match a player has to kill many enemies. This strategy is very costly because it results in the death of many soldiers. Many precious allies are sacrificed. Many healthy cells, organs, tissues are destroyed.

In chess you start the game with many pieces. By the end of the game you are left with less than 10% of your army intact. There is a lot of death and destruction. Conventional medicine uses direct confrontation. A person gets a diagnosis and is told that we have to either cut you, burn you or radiate you then wait and see whether you survive. We need to burn you in order to destroy an enemy called cancer. We are going to burn everything that's around the enemy, including healthy cells and organs. The shaman, medicine man and medicine woman who wishes to restore life does not prescribe to this strategy. It is too violent to be contemplated by the followers of Sedna and Aset.

Chess & wars

During the Vietnam War, American president Lyndon B. Johnson sent more than half a million soldiers to Vietnam. The U.S. had superior weapons and manpower. American strategists and generals flooded Vietnam with millions of bombs. Although the Vietnamese army was smaller and had less resources it won the war. The Vietnamese generals fought for territory and avoided direct confrontations. They went for territory and encircled American soldiers. The U.S. had bombs, soldiers and high-level equipment. It did not have territorial advantage.

The same happens to the big monster called cancer. Unless it metastasizes cancer does not have territorial advantage. Cancer is a smart enemy that requires a very smart strategy and approach. Direct confrontation is not ideal because it causes a lot of destruction and helps cancer to prosper. The condition called Cachexia is created by toxins such as chemo. This disease is very serious because it means toxins have gained territorial advantage. The patient's body disintegrates. The bone marrow gradually collapses. When tumors spreads to other areas of the body there is also an accelerated disintegration of the body. Compounds such as Turmeric, juicing and coffee enemas are excellent at preventing cancer's territorial advantage.

Conventional medicine has been playing chess with cancer for years. It wins a few battles and loses many wars. Using chess, a direct confrontation strategy, the cancer is violently attacked through surgery, radiation and chemotherapy. The goal is to force the cancer to surrender. Many cancers trick doctors and patients by offering a temporary surrender. Please remember that cancer is a trickster. Cancer uses deception to lure people into a deadly trap. If you listen to the stories of heroes who used conventional methods, you will learn that many were told that your "cancer is in remission." A few months, sometimes years later the big monster shows up and causes serious and fatal damage. Many patients are told that they will die in days. Such negative statements inspire them to surrender psychologically. Once the mind accepts a negative outcome, the body follows. The same happens in chess. To win a chess game a player has to first win the psychological war. A silent and invisible war.

The strategy used by chess players is not ideal because it causes a lot of destruction. It relies on violence and winning at all costs. If you use chemicals to attack the monster you risk leaving your immune system exhausted. An exhausted immune system will be unable to respond to future attacks. HIV patients give us clues about the power of the immune system. HIV patients are not killed by the HIV virus. They die because their immune systems becomes too intoxicated and weak therefore it cannot fight something as small as a cold.

Go - A Chinese approach to conflict

There is a wonderful and effective alternative to direct confrontation. It comes from Ancient China. There is a very Ancient Chinese game called Go. In Go a player starts with an empty board then slowly fills it with pieces. The goal is not to kill people. The main vision is to conquer territory. In Go you use very few pieces to acquire as much territory as possible. The goal of Go is to win the war not small battles. Go is a resource oriented strategy. Vietnamese generals used Go to defeat an army that was a million times bigger than theirs. U.S. generals played chess. Vietnamese leaders played Go. In Go there are no queens or kings. Every single piece is valuable. If we were talking about the immune system we would say that every single cell is valuable. Every organ is valuable therefore it should be taken care of rather than destroyed.

An experienced Chinese general who uses Go as his main strategy would not attack the cancer directly. Instead the practitioner of Go would acquire as much clean territory as possible. The cancer cannot prosper in a clean and healthy environment, therefore, it would be a matter of time until it surrendered to endless streams of organic juices, vitamins, good emotions and enemas.

The Art of War

The most well-known practitioner of Go was a General and mentor called Sun Tzu. He wrote a book called "*The Art of War*". The Art of War is the most used military strategy manual in the world. Every American, British, French, Chinese, European, Israeli high rank military officer knows Sun Tzu's principles. Go and "The Art of War" prioritise conquest of territory rather than direct attacks and prolonged conflicts. Sun Tzu wrote: "*It is more important to outthink your enemy that to outfight him.*"

He also said;

- "If you know your enemy and you know yourself, you need not fear the result of a 100 battles.
- If you don't know your enemies but you know yourself you will win a few but lose many battles.
- If you don't know your enemies nor yourself, you will be imperiled in every single battle."

Sun Tzu's teachings are essential. They prepare us for the ferocious psychological war that takes place in step 8. If you don't know yourself and the hero inside yourself, you will be in serious trouble... If you don't know your enemy, you will also be in trouble. If you don't know how cancer operates and attacks the body, you will not know the best ways to defeat it. Cancer is the product of a weak and deficient immune system. You should do all you can to know your enemy because that type of intelligence guarantees success. Stage 8 is total war. Prepare yourself by reading and studying. Ask yourself, do I really know my enemy?

The big monster is a trickster, a lover of sugar, toxins and negative emotions, a ruthless destroyer that does not care about emotions, tears, age, gender, social status, etc. Cancer and its allies use deception. They promote La Dolce Vita as the ideal Vita, the ideal life. Cancer fools people to believe that it is no longer inside their bodies. People relax and lower their guard only to find themselves dealing with a more aggressive monster. Know your enemy and you shall win. A philosopher is someone who asks smart questions.

Key questions

- What causes cancer?
- Which foods help the body to fight cancer?
- What are the weaknesses of cancer?
- What makes cancer strong?
- What weakens cancer?
- How many books about cancer did you read?
- How many videos about cancer did you watch?
- Who produced those videos?
- What do they teach?

Step 8 has 3 steps

Aset, Wsr and their son Hrw were the original trinity. The mother, the father and the golden child. The Hero. This trinity inspired the creation of the Mer Cut Sr, a monument which the Greeks renamed Pyramid. Number 3 is the source of many wonderful things. It gives us 3 steps that are carefully hidden inside step number 8.

We have been preparing ourselves, we have been refining ourselves, we have been learning and now comes the time to battle the monster. We have been given the thread and now we enter the labyrinth. We stand in front of the monster and engage. The battle might last 9 months or 9 years. It doesn't matter how long it lasts. It has to take place. Either the patient or the monster will die. Sun Tzu's said: "*What's important in war is victory not prolonged operations.*"

An effective method should enable you to defeat the monster in less than 5 years. Consistent application, discipline, the right tools and emotions would enable you to overcome the monster in less than 5 years. The strategy of having 13 enemas and 13 juices with supplements every single day seems intense. Yes the strategy is intense, it is also necessary and effective. It is also an ideal strategy to prevent and repair... The 3 parts of step 8 are;

- Ordeal
- Death
- Rebirth

Part 1 Ordeal

The root word for ordeal is 'ordene', Latin 'ordinem', 'ordem', 'order'. The earlier from is 'Ord', it means to arrange. Source www.etymonline.com

We go to war in order to restore, attain the ideal order. The ordeal is essentially the climax. The conflicts between healthy cells, the immune system and free radicals reach their peak on stage 8.

This stage will result in the death of either the hero or the monster.

When Theseus went into the labyrinth, he knew that he was entering a dangerous place. He was going into the house of death. He knew that he would either kill the monster or be killed by the monster. The same applies to the monster called cancer. We will either kill the cancer or the cancer will kill us. A great general does not go to war expecting to die or lose a battle. Planning is his or her secret weapon. A well prepared general knows that his or her plans and the available resources are strong enough to guarantee victory. Intelligent generals spend years preparing themselves for a great battle. They don't wait for things to happen. Like them you should not wait to see if you will ever get a specific disease. "Be proactive".

Part 2 Death

"Many people believe that a kind of death is experienced during vital transitions. A person is believed to die to the old life, before he or she is resurrected in the new."

- The Religions of Small Societies- Professor Ninian Smart - Narrated by Ben Kingsley.

Gilgamesh the King of Ancient Uruk, was invited by his best friend and ally Enkidu to go the forest. Shortly after they got into the forest, the two brothers were confronted by Humbaba. Humbaba was a fearsome monster. He was the guardian of essential mysteries. Enkidu and Gilgamesh fought against Humbaba. It was a violent fight. In the end they succeeded in killing Humbaba. The brothers were relieved when they saw the monster falling to the ground. After killing Humbaba Gilgamesh and Enkidu returned home and were received as heroes. Everybody was happy to see them back home.

Less than 1 year after helping Gilgamesh to kill Humbaba, Enkidu fell sick and died. Please remember Enkidu and Humbaba were two archetypes. They were two aspects of the human personality. The death of Humbaba symbolised the death of the monster that was inside Gilgamesh. The same happens to many cancer patients. The death of the big monster inside them is also the death of the old self. Heroes who conquer the monster are transformed by the experience. They become wiser and give up old habits. The toxic self addicted to junk food and sugar is discarded. Heroes are people who conquer their own lower nature.

The patient has to die in order to create the space for the hero. A patient and a healed person are two different individuals. The death of the old self heralds the birth of a new person, a more intelligent, strategic and confident person. A patient is not the same person as a cancer survivor or cancer conqueror. They have different names.

Part 3 Rebirth

"*Cancer is not a death sentence.*" - Dr. Rashid Buttar

The Truth About Cancer YouTube channel.

Dr. Rashid Buttar - "There's one recurring theme that I hear from them. After they've gone through this challenge, they relate to me how grateful they are that they had this disease. How it transformed them, how it changed their life, how it allowed them see a different perspective that had they not seen, their lives wouldn't be where it is today, where their lives are today. And that gratitude, that appreciation for having gone through that experience, that's really, cancer is a wake up call. I believe that in 20 years nobody is going to be scared of cancer, it's gonna be like getting a cold. But it's a wake up call. When you get cancer you need to do something. It's God giving you the ultimate email, but it's like you know, it's something that takes the wind out of your sail as soon as you hear it. It's not a death sentence. It's only a death sentence if you believe it's a death sentence."

Any person that goes through a challenging experience, learns certain skills that have the potential to make him or her a hero. Fasting and food deprivation transformed me into a new person.

Fasting

In 2016 I spent 3 months juicing and fasting. On the second month of my fast I experienced a very profound transformation. It was both psychological and biological. The biological transformation was visible. I lost a lot of weight. I looked younger. My skin was very clean. The psychological transformation was very profound. I also mastered self-control. The knowledge that I could resist food for 3 months was a source of organic self-esteem and confidence. The experience prepared me for the future. I did not have cancer. I was following Dr. Sebi's fasting program. I learnt a lot about myself and food. I started to teach people how to get into long-term fasting.

In prolonged fasting, 60 or 90 days, there is a death of the old self and the birth of a new and very confident person who knows how to protect himself or herself , his or her family and friends.

Heroes that reach part 3 of step 8 experience several types of transformation. Many give up their jobs and become mentors and healers. Others become authors, inspirational speakers, healers and conductors of souls.

The evolution of a sincere seeker

After losing his parents and grandparents, Ty Bollinger decided to learn and help others to defeat the Minotaur. He collected a large quantity of information that enabled him to write a book. He evolved from orphan to author, speaker, teacher and healer of souls. Tamara St. John, Chris Wark, Dr. Veronique are prolific authors and educators. Like every hero they experienced physical and psychological challenges, trials that transformed their thinking, and inspired them to adopt a new philosophy.

The rebirth is not just physical. There is also an intellectual, psychological, emotional rebirth. The sincere seeker, patient that goes into the labyrinth is not the same person that comes out. There is a very positive transformation. Theseus went to the labyrinth as a young man. He came out as a man, a warrior and leader of a nation. After killing the Minotaur, Theseus became a man after sleeping with Ariadne. That was his first love experience which marked his transition from youth to maturity. When he arrived in Athens he was proclaimed King.

In mythology, the loss of consciousness, sickness, temporary death, the trip to the Netherworld is an opportunity to learn essential mysteries about life. The same happens to heroes who defeat a big monster called cancer. Step 8 is the stage of profound transformations.

Step 9 Reward – Healing

When the deadly battle between the Minotaur and Theseus ended, 14 young men and young women were saved and allowed to return to Athens. They were received by their astonished friends, relatives, parents, brothers and sisters. Theseus saved his life and and the lives of 14 teenagers, who were about to be eaten alive by the Minotaur.

Rescuing a victim from the labyrinth and saving a life is one the greatest rewards a hero receives. There is also the personal and public recognition. The wife of the kemetic king became an asset after rescuing her husband. Max Gerson's reputation grew after he cured more than 400 patients who were suffering from tuberculosis.

Betsy Dix - The Truth About Cancer

"Dr. Buttar has brought something to my family that we thought we couldn't have. After the diagnosis last year, psychologically, mentally I just thought I was on my way out..."

The story of Betsy Dix had a very happy ending indeed. Dr. Buttar and his team saved Betsy Dix from premature death. The unconventional treatment given to Betsy, saved more than 1 person. It saved Mrs. Dix's children from growing up in a hostile world without a mother. It also saved her husband from a forced and very painful separation. In both mythology and the real world, the sincere seeker who spends years striving to refine his or her habits is rewarded with longevity. Longevity leads us to Longa Vita. Long life.

In order to enjoy a long and healthy life, the hero must reject the idea of premature death. Many ambitious men and women are told that if they don't accept the invitation to use conventional methods, they have less than 1 year to live. I have heard stories of people who were told that they had 6 days to live. They accepted the invitation to go to the world of no return. Within 6 days of accepting the invitation they died. If a person was told that, "the last person I saw who had a problem similar to yours followed the program and is still alive and well today." This type of positive talk has the power to inspire a person not only to believe but also to pursue longevity. It triggers the "Placebo effect".

Ancient sages used mythology to remind us of the need to save our lives and strive to save others. When we work hard and succeed in defeating the monster, we are not only saving ourselves. We are also saving our friends and relatives from the depression and trauma that follows a funeral.

We become heroes when we save a life. That's the organic life purpose of every human being. That's why we should research subjects, such as;

- Coffee enemas
- Meditation
- Raw organic foods
- Reading and learning
- Supplements
- Nutrition

The study of the above disciplines requires money, patience and time.

Why would someone spend days and nights doing enemas and drinking juices? Because he or she wants to become a hero and enjoy a long and healthy life.

An ambitious person realises that without vitality he or she will fail to fulfill his or her creative, intellectual, social and financial potential. People who are prepared to make big sacrifices and even risk their own lives will be rewarded with longevity. That's what happened to Eleio, a hero from the Native Indians that lived in Hawaii.

"From Hawaii came the story of a shaman called Eleio who, seeing a beautiful maiden one day, followed her to a cliff top burial ground, where she revealed that she was the spirit of a girl who had recently passed away. After telling her parents what he had seen, Eleio entered a trance in which he was able to re-establish contact with her spirit and draw it towards him. Finally, he succeeded in reuniting it with the girl's dead body by pushing it through the soles of her feet, at which point the girl revived. Subsequently, she and Eleio married."

- p124 The Great Themes - World Myth. Myth and Mankind.

The story of Eleio and his wife also had a very happy ending. The hero married the lucky bride. The reward is not cheap or easy to get. Defeating the big monster called cancer is a very difficult entreprise. There are many changes to be made. New habits have to be introduced. A new paradigm, a new way of thinking has to be adopted. To get the greatest reward that a person can have in life, the old self has to go.

"As long as their bodies are clean and they are not putting the toxins in their system and they are cleansing their bodies on a regular basis,

that is the solution and the secret to preventing and eliminating degenerative diseases and cancer."

- Dr. Group - iHealthtube.com YouTube channel.

The Truth About Cancer has amazing stories of heroes who got the big prize after following the instructions of their mentors. We also have the remarkable story of Mildred Nelson. Although she is no longer alive, Mildred Nelson's legacy continues to save lives through the clinic that she opened in Mexico. She worked very hard to save lives. She spent more than 40 years healing people. She has been rewarded with a place in eternity. Below is a fragment of her patient's journeys.

Content extracted from the YouTube channel - The Truth About Cancer: A Global Quest - Episode 1:

"I am Liz Jonas. And my sister was Mildred Nelson. I have no medical background. Mine is business, Mildred was the medical one in our family. My mom had cancer. Ovarian and uterus and they had planted radiation in her body and burned her very bad and told her to go home and die. My dad heard about Harry Hoxsey who was in Dallas, Texas and we lived in Jacksboro which is about 90 miles. So my dad called my sister. She was the oldest in our family. There were 7 of us. And asked her to come and drive for him. He was an old-time rancher. And she said, "What are you going to Dallas for?" She said, "To get parts for the tractor?" He said "No, I'm taking your mother to the doctor." So she came and drove. And through the day, Hoxsey found out she was a nurse and offered her a job, and my dad told him,

"No, she doesn't want to work for you, she thinks you are a quack." He offered for her to go and look in all his files but she didn't. And she couldn't talk my mother out of this, so she decided to go to work for him to prove he was a quack and to save her mum. Our mum lived to be 99 years old".

The above story gives details of Mildred Nelson's journey from skeptic to healer. Although Mildred Nelson's family was skeptical about natural treatments, mother, father and daughter were left with no other alternative after conventional doctors told them that they had done everything that they could. The family drove to Harry's clinic that was located in Dallas. The entire family was initiated. When they departed they were skeptical. After Harry's initiation the entire family was converted to a new way of living that enabled Mildred's mother to remain alive until she was 99 years old.

The Truth About Cancer: A Global Quest - Episode 1:

David Olson - "8 and half years ago, back in August of 06, I couldn't lay down. Matter of fact, Zack was with me on a motor car trip on the railroad. And the seatbelt started hurting on the way back from the trip. We were doing about 300 miles and the seatbelt started feeling tight. And the next week I had another trip and coming back the seatbelt was also tight. And shortly after that I couldn't lay down. And I went to the Mayo Clinic and was diagnosed. On the first time they said I didn't have cancer. And in a two week period they found that I did have cancer pretty bad.

I had Hodgkin lymphoma. I had it in the esophagus, the liver, the kidney, the lymph nodes, all around the arm and in the groin. I had a tumor bigger than a volleyball in the stomach and then in the bones stage 4. Doctors gave me 3 days to 3 months. One doctor said; you know, the last guy that we treated like you made it 3 days. So, it was not a very good forecast. So the day I found out I had it in my bones. I found out that at 2 O'clock right up on the 10th floor of the Rochester Mayo Clinic at the Gonda building, things looked very bleak...

It has been 8 and half years later, and I've not had cancer for 8 years and 3 months. They have not found it. Mayo Clinic couldn't find it. They haven't found it here. There is no cancer that's visible anymore. We started at the Mayo Clinic, had 13 doctors at Mayo Clinic and they gave me the same forecast of 3 days to 3 months. And I went up to the University of Minnesota and then to Fairview hospital and the Masonic Cancer Centre.

I received a death sentence from 17 doctors. And the 18th one down here, Dr. Gutierrez (in Mexico) it was no big deal to him. It was bad yes, but nothing special. As far as I know I was taking more medicine than any other patient that I ever talked to so far. I talked to a lot of patients from down town that had been sent down here and other patients. I was taking the strongest dose than they had but I have never missed a day at work. It never affected my ability to do whatever, but it made the total difference in life. And this life is fantastic. I got 3 grandsons but only one can come with me once in a while, the other two are very busy. And this one (grandson) comes with me and we do a lot of things together."

The fearful patient who was attacked by the big monster was told that "he should go home and prepare to die by 17 doctors." He was desperate to find a healer and was lucky to be taken to the Hoxsey

Clinic in Mexico. There he found doctors who are used to dealing with "terminal patients." They examined him and gave him the instructions as well as the tonic. He believed in them and was rewarded with longevity.

He was given the greatest gift a human being can enjoy. That's life and the ability to be with his grandchildren. The stories of heroes have a hidden message. They teach us that to get the greatest reward in life, we must believe in the hero inside us and remain positive. We must not give up. The man did not surrender to the negative thinking that greeted him wherever he went. He kept searching for a solution. He was a sincere seeker who embraced the Hero's Philosophy. The Hero's Philosophy is based on optimism, initiation, biological as well as psychological cleansing.

STEP 10 - RETURN

"We've encountered a significant number of doubters along the way. Skeptics, doubters. We have what we refer to as the awkward pause. This occurs when you're talking to, say a friend or a family member or even a stranger, and you say oh my goodness my husband has stage 3b colon cancer and we're treating it holistically. And suddenly it's radio silence, their faces are just blank."

- Cancer survivor interviewed on The Truth About Cancer.

After spending weeks, months sometimes years learning and collecting the mysteries and treasures hidden inside the special world, the hero will get the knowledge that he or she needs to restore the lost vitality. The next step is the return journey. Why return? Why not keep the secret to oneself? Why risk getting into trouble by contradicting pessimists and tricksters?

The answer is very simple but also very profound. We don't go to the special world in order to satisfy our egos. We go there to heal ourselves psychologically and biologically. The return gives us the opportunity to heal ourselves socially by striving to save our friends and relatives. We go to the special world in order to learn how to defeat the monster and rebuild our immune system. The wisdom that we collect during the journey is a valuable asset that we could use to inspire others and help them to heal themselves.

The skeptical man or woman that refuses to learn becomes spiritually poor and toxic. Both ancient and modern heroes leave their homes and go on a quest. Once they get the gold they return home. They don't keep the gold for themselves. The goal of the quest is to save not just oneself but to rescue others as well. Mothers who succeed in defeating the monster will become a great source of inspiration for their children. The grandfather, the grandmother, the father, the brother, the sister, the cousin will become a lighthouse for many people. A conductor of souls rather than a victim.

Before we look at the return of the modern and ancient hero we shall look at the origins and etymology of the word return. We return to Re, the grandfather of Aset and the first ruler of Kmt.

Please remember that the main solar principle of Ancient Kmt was called Re. Re was the visible form of the creator. Many cultures, Greek, Roman, Persian adopted the principle of Re after invading the country. Re became a universal principle. We find Re as a prefix for many words that we use today. Example; return, recover, remission, rely, Rey, ray, radio, ratio, refuse, reject, renounce, renew, restore, rethink, re-election etc.

From Re we get the word return. Return is a union of two words. Re + turn. Re is the circle and solar principle which will turn back. The turning back gives us the word return. You look back at the place where you began your journey. You started your journey inside the home of your family, community, country. When you finish you will look back. You turn. You will adopt the principle of Re and you will Return. You become Re, a source of light that turns back. Orpheus was punished for turning back. The King of the World of the Dead did not want Orpheus to become a prolific saviour of souls.

According to ancient priests and priestesses who lived in a city called Iunu, the creator, symbolised by the Sun, left the world at sunset, went to the underworld where he met ferocious monsters. With the help of essential allies, principles and archetypes the creator returned the following morning. He was hailed as a hero, a bringer of light. The same happens to heroes who sacrifice their egos and learn how to heal their minds, souls and bodies. Re experienced the 3 essential stages of spiritual, intellectual and biological development.

- Departure at sunset
- Initiation in the evening
- Return in the morning

On his return Re brought with him the daylight that died at sunset. His ability to return to the world with the daylight made him a hero. That's the principle behind the word hero and return. In Mdw Ntr the word Hrw means daylight. Hrw has been translated to hero. A hero is someone who brings the daylight back into a diseased body.

An ambitious individual who wishes to accomplish something remarkable, a great goal, will have to start a journey. It doesn't matter whether the person wishes to defeat the monster or prevent its arrival, win an Olympic gold medal, become a mother, a father, a healer, a doctor, a politician, a businessman or businesswoman, the ambitious individual will follow the path of Re. Departure, Initiation and Return.

The return in mythology

After killing Humbaba, Enkidu and Gilgamesh returned to Uruk. They were not aware that their lives would never be the same again.

There were physical, psychological as well as social changes awaiting them. The ancient message is hidden in their story. After killing the monster, the heroes returned to Uruk and shared details of their life changing adventure with friends and relatives. Gilgamesh and Enkidu were well received by their people. They were seen as heroes and saviours. Like them you must return to your family, office, village, town and share the wisdom hidden inside this book. "When you teach once you learn twice."

Not everyone was pleased to see the heroes or contemplate their new lifestyle. A profound psychological and intellectual transformation is not something that most people want. This ancient truth is something which every modern hero should be aware of. There are many people who are chronically addicted to ignorance therefore they are not prepared to embrace a new philosophy, a refined experience that rejects processed foods, meat, pizzas, pretending, poultry and pasta. They are opposed to progress and any forms of intellectual prosperity. Heroes who discover and use the mysteries of the special world to heal their minds and bodies become special people, followers of a special diet and enjoy a special experience. They also appear strange to their friends and relatives who are stuck inside the artificial and lifeless ordinary world. A hero should be aware that he or she will face opposition and criticism from people that profit from ignorance.

The return of the mother

On the 9th month of her pregnancy a young lady was given the signals that it was time to bring the baby to the world, to give birth and become an Aset. She started feeling kicks, contractions and sharp pains. She complained. She was taken to a hospital where she gave birth to a wonderful baby. After the birth of her first child, the new mother returned home where friends and relatives awaited her. Unknown to her, the young lady and new mother followed the path of Re. Her pains forced her to depart. At the hospital the midwives initiated her into ancient mysteries. A few days after giving birth she returned home with the greatest prize of her life, a child that has the potential to become a hero.

The hero left home as a pregnant woman. She returned as a hero who brought a new life to the world. She left home as a patient who was in pain. She returned home as a giver of life, a mother, a teacher, an Aset who saved a baby from perpetual obscurity.

Every culture and country has a hero who returned home after completing his or her mission. In sports, a football team will travel to a country. They will spend weeks battling ferocious enemies. One day they will get to the final. The final confrontation will be very hard indeed. It will also be very emotional. They will be watched by billions of people around the world. After defeating their enemy, they will lift the trophy. The following day they will pack their belongings, go to the airport, and start the return journey. That's step 10 of their heroic journey. Step 10 is very interesting indeed. It is very esoteric. Number 10 is a gateway to longevity and eternity. Number 1 symbolises the individual that's standing, the zero is the circle, the womb, the path to eternity.

Number 10 an esoteric, mysterious number

If we look at the Hero's Journey, the Universal circle of influence, we see that number 5 is in the middle of the circle. Number 10 is also in the middle of the circle. They are two pairs of opposites. Number 5 is on the right side of the circle. Number 10 is on the left. Number 5 is the gate that enables a dreamer, a seeker to enter into the special world, the world of Maat. The domain of harmony, health and happiness. Number 10 is the gate, the door that enables the healed person to exit the special world. 5 enables you to enter into the world of mysteries. 10 is the door which takes you back to where you came from.

There is always a beginning and an end, a final day of every experience. The final day of person's life should be filled with joy not pain. We are meant to cherish our memories not to depart in fear, tears and agony. A person who wishes to study and acquire wisdom will go to a library. He or she will spend hours reading books about the subject of his or her interest. After spending many hours in the library, the seeker, the patient who suffers from a common disease called ignorance, the son or daughter who is intellectually thirsty will discover exciting mysteries. Once the patient gets the knowledge or "the cure" step 10 appears. The journey of the hero is a cyclical and universal experience. It is an ancient ritual that reconnects the individual to the ancestral memory. When we reach the end of every quest, we take the first step of our return journey. We must return home and share the gold that we've discovered. One day we shall return to the world of the ancestors. Do we return as victims or heroes?

The mother, the father, the grandfather, the brother, the sister, the breadwinner wakes up at 6 o'clock in the morning and goes to work. Around 6, 7pm in the evening the front door opens and the hero, the breadwinner returns home. The hero's journey is also a universal ritual that takes place every single day, every single hour, in every single village, country, house, every forest and street in the world.

The blood as a hero

The blood that carries vitamins, oxygen and micronutrients to vital parts of our bodies goes through the liver every 5 minutes. After 5 spending minutes nourishing the sacred and perishable shrines that we call organs it returns to the starting point. That's why the liver is one of the most important organs of the body. That's one of the unquestionable reasons why the liver should be given priority. The regeneration of the liver can be attained through herbs such as Milk Thistle, Turkey tail mushrooms, coffee enemas, beetroot juice, alpha lipoic acid, Glutathione, vitamin C, Dandelion root. These are some of the strategies used to revitalise the liver. The liver could be seen as a principle, a Ntrt, a "Goddess" that should be worshiped every single day of the year. 5 x 2 = 10. The union of two pairs of opposites, the left and right central points of the circle gives us number 10. In basic numerology 10 will be reduced to 1. The pioneer. That's Max Gerson, Dr. Sebi, Rene Caisse, Ty Bollinger, Inspector Dupin, Sherlock Holmes and many others.

Number 10 is a very esoteric and rich number. In numerology number 10 is reduced to 1. One is the number of leadership. The zero behind the one symbolises the circle and journey that leads the pioneer to eternity. You don't reach eternity without longevity.

We could speculate that number 1 symbolises the male, zero the female, the womb and sacred door to eternity. 1 is also the number of the pioneer who takes the first step and tries to establish an empire, a clinic, a school, a family, a civilisation, a philosophy etc. Heroes such as Imhotep, Linus Pauling, Otto Warburg, Dr. Matthias Rath, Dr. Aleksandra Niedzwiecki, Max Gerson, Dr. Sebi, Dr. Johanna Budwig,

Rene Caisse, Dr. Veronique, Queen Afua, Dr. Mercola, Ty Bollinger, Dr. Robert Gorter, Leonard Coldwell, Charlotte Gerson are pioneers in their own way. They overcame formidable obstacles and found ways to share wisdom which they collected during their healing journeys.

We can see number 10 in global politics. The Prime Minister of England, a person whose role is to lead the country, lives in a house located in Central London. The house is referred to as "Number 10 Downing Street". The word prime can be traced to Latin. It means 'primo'. In Latin 'Primo' means 1st. The word for 1st in both Spanish and Portuguese, is 'primeiro', 'primero'. Primeiro leads to 'primo', 'prime', 'primordial', 'primavera', 'principal'. There was a very prominent Jewish writer called Primo Levi. Number 10 is deeply linked to leadership. The aspirant who reaches this level is almost ready to be the leader of his or her circle of influence.

The dreamer who reaches step 10 is also ready to become a leader of his, her family, society, community, generation. The dreamer, the sincere seeker who jumped into the special world and accepted the invitation to change his or her beliefs and habits will learn the secrets of longevity. The wisdom and experience will transform the person. The hero will have the necessary skills and knowledge to become a leader of his or her family, generation and even country. That's exactly what happened to the ancient queen Aset. She went to Byblos to rescue her husband. Wsr, returned from the world of the dead. Jesus, went to "Egypt", Buddha, went to the streets then spent hours under a tree until he attained Nirvana, Theseus, went to Crete, Max Gerson moved from Germany to US. He also grew up on a farm, Dr. Sebi, cured himself of diabetes after leaving Honduras for California. Rene Caisse, cured her aunt and mother, Mildred Nelson, helped thousands of people after moving to Mexico, Robert Gorter, cured himself of an aggressive cancer, He was in Berlin then opened a clinic in Cologne. Ty Bollinger, became a mentor after losing his parents and grandparents. He travelled to many countries in order to learn from experts. The list of victims who were initiated, became heroes then pioneers, leaders of souls and mentors is endless. They became heroes after following the sacred sequence.

On step 10 of the Hero's Journey, the hero packs his or her belongings and prepares to return to the ordinary world where his or her friends and relatives live. Many patients who go to hospital will spend several weeks receiving treatment. One day they will be told that it's time to return home. They will return home where they will see their bodies experience a gradual disintegration. They cannot share that wisdom because it is not healing. That's one of the reasons why many fail to become heroes or pioneers. Please remember that a hero is someone who saves another person's life. To save another person's life a student, an initiate, patient, nurse, doctor, mother, father, daughter, son, should spend a great deal of time studying, researching and practicing a specific philosophy. My mother, my father and a few friends went to hospital to get treatment. They did not return. I had the opportunity to become a victim of their death. I could have allowed the grief to consume me. I could have become very toxic and sick. Instead I choose to do something about it. I wanted to learn from my experience. I said yes to the call to the adventure. It was not easy to liberate myself from the ordinary world. 99.9% of my friends and relatives live there. I had to depart and detach myself from childhood friends who said "No" to the great call. If you watch the movies The

Matrix and Back to the Future you will see the hero being constantly asked to answer the call to adventure.

In mythology, the hero usually returns home with the secret about how to heal society. He or she is what Joseph Campbell calls the "boon-bringer". The healed hero becomes the guardian, knower of ancient wisdom. An ancient mystery that's essential for the well-being of the collective, the family and generation. That's why the hero cannot skip step 10.

In the Epic of Gilgamesh both Enlil and Shamash were furious with the adventurous brothers because they killed Humbaba, the "Watchman". A person who cures him or herself from a serious disease will also become a "Watchman or Watchwoman". A teacher of essential wisdom.

The Canadian healer, and ferry woman

We contemplate the wonderful journey of Rene Caisse. She went to a hospital to work as a nurse. She returned home as a healer. She became the mother of a new generation of naturopaths. She also became a powerful source of inspiration of many natural doctors.

During a warm and dry October afternoon, I was in Kensington with my sister who was keen to find a wonderful suit. We went to the local Zara store and there we found a wonderful blue suit. While she was trying the suit, a very happy and smiling lady approached me and said. "She looks wonderful. The suit is wonderful." "Thank you." I said. "Where is your accent from?" I asked smiling. "Canada. I am from Canada." "Wonderful." I exclaimed. "I am sure you are familiar with Rene Caisse." "Ohh yes." She said smiling. "She saved my life.

Although I have never met her, I am very grateful to her. I drink her tea every single day of my life."

Although Rene Caisse died many years ago, her name, memory and spirit returns and saves many lives through her tea. The Essiac tea. Rene Caisse was a pioneer. Number 1. The first lady in history who spent 50 years helping people to cure cancer for free. Like Aset, she was "La prima Donna."

Step 11 Resurrection – Recovery

"There are several important themes here, but the most vital one is that the shaman becomes sick in order to heal. He is a wounded healer. Similarly the theme about the bones suggests that one must be dismembered and re assembled in order to become a new person... Death and resurrection."

- The Religions of small societies - Professor Ninian Smart - Narrated by Ben Kingsley.

We contemplate the journey of Aset again in order to find more hidden lessons and clues. That's the main reason why we keep going back to these sources again and again. Aset is the central reference. Her husband, Wsr was cut into 14 pieces by his younger brother Sutek. Aset collected the 13 fragments then healed her husband. Wsr, the grandson of Re, oldest son of Nut the sky Mother, returned to the world of the living. He resurrected and reclaimed his throne.

A very interesting detail about the journey of Wsr. Shortly after he was proclaimed the king of the "Two Ladies" he told his closest allies that he wanted to return to the Nether World. He returned and became the "King of Kings and the Lord of Eternity."

Before we proceed we shall examine the origins of the word Resurrection, the name of 11th step of the Hero's Journey. The main principle of the Ancient African solar cult was called AmenRe. Amen means hidden. One of Amen's symbols was the image of an old man with a stick. He symbolised the oldest form of light that transitioned during the last hours of sunset.

With the help of 12 principles, the glorious Re, the victorious source of light re-emerged during the early hours of the morning. Re the visible light that comes in the morning, the Sun, is the resurrected and irresistible light that comes to shatter the shadows, ignorance. The new light is the hero.

What's the relationship between Re, cancer and disease?

We start our healing journey as patients. We find a mentor who teaches us how to rebuild our immune system. There is a death of the old-self and the birth of a new individual, a new consciousness. The resurrected man or woman is called healed, cancer free, cancer conqueror etc. That person has a new light in his or her eyes. After 2 years drinking 13 daily glasses of juices and hourly enemas, your skin will become very shiny indeed.

The return of an immune system

The immune system is the most important element in the human body. When the immune system loses its ability to fight, the life of the person is in grave danger. Patients affected by cancer or ambitious individuals who wish to preserve or renew their vitality are advised to take high doses of vitamin C and vitamin D3. Both vitamins help the immune system to recover from a prolonged and vicious attack by the allies of the big monster. Although both vitamins are essential, vitamin D is the father of all vitamins.

We looked into this vitamin on step 1. Re is the supplier of vitamin D and organic foods that contain essential micronutrients. Any rational person that wishes to recover or prevent the death of his or her immune system has no option but to take vitamin D3 supplements.

The word resurrect means, to resuscitate, renew, re-establish. A person attacked by cancer will lose an inner and essential light that enables his or her organism to function. In order to recover the lost light the ambitious man or woman will need the help of Re. Please remember that Re is a universal and timeless principle that affects every single living being. Re is not a God, therefore the principle is not in conflict with the religious beliefs of a patient.

A prolonged exposure to 13 glasses of organic juices, 13 daily enemas + supplements has the potential to help a person who has lost his or her light to resurrect and return.

13, the number of glasses of organic juice prescribed by the Gerson philosophy is very interesting. Aset spent 70 days healing her husband. After 70 days he resurrected. Wsr provided the world with the 1st written account of a resurrection. Wsr was also cut into 14 pieces. 1 piece, his phallus, was swallowed by a fish therefore his wife recovered only 13. The number 13 shows up again in the Upanishads. One of the most influential philosophical books in the world prescribes 13 principles. When reduced number 13 becomes 4. Four is the number of primordial elements that enable life to exist. That's water, air, fire and earth.

The ancient people of North Africa worshiped many principles rather than a single deity. Each principle is a fragment of Mdw Ntr, Mother Nature. The most prominent principles were seen as the mother and father of the entire civilisation. They were Aset and Wsr (Asar). They both had wonderful temples dedicated to them. The temples are still standing today. Aset was usually depicted as a mother breastfeeding her son Hrw. Aset's husbands main symbol was a phallus called Teken. Greek and French invaders renamed it Obelisk. If you take a walk in central London, Vatican City, Washington DC, you will see Tekens that were taken from Kmt during the 19/20th century. The first Teken was commissioned by an African Queen whose ancestors came from Punt, modern day Yemen and Eritrea. She was called Hatshepsut. There were very intelligent people who spent a great deal of time and money collecting Tekens and placing them in the center of prominent cities such as Vatican, Washington DC, Paris and London. They believed in the principle of resurrection symbolised by the monument.

Waking up from deep sleep

The husband of Aset was tricked to get inside a wooden chest. The chest was locked and thrown into the Hapi Itrw, (river Nile). He fell asleep.

In Kemetic African mysteries and in the culture of Native American Indians a person does not die. Instead he or she goes to sleep. Wsr transitioned from being awake to sleeping consciousness. He moved from the ordinary world to the special world.

The word death is alien to ancient cultures. The ancients spoke about a transition. Every evening, we return to our bedrooms and go to sleep. That's exactly what happens to all of us every single day. We go to bed at 9 pm whenever we are able, and return the next morning at 6 or 7 am. While we sleep our immune system is restored. The healing takes place in darkness. The Minotaur that confronted Theseus lived in perpetual darkness. The Minotaur was a source of treasure, heroism. A cure.

In order to resurrect her husband, Aset asked her nephew called Empu to embalm the body of his uncle. After the 13 pieces were reassembled she asked her sister and nephew to leave the room. She used an artificial phallus to awake him. Wsr was asleep and Aset resurrected him with the help of her allies. What has all of this got to with cancer and sickness? We get cluses by looking at the journey of Tamara St. John.

Tamara St. John is a hero who cured herself of breast cancer. She said that when her cancer became very aggressive she slept for 15 hours every single day. After she started juicing and detoxing she gradually recovered. Tamara St. John's inner light and immune system was forced to sleep by cancer. The juices and detoxing helped her to resurrect her badly damaged immune system. She resurrected an almost dead immune system.

It is not the human being that dies but the immune system. The goal of every natural healer and therapy is to resurrect the immune system. Her immune system was weak therefore she fell asleep. When micronutrients, vitamins, flaxseed oil and cottage cheese repaired her badly damaged immune system, she gradually resurrected. She resuscitated. She returned to the world of the living.

The Hero's Journey of Paul Schofield

Page 113 of the book *The Gerson Therapy* written by Charlotte Gerson and Morton Walker, tells the story of a man called Paul

Schofield. Mr. Schofield was 38 years when he was struck by acute infectious hepatitis B.

"...so he set himself up with a Norwalk Juicer, Dr. Norman Walker's famous hydraulic pressing device and started the Gerson Therapy on his own. In proceeding with Dr. Gerson's instructions, Paul Schofield drank great quantities of juice, consisting of an 88-ounce glass of carrot and apple or green juice, every waking hour of his day - a minimum of thirteen glasses, and sometimes more...

I immediately began to feel better. My liver enzymes test readings improved... Within two months, when my physician re-examined me, his verdict was that I was no longer remained infectious; my blood counts were normal."

Paul Schofield is a fine example of a hero that succeeded in resurrecting his immune system. When an immune system is repressed, it loses its ability to fight against diseases. A natural therapy has the potential to resurrect an individual's immune system. Mr. Schofield's journey is very interesting. He completed the 12 steps of the Hero's Journey. His first mentor was his "massage therapist from whom he received rubdowns. The massagist told Mr. Schofield to read the book "*A Cancer Therapy: Results of Fifty Cases.*"

13 glasses filled with life

After reading the book written by Max Gerson, Mr. Paul Schofield initiated himself into Gerson's Philosophy. He accepted the invitation then jumped into the ocean made of organic juices and enemas. Mr. Schofield's story is a great source of inspiration for ambitious men and women who wish to experience step 11. His journey teaches us that there is a biological, financial, intellectual, spiritual and psychological resurrection. That's the whole person rather than a single organ. It is a holistic approach to healing. You cleanse the whole house not just a few rooms.

Coffee enemas are central to the Gerson therapy. One of the known effects of coffee enemas is the ability to change a person's mood. An enema forces the bile to release toxins. After the toxins are released fresh oxygen is sent to the brain. There is a euphoria and a sensation of happiness and cleansing that lasts for several hours. This effect is known to cure depression and addictions. A happy soul is a healthy soul. This idea is a central element of Epigenetics and Inner Engineering philosophies.

The sad personality that afflicts the patient, dies and is replaced by a happier and positive human being. Positive energy is one of the many and natural sources of healing diseases. Positive energy leads to jubilation. Jubilation is a bridge to resurrection.

One of the means to activate the natural state of euphoria and release endorphins is the combination of coffee enemas and organic juices. The 13 glasses of organic juices + the coffee enema = 14. Please remember that the husband of Aset fell into a deep sleep after his body was cut into 14 pieces. The greatest asset of her country resurrected the king after the 14th piece was united with the 13 pieces which Aset was able to locate.

13 glasses + 1 person = 14. That' a mysterious formula. This is one of the mysteries hidden in the story of Wsr. Our goal is not to read myths literally. Instead we should strive to discover the mysteries hidden in every name, every number. Ancient mysteries have the power to inspire and help us to achieve remarkable things.

The Native Indians, Shamans said that in order for a person to be healed he or she "has to be dismembered." Dismembering could mean the cutting off of old habits, diets, ideologies, practices, preferences, toxic personality etc. A person has to be dismembered in order to be resurrected. Cancer could be seen as a natural tool that precipitates the dismembering of the old self.

Dr. Buttar said "that cancer is not a death sentence." Cancer is a tool that Mother Nature uses to inspire the individual to embrace personal transformation and evolution. The evolved, transformed individual is also the resurrected man or woman.

Evolved refers to a person who has given up 10, 20 years, sometimes 50 years of bad habits, such as love of sugar and animal protein. The paintings of Wsr shows a green man. Greenery is the source of life. Spirulina is a source of life, sea kelp, kale, lettuce, cucumber, chlorella is a source of life. They are all green. Milk thistle enables the liver to resurrect. Mother Nature holds the key to the principle of resurrection. It doesn't matter how damaged our immune system is, we should always try our best to repair it. We can do it if we combine 13+1 - 13 glasses plus 1 person; 13 enemas plus 1 person; 13 books plus 1 person.

STEP 12 - THE ELIXIR

"AMRITA is the elixir of immortality that features in the popular Indian myth of churning of the ocean. The tale tells how, when the authority of the old gods was weakened, the Asuras, or demons began threatening to usurp their power. The great god VISHNU, the preserver of the Universe, suggested that the Gods revitalise themselves by drinking the miraculous elixir, Amrita, which they would have to produce..."

- p346 The Ultimate Encyclopedia of Mythology - The Myths of South and Central Asia.

When Wsr, the first King of Kmt awoke from the deep sleep, he embraced his wife. They spent the evening together. They celebrated their reunion by making love. 9 months later Aset gave birth to a boy whom she called Hrw. Please remember that Hrw is the root word for 'hero'. Hrw was the child of the first queen and king of Kmt. It doesn't matter whether the child is a boy or a girl, he or she has the potential to become a hero. The mother, the father and the child. Your mother, your father and you. You are the hero. The hero is within you not outside you. You are the hero.

Hrw was depicted laying on the lap of his mother and drinking organic milk, which was flowing from her breast. Breast milk is the elixir of every healthy baby. Breast milk contain Selenium and essential vitamins that help a baby to remain healthy for many years. The elixir is a drink, a liquid that has healing properties.

AMRITA, Amor a la vida

To understand the last step of the Hero's Journey we look into the origins of the word 'love'. The Italian word for love is 'Amore'. In Spanish and Portuguese the word for love is 'Amor'. From amor we get the expression "Amor a la vida." Love of life. If you really love your life, you will do whatever you can to protect it. That means giving up the old self. "Shedding off the old skin."

The Italian, Spanish and Portuguese words for death is 'morte', 'muerte'. A morte literally means, the death. Amore means love. "Amore mio", my love... The two words are deeply linked. The origins of both amore and morte are Indian, Sanskrit.

In Ancient India the sacred drink, the elixir of immortality was called Amrita. Amrita was a sacred drink that saved a person from death, morte. A person who was keen to save his or her lover, amore, from permanent death would give him or her a liquor called Amrita. The word AMRITA is etymologically linked to amore, amor and a morte. Please remember that Ancient Indian culture had a very profound influence on European culture. The evidence is found in the language. Example:

- Indian - Mantra is a chant used to inspire and instruct the soul to be healthy. In Portuguese manta means 'bedsheet', to cover.
- Indian - Madri was the name of Prince Arjuna's step mother. In Spanish - Madre, means mother. Real Madrid in Spanish is royal (Madre) mother.

- Indian - The sacred scriptures are called Vedas = Spanish, Portuguese - Verdade means truth - Also Vida = life. Verde = green. The word for sees in Italian is Vede.
- India - Vivasvat was an aspect of Survya. Spanish, Portuguese = Viva la Vida.
- India - Amrita is the elixir, source of health. In Portuguese Rita is the name of a female. A lover of Rita says Amo a Rita (Amrita).
- India - Assuras - Iran, Ahura Mazda - in Greece it became Agora, Portuguese/Latin, Spanish - Agora, Hora = it means hour. Ahora/Agora means now.
- From Surya we got Asturias.
- Bhagavad Gita - Gita means song in Ancient India - Gita is slang for money in Portuguese, Gita+nos = Gypsies in Spanish - Gitara - Guitar in Portuguese and Spanish.
- Gatas - Ancient Persian for sacred songs. Gatas = female cats in Portuguese. Tasting in Spanish.
- Kama Sutra - Love manual in India. Cama means bed in Portuguese and Spanish.
- Haoma - Ancient Iran, sacred drink - It became Aroma in English, Spanish, Portuguese.

Amrita is the elixir that enables the hero to restore vitality in his or her body. From India we also got a liquor called "Soma". In Portuguese the word soma means 'to add'. Soma is the root for the English word 'sum', 'summary'. To be healthy we have to add something into our immune system. We could add 13 glasses of organic juices + supplement. That's the Soma.

The Hero's Journey: a person leaves his or her familiar surroundings, old habits in order to find the elixir. There is a departure, detachment from old ideas and ways of living. The departure is followed by initiation, learning how to prepare the elixir, the Soma. In Persia we got Haoma. We could also speculate that the "Soma" was a drink with a very nice Aroma. Haoma and Soma are possibly the same juice. One from India and the other from Iran. Ancient Indian and Iranian cultures are twin sisters. The word Iran means the land of the Aryans.

It doesn't matter where he or she goes, the sincere seeker is initiated into an ancient method, the ritual, preparing the Elixir. The method, the therapy contains an elixir that must be added (Soma) into a diet and the body.

The sister of Maat was a lioness called Sekhmet. There was a point when Sekhmet lost her temper and started to attack people. She was given a special drink which healed her psychological disorder. A doctor in Kmt was called the priest or priestess of Sekhmet. Sekhmet was a warrior that waged war against disease. She had a drink and festival associated to her.

Examples of modern elixirs:

- Intravenous vitamin C
- Kombucha
- Spirulina
- Chlorella
- Beetroot juice etc.
- Milk thistle

- Organic apple juice with organic watermelon + celery + 1 spoon of turmeric
- Essiac Tea

The elixir is the wisdom that helps an individual to heal not just his or her body but also the bodies and minds of an entire society and generation.

Max Gerson departed from a conventional method of healing migraines. He spent years searching for the elixir. When he completed his initiation, he returned home and shared the wisdom with patients, friends and relatives. He used the elixir to save many, many lives and generations. The idea of using an elixir to restore vitality into a body may seem illogical to the skeptic, however the journeys of the heroes who defeated the big monster contain many references of an elixir.

Lonnell the American hero who cured himself of prostate cancer told "The Truth About Cancer" that he learned how to make "Kombucha."

In a wonderful book called "*Hinduism*" Professor Gregory Kozlowski says the following;

"During the Vedic Age, that is from the 19th century BCE through the 6th century BCE. The most common recreation activity was the Soma ritual. Soma was a liquid produced by crushing some form of vegetation. Specialised priests collected the plant as they sang hymns about searching for and cutting down the Soma plant. The priests who pressed the juice, sang special hymns while they performed their tasks. Other priests built a ritual... and wooden huts each of which covered a sacred fire pit. Here the soma would eventually be poured. No one today knows exactly what plant provided the Soma juice. Many scholars believe it was Marijuana, because Cannabis juice known in India today

as Bhang continues today in modern times to form part of celebrations such as the Holi Festival in early spring. Other experts argue that the ancient Soma juice was obtained from hallucinogenic mushrooms. Whatever the source, Vedic hymns often celebrate the way that drinking Soma inspires the poets, priests, worshippers and the Gods themselves."

Hinduism, written by Gregory Kozlowski,

narrated by Ben Kingsley - Audible

An Elixir called Essiac Tea

During the second decade of the 20th century, a nurse called Rene Caisse went to work. She was taking care of a patient when she noticed a scar. She asked about the origin of the scar. Her curiosity lead to the discovery of a drink which was later called Essiac tea. Essiac is used by many people around the world to fight the big monster and prevent diseases.

The ambitious individual who accepts the invitation to leave the world of decay will be initiated. He or she will be given the knowledge regarding how to create the "elixir".

Although he did not meet Max Gerson personally, Paul Schofield read the book then followed the instructions of his mentor. He created an elixir which he drank daily for several months. Tamara St. John used an elixir to heal her breast cancer. In both mythology and the real world the elixir tends to be a liquid. Why a liquid?

More than 70% of the human body is made of liquids. A liquid has the power to penetrate and cleanse every single corner of the temple, the body. A liquid goes directly to the bloodstream, it penetrates every organ and nourishes the cells. It brings vitality.

In Ancient Indian mythology, we learn about a drink called Amrita. Amrita was a sacred drink, the drink of the Gods. Whoever drank Amrita regained vitality. The word Amrita sounds like America. In their excellent book called "*The Hiram Key*", Christopher Knight and Robert Lomas tell us that:

"Knight Templars that escaped Papal persecution sailed to the American continent and settled in a country which they named in tribute to a star called Merica. Merica is the morning star also known as Venus."

Venus was the name which the Romans used to refer to Aset. We find Venus in the word Venice. The founders of Venice worshiped the star Venus, that's why they called their city Venezia. Venice is linked to the sea. Sailors use stars a means of orientation. In both the sea and land you will be lost without navigation. In the world of disease you also need orientation, that comes in the form of initiation. Aset and her husband were associated to two prominent stars. The husband of Aset was associated with the constellation of Orion. Prominent temples were orientated towards the constellation of Orion.

From AMRITA, we got words such as 'Merica', 'America', 'Amarante' 'amante', 'diamante', 'amor a vida'. Amor a vida. If you love your life and want to preserve it, you should learn how to make your own AMRITA.

In Ancient Persia, there was a drink called "Haoma". The drink enabled people to descend and transcend then leave the ordinary world and access the special world. Haoma reminds us of Soma. We could also speculate that from Soma, Haoma, we get the name of the city Roma. When you get into juicing, please make sure that your juices have a nice Aroma.

The Elixir of Shamans

One of the most talented painters of the modern world was a man called Pablo Amaringo. Mr. Pablo was born in Puerto Libertad, deep in the Amazon forest. Like Enkidu, Mr. Amaringo grew up among plants and the sounds of streams of rivers as well as mysterious animals. Mr. Pablo was 10 years old when he drank Ayahuasca. Please be aware that we are not advising you to drink Ayahuasca.

"He was 10 years old when he first took Ayahuasca - a visionary brew used in shamanism to help him overcome a severe heart disease. The magical cure of this ailment via the healing plants led Pablo towards the life of vegetalismo in which he worked for many years."

"For me personally though, they mean even more than this. Plants - in the great living book of nature, have shown me how to study life as an artist and shaman. They can help all of us to know the art of healing and discover our own creativity, because the beauty of nature moves people to show reverence, fascination, and respect for the extent to which the forests give shelter to our souls. The consciousness of plants is a constant source of information for medicine, alimentation and art. An example: the intelligence and creative imagination of nature. My education I owe to the intelligence of these great teachers..."

Pablo Amaringo, interviewed by Howard G. Charing and Peter Cloudsley.

The book Hinduism written by Dr. Kozlowski teaches us that the people of Ancient India worshiped plants. "One verse from the Atarwa Sa Gita celebrates the special properties of the Apamarga plant: We take hold of you, ohh victorious one, ruler of all remedies. I have made you ohh Apamarga plant, the bearer of a 1000 benefits. Always conquering, always warding off curses, I have brought you together with all the healing plants, saying May they protect me from those evil..."

Hinduism, written by Gregory Kozlowski,
narrated by Ben Kingsley - Audible

An ancient culture and knowledge

Ancient people knew how to produce drinks that had the power to heal both the mind and soul. Shamans used to drink certain liquids in order to leave the ordinary world. The message from the ancient world is the following: The special world contains a special drink. On step 12 of the Hero's Journey, the hero returns home with the knowledge of how to produce a drink that restores the vitality of the immune system. The elixir does not have to be just a drink. It could be a diet, a book that shows others how to prepare a drink.

The Harry Hoxsey clinic supplies a tea that contains herbs. Some of the herbs used in Hoxsey's tonic produce the same effect as those found in Essiac tea.

How do you prepare a "Soma", Amrita in the 21 century?

The juice lady

Cherie Calbom is a prolific writer who specialises in juicing. She wrote several books on the subject. She is great mentor to have if you are keen to know how to prepare your own Soma. Jay Kordich was a hero who attained longevity and health through juicing. He was a prolific creator of juicing machines. Jay Kordich, a hero, author, mentor was known as the father of juicing. Mr. Kordich was born in 1923 and died in May 2017. He was 94 years old. That's the power of the "Soma" Amrita and organic living. Mr. Kordich's longevity is evidence that the "Elixir" works.

A healer who knows how to prepare the tonic

In Indian mythology, Vishnu was the mentor, the old man who advised the young Gods to drink the Amrita, the elixir. The demons were called Asuras. Asuras is the root word of 'assure' assurance, 'azul', 'azure', and 'Asturias'. The Asuras were keen to destroy both the individual and the collective. In the human body, the Asuras are called free radicals or cancer cells. They are also keen to weaken and destroy the individual and the collective symbolised by the person's family.

Vishnu was known as "the preserver of the Universe". Our body is the visible universe. Free radicals are asuras. Human beings should be the preservers of their own Universe. The conditioning which takes many years to reject, persuades many people to neglect the preservation of their bodies.

The message of the ancient mentor was very simple. "Drink the Amrita, the Soma, purify yourself". We find the elixir with Harry Hoxsey, Max Gerson and almost every single naturopath, and healer in the world. All of them talk about a special juice that cleanses and revitalizes the body. All of them recommend an elixir. The union of an elixir and detoxing is a vital combination because it cleanses the body.

Lonnell the hero from the United States who cured himself from a monster called prostate cancer, drank chlorella, kombucha, avoided junk foods and solid cooked foods. Although he did not take any conventional treatment he is still alive 18 years after the diagnosis. The lesson is there. Any patient or dreamer who wishes to defeat the monster should drink an elixir. The elixir comes in the form of juices that contain fruits, vegetables, herbs, powders, oils etc. Milk thistle is a fine example of a modern Soma. Milk Thistle protects the liver, an essential organ. In ancient Kmt the liver was seen as a Ntr, an essential principle therefore it was preserved in the "Canopic jars". In the modern world humans destroy their lives and livers through endless drinking. The culture has changed. Most of the progress is superficial, useless and artificial. We must return to Mdw Ntr. Mother Nature.

YouTube has many videos of people who claim to have cured themselves of cancer. Almost all of them say that they spent several months, sometimes years juicing. Beetroot, grapefruit, celery, carrots are some of the juices mentioned. Beetroot juice is one of the most used elixirs by people attacked by the big monster. It contains folic acid and helps the liver to detox. Graviola (soursop) are other popular juices mentioned by YouTubers. Vitamin B17 is what makes this juice an attractive asset to dreamers who wish to defeat the big monster. Spirulina, Chlorella, Graviola, all contain vitamin B12. B12 helps the body to repair DNA cells. Glutathione is also a liquid, a powerful antioxidant, an elixir that goes to every organ.

The Juice Lady's Liver Cleansing

The Juice Lady's Liver Cleanse Recipe - Cherie Calbom - The Truth About Cancer YouTube channel:

Ty Bollinger - "One of our favourite juices, I need to get your approval here since you're the Juice Lady. One of the juices that Charlene especially loves, my wife, is fresh orange juice, fresh lemon juice and then garlic and ginger. And we just put it in the vitamix blend it up. We put about 10 cloves of garlic, couple of big things of ginger and maybe half a thing full of juice, blend it up with ice. And it's like a, it's a smoothie. It's so good.

Cherie Calbom - "That sounds wonderful. Well I've been doing one in the morning, this is a liver cleanse, a gentle, gentle liver cleanse shake...
I've been doing this one because I'm starting on my summer liver cleanse. Any time of year is a great time to cleanse but summer is just wonderful, spring and summer when it's warmer, and we can definitely eat lighter because it's just warmer. So I'm doing one, but my morning shake is the juice of one lemon and one lime, and you can add orange too if you want to. For me that's just too much sugar and my body doesn't like sugar at all, even orange juice. But you can put orange juice in there for sure. And then you add about a cup of water, a bunch of ice cubes, as many as you want to make it the temperature you want. A tablespoon of olive oil, one garlic clove and a little chunk of ginger. And that's day one. Day two, it's two cloves of garlic and two tablespoons of olive oil. And then day three, three and three. Four and four. Day five, five and five. Five garlic cloves, five tablespoons of olive oil and the rest is the same. Don't breathe on anyone that day."

Ty Bollinger - "Oh because of the garlic."

Cherie Calbom - "No I'm just teasing you."

Ty Bollinger - "You need to make sure your husband or wife is drinking with you right?"

Cherie Calbom - "Or chew on parsley. That takes away the garlic breath. So that is along with a carrot salad, a beet salad, and a potassium broth soup, and a beet juice drink, and a green juice drink, that is your liver cleanse. Gentle liver cleanse program. And then you can add salads and soups and stir fries. But it should be an all vegetable week. And so this is my one day, I'm not doing that today but I'm going to pick back up and complete my liver cleanse for the rest of the week."

Ty Bollinger - "You're in the middle of it then?"

Cherie Calbom - "Yeah, I took a day off. But it's a wonderful, gentle, very gentle, liver cleanse. There are many others that are more heavy duty with herbs and different tinctures that you can add in. But if you want to do a gentle one, that is a great way to start working into it. Beets are wonderful for the liver. They are known as a liver food, liver cleanse food, along with many others. The dark leafy greens, and carrots, and olive oil, lemon juice, all of that is just wonderful for liver cleansing. And with my carrot salad and beet salad, I make them with the pulp. So I juice a beet first and pull out the pulp. And then I juice all my carrots to get a cup of pulp. And then add lemon juice and olive oil dressing to each of them, they're separate. I put cinnamon in there, in my dressing, because it just sparks up the flavour a whole lot. I love cinnamon. And then you eat your beet salad a couple of tablespoons at a time throughout the day. Your carrot salad you can eat all at once. But it's done for you. It's so fast. You know it's all done for you with the juicing."

Ty Bollinger - "And it really cleanses the liver? All these steps together."

Cherie Calbom - "Yes. And if anyone has had chemo and radiation, extremely important that you cleanse your liver. And I say to everyone who has cancer, has had cancer and has been through chemo, and or radiation, you must, must, must cleanse your liver. Cleanse your whole body. Because those things are so toxic. And if you don't it's going to stay in your body and it could contribute to cancer coming back. Along with all the other toxicity that was there and contributed to cancer in the first place."

Ty Bollinger - "So really good advice to cleanse that liver. Because the things that we are using, the conventional treatment, actually could be carcinogenic. They are actually known to be carcinogenic."

Cherie Calbom - "Yes. Highly toxic for the body. But before you cleanse your liver and we talked about it earlier, always cleanse your colon. Because we want that channel of elimination very open and as clean as possible. So that when the liver starts dumping the toxins it can get on out, get through your body."

"The real key to final stage of the Hero's Journey is the Elixir. What does the Hero bring back with her from the special world to upon her return."

- p220 The Writer's Journey - Christopher Vogler

If you visit the Gerson Institute website then click on "supplies - coffee - enema - supplies" you will read the following message: "Eat clean and live clean." You are advised to cleanse your body.

You cleanse your body through the elixir. You cleanse your soul by sharing the elixir with others. Studying, reading, meditating are powerful ways to cleanse the soul.

Please be aware that not everybody wants to eat clean and live a clean life. Toxic foods are very addictive. Many people are addicted to toxins and chemicals, negative thinking and pessimism that comes from breaking news and weather forecasts. That's why the number of people attacked by the big monster is increasing. People are not drinking the elixir. They are doing exactly the opposite. Fizzy drinks, processed drinks, coffee, alcohol etc. Not everybody is keen to save themselves from premature death. Many wonderful human beings are conditioned to believe that they will die early. Sadly many buy into the pessimistic idea that sees life as a " great depression." There is no adventure or "Vitality of Experience." Only prescribed medications, which intoxicate the organism and weaken the immune system.

Many people are not willing to give up dangerous foods such as meat and alcohol, wine, beer and a few other visible enemies.

Be bold, detach yourself from negative thinking. Learn to listen to your soul and body. Master the art of cleansing and living well. Re-educate yourself about nutrition and longevity. Strive to find the "elixir" that will transform your life.

Wisdom as an elixir

The Sumerian hero Gilgamesh went on a long and difficult journey. His goal was to discover the secret of immortality. He found the Tree of Life and lost it after it was eaten by a lucky snake. He returned home with a different type of elixir. The elixir that he brought to his people was wisdom. He taught the people of Uruk not to become prisoners of their egos. He also taught his students and followers how to live a clean life. That was the elixir that he took home with him.

It will take you years to complete the Hero's Journey and discover the "elixir". It's never too early or too late to start your Hero's journey. You need to cleanse your mind. You could and should move the rock that's located deep in your mind, in your city, village, generation, family, office etc. That's one of the first obstacles, the trials which every hero is forced to confront. Below are some examples of the types of elixirs that you can use to cleanse both your mind and body.

Examples of elixirs:

- Beetroot juice - for the liver
- Black seed oil
- Essiac tea
- Hoxsey tonic
- Hydrogen peroxide - used in Oxygen therapy (35% food grade only)
- Intravenous Vitamin C
- Organic medicinal coffee (for coffee enemas)
- Vitamin D3
- Turkish Tail
- Kombucha
- Chlorella
- Spirulina

Please visit our website www. theherosjourneyhealth.com in order to learn how to make an elixir.

Key questions

- What is your elixir?
- What is your Soma?
- What is the drink that's purifying your body?
- What does it contain?
- Are the ingredients organic?
- Who initiated you?

The wisdom of an experienced healer

The skeptical man and woman, who makes a living being skeptical, being negative and rejecting the beauty and power of Mother Nature will say: "This is not scientifically proven."

He or she will also say that "the idea of using plants to heal the body and the mind is nonsense." Such thinking is detrimental to your future, therefore you should detach yourself from it. We shall follow the instructions of experienced mentors.

One of the most remarkable healers and leaders of souls of our time, is a man who has dedicated more than 30 years to the very complex subject called "cancer and chronic diseases". He is a qualified and highly experienced Neurosurgeon who deals with cancer patients every single day. He wrote an essential and remarkable book called "*Natural Strategies for Cancer Patients*" On page XVIII of his introduction Dr. Russell L. Blaylock says the following:

"Many flavonoids, and some vitamins, can also inhibit enzymes that play a vital role in the tumor invasion of surrounding tissues. Still other plant chemicals and certain vitamins can significantly boost the immune system, especially the cells that normally attack cancers. All of the flavonoids found to suppress or even destroy cancer cells can be found in commonly eaten fruits and vegetables. They are especially abundant in certain vegetables often referred to as cruciferous vegetables, such as cauliflower, Brussels sprouts, and broccoli. It is now evident that these plant chemicals, vitamins, and minerals can attack cancer cells at all levels, but at the same time have no harmful effect on normal cells. In fact, they powerfully protect normal cells from becoming cancer cells."

The experience and wisdom of a modern healer, shaman confirms the truths revealed by mythology. That is: Our ancestors knew exactly what they were talking about. Do your duty and do it well. Strive to learn how to create an elixir, a Soma that will penetrate and heal the essential organs of your body, mind, family, circle of influence. Society, community and generation. Create an elixir that will heal your mother, father, brother, husband, sister, friend, work colleague, lover, wife, cousin, neighbour, mentor, son, daughter, employee…

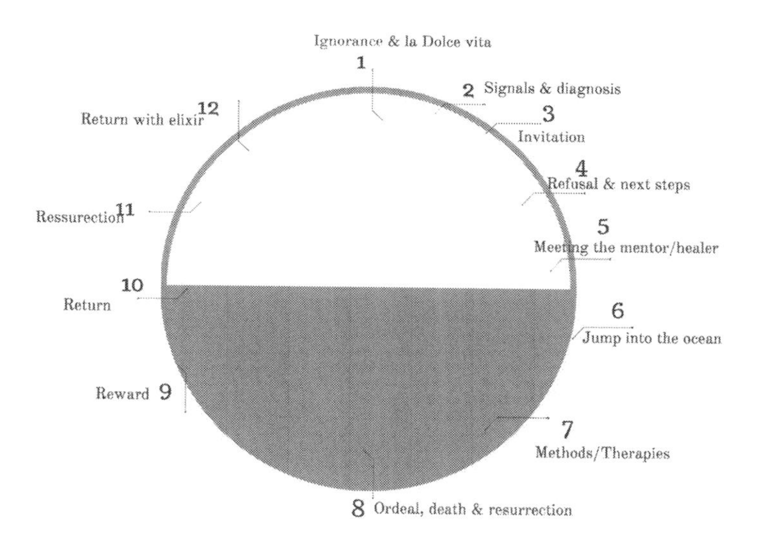

CONCLUSION
How to Become a Hero

"Siddhārtha Gautama, the Buddha, (enlightened one), lived in northern India from c.560 to c.480 bc. The son of a nobleman, he embarked on a quest for spiritual enlightenment at the age of twenty nine. His core teaching became known as the Four Noble Truths. In summary, the Buddha said that the universe is a place of suffering and pain, caused by a complex chain of causation that manifests itself as desire. We are doomed to experience samsara (rebirth) - a concept shared by Hinduism - and a continuation of suffering unless we break the cycle of practicing the Eightfold Path of right views, right intention, right speech, right conduct, right livelihood, right effort, right mindfulness and right concentration."

- p13 The Riches of the Indus - The Eternal Cycle - Indian Myth - Charles Phillip, Michael Kerrigan, Stuart Blackburn.

We will conclude the Hero's Journey by examining key aspects of Siddhārtha Gautama's journey. We will look into his story again with the eyes of a dedicated expert. Our goal is to turn the contemplation into a ritual. Like an experienced detective, Sherlock Holmes, we examine every line of the story. We want to find clues, threads that will help us to complete our own journey.

Siddhārtha Gautama was a prince from the Shakyamuni clan. He left the luxurious palace of his father and became an ascetic. He renounced power, opulence and became a mendicant. He went on a journey of self-discovery that enabled him to heal himself and find the keys to heal others.

Like Siddhārtha you could also go on a journey in order to learn how to heal yourself and your loved ones. You don't have to leave your "palace" and wonder the streets of London or New York, Lisbon, Liberia, Liverpool, Lesotho, Lima, Lagos, Madrid, Manhattan etc. You don't have to go begging people to give you money. That's already been done. Your type of renunciation could be more psychological, strategic, intellectual rather than material. You will have to throw away the microwave. Throwing away your microwave would signal the material sacrifice. The sacrificial principle has to be applied. There are no shortcuts.

The negative thinking, mindset that has been developing in your subconscious mind should not be ignored. You have been exposed to words, ideas, foods, ideologies, beliefs, images that are detrimental to your psyche and inner self. All of us have habits that are not ideal for our health and future. Many ambitious people eat healthy foods and exercise however they have no idea what supplements are powerful enough to prevent and correct the damage done by cancer cells.

During the initial stages of the Hero's Journey, we give up what we consider "bad habits". The addiction to sugar, television are some of the habits that have the power to derail our progress. TV for example, teaches us that foods filled with sugar and meat are tasty. They might be tasty. They are also very damaging to the human organism. The famous TV chef whom I had the pleasure to watch and listen to on

BBC, never mentioned the consequences that might follow her "delicious dish."

There was fried sugar, fried butter, and syrup in the dessert. If you spend 5 minutes listening to the masters of the special world, you will hear a recurring message. Every single healer tells you to stay away from sugar because sugar feeds cancer cells. I suspect the famous chef forgot that detail.

Below are some of the pillars which are part of the Hero's Philosophy:

- Rituals & Mantras
- Meditation
- Cleansing and studying

Rituals & Mantras

"The sacrifice is a mechanism for producing a result. Sacrificial action (the Sanskrit word for 'action' is Karman). If performed correctly, produces future benefits for the sacrificer."

- The Bhagavad Gita - Translation by W. J. Johnson

To become a hero you need to develop healthy rituals and mantras. You will need new music, new words and a new vocabulary. Attend one of our seminars or visit our online school:

www.theherosjourneyhealth.com

You could also use rituals and mantras to reconnect with your soul. Please remember that the subject called disease is 80% psychological and 20% physical. The mind heals the body not the other way around. You need morning, afternoon and evening rituals. You also need weekend rituals. Be bold and incorporate foods into your rituals. Kiss your fruits and vegetables and thank them for bringing you health. Thank your friends, relatives, ancestors, sing and celebrate life. Below are examples of Mantras which you can sing in order to instruct your soul and body to heal itself;

I heal my body
I heal my mind
I heal my soul
I am a hero
I am a hero
I am a hero
I am healthy
I am happy
I am wealthy
I heal my body
I heal my mind
I heal my soul daily
I am happy
I am blessed
I am successful, I am completing my journey, I am healing my body

I am a hero
I am a hero

I am a hero

Please spend 20 minutes every day repeating this mantra. Chant once in the morning, once in the afternoon and shortly before you go to bed. This mantra will reprogram your subconscious mind.

Find a mentor

You've heard stories of heroes who defeated the big monster. Maybe you, your friend or a relative are being attacked by the big monster, we are all being attacked by some form of a Minotaur, depression, addiction to sugar, addiction to TV, ignorance, financial stress, aging etc.

Do you want to know how to become a hero, how to defeat the big monster and restore balance into your body? The answer is very simple.

Find a mentor, a ferryman, a ferrywoman, someone who will help you to cross the first threshold. Find an experienced mentor, a helper, a teacher that will help you to leave the ordinary world. That's the world of decay, disease, degradation, dissolution, destruction, and death. The hero's journey is not a lonely journey. We are social animals, we are designed to interact and learn from others.

Please look at the diagram and find where you are. Live like a philosopher, develop the habit of asking excellent questions.

- Who are your mentors?
- Who is guiding you?
- What's the spiritual goal of the person who is advising you about your health?

We all need a mentor, a Buddha, an Aset, an Ariadne, a Spider woman, a teacher who will help us to discover essential and lifesaving, clues, tips and mysteries.

A lady that works in the local mini market told me that she did not take supplements because her doctor told her that "they don't work". She bought into the delusion and deception that leads to biological destruction.

Search and you shall find

Depending on your location, it might be difficult to find a mentor in your area. Geography should not stop you from reading and watching lectures or attending seminars dedicated to health and wellness. You can also learn a lot by experimenting and trying. You could also find a local naturopath that lives in your country, city or village. Be proactive and take the necessary steps to protect your health, the health of your mother, father, daughter, brother, son, cousin, sister... Accept the wonderful idea that you need re-education. The more you re-educate yourself, the more valuable you will become to yourself and your inner circle. You will become an Aset to your wife, children, husband, friends, generation...

Inner Engineering and Mind Power

"As long as your inner life is enslaved to external situations, it will remain a precarious condition. There is no other way for it to be. What then is the way out? The way out is a very simple change in

direction. You just need to see that the source and basis of your experience is within you. Human experience might be stimulated or catalysed by external situations, but the source is within. Pain or pleasure, joy or misery, agony or ecstasy happens only inside you. Human folly is: People are always extracting joy from outside."

- Inner Engineering: A Yogi's Guide to Joy - SadhGuru

Sadhguru is a remarkable mentor, a hero, healer, poet, Yogi, prolific author, entrepreneur and pioneer. He was born in India on the 3rd of September in 1957. He is the creator of a philosophy called Inner Engineering. Inner Engineering is a life changing philosophy that has the power to cure diseases and transform lives. The central idea of Sadhguru's philosophy is the following: "You can and should engineer your life through your mind and your thinking. They both affect your behaviour. It is a powerful philosophy."

Mind power

Mind Power is a philosophy developed by a Canadian hero called John Kehoe. Mind Power goes beyond positive thinking. Can you heal yourself using your mind? Is this really true?

The skeptical who has never used mind power will say that the idea of using the mind to cure oneself of a serious illness is nonsense. In his wonderful and highly influential book "Mind Power into the 21st Century", the healer and leader of souls John Kehoe told the following story:

"Dr. Patricia Norris of the Karl Menninger Foundation, who teaches patients to use mind power to combat disease, tells the story of a nine - year-old boy who cured himself of a malignant tumor using a "Star Wars" visualisation technique: Garret Potter was a terminal case - it was estimated he had only about six months to live. He had a virulent, malignant type of tumor. Radiation treatments had failed. Surgery was out of the question because of the tumors location. If he fell down he couldn't pick himself up. Using his mind he visualized his immune system as powerful. It was a Star Wars - like visualization - he saw his brain as the solar system and his tumor as an evil invading villain. He visualized himself as the leader of a space fighter squadron fighting the tumor and winning.

"Garret used the technique for twenty minutes each night. At first his condition worsened and then it gradually began to get better. Five months later a brain scan was taken. The tumor was gone.

"The visualization technique was the only therapy employed after it had been concluded that radiation therapy had failed." - Page 117, Mind Power into the 21st Century - Techniques to Harness the Astounding Powers of Thought - John Kehoe
The Power of Your Mind + 4 Techniques to Control Your Reality (law of attraction) - YouTube channel Your Youniverse.

John Kehoe - "So this morning what I'm going to be talking about, is I'm going to be talking about the powers of the mind. And this is a subject that I'm absolutely passionate about. 25 years ago I discovered some very interesting intricacies about the human mind and the human psyche and how the powers of the mind can begin to influence and affect the things that happen to us in our life. And this was a revolutionary concept for me, it made me understand our purpose, our destiny, our personal power and in order to work with the powers of the mind, you have to understand first of all that, everything in physical reality is made up of vibrations of energy. This stage here is made up of vibrations of energy, the seat that you're sitting on is made up of vibrations of energy, the clothes that you're wearing are made up of vibrations of energy.

The walls are made up of vibrations of energy. That everything in the physical universe is made up of vibrations energy, everything. An our thoughts also are vibrations of energy. Our thoughts are the most dynamic most fluid, most powerful substance in the entire universe. And when you begin to think a thought over and over and over again, imprinting it on the conscious level, what happens is this begins to make an imprint into the subconscious and once it begins to imprint into the subconscious, it's like a tuning fork, a vibration of energy, attracting to you the people, the circumstances, the events, the synchronicity that matches the images that you have within.

You have very real power, to create and manifest. Once you understand the dynamics of consciousness and physical reality and you begin to train and practice with the natural powers that each and every one of us have been born with. You see everything is, in our life is made up, we're living simultaneously in two different worlds. This is the, this is the place that we're going to start at this morning. We live simultaneously in two different worlds not one. We live in the inner world, the world of our thoughts beliefs and reactions and we live in the outer world, the world of circumstances and situations."

The Power of Your Mind + 4 Techniques to Control Your Reality (law of attraction) - YouTube channel Your Youniverse.

The last line where he talks about the inner and outer world is very interesting. It also reminds us of the need to be the masters of the "two worlds." That is the Ordinary world and the Special world.

Meditation

The word meditation comes from an ancient tribe made of wise men and women. They were called the Medes. The medes were invaded by Greeks who copied some of their rituals. Medes is also the root word for 'medication', 'medicine', 'mediterranean', 'miedo' and 'medo', 'media', 'mediator'.

One of the richest Florentine families was called the Medici. They were responsible for the Renaissance. They funded schools which were later attended by Michelangelo, Da Vinci and many other prominent Italian artists. The Medici family was in some way connected to the wise tribe called Medes.

The origins of the Medes is not certain. Some historians say that they were from Libya, others say that they were from Ancient Persia, modern day Iran. During an interview conducted by a prominent Jewish philosopher called Jeffrey Mishlove, an Iranian American historian and philosopher called Jason Reza Jorjani said that the "Medes were based in modern day Kurdistan".

The Medes were very clever people. They were experts in ancient wisdom. They were students of essential subjects. The Medean tribe was made of experienced and sophisticated priests and priestesses. They were experts in astrology, ancient psychology, rituals and numerology. They were advisors of kings and queens.

The word Medes leads us to 'meditation', 'medication', 'medal', 'medallion', 'mediocre', 'media', 'medicinal' etc. Meditation is the oldest remedy in the world. Pregnant women spend 9 months meditating on their child. Chess players meditate on their next move. Meditation is the starting point of everything that's great and excellent. It doesn't matter whether you're healthy or unhealthy, please get yourself into meditation.

What's the first step?

The first step is to switch off the TV, the radio, the iPod, the phone and sources of psychological and emotional distractions, such as "Social Media". Cut off all the noise around you and allow the interior voice to emerge. Meditate. Think. Become a prolific creator of ideas. We are humans and are surrounded by negative elements. Sometimes we are also surrounded by negative people who are also struggling to deal with their own inner conflicts. We must develop techniques to heal our emotional wounds. A healthy emotional self will create the space for positive and healthy ideas, healthy psychology, healthy soul, healthy body, healthy future.

It doesn't matter whether you want to protect yourself, a friend or your family. You should find time to meditate. Some people go for a run, others cycle, many others go swimming. Many people practice yoga for hours. Do what works for you. I like to go for long walks. I also enjoy running, listening to audio books and reading. I also like teaching and sharing.

Stephen R. Covey said that, "when you teach once you learn twice." It doesn't matter how you start, there should be some kind of movement that takes you away from your comfort zone. The ordinary world. Please remember that there are 12 steps. You should never skip any of the steps or try to rush. There is an ancient and sacred sequence. A path left by the ancestors. Follow the sequence and you shall prosper.

Shedding the old skin

After discovering the Tree of Life that was planted in the bottomless sea, Gilgamesh took the elixir, celebrated then returned to dry land. He was very pleased indeed. Together with Urshanabi the ferryman, Gilgamesh started the return journey. The student and ferryman spent days travelling.

During his return journey Gilgamesh decided to take a break and have a bath. He took the Tree of Life and put it in a place which he considered safe. He then dived into a lake to enjoy a bath. He was enjoying himself when a snake was attracted by the irresistible and powerful aroma of the plant. The treasure that Gilgamesh risked his life to find was slowly eaten while he was cleansing himself. As soon as it ate the Tree of Life, the lucky snake became immortal. The snake shed its old skin and regained its youth.

Shedding the old skin is an ancient ritual performed by snakes from all over the world. What's the meaning of "Shedding the old skin?"
It means personal growth and renunciation of the old self. Every year millions of people living in India perform a collective ritual of purification. The ritual takes place in a sacred river, the Ganges. The waters of the ancient river cleanse the old body, mindset and soul.

Ancient sages used the Epic of Gilgamesh to teach us a very important lesson. We should strive to renew and refine ourselves.

Shedding the old skin means renouncing the old self. The meditation that you do in Step 5 is to help you to get rid of old beliefs, ideas, toxic friends, bad habits, manners, negative intentions and memories. The positive aspects of your personality should remain and be refined. The negative should go. Eating meat and dairy products is an essential renunciation. Sugar, processed foods, non-organic foods, toxic music, old emotional wounds and conflicts, carefully hidden in soap operas, crime dramas, and all kinds of movies should go.

All this negative, disease making "stuff" has to be thrown into the dustbin of your personal history. You cannot heal yourself from a disease if you persist in clinging on to old grudges and habits. You won't be healthy if you persist in drinking the wrong elixir, such as milk or alcohol.

Drinking milk is not compatible with good health. Milk contains hormones that are harmful to human health. Some hormones found in milk are linked to certain cancers such as breast cancer, hormones and oestrogen related diseases. Milk also contains toxins used to keep the milk fresh.

You will struggle to heal your body if you fail to cleanse yourself deeply. The old skin must go. Your quest is optimal health. It won't be easy to shed the old skin because you have spent the last 10, 20, 30, 50 years of your life being brainwashed not to believe in the hero that's inside you. You are told that you are everything but a hero. You have been persuaded that you are a hopeless victim. You are not a victim. You are a hero.

You should strive to shed that negative personality which has been created through adverts, false education and propaganda.

I used to read newspapers every single day. One day an old wise lady told me that her younger brother fell into depression after getting himself hooked to breaking news. That was a call to adventure which I gladly accepted. I exchanged newspapers for books, Breaking News for poetry, medical drugs for supplements, toxic thoughts for mantras and positive affirmations.

Prepare yourself and be grateful

In the story of Gilgamesh we are told that when he met his mentors, the couple that survived the great flood, Gilgamesh was told to go and have a bath in a lake in order to purify himself. Theseus was also told to go and have a bath in the river in order to purify himself. Wsr was thrown into a river and forced to purify himself. The thread is in the water, a liquid, an elixir.

You don't just jump into an ocean, a river, a sea. You don't just move from step 1 to step 6. There is a sequence which leads the sincere seeker to longevity and heroism.

Muchas gracias - gratitude

You should take a spiritual and emotional bath before you jump into the ocean. The same strategy is applied in the world of swimming. Before jumping into a swimming pool you are asked to have a bath. "You must shed the old skin." You should be grateful for being alive. You could say thank you to everybody that's helping you. It doesn't matter whether they helped you in the past or are doing it in the present. It doesn't matter whether they are online or offline you should be grateful to everybody that's trying or tried to help you. Gratitude is the correct attitude. Gratitude creates the right conditions for a new season in your life.

At the end of winter the soil is grateful for the rain. Shortly after the last days of winter, the healthy and rested soil gives birth to plants and foods. That's the resurrection principle. The new and sunny season is called spring. Winter is an essential ally of the soil. Please remember that your mind is one of your greatest allies. You should be grateful and take care of your mind daily, by reading and listening and contemplating beautiful things and subjects such as the Hero's Journey.

How to become a hero for your family & friends

A year ago I was chatting with a postwoman. She asked me, "How do I prevent breast cancer?" I told her that - "You need to cleanse your system and ensure that it has plenty of minerals. There are 90 minerals that the body needs in order to be very healthy. How many do you take?" I asked.

She looked at me, smiled then said; "I don't even know the name of the first one."

Minerals are essential for optimal health. They can be found in clean water, clean and organic soil. The body needs minerals in order to function properly. Minerals used to be found in organic foods, in plants and vegetables. The soil of the modern world is now polluted and damaged by endless rivers made of pesticides. The once fertile and healthy land is no longer producing the required minerals. No minerals means deficiency. Deficiency means a weak immune system. A weak immune system means disease. Disease is another word for cancer.

Craving Sugar? This Is What Your Body Is Telling You! - iHealthTube.com:

Dr. Peter Glidden - "Well remember there's two things at play here. Yes you're absolutely right. But number 1 we need to reduce the amount of sugar that's in the diet, absolutely, right. But more importantly than this, from my way of looking at things, if your body is minerally deficient, which everybody's body is, because nobody is taking mineral supplements, and remember the minerals are not in the soil anymore. So everybody's minerally deficient. Even if you're consuming exactly the right amount of sugar, it's only a matter of time until your body becomes inefficient at metabolising it, because it lost the minerals that it needs to do that. So more important than regulating how much sugar you eat, is regulating how many minerals are in your body. That's a much more important thing to do."

Supplementation

When the big monster strikes, a person gets signals, symptoms. Symptoms are a manifestation of weakness. Symptoms are a signal that disease has been in the body for a long time. It takes years for tumors to develop. Every single day the body will fight and succeed in defeating small monsters. The exhaustion of the body results in serious sickness and accelerated decay. To avoid sickness you must get deep into a subject called supplements. Find a good supplier of supplements and buy them.

There are 90 essential nutrients that the body needs:

- 60 minerals
- 16 vitamins
- 12 Amino acids
- 2 Fatty Acids

Dr. Peter Glidden is an expert on this subject. He is on YouTube and Amazon. He is a prolific author, teacher and healer. He has been helping people for a more than 40 years. He is a very good mentor. Dr. Glidden recommends a supplier called "Youngevity" as an ideal source of mineral supplementation.

Iodine, Selenium, Vitamin D and Apoptosis

Dr. Bob DeMaria's comments are vital. They teach us that we can turn on and off the gene that promotes cancer. This is one of the secrets of longevity. Some of the oldest people in the world are from Japan. Japanese people, especially those that live by the coast consume high levels of Iodine. Iodine is one of the secret weapons that an ambitious, father, mother, brother, sister, lover, teacher should use in order to stop the development of free radicals. There are powerful strategies capable of preventing the arrival of the big monster. One of them is the mighty Iodine. In Japan the source of vitality is Iodine. In ancient India it was the Apamarga plant. In Babylon Gilgamesh searched for the Tree of Life. The Native American Indians also use plants such as graviola. Wherever we go, we find wise men and women using healing plants. That's another essential clue.

The experienced leader of souls

Dr. Peter Glidden - 5 Things This Doctor Would Do If Diagnosed with Cancer - iHealthTube YouTube channel:

"Supplementation with the mineral Selenium at 200 micrograms a day reduces the occurrence of breast cancer by 82%. Reduces the occurrence of lung cancer, even if you're a smoker by 30% I believe. It reduces the occurrence of colon cancer, 50 something percent, reduces the occurrence of prostate cancer by 60 something percent. So, there is so much clinical evidence to support the notion that Selenium helps you not to get cancer and it's one mineral out of the 90 essential nutrients that you need. Inquiring minds want to know, number 1 why don't the Susan G. Komen women know that? Why aren't they marching for Selenium supplementation? Because you know what that means. If every girl in this country took one Selenium capsule from the time of birth through their life, in one generation we'd eliminate breast cancer by 82%."

Dr. Glidden has been helping people to defeat the big monster for more than 30 years. His experience teaches us that it doesn't matter what kind of monster you are dealing with, there are tools, weapons, allies, juices, supplements ready to help you. Vitamin D3, vitamin C, Selenium, Iodine, and Glutathione are essential allies. You should never go to war without them. There are more than 10 different methods and therapies a person can use to defeat the big monster. All you need to do is to find the right mentor, a teacher who thinks outside the box. That means outside the ordinary world.

Many people think that table salt contains Iodine. Nope. Table salt is industrial. It doesn't contain Iodine. That's one of the reasons why many people are Iodine deficient. You should consume Himalayan pink salt and sea kelp in order to get high-levels of Iodine. There is a supplement called Lugol's Iodine. These are powerful sources of Iodine. You also need Selenium. Brazil nuts, the organic ones, contain Selenium. They are also very tasty. Selenium is great for men who are struggling with fertility issues. I love Brazil nut milk. The best milk I have ever tasted was homemade. I made it myself. I used Brazil nuts to make it. Hum, very nice indeed.

Fasting

"*Let the soil rest from so much digging.*" - Wayne Dyer

Fasting is an excellent strategy to starve cancer cells. Cancer cells need sugar and if a person stops eating sugar, cancer cells lose one of their main sources of food. Fasting enables the body to rest. A rested body is a healthy body. Obesity does not allow the body to rest because it is constantly under pressure, working hard to do simple things. That's one of the reasons why obese people are always tired and in bad mood.

Give your body a rest

A few years ago I was researching the subject of fasting and I came across a very interesting statement. "Try to drive a car for 365 consecutive days and see how it performs. Try to drive your car for 50 consecutive years without stopping and see how it performs." That's exactly what people do to their bodies and minds.

5 years ago I got into fasting. I started by eating only 1 meal a day. I gradually moved to 3 days of water fasting. Next came 7 days of water fasting, gradually increasing. Once I reached 10 days, I moved to 15 days. When I reached 15 days I stopped fasting. I spent 2 months eating only 1 meal a day. Then in 2016 I fasted for 3 months. I succeeded because I felt psychologically and biologically ready. It doesn't matter what you aim to achieve in your life. Whether you wish to write a book, win a marathon, heal your body, get rid of depression and anxiety, drive the big monster out of your body, you will need fasting. Fasting starves cancer cells and cleanses the body. There are several types of fasting.

Intermittent

This type of fasting consists of skipping breakfast and lunch. You spend 8 hours without consuming solid foods.

Juice fasting

Juice fasting consist of replacing solid foods with fruit juices. Organic homemade juices are the best as they don't contain artificial sugars and salts. Juice fasting is a powerful strategy to cure diseases. The sincere seeker floods his or her body with essential micronutrients.

Water fasting

This is the most ancient and popular type of fasting (ideally alkaline water) Dr. Walter Longo wrote that females need at least 2 days of fasting in order to restart their liver and the immune system. For males it is 3 days. After 72 hours of fasting your organism will start to eat stored fats. Fat causes inflammation. Inflammation is one of the main causes of cancer.

Eat raw foods only

Two years ago I went on a 10 days water fasting exercise. After I finished, I spent 20 days eating raw foods. I was lucky to get access to organic fruits and vegetables therefore I ate a lot of raw organic foods. Eating raw foods changed my life and the way I see nutrition. I learned to appreciate good, tasty fresh organic foods. I learned to give up the idea that you need cooked foods in order to be healthy. I also learned more about micronutrients. Micronutrients are found in fresh and raw foods. When food is cooked at high temperatures micronutrients are killed. Raw foods contain essential micronutrients. That's why they are tasty and very healthy. Raw diet is also very powerful. Very powerful indeed. The cure of many diseases.

The journey of Jay Kordich

Jay Kordich was a very sick patient who used raw foods and daily juicing to heal his body, mind and soul. He spent 2 years juicing organic vegetables and fruits. After healing himself of a "serious disease" Jay Kordich became a hero, a mentor, professional juicer, healer and inspirational speaker.

If you or your relatives are trying to prevent an illness, you would do well by adopting a 100% raw foods diet. Ideally they should be organic. It doesn't matter whether you are fighting the big monster or you are keen to prevent disease you should eat as much raw foods as you can.

How do you get into raw food? Start by setting a very small and tangible goal. It could be a weekend dedicated to raw foods. When you accomplish that goal move to 3 days. Then add 1 more day. There will be a point when you reach 7 days. Like most ambitious entrepreneurs in the world, I started small. Once I got used to it, I succeeded in spending 3 months eating raw foods only.

A raw foods diet may help you to:

- Eliminate inflammation
- Fill the body with essential vitamins
- Boost your immune system
- Prevent cancer
- Remove stress
- Heal and eliminate an existing condition
-

What should I eat?

- McIntosh Apples
- A lot of salads
- Apricots
- Avocados
- Beetroot
- Broccoli, broccoli sprouts
- Purple cabbage
- Cucumbers
- Cauliflower
- Kale
- Parsley
- Grapes
- Melons
- Blackberries
- Blueberries

- Cranberries
- Strawberries
- Red currants
- Oranges
- Raspberries
- Turnip greens
- Spinach
- Onions
- Nuts
- Tomatoes
- Bananas
- Brazil nuts
- Walnuts
- Cashews
- Seeds
- Eggplant
- Organic Flaxseeds

Eat as many raw organic foods as possible. The health benefits are immense. Please make sure you avoid the infamous "Dirty Dozen". Stick to organic foods only.

Before getting into the special world

The mentors of the ancient world told us that we need to cleanse ourselves. We need to detox. We should learn from the experts. Dr.

Veronique Desaulniers is a hero who defeated the big monster. In one of her videos called "Benefits of Coffee Enemas" she says the following:

"Personally I have been doing coffee enemas for over 10 years. Prior to that I was doing colonics and home colonic irrigation, so I understand that the colon is very important to keep clean. The benefits of using coffee is because of these 2 things.

1 is coffee nutrients;

- Kahweol Cafestol
- Palmitic acid

And what these nutrients do, is they really help to stimulate the liver. Specifically phase two detoxification. Now, there's different phases of detoxification.

Phase 1 in the liver and then, phase II is where you get into the nitty gritty: detoxification of environmental chemicals, urbanistes, pesticides, heavy metals. And a lot of people have a compromised phase II detoxification process which is why the coffee enemas are so beneficial because it helps to stimulate that.

Another benefit of the coffee enemas is that it stimulates glutathione production. Now Glutathione, specifically is your body's primary antioxidant. It is something that you produce inside your cell and the more you produce of that the better it is for your cells to detoxify...

Another benefit of the coffee enema: is that it decreases specific enzymes. Now, we have enzymes that we need and they are good enzymes. But there are specific enzymes that help to stimulate tumor production and tumor growth. The benefits of coffee enemas is that it decreases the production of the enzymes that are pro-carcinogenic, so there is another reason. And I can tell you story after story of people who resisted the coffee enemas, didn't progress very well. Once they started doing the enemas they saw a big shift in their health."

Dr. Veronique is the author of the book "*Heal Breast Cancer Naturally*" her website is: www.breastcancerconqueror.com

Prometheus and the promise of longevity

From Ancient Greece we get the story of a hero called Prometheus. Prometheus committed a terrible crime against powerful Gods that ruled Heaven and Earth. He stole their sacred fire and gave it to humankind.

In Greek mythology, fire was a treasure of the Gods that was not supposed to be used by humans. Fire symbolises wisdom, clarity, consciousness. Shadows symbolise ignorance and confusion. Humans were supposed to be kept in the dark until the end of time.

Prometheus stole the fire from the Gods and gave it to mankind. The Gods were not pleased. They punished Prometheus by bounding him to a rock. Every day a hungry bird came and ate a piece of Prometheus's liver. Although a chunk of his liver was eaten daily, Prometheus did not die because his liver grew back during the evening. That's the principle of regeneration, and resurrection. The story of Prometheus was a lesson about the ancient principle of regeneration and the importance of the liver.

We can easily discover this principle by looking at how the word Prometheus is spelled in Portuguese which is a language of Latin origin. Latin was deeply influenced by Greek language.

The Portuguese word for promise is 'promessa'. Ele prometeu literally means he promised. The verb promise in Portuguese is 'promete'. Prometer means to make a promise. Prometer is the present tense, Promoteu is past tense. Prometheus the hero whose liver kept regenerating, growing. Prometheus is the root word for 'promise'. There is a promise that the liver will grow back again. That's one of the the mysteries hidden in the story. The Greek word for God is

'Theo'(Theos). Prometheus = Prome + Theus. We could speculate that 'Theus' is plural for Gods. We have the promise of the Gods.

If you commit a crime against your own liver you risk losing your life because the liver is a very influential organ. You can always help your liver to grow again through juicing and coffee enemas, as well as essential minerals and supplements, such as Milk thistle.

You should always take care of your liver. Foods such as beetroot, grapes, vegetables, blueberries, grapefruit, herbal tea, Milk thistle, Dandelion root are all excellent allies of the liver. Alcohol, drugs, toxins, junk food, fizzy drinks will wreck your liver. It takes a long time to destroy a liver. It doesn't matter where you are, if you can read this book you still have time to cleanse and heal your liver. Fast, eat organic foods, meditate and use positive thinking to program your mind to heal your body.

"The body succumbs to disease when it is acidic. Acidifying the body compromises the mucous membrane that protect organs, which leads to the development of chronic disease. Through the difference areas of the body we have various pH levels, we need to consume alkaline foods that maintain the pH 7.4 (a range between 7.35 and 7.45) that the body maintains in the blood."

- p18 Alkaline Herbal Medicine - Aqiyl Aniys

There is a lot to learn about some of the subjects discussed in this book, such as longevity, healing, mythology and the Hero's Journey. We created an online library that contains lessons about detox, herbs, supplements, minerals and great strategies for you to remain healthy. The library will help you to understand and implement the Hero's Philosophy.

Please join us at www.theherosjourneyhealth.com. Contact us and share your opinion about the contents of the book and your "Hero's Journey". Strive to become a hero. The Hero's Philosophy is sublime because it was extracted from an ancient and sacred experience. It is an amalgamation of universal and life transforming principles. You are Aset, you are Gilgamesh, you are Theseus, you are Wsr the resurrected husband of Aset, you are Ariadne, you are Theseus the slayer of Minotaur, you are Arjuna, you are Prometheus, you are Eleio, you are Perseus, you are Sedna, Ishtar, Daedalus, Enkidu, the Spider woman, you are Dana, you're Brigid and all the heroes who came before you. You have the potential to become the hero of your family and generation.

Thank you for reading our book. Please get in touch and share your Hero's Journey.

The next logical step

Below are the 7 principles of the Hero's Philosophy:

1. Emotional cleansing
2. Spiritual cleansing
3. Cultural cleansing/study
4. Mind mastery
5. Detox & supplementation
6. Organic living
7. Teaching, healing & sharing

We are delighted to introduce you to the Hero's Philosophy. Please strive to become a hero of your "Inner Circle". Enjoy the journey. Our next book is called "The Penguin Entrepreneur".

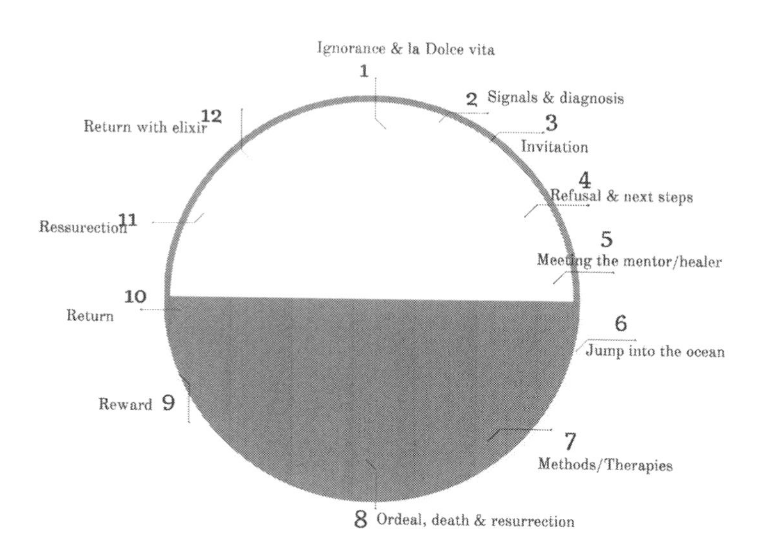

Bibliography & Further Reading

Alkaline Herbal Medicine by Aqiyl Aniys, 2016.

Ancient Egypt - the light of the world by Gerald Massey, 1907.

Beating Cancer with Nutrition"by Patrick Quillin PHD, RD, CNS

Become a Key Person of Influence by Daniel Priestley, 2010.

Cancer as a Metabolic Disease: On the Origin, Management, and Prevention of Cancer by Thomas Seyfried

Cancer Step outside the Box by Ty Bollinger, 2006.

Classical Religions and Myths of the Mediterranean Basin by Dr. Jon David Solomon - Narrated by Ben Kingsley - Audible, 2006.

Effortless healing: 9 Simple Ways to Sidestep Illness, Shed Excess Weight and Help Your Body Fix Itself by Joseph Mercola, 2015.

Egyptian Grammar by Alan Gardiner, 1957.

Epics of Early Civilisation - Middle Eastern Myth - Myth and Mankind by Allan Lothian 1999.

Fat for Fuel by Joseph Mercola, 2017.

Flood Your Body with Oxygen by Ed McCabe, 2004.

Greek (Myths and Legends) by K.E. Sullivan, 1998.

Hinduism by Dr. Gregory Kozlowski, Audible 2006.

How to Read Egyptian Hieroglyphs by Mark Collier, 1998.

Inner Engineering: A Yogi's Guide to Joy by Sadhguru, 2016.

Keto for Cancer by Miriam Kalamian

Life in Ancient Egypt by Adolf Erman, 1998.

Mejat Wefa by Rhkty Amen, 2013.

Middle Egyptian by James P Allan, 2000.

Mother Earth, Father Sky - Native American, Myth and Mankind by Tom Lowenstein, 1998.

Mythos by Stephen Fry

Myth and Symbol in Ancient Egypt by R. T. Rundle Clark, 1978.

Natural Strategies for Cancer Patients by Russell L. Blaylock, M.D., 2003.

Pro. Arnold Ehret's Mucusless Diet Healing System: Annotated, Revised, and Edited by Prof. Spira, 2014.

Tomorrow's Cancer Cures Today - 25 secret therapies from around the world by Allan Spreen, M.D. 2009.

Triumph of the Hero - Greek & Roman Myth - Myth and Mankind by Tony Allan, 1999.

The Bhagavad Gita: A new translation by W. Johnson - Oxford world's classics, 1994.

The Cancer Survival Manual: Tomorrow's Cancer Breakthroughs Today, by Rachael Linkie, 2012.

The Cancer Revolution. A ground-breaking program to reverse and prevent cancer

The China Study by T. Colin Campbell, 2016.

The Complete Tales and Poems of Edgar Allan Poe - Penguin

The Eternal Cycle - India, Myth and Mankind by Charles Phillips, 1999.

The Gerson Therapy by Charlotte Gerson and Morton Walker. D.P.M, 2001.

The Great Themes - World Myth - Myth and Mankind by Tony Allan & Charles Philips, 2001.

The Hero with a Thousand Faces by Joseph Campbell, 2012.

The Hiram Key by Robert Lomas & Christopher Knight, 1996.

The Portable Walt Whitman edited by Michael Warner

The Red Headed League - Sir Arthur Connan Doyle

The Sumerians Their History, Culture and Character by Samuel Noah Kramer, 1971.

The Truth About Cancer by Ty Bollinger, 2016.

The Way to Eternity - Egyptian Myth - Myth and Mankind by Allan Lothian & Fergus Fleming, 1999.

The Winning Formula by David Coulthard, 2018.

The Writer's Journey by Christopher Vogler, 2007.

Tripping Over the Truth by Travis Christopherson

Wise Lord of the Sky - Persian Myth - Myth and Mankind by Tony Allan, 2000.

The 1 Minute Cure by Madison Cavanaugh, 2008.

Documentaries

The Truth About Cancer - Episodes 1, 2, 6

The Quack Who Cured Cancer

iHealthtube.com YouTube channel

Dying to Have Known - Gerson Media

Mythos by Stephen Fry

ABOUT THE AUTHOR

Nelson Lecuane - Sn Hrw Mry Amen
is a filmmaker, researcher, writer, educator, screenwriter, and speaker. He is the author of 5 books. The books explore subjects such as mythology, heroism, ancient history, ancient cultures, strategic thinking, natural health, entrepreneurship and personal development. He was born in Africa, Mozambique and currently lives in the UK. He is the author of the Penguin Entrepreneur Philosophy and co-founder of the Penguin Entrepreneur Academy. Nelson is passionate about helping others, mythology and ancient cultures.

Printed in Great Britain
by Amazon